MAGPIE

AND OTHER STORIES

MAGPIE

AND OTHER STORIES

SARAH HEGARTY

T

Troubador Publishing Ltd
Unit E2 Airfield Business Park,
Harrison Road, Market Harborough,
Leicestershire LE16 7UL
Tel: 0116 279 2299
Email: books@troubador.co.uk
Web: www.troubador.co.uk

ISBN 978-1-80514-500-4

British Library Cataloguing in Publication Data.
A catalogue record for this book is available from the British Library.

Printed and bound in Great Britain by 4edge Limited
Typeset in 11pt Minion Pro by Troubador Publishing Ltd, Leicester, UK

For Mark, Tom and Rory

Versions of some of these stories have been published as follows:

'Paradise Acre' appeared in *Utopia* (Momaya Press). 'Magpie' (as 'Vigilante') appeared in *The Book of Euclid* (Cinnamon Press). 'In the Blood' was first published in *Reaching Out* (Cinnamon Press). 'Proof' appeared in *Hysteria 2*. 'A Thousand Grains' was first published in *The Mechanics' Institute Review 14*. 'Off the Shelf' appeared in *Mslexia*. 'Looking for Michael' was published online at www.exeterwriters.org.uk. 'The Ishtar Pin' was a finalist in the Manchester Fiction Prize and published online at www.mmu.ac.uk/writingcompetition/winners/2021

Contents

All at Sea

You don't look up when I trudge towards you across the beach. The sand's warm under my feet, the sun not yet blistering. You're leaning over your wooden square, fiddling with seaweed, stones and Christ knows what else. How complicated can it be? Lines of sticks and shells, marching through our days.

'How do you know it's right?' I asked once. That was near the beginning – you were only on the second row. 'I started it the day after we got here,' you said. 'So we can keep track.'

Now the weeks are into double figures. I suppose that's a kind of miracle.

I dig my toes into the pale powder, upending a stumpy bit of your driftwood edging. 'You remind me of the – what were they called? Those people, who worked out the calendar, for two thousand years, to the end of the world.'

Your real feet tread on your shadow feet. 'Mayans.'

'That's it. The Mayans.'

I take up my spot in the shade, under the plastic sheet we rigged up. There's a great view: white sand, palm trees, blue sea. I long for concrete and tarmac.

It would make a good photo. A selfie would be better. The girls would be, like, WTF? OMG! U OK?

I press my knuckles into my eyes and hold my breath until the lump in my throat goes away. Our phones are long gone. My umbilical cord, Mum used to call it. My whole life was on there. I couldn't imagine being without it.

Amazing what you get used to.

This was the best place to set up camp, you said. Anyone landing would come in here. The other coves are too rocky. You'd been for a run – it must have been the first morning – and come back, sweating. Excited. You'd found water, and coconuts. There were fish.

'We'll be fine,' you said, and hugged me. 'It's an adventure.'

*

Below the sheet, strategically positioned to catch the dew, is the plastic basin. This sounds lame, so I'd never tell you, but when I spotted it on the sand my heart literally leapt. That basin was like a secret message – as if it had floated straight out of the salon to find me. I ran towards it, but when I picked it up, it was green and manky. It'd been at sea a while.

Some souvenirs have washed up, though: a few cushion covers, with the company logo, and the back of a white deck chair. No clothes, unfortunately. I'm still wearing the knickers and shirt I was sleeping in. Every time I wash them the holes get bigger, like bubbles you could make a wish on.

You stop mending the netting and sit next to me. Before we got together, I loved it when you did that, although I tried to play it cool. 'Treat 'em mean, keep 'em keen,' Mum always says. I'd spotted you from the PampaZone window: the dead spit of Jamie Dornan, dark hair shiny in the sun as you patrolled the pool. You stopped the punters sneaking glasses out to the loungers, and made sure the teenagers didn't bomb each other. But you always had a laugh. You weren't up yourself like the other lifeguards.

In between threading, and waxing, and layering on the Shellac and Gelish for my ladies, me and the girls used to joke – if the worst happened, we wouldn't mind being stuck with you.

But this isn't *Love Island*.

Your arm round my shoulders is hard. It hurts where it rests on my collar bone. You smell of sweat, and woodsmoke. You used to smell of sun block. You were always careful in the sun. Now we're tanned, all right: more than we could ever have imagined. Our cracked lips touch. We're still trying.

You pull away. 'At least the roof's holding. I'll get some wood for the fire.' The woodpile is your pride and joy; you've even found a tarpaulin to keep it dry. The throwaway culture has been good to us.

It took you hours but you managed to make a fire, using a piece of glass and brushwood. We don't let it go out. So now it has to smoke, day and night, next to our Ideal Starter Home – the cave we found, at the bottom of the cliff.

At first, I was scared the smoke would attract the wrong sort of neighbours. I couldn't believe there was no one else here. I've watched too many weird films where it turns out they're trapped in a giant experiment. We spent the first few nights lying awake, waiting for an ambush. No one came. You think the smoke will be spotted from a plane, or ship. We wrote a giant 'HELP!' in the sand. But the tide washed it away. We kept it simple after that and made a big cross, above the tideline, out of stones and shells, and anything that wasn't edible.

*

Sometimes I think about how we got here. Time played tricks that night. It sped up, then it slowed right down. A deafening bang. Darkness. Alarms, wailing. Everything sliding, going sideways. We crawled across your floor, and got the door open. A bloke in tartan pyjamas with a lifejacket on was staggering like a drunk along the passageway. You grabbed two lifejackets off their hooks. Outside, the deck was a massive climbing wall, bodies crawling upwards towards the hand rails, shiny in the moonlight. At the top, figures stood, staring at the black water, as if they didn't know what to do. Women were crying, hugging each other. A man kept shouting, 'What about the boats?' Someone dived off. Others were scrambling down the ladders, towards the sea, past the lifeboats, stuck on the side like barnacles. You pulled me with you. We climbed over the side and onto the slippery rungs. 'Don't look down,' you said. 'We'll have to jump.' I closed my eyes and tried to pretend it was ten years ago and I was 18, going down that flume ride at Thorpe Park, but really I thought, *This is it, the end.* I took a deep breath – and went. It felt like falling down a well. The drop and then the slap and sting of seawater, cold, salty, in my mouth; in my eyes. Then I was back above water, my arms thrashing, lungs gulping air. People floated past, hanging onto anything they could find. There were splashes, when someone dived or jumped; the stomach-churning thud of a body hitting an obstacle. You were beside me. 'Swim!' you shouted, above the screams, and the strange moaning sounds from the ship. It sounded like a dying animal. Things kept bumping into me: hard, soft – I couldn't tell what they were. We kicked, pushed ourselves forward. I couldn't keep up with you. You tied our jacket cords together and pulled me along. After a while the screaming stopped. The silence was worse. Something hit my side, winding me: a length of smashed wood. You stopped, and we floated, holding on to each other in the moonlight. Like the most romantic date ever; except we were in a nightmare. I was shaking, with cold and fear. You rubbed my arms, to keep the blood flowing. You calmed me down. 'We're alive,' you kept saying. 'We'll be okay.' We told each other stories, to stay awake. We always ended up talking about the ship. Our mates on the crew. The passengers.

What the hell had happened?

How on earth did all that stuff float in the first place? The climbing wall, the restaurants and bars, the dance floor, the therapy rooms and pools. And all those people. All of it, sitting there, on top of the ocean. Then, suddenly, it wasn't.

I thought of sharks. Did they live in the Indian Ocean? Luckily, we had no injuries; we weren't bleeding.

Sunrise is different, over the sea. There's nothing in the way. You get the light, before you see the sun. The sky turned pale grey. I couldn't bear to look. In the dark there had been people, debris, noise. Now there was nothing. We'd left the wreckage behind. We were completely alone.

The sun rose, quickly, and our skin began to burn.

We had no water. That was all I could think about, trying not to picture the endless water below us. So many times I'd stared out of the salon window, feeling hot and sticky in my work clothes, watching the sea change colour, imagining diving into the cool, greeny-blue. I would have given anything to be back there.

My face and arms were sore. I tried to wash off the salt, but that made it worse. I stuck my finger in the sea and wet my lips. You let me do that.

We'd only been a day out of port. The ship must have sent a distress signal. Surely somebody would find us? But we couldn't stay in one place; we kept drifting.

'It's all right,' you said. 'They'll look at the currents. They'll work out where survivors will be.'

I tried blowing the whistle on my lifejacket, but the sound was so feeble it made me want to cry.

'Save your energy,' you said. 'You'll need it.'

I watched the stripe of navy-blue horizon, willing a ship to appear. The sky was bright blue, streaked with white, wispy clouds. The sea was calm. It was beautiful. It went on forever.

The sun slid across the sky, and when we swam, we followed it.

Later, it must have been later, the wind got up, and the sun went behind clouds. Waves broke over us; small at first, but they got bigger. I turned my head at the wrong time and swallowed a mouthful of seawater that left me gasping. I didn't mean to, but I started to cry. I felt like giving up; slipping out of my jacket. But you wouldn't let me go.

You spotted a shape – rocks. Somehow you found the energy to power us towards them.

The rocks got bigger. An island.

'It's straight out of a film,' you said. 'Palm trees and everything.' The light was going by the time we staggered onto the beach, and collapsed on the sand, and I closed my eyes and felt the sea, still moving, under my ribs.

That night, we slept beside some bushes at the top of the beach. First thing the next morning you made your fire, and started on your calendar.

'We're so lucky,' you said. 'What about those poor bastards trying to cross the Channel in leaky boats? Remember that little kid's body, washed up in the Med?'

'Everyone knows they're there,' I said. 'What about us?'

*

Were people picked up? Is anyone still looking?

There'll be a record somewhere – the staff and passenger manifest, with our names on it. We used to laugh – we covered the alphabet from A to Z – Abby and Zach.

Soon there'll be three of us.

I didn't want to tell you at first. I couldn't believe it. I thought it was worry that had stopped everything. Then I realised – and felt stupid. Panicked. Terrified. I mean – one day, sure. But not here. Not now.

I thought it might sort itself out, as Mum would say. I tried giving it a helping hand by running up and down a sand dune, in the heat, until my head was pounding and I had to lie down. You wondered what I was up to and I said I was trying to keep fit. When you were busy fishing one day, I drank sea water, and threw up. I tried that a few times.

But it's determined, all right. Must get that from you.

'We can't have it,' I said. 'I don't want it.'

'We'll manage,' you said. 'People do.'

'We've got nothing!' I yelled. 'What if something goes wrong?'

'We'll be rescued, you'll see.'

Now you're making a cradle.

Sand is surprisingly hard to sleep on. The cave is cold, and damp. You're on your back, snoring. The sound echoes off the walls until it feels like the whole space is growling.

A finger of moonlight creeps down the rock, and the wet patches gleam. I slide out from under our palm leaf cover and move carefully past you. I step round the smouldering fire, and follow the track, past your calendar, to the beach.

I have my own clock now: my own calendar, counting down. An uncertain future yawns ahead, dark and deep as a tunnel.

The tide is up. A wide, silvery stripe floats on the black sea.

Water laps my ankles, my thighs. It's shockingly cold.

My ripped shirt clings to the curve of my belly. I remember drifting helplessly in that endless space.

A wave slaps my chin. I open my mouth, taste the shock of salt. I swallow it down. Another mouthful surges into my throat. There's water in my nose, in my ears. I push my face under. I try to open my eyes but I can't. I stumble, fall, arms flailing.

I back out, coughing and retching, wheezing for air. I bend double, splattering seawater over my feet.

At the top of the beach, the woodpile hulks under the tarpaulin. I lift the heavy cloth and crawl underneath, curling myself into a ball.

In my dream, the sun beats down on my head. The sand's hot and grainy under my knees. I'm digging up your crappy calendar, shoving my fingers into it until they bleed, hurling wood and shells and stones into the air, screaming my head off. *It's gone! It's gone!*

I wake, crying. Sweat on my skin. I push at the tarpaulin. Sweet, cool air seeps in and I drink it down.

I can't do this.

The dark presses on my eyes.

This isn't a dream.

What's that?

I put my hand to my belly.

A flutter, a swoop.

Morse code. An SOS from a distant sea.

My heart trips.

I wait. Silent, breathless.

The message comes again, more urgent this time.

Lily

Once he's out of sight, Bill lights a cigarette and takes a deep drag. He pulls on the upright bar to open the gate onto the Downs path, and a swift knife of pain along his left arm makes him gasp. He leans on the gate and breathes hard until the pain goes. Then he edges through, onto the track, and sets off, avoiding roots, flicking stones into the hedge with his stick. Not bad for an eighty-year-old.

In the field beside him, a crop he can't identify – wheat, barley? – has shot up, its leaves startlingly green. Eleanor's right, the countryside is always changing. He'll ask her what they're growing up here; she'll understand that he's adjusting to the move. A lifelong townie, he misses pitched roofs and neat parcels of garden. All this space makes him feel small.

The track turns into a narrow lane. Trees have grown across, forming a shadowy tunnel. Mickey's voice is back in Bill's head: 'We'll make a man of you yet!' He remembers the bitter smell of hops. He was just a kid. The others are long gone. If he dared to tell Eleanor, would it all go away?

She's at the kitchen table, in her sweatshirt and jeans, reading her iPad. He's suddenly aware of the fifteen years between them and grateful for her steadfastness. He bends to kiss her silvery-blonde hair, damp from the shower.

She takes out her ear buds. 'Did you commune with nature?'

'You know me.' Bill glimpses the screen. Behind the newsreader, burned-out cars are scattered across a road. An apartment block stands, open to the blue sky. He feels the familiar dread under his ribs. On a mound of rubble a young man's body lies, face down. Will that family want revenge? Is forgiveness ever possible?

Now Bill hears the old pram, creaking down the street, pots and pans clanking; the whole contraption swaying, threatening to come apart. His cousin Mickey, twisting Bill's wrists: 'Billy White by name, Lily White by nature!' Even picking hops that summer, Bill's hands stayed pale, criss-crossed with stinging cuts from the woody bines.

'Bill!' Eleanor sounds irritated.

Has she guessed what he's thinking? 'What?'

'Have you taken your tablets?'

'Don't fuss.'

*

The hoppers' trains left at dawn, from London Bridge. The rattling carriages were packed. Bill stood, squashed by the window, between Mickey, and Mickey's mate Ron. When the train lurched, Bill fell into them. He'd lain awake all night, worried he'd miss Mickey's knock. Tiredness made him clumsy.

'Watch it, you little git.' Mickey pinched Bill's ear.

Ron scowled. 'Why's he coming, anyway?'

'One less kid in the house for his old ma.' Bill's twin brothers were three weeks old. Mickey lit a roll-up, and blew the smoke at Bill. 'We're going to be your mum and dad for a week.'

Bill wanted to say, *No you're not, you're only nineteen!* But he didn't dare.

Ron smoothed his hair, dark and shiny with Brylcreem. 'He'd better not cramp our style, Mick.'

'He won't.' Mickey grinned. 'We might even show him our HQ.'

Bill blinked hard. 'You mean, like an army one?'

'Where we plan our campaigns.' Ron looked at Mickey. 'If it's still there.'

'We'll find somewhere,' Mickey said. 'Ain't that so, Lily?'

Bill put on what Ma called his 'grown up face'. 'Definitely.'

Mickey laughed. 'No more toy soldiers for you, mate.'

The train moved above narrow streets of roofless houses. Wallpaper flapped, like bloomers on a washing line. It looked like the war had ended yesterday, not nearly ten years ago. Churchill should get a move on and sort it out, Bill's pa was always saying.

On a pile of rubble, kids were playing tag. For a moment, Bill envied them.

'Look at that,' Mickey said. 'Bloody Jerry. Hunted us like rats.'

Mickey's nan and little sister had been too slow, one night, to get to the Tube shelter. That was why Mickey's mum *wasn't all there*. And why Mickey was trouble. 'Hot-headed,' Bill's ma called him. She didn't know the half of it.

The cluttered streets gave way to pairs of houses, with gardens that reached almost to the railway. Then: enormous yellow fields. In the distance a toy tractor, bright blue, crept up a slope. Beside the track were clumps of trees; their leaves brushed the train windows.

Mickey stared out. 'D'you know, in France, they found Jerries, hanging in the trees, still in their bleedin' parachutes.'

'Too bloody good for 'em,' said Ron.

Bill imagined cold air rushing at his face and the stab of thorny branches on his legs. Leaves, covering his mouth, suffocating him. He shivered. And if he was caught... he could feel the brick wall at his back; see the line of rifles, each with its single, staring eye.

They walked to the hop fields from the station, the whole gang of them, pushing their makeshift carts. The women's chatter filled the lane. Pram wheels squeaked under their loads.

*

'How can violence solve anything? They never learn.' Sally from the old vicarage holds out her wine glass for a refill. 'Bloody stupid men. I'm sick of them all.' She adds, too slowly, 'Present company excepted, of course.'

'I agree.' Eleanor puts the poached salmon on the table. 'I can't bear the way they go on about the rules of war, as if it's a game.'

'Of course there are rules,' Bill says. His voice surprises him. He doesn't look at Eleanor.

Sally shrugs. 'If the soldiers refused to fight, there'd be no war.'

'Some of them did refuse,' Bill says. 'It made no difference.' Aware that he's being listened to he adds, 'Most of those kids are conscripts. They've got no choice.'

'They're using torture.' Sally's husband Paul joins in. He's made his money in caravan parks and looks down on Bill as a retired bean counter. 'They know what they're doing.'

Eleanor hands round the plates. 'They'd just say they were following orders.'

'As if that's an excuse,' Paul says.

'It's not an excuse.' Bill can't help himself. 'It's a fact. Who knows what we'd do? It takes courage to stand up.'

There's a silence.

'Talking of courage,' Sally says, 'there was a half-dead rabbit in the lane yesterday. I put it under my front wheel.'

'Now that's brave!' says Eleanor.

'Something always needs killing in the countryside,' Paul says.

Eleanor laughs. 'As long as you don't expect Bill to do it.'

He doesn't point out the irony of her wanting him to be violent. She's put little candles on the table: the one nearest him is guttering in a pool of wax. Bill licks his finger and thumb and pinches out the flame. It leaves a black mark on his fingertips.

'Must we have candles?' he says. 'Health and safety, you know – with the wooden beams.' He gets up and snaps on the overhead light.

Eleanor frowns: the look he knows too well. 'Are you okay?'

'Yes. Fine.'

*

Hop-picking was harder than hauling sacks for the coalman, or loading crates onto the milk-cart. The woody, hairy bines were heavy, and had to be pulled off their supports, where they clung like limpets; the yeasty smell off the hops made Bill's eyes water. At five o'clock on the first day, when the farm manager shouted, 'Pick no more bines!' Bill's hands were covered in stinging welts, and his shoulders ached. But the canvas bin beside him was full of bright green treasure. He pictured how his ma would smile when he handed over his earnings at the end of the week.

He shared a hut with Mickey and Ron. The first night, Mickey dragged Bill's straw pallet away to the far wall, and pushed the other two closer together. Then he and Ron sat up smoking, talking about people Bill didn't know, and Bill fell asleep imagining the two of them were his big brothers. He dreamed of galloping on horseback over a grassy plain, in their gang of three, guns at the ready in case of ambush.

One night Bill woke to silence. Moonlight streamed in over the door and fell on the two empty mattresses across the room. An owl hooted, too close. Bill pulled the scratchy blanket up to his chin and shut his eyes tight. He pinched the inside of his arm to keep himself awake and wait for Mickey and Ron.

The next morning, they still weren't back. The small hut was too big; too quiet. Bill was horrified to feel his eyes fill with tears. He got dressed quickly and hurried outside. Anxiously he scanned the yard. Women chatted in groups by the lavs. Kids ran in and out of the tables laid with porridge bowls and loaves of bread. There was a long queue for the tea urn. Relief surged through him. There they were, dark heads together, sharing a roll-up and laughing. They hadn't gone and left him behind.

Bill ran over and tugged Mickey's shirt sleeve. 'Where were you last night? Did you go to your HQ?'

Mickey cuffed him. 'Mind your own, Lily.'

On the last night, the hoppers sat round the fire. Shadows jumped, making the faces Bill had got to know strange again. The strangeness gave him courage. He was tougher, stronger; no longer the weedy twelve-year old who'd come down on the train a week ago.

Two older women started the singing. Their voices rose in the soft air, and for a moment all the hard work melted away. Bill was almost sad to be leaving, although the promise of home was there in the words.

'Bugger the bloody *Lambeth Walk*.' Mickey stood up. 'Bed time, Lily.'

'I'm coming with you,' Bill said.

Ron gave Mickey a loaded look. 'Not tonight!'

'You promised!' Bill scuffed his plimsoll in the dirt. 'Otherwise I'll tell.'

'Tell what, you little shit?' Ron swiped at him, but Bill dodged away.

'All right.' Mickey sighed. 'Come on.'

He led them away from the yard. The singing grew fainter. They crossed a field, climbed a stile, and turned into a narrow lane. The hedgerow met the trees in a dark tunnel. Mickey stopped, and ducked under a branch. Hidden in the bushes, as if it had grown out of them, was an old hut. He pulled at the door. 'Welcome to our HQ.'

*

Eleanor's curled on the sofa under a blanket, watching TV.

Bill, on his way out for his evening cigarette, can't help glancing at the screen. A young woman he vaguely recognizes is muttering into her mobile. Beside her, a man in white coveralls peers into a deep hole. At the bottom, under a scattering of soil, are human limbs. He looks away quickly.

'The hands have been cut off, and there's no teeth.' Eleanor rifles in the box of chocolates left over from the dinner party. 'They'll have to do DNA profiling.'

'Don't you get fed up watching this stuff?'

'It's entertaining. Escapism.' She pats the sofa. 'Come on. You might like it.'

'You know I hate these things.' He tries to smile. 'I mean – if it was real… you wouldn't want to watch it then, would you?'

'For God's sake, Bill.' She offers him the chocolates. Her manicured nails are vivid drops of blood. 'If it was real, it'd be all over the news.'

'Yes. Of course.' He feels his heart knock; the old fear. 'El? I wondered –'

'Ssshh. I missed that bit.'

*

Mickey and Ron went in first, stooping. Bill followed. There was the smell of damp wood. The door closed, and for a moment he could see nothing.

Mickey lit a candle. 'Here's – bloody hell!'

An old mattress, with a blanket, took up half the space. Under the blanket was a lumpy shape. Mickey bent down, and carefully pulled the cover back. There was a man. Curled up, asleep. A skinny, dark-haired man, in poor clothes. Next to him was an empty whisky bottle.

Mickey put the light near the stranger's face. The man's skin was dirty. 'He's not a hopper,' Mickey said. 'Where's he from?'

'Tramp,' said Ron.

'He looks like an Eye-tie,' whispered Mickey. 'Or a Spic.'

'Enemy alien,' said Ron. He went to kick the man awake, but Mickey stopped him.

'Maybe he's a Jerry,' Mickey said. 'Escaped from a camp.'

'There's no more camps,' Bill said. 'They shut them years ago.' He'd seen it on the Pathé news at the Gaumont: all the Jerries had gone home, apart from a few who liked it here and wanted to stay. There'd been pictures of them, in the paper, having Christmas dinner with local people. 'Good Christian families,' his ma called them. Pa said they were 'do-gooders'. That sounded bad.

In the candlelight the man was a bony shadow on the mattress. Could he be a Jerry, who wanted to stay?

Mickey sniffed the bottle. 'Whoever he is, he's out for the count.' He set the candle in an empty jar, took something from his pocket, and tied the stranger's wrists. Then he glanced at Bill. 'Keep an eye on him, Lily. We've got business to see to.' He followed Ron out, and turned in the doorway. 'Said we'd make a man of you.'

The candle flickered in the draught.

Bill sat next to the stranger, his back against the damp wall. His heart thudded under his ribs. He didn't dare move, in case the man woke up. He was in Mickey and Ron's HQ! He counted to a hundred, and back again, a few times, to calm himself. It was a good HQ. It felt secret. There was no window, and the walls were covered in leaves, growing in from outside. Bill was glad of the candle, though it threw odd shadows. The man's breathing was steady and even. Was he really a Jerry? He looked like anyone else. Ma would have said he'd 'fallen on hard times'.

Mickey would tease the bloke, maybe push him about a bit, and let him go.

Watching the man, lost in sleep, reminded Bill of sitting on Ma and Pa's bed, beside the twins' cot, waiting for them to wake up. Longing for home overcame him. He pressed his fists into his eyes.

*

Bill wakes, his pulse fast in his throat. He can't breathe. It's as if a rag is stuffed in his mouth. He stares into the dark.

Beside him, Eleanor snores quietly.

He needs air. He sits up, and eases his legs from under the duvet. Eleanor doesn't stir. Slowly he crosses the carpet, closing the door carefully behind him. In the kitchen he pulls a jumper over his pyjamas, and puts on his Barbour and wellies. He finds his stick by the back door, and steps into the cool morning.

He lights a cigarette, and moves off down the lane. In the still air the hedgerows shimmer, busy with birds. If he screws up his eyes, it could be a late summer's evening.

*

When Mickey and Ron came back, they smelled of beer. They brought more candles.

Mickey had a stick. He prodded the sleeping stranger. 'Hey, pal. Wakey wakey!'

The man's eyelids fluttered open.

Bill had a heavy, cold feeling in his stomach. He stepped back, and crouched in the corner.

'What are you doing here?' Mickey stood over the man. 'This is our place.'

The stranger tried to get up. Then he realized his wrists were tied. He looked from one to the other of them, puzzled.

With the stick, Mickey pushed the man backwards. 'For your own good, pal. Where are you from?'

The man said something they couldn't understand.

Mickey went nearer to listen. 'What's that?'

The stranger tried again. Bill thought he heard, 'bitter'.

Mickey looked up, grinning. 'Hear that? He is a bleedin' Jerry after all.' He shoved the man's shoulder, hard. 'A bloody Jerry, in our HQ.' He turned to Bill. 'What do you think of that, Lily?'

The foreigner muttered something. Ron leaned over him. 'Speak English, mate!'

'Don't know any, does he?' Mickey laughed. '*Nein, nein!*'

The man darted a look at him, and struggled upright.

'First lesson coming up!' Mickey swung his fist. There was the crack of bone, and the stranger fell sideways, like a broken doll.

Bill had never seen one man hit another. The air seemed to shake with the force of it.

The foreigner lay on the mattress, moaning.

'Filthy Jerry scum.' Mickey took a rag from his pocket, and pushed it into the man's mouth.

'What are you going to do?' Bill asked. It was hard to speak. His throat was dry.

When Mickey struck the first match, holding it up near his face, he looked like the villain off the poster for *The Third Man*. He bent to the stranger, and put the match to the man's hair. There was the sickening smell of rotten eggs. A dark stain spread across the man's rough trousers. His face twisted and he began to cry.

'Dirty bastard.' Ron kicked the man's leg. There was a muffled groan.

'We can stop now, hey, Mickey?' Bill's voice wavered. 'What if someone finds us?'

'No one comes down here.'

The prisoner's eyes were pleading. His head was marked with blistering, raw patches, where Mickey had burned the hair off.

Mickey leaned down to him. 'Hear that, Fritz? No one's coming to find you. No bleedin' Luftwaffe cavalry.'

The stranger closed his eyes, and whispered to himself. Was he praying? Prayers wouldn't work. Not against Mickey and Ron.

Bill wanted to stick his fingers in his ears. He should run and get someone. There were coppers, somewhere – they were sent down from London with the trains.

What would he say? He was in on it. And Mickey had no time for snitches.

'Do his fingers, Lily.' Mickey shook the box of matches in Bill's face. He struck a match and held it near Bill's fingertips.

Bill recoiled from the heat.

Ron laughed. 'Otherwise we'll do yours.'

Bill took the box and tried to strike a match, but his hands shook and he dropped it. Mickey struck another and passed it to him, the heat of it up near his eyes. Ron held the prisoner still, and Bill touched the flame to the man's thumbs. The skin glowed, then bubbled and blackened. Bill thought he'd be sick. The stranger squirmed and cried, his legs thrashing the floor. The small space stank of shit.

When the matches were almost gone, Mickey pulled the rag from the prisoner's mouth. 'What's that, Fritz?'

The man gasped for air, as if he was drowning.

'You want a drink?' Mickey's voice was friendly.

Bill felt his heart lift. The foreigner was going to be all right.

'Oh dear.' Mickey turned the whisky bottle upside down. 'Shouldn't have guzzled it, should you?' He stuffed the rag back in the man's mouth, and threw the blanket over him. He winked at Bill. 'Bet you've got a hanky, haven't you Lily?'

Bill found one in his pocket.

Mickey wiped the empty bottle. 'Can't be too careful.' He picked up the jam jar and candles.

Outside, Mickey and Ron rolled a log from the hedgerow. Mickey looked up. 'Come on Lily! Don't just stand there.'

Bill couldn't move. Tears welled in his eyes. 'Can't we let him out?' he whispered.

'This is the best way.' Mickey grabbed Bill's hands, and pressed them down on the bark. 'Put your back into it.'

The log fell into the door with a heartbreaking thud. Ron covered the entrance with brambles, and they started back across the field.

The fresh air hit Bill like a train. He doubled over, and vomited into a ditch.

The moon was up. They crept across the yard, and slipped into the hut. Mickey patted him on the back. 'Can't call you Lily no more, can we?'

Bill lay down. He didn't dare close his eyes; behind them was the stranger, wounded and dying, alone in the dark. Why hadn't Bill helped him?

Later, when he was sure Mickey and Ron were asleep, he got up and crept towards the door.

A hand gripped his ankle.

'Not worried about our friend, are you?' Mickey pulled him down. 'Don't you forget, he'd do the same to you.'

Bill crawled back to his mattress, stuffing his hand in his mouth to stop the sobs. Through the gap above the door he watched the night sky and felt the stars' cold gaze.

*

Ahead, on the path, sunlight flickers through the trees in a kaleidoscope of green. A brown rabbit lollops out of the undergrowth. As Bill nears, the animal staggers in a circle, leaning to one side. It falls over and lies, unable to get up. *Something always needs killing in the countryside.*

It's easy to approach the creature. It growls half-heartedly but doesn't move.

Bill bends down to the rabbit and grasps its hind legs. The

fur is surprisingly coarse, the bones light. 'Come on, old pal.' Leaning on his stick, he lifts the animal and its ears flop down, revealing patches of angry skin. Fighting nausea, Bill brings the rabbit's head level with his own. The eyes are swollen shut, the head jerks round. The creature struggles feebly in his grip.

'It's all right.' By the hedge is an old oak. Bill stands, his arm wide, ready to swing the rabbit at the tree trunk.

This is the man Eleanor wants him to be. This is how he'll start the conversation. Confession must bring absolution. Dare he ask for that, after all this time? Can courage now make up for his lack of it, all those years ago?

The rabbit's not heavy but it takes all Bill's strength to hold the animal out in front of him. His chest and arm ache.

Without warning, the creature screams.

Bill lets go.

The rabbit falls into the ditch and lies, twitching.

With his stick Bill pokes around in the undergrowth and finds a hand-sized stone. He turns back to the ditch.

The creature is on its side, lying still.

Bill drops the stone. Relief surges through him and he leans against the tree.

From somewhere, a bird calls, the notes high and pure. The sky is pale blue and white, bright with the promise of a new day.

Glad of his stick Bill moves slowly down the lane, his breath tight. The pain in his arm will pass.

Perhaps it takes courage, just to keep living. He'll tell Eleanor everything and she'll understand. He can hear the words, forming in his head.

Green Fingers

I hear his angry tapping every day. Like the signal of a forgotten prisoner, his typing echoes in the silence. He sits at his desk under the courtyard staircase, out of the sun because of his pale skin. He's writing the history of this house: the story of everyone who's ever lived here.

I wonder how it will end.

His Spanish was always good, although now if I speak quickly, he looks blank. When I ask, 'How is your wife?' I say it nice and slow. I want to make sure he understands.

*

They arrived one July afternoon five years ago, their big hire car nosing up the street like a curious bull. They grabbed Luis's old house as soon as they saw it. Didn't even haggle, Luis said.

Later, Luis brought the husband into the bar. He was tall and narrow-shouldered, his face as pink as his shirt. He ordered a beer and introduced himself as William.

'You can call me Guillermo,' he said.

'I'll call you my Lotto ticket,' Luis said to me, under his breath. 'These are your neighbours,' he went on, pointing to Miguel who was sitting at the counter, and me behind the bar. It was my day for washing glasses. 'Miguel lives opposite, with his wife, Gabriela. He does many things. Taxi, plumber, builder – whatever you want, Miguel can do it!'

William smiled. 'That sounds useful.' His eyes were light and hard.

Luis turned to me. 'Maria lives next door to you. She knows everything about our street.'

'I've lived here all my life,' I said, stacking glasses on the bar top. 'Seventy-five years, in the same house.'

'Great.' William nodded at me, his hands in his pockets. His fair hair was thin on his head and his skin showed through, smooth as a baby's.

I was going to tell him that I was the last of five, the one who stayed to look after the parents. About my oldest brother who was killed in the war and my sister, a teacher, who helped me learn English. That she's in Madrid. But William was looking around the room.

'You've bought the lucky house,' I said. I knew that would get his attention.

He smiled and reached for his beer. He drank from the bottle. 'Go on.'

'My mother said that in the courtyard there's an old pine. As long as it grows there, you will have your' – I couldn't remember the English – '*deseo del corazon*.'

'The desire of your heart,' Luis said.

'Heart's desire,' William said. He looked at Luis, waiting for him to laugh.

Luis smiled. 'Maria knows all the old stories.'

'Sounds good!' William raised his beer bottle. 'To all our heart's desires!' There was a movement behind him, and a young woman stepped forward. 'This is my wife, Helena,' he said.

She was darker-skinned, thin as a stick. Straight, black hair hung round her face. With her were two serious-looking children: a dark-haired girl of seven or so, and a younger, paler boy.

'Anna and Jamie, say hello,' William said.

Helena put her arms round the children awkwardly. They said nothing.

That evening, as I watered my plants, I thought about the family moving in next door. It was a long time since children had lived there. I could help them with their Spanish.

*

But they didn't move in. They came back at Easter, William wanting a plumber and an electrician when it was fiesta time. The sound of drilling and hammering echoed in the street.

'Where do you buy good furniture?' he asked.

'In the town,' I said, but he made a face.

I gave them a tablecloth as a welcome present, to cover the wooden table they ate at. They never used it. But they were always asking me where to find the best this, the real that.

It was lucky for them that Miguel lived so close. He was always in that house. The tap was dripping – ask Miguel; they needed shelves – ask Miguel; a problem with the water tank – ask Miguel. Sometimes Gabriela came too, and they all sat together drinking beer.

'You could make a fortune in London,' William said to Miguel one day. They were out on the terrace. I was in the kitchen. Helena had asked me to cook 'real paella'.

'A fortune?' Miguel sat up straighter. 'That's true?'

'Well – I mean, with your skills,' William said. 'It's hard to find good people.'

'Good people!' Helena laughed, but her voice was hard. She touched Gabriela's arm. 'Isn't that what we all want?'

Miguel saw me watching. 'I think it means something different here.'

I wondered if they would stay this time. Then I overheard William say something about 'keeping an eye on the place'.

The next day Helena said they were going back to England, but would I be their housekeeper. I liked the word. Keeping the house. I thought about it. Then I said yes.

'You're a treasure, Maria,' said William. '*Nuestra tresor.*' He looked pleased with himself. He stepped forward, as if he might shake my hand, then stopped. 'Good,' he said. 'Excellent.'

*

After that we didn't see them until July. By then it was hot, but they carried on just the same: while William did his typing, or drew diagrams of how the house could look, Helena went shopping. Sometimes she and Gabriela took the children to the beach, or they went out early, sightseeing. The children must have had their siesta in the car.

One afternoon we were in the kitchen. Helena was kneeling on the floor, unwrapping old plates she had bought in a market somewhere. The children were outside, arguing in the heat. The sound of William's typing echoed through the house.

'He doesn't want a computer?' I asked. 'Is it because of the electricity?' Our supply in the street was unpredictable.

Helena laughed. 'No, no. He says typing makes him feel like Hemingway – you know, the famous American author, who loved Spain.'

'My sister likes his work,' I said. 'But a computer would be more peaceful.'

The noise was worse because one of the downstairs walls had been removed to make a bigger room, but it was unfinished. Wires hung from the plaster.

Helena handed me a plate to wash. 'Do you think we're crazy, Maria?'

I gripped the slippery china. 'You find a lot to do in this house.'

'William likes to start things,' she said. 'But then he doesn't know how to finish them.' She gave me another plate and it slipped, smashing on the tiles. 'Oh!' She started to cry.

'*Senora.*' I bent to help her. She put her hands to her face, and her sleeve fell back. On her arm was a row of bruises, like dark fingerprints.

That evening was the first time I heard them arguing through the wall. Her voice was sharp; his was soft, like water dripping on a stone. But it would cut a groove.

The next morning, when I took him his coffee, he was standing by the desk, studying his drawings of the house.

He looked up. 'Are you sure this house has never been altered, Maria?'

'You have plans, *Senor*?' I put the coffee cup down on the sketches. 'Nothing has been built here for four hundred years,' I said, not bothering to keep the pride out of my voice.

William took his coffee and walked over to the window. He kept his back to me. 'Well, perhaps it's time we started, then. Nothing major, not the house, as such.' His talk was full of meaningless words like that. You had to pick them out here and there, like bad tomatoes from a bowl.

'What are you thinking of?' I glanced at the pages but I could make no sense of them.

'Well, Maria – one thing we always wanted, my wife and I' – he came back to the table and prodded his drawings – 'this house, here – it's our little bit of heaven, as it were. And to make it complete – we both feel' – he stressed the 'both' – 'we need a pool.' He looked up at me, pleased with himself.

I thought of water pouring over rocks and men digging, more broken things. 'You know how precious water is here, *Senor*.'

'Oh yes, yes. We'll pay, of course,' he said. 'Do you think Miguel could do it?'

*

The next day they were all on the terrace. Helena and Gabriela sat under the parasol, talking, while William and Miguel walked up and down, William waving his arms about, no doubt telling Miguel about the pool – where the walls would go, how deep it would be.

As they came back towards the kitchen, I heard William say, 'You'll have to clear the whole area, of course.'

I hurried outside. '*Senor!*'

He turned. 'Maria. Yes?'

'Don't you remember? The lucky tree.' I made him follow me back up to the top. The sun was already burning, and his face ran with sweat, like fat on a suckling pig. 'Here it is.' The little tree squatted in the corner. The short branches were almost bare of needles, but its roots were firm in the soil. 'It's very old.'

Willliam glanced down. 'That's not a tree. It's a shrub. And it's half dead!' He looked over the wall at the town spread below, the small square roofs like playing tiles in the sun. 'I didn't know you were a gardener, Maria.' His voice was unfriendly. 'You should go to England. Everyone's crazy about gardening there.'

'Perhaps I will,' I said. 'I would like to see your country.'

He said nothing.

'*El deseo del corazon,*' I said. 'I told you the story. My mother told it to me. It's brought good luck to this house.'

'What kind of luck?' he asked.

I wanted to say that Luis' mother lost no one in the war; she lived to ninety, and was blessed with grandchildren. But I knew that wasn't the kind of luck he meant. 'It's hard to explain,' I said.

'People make their own luck.' William crouched down and snapped off the end of a branch. 'It's an old dwarf pine.' He threw the twig over the wall and smiled an empty smile at me – an old woman who's lived in the same house, in the same street, all her life. 'Just a fairy tale, I'm afraid.' He indicated the terrace with a sweep of his arm. 'That's my heart's desire – a pool.'

I bent to the tree and rubbed its needles between my finger and thumb. The smell of pine was faint, but it was there. I remembered my mother telling me the story her mother had told her. How she had always envied Luis's mother.

'Perhaps you are right,' I said. 'It's only an old tree. Your pool is more important.'

He laughed. 'I knew you'd come round in the end.' He kicked the tree. 'Its luck has run out.'

*

Two days later, Miguel and Salvatore started digging. Sun caught their spades as they sliced through the plants and the dry soil. While the men worked, Helena and Gabriela made them cool drinks, or took the children out, away from the noise. By the end of the week, the garden had gone.

I had to pick my way over piles of rubble to water the vine William was trying to grow against the far wall. On the debris heaped in the corner was the little tree, earth clinging to its tangled roots. It weighed almost nothing.

*

'Maria, can you look after the children for me?' Helena was on her way out. 'Gabriela's going to help me choose tiles for the pool. We won't be long.' The heavy front door banged behind her.

While the children had their siesta, William typed. It was the only sound in the street – not even a dog barked in the heat. The small digger Miguel had hired was silent in the rubble, bent forward like a scavenging bird.

I woke the children at five o'clock and we went out to the courtyard. The air was warm and still. The sun had moved round, and the space was shady. The red and orange flowers made the pots look like fiery cauldrons.

Jamie lay on the ground, dropping small stones into his truck and pushing it backwards and forwards. Anna sat at the table, drawing.

'Do you believe in nonsense, Dona Maria?' she said, without looking up.

'Nonsense, *mija*? I hope not.'

She nodded. 'That's what I thought. And Daddy said there's no such thing as witches, even in this funny old place.'

'Your daddy is very clever.'

'I know. Mummy said he should be careful.'

'Did she?'

'We're getting a pool,' Anna said. 'You don't want us to, do you?'

'No.'

'Why not?' She scowled at me with her mother's dark eyes. 'It's our house and we can do what we like.'

'Of course, *mija*.'

'Anyway, Daddy said it's his heart desire.'

'What's a heart desire?' asked Jamie, tipping the stones out of his truck.

'Heart's desire,' I said. 'Something you want more than anything else.'

'That's *easy*.' He pushed his truck into the stones. 'No school!'

'Don't be stupid,' Anna said. 'You'll never make anything of yourself.' She looked at me. 'What's yours?' she asked.

'I'm not sure I can tell.'

Helena and Gabriela were back after seven. They came in carrying small cardboard boxes, one on top of the other. Gabriela stacked them on the kitchen floor, while Helena opened the fridge and took out a bottle of wine.

'It was so hot today!' She pushed her hair off her forehead.

'Look, Maria.' She opened one of the boxes, and took out an ordinary green tile. 'Isn't that beautiful?'

Gabriela nodded. 'It is a skill, to be able to make things.'

Helena passed her the wine and a bottle-opener. 'Lucky you, married to Miguel.' They both laughed, as if they shared a secret. Helena turned to me. 'Were the children good?'

'Of course,' I said. 'But they missed you.'

She took the glass Gabriela gave her. 'Their father was here, wasn't he?'

That night William's and Helena's voices were loud through the wall. Even my radio, turned up loud, couldn't drown them out. I couldn't understand the words but I heard a name I knew.

I was glad to leave for my holiday with my sister in Madrid. I needed to forget about William and his pool.

*

When I returned, two weeks later, everything was quiet next door.

I let myself in to the house as usual. I called out, 'Hello!' No one answered. I tiptoed through the rooms, careful as a burglar. At any moment, I expected the children to surprise me. But my shoes echoed on the tiles. In the kitchen, I slid back the latch and opened the shutters.

The terrace was a building site. The mechanical digger had gone. There was no sign of Miguel or Salvatore. I opened the door. On the air was an odd sound, an animal grunting. I walked up to the top of the steps and looked down. William stood in the bottom of a half-dug pit. He was bending over a spade, his pale hands gripping the handle. One foot, in its tennis shoe, was pushing the blade into the stony earth.

'*Buenas dias*!' I called.

He looked up, startled. 'Maria!' He waved me over to him.

I made my way to the edge of the pit. There were no steps yet; you had to jump in and out. '*Senor.*' I stood by the deep end. 'You are working hard.'

'*Si!*' William leaned on the spade and wiped his forehead with his arm. His shirt was dark with sweat. 'Unfortunately, I've had to – let Miguel go. The job wasn't working out. So' – he indicated the rocky space – 'I'm going to finish this myself.' He jabbed the spade into the ground. 'It'll take me a bit longer, but – I know I can do it.'

'Where are the children?' I had to ask.

William watched the spade, puffing up clouds of grey dust. 'They've – they've gone back home. To England. My wife felt – she thought – the house wasn't ready.' He pushed small rocks into a pile. 'She'll be back when – when –' He looked up at me, and smiled. 'When the pool's finished.'

*

Helena and the children are not back yet. Neither is Gabriela. Miguel rarely comes to the bar. Willliam looks tired these days; too much sun does not suit him. But the doctor says I am doing well for my age. I still enjoy my garden: my neighbours say I have *mano para las plantas* – green fingers. In my courtyard, the old pine is thriving.

William often stands outside, staring at the shell of his pool. It lies there like a dirty wound, waiting for water. He told me, the other day, that he's thinking of selling. But who would want his house, with its half-dug pool, its broken-down walls?

He never looks at his drawings. He's forgotten all his Spanish.

'When will your wife be coming back?' I ask him. 'How are the children?' But he doesn't answer.

Looking for Michael

'What brings you to Kenya, Jill?' Dana's question hangs in the air behind me.

She appeared at my door ten minutes ago, opening it as she knocked. I was sitting at my desk, thinking about Michael.

I can tell my visitor's scanning the small room, searching for photographs of adult children, or grandchildren; proof that someone *cares*.

I keep my back to her. 'You know – to do my bit for humanity.'

At least I'm conforming to type: the stuck-up Brit, cold-shouldering the friendly Aussie. Since we arrived, a week ago, I've watched Dana working her way round the other volunteers, extracting their stories with a cheery smile and a pat on the arm.

The bed squeaks. I turn round. She's parked herself on the thin bedcover, her thighs spilling out of her shorts. I imagine her sweat on the sheet.

Her freckled face is as innocent as a child's. 'Do you have a medical background, then?'

'Yes.' *A long time ago, but that's none of your business.*

Beside me on the desk is Morag's farewell present, in its worthy recycled paper; a flat, square parcel, ticking like a time bomb in my heart. I was about to open it when Dana burst in. I presume it's a book: my daughter-in-law has a book for every occasion. She pressed the package on me as we kissed the wrong cheeks on what feels like the other side of the world. My granddaughter hugged my knees. I was glad when the taxi beeped at the gate. I walked down the path without looking back.

Dana's foot, in its pink flip-flop, lands on my copy of *Out of Africa*. She picks it up. 'What's this about?'

'Haven't you read it?'

'I don't think so?' She shakes her head and her mousy hair, in two ridiculous bunches, swishes at her jaw. 'Is it good?'

'I used to think so. It's – poignant. Love and loss in colonial Kenya.'

Dana's face closes down. 'Not exactly relevant to us, then.'

Maybe not to you. It's certainly a different world from Good Hope Clinic, with its endless stream of enthusiastic volunteers, applying a sticking plaster to the country's gaping wound.

I turn back to my desk and open my notepad. I had half-thought of keeping a journal here, but who would read it?

The bed sighs as Dana stands up. 'Time for my shift. I'll let you get on.' She opens the door. Cooler air drifts in from the corridor. 'Well, you take care, now, Jill. If you ever feel like a beer, just give me a call. *Tutaonana!*'

'What?'

'It means, see you later.' She looks exasperated.

'I thought it was *kwa heri*.'

'That's goodbye.'

'*Tutaonana*, then.'

I intended to try to learn Swahili before I got here, but I'm not a natural linguist. I envy those who can tune into different tongues. I would rather people who spoke to me in broken English said nothing. But then, I've never been a talker. Not like Michael.

They didn't stress, at the introductory session, that we had to learn Swahili. My age didn't matter either. I was interested and I had the funds. When they found out I used to work in paediatrics – even though my qualifications were out of date – they were keen to sign me up.

I didn't mention Michael on all the forms I filled in; just said I had no dependants. My reasons for volunteering? I lingered over that one. *To understand what my son found in Africa.* In the end I wrote, *To give something back.* But then I wanted to cross it out. Haven't I given enough?

On the way from the airport, as our minibus lurched and crawled through the Nairobi streets, I searched the billboards for a picture of Michael, or his name. There was nothing, just ads for mobile phones and Coca-Cola, and warnings about Aids. He wasn't news. And how could he be? It was three years ago. People are dying all the time.

There were five of us on the journey: me, Dana and a Swedish girl were coming here; two young French guys were being dropped off on the way. While they tried to talk to each other I stared at the city through the open windows. The smell of heat, fried food and diesel fumes drifted in. I wanted someone to look me in the eye. I wanted to ask them, *what do you want from us?* But everyone was preoccupied. Women in brightly-coloured dresses weaved through the traffic, loaded baskets on their heads; others bent over stalls piled with vegetables and fruit. Skinny dogs hunted, nose down, in the gutters. This was what Michael saw. Cars and trucks came at us like images in a computer game. I remembered him as a kid sitting cross-legged in front of his PlayStation, lost in a parallel world. I was always glad when he was occupied. I squeezed my eyes hard against the picture. I put my jacket behind my head and tried to sleep, jolting in and out of disjointed dreams.

Four hours later, we pulled up in front of the clinic. Its squat, white buildings sat in a strangely familiar landscape of grassland and flat-topped trees. I recognised Dr Mboto, the medical director, from his blurry picture on the photocopied letter. 'Welcome to Kenya!' he said, as we stepped down onto the worn grass. He had a warm smile and a crunching handshake.

We trailed behind him, dragging our luggage, as he led us through the clinic grounds to the accommodation block. 'We're very pleased you've come,' he called over his shoulder. 'I hope you will be comfortable here.'

It was late afternoon, but still hot. I thought of Morag and Lucy at home with the central heating on, windows and doors shut against the cold, and my heart tripped.

*

Just walking from my room to the main block makes me sweat. I'm glad to reach the cool of the dispensary. Mary, one of the medical assistants, stands under the ceiling fan, laying out tubes of eye cream and antiseptic ointment on a battered tin tray. Under her worn white coat, she always seems to wear her Sunday best; I'm sure she despairs of my drab outfit of t-shirt and loose trousers.

I reach for a pile of leaflets on how to prevent HIV, and she puts her hand on my arm. 'Good girl! You left your rings behind.' They advised us not to bring anything valuable.

'I don't have any rings.'

Mary puts down the tray. 'No husband?'

Through the open window I can hear women chattering, kids calling and shrieking.

'Just a son.' I hold the door to let her through.

'A special blessing.' She swings through to the clinic.

Our patients understand the meaning of the word. They walk miles to get here. Then they wait, immobile in the hot shade. Their children run in the dust, kicking up tiny sandstorms. The older ones look at me with serious eyes when I check their pulse, or take their temperature. They don't speak.

It's a long afternoon: eye infections, diarrhoea, fever, racking coughs, complications from poor nutrition. We do what we can, with what we have. The contrast between the supplies we ration and the contents of the medical bag in my room strikes me again. I've got tubes of antiseptic and antihistamine cream; pills for diarrhoea; alcohol swabs for scratches and bites. I've had all my jabs. I've taken my anti-malaria pills, just in case. A line from *Out of Africa* comes back to me: something about white men trying to insure themselves against fate. But that's not true. Michael didn't.

There's no dusk; the light goes, suddenly, like a curtain falling. I'm stacking chairs in the waiting room so I can mop the concrete floor when an old lady shuffles in. She puts a rolled-up bundle on the table by the door on top of the pamphlets on hygiene and how to use condoms.

'*Salama, daktari*,' she says, through stumps of teeth. '*Tafadhali, naomba msaada?*'

'*Salama. Sisemi Kiswahili.*' I stumble over the unfamiliar words. I repeat it in English. 'I don't speak Swahili.' But I can guess what she's asking.

The bundle is a threadbare blanket. She opens it slowly. In the folds, curled like a fossil, lies a small boy. She strokes his arm. 'Mother dead.'

The child's closed eyelids flicker. His skin is hot and dry. 'How old?'

'*Mbili.*' She holds up two crooked fingers. He looks less than a year old. She picks him up and holds him out to me. He doesn't cry.

Without thinking I take him. He weighs almost nothing. I feel his bones against my chest. He smells of vomit.

The old lady prods my arm, and signals that the child's bowels keep emptying.

He's dehydrated, and feverish. He should be on a drip, but I doubt his body would take it. I wonder how many times Michael stood in a room like this and looked into an old face or a young face and said – what? Did – what?

The old lady picks up the blanket and drapes it over her shoulder. She looks at the floor and at the door, anywhere but me. And now I see. This is her grandson. She's a grandmother too.

'Okay.' I touch her arm. 'Okay.'

I wrap the child in a clean towel and carry him to the dispensary.

Mary's checking the contents of a cupboard against a list. She looks up when I come in.

'Can you give me some rehydration salts? He's had vomiting and diarrhoea.'

She checks his pulse and shakes her head. 'No good.'

The boxes are right there behind the glass. 'Please? I won't need much.'

She shrugs and passes me a box.

Still holding the child I tip the powder into a tin jug and measure in boiled water. It takes longer with him on my hip. It feels strange, to be doing things one-handed again, after all this time.

At the back of the clinic is a room with a couple of empty beds. I sit on a chair, the child propped in the crook of my arm. He feels like a husk. I dip a spoon in the jug, and touch the tip of the spoon to his mouth. A trickle of water slides in. I do it again. A few drops go into his mouth, more onto his skin. He barely moves.

Mary peers in, and gives me a look that says I'm wasting my time, but she comes back with a bowl and a damp cloth, and I touch the cool cloth to the child's forehead. I give him a little more water. That stays down. He seems to be cooler. His breathing is shallow, but regular. I stroke his small hand, willing him to survive, trying to let him know I'm here.

In this lamplit cocoon we're the only people in the world. I remember what I used to do when Michael was ill.

I tell the little boy about Karen Blixen's farm, at the foot of the Ngong Hills: the trees, the flowers, the wild animals that used to live here. I give him a few more drops of water. He seems more willing to swallow. I lay him down on the bed and put a thin sheet over him. 'She came here, a long time ago, and tried to grow coffee, but it didn't work.'

I remember the story about Chief Kinanjui, and tell my small patient how the chief held court, smoking cigars, and wore a cloak of monkey-skins. 'The land belonged to his people.'

In the shadows I see Michael. *Open your eyes, Mum. They're still living with the legacy.*

I'm doing something, son. I'm trying to do what you did.

I'm proud of myself, sitting in the gloom with this little boy, cooling his limbs with the wet cloth. I watch the thin skin on his ribcage rise and fall.

Fever's unpredictable. It always spikes in the small hours of the morning. But the child is calm. He lies still, curled under the sheet. I close my eyes.

Karen Blixen's a terrible driver. We're in her big old car, hurtling down a rutted track. There's been a robbery at the clinic, and Michael's hurt, but if we can get to him in time he'll survive, and I'll bring him home. But the road signs for the clinic have disappeared. A lion springs out of the dark and we swerve off the road. A tree trunk looms up in the headlights. I open my mouth to scream at Karen, but no sound comes out.

'Jill!' Someone's shaking me. I look up, into a freckled face. 'Go to bed! You're bushed.'

My heart's racing. The panic of my dream settles into the familiar ache in my chest. I remember where I am. Beside me, the bed is empty. The sheet is soiled.

'He's gone. His grandmother's taken him.' Dana moves between me and the bed, as if to break the spell. 'You need to sleep. Come on.' She reaches to help me out of the chair. I take her hand and get up stiffly, my legs as spindly as a puppet's.

We walk like two old people back to my room. The sky is lightening, birds starting to chatter and call; soon the relentless sun will be back.

'This bloody place.' I want to scream. 'Do you ever get used to it?' I feel stupid, as if I've been in a waking dream that everyone has tried to tell me would end this way.

'I don't know.' Dana sounds weary. 'You know about hospitals. It's just harder here.'

'Maybe I shouldn't have come.'

'That depends.' She stops by my door.

'What do you mean?' I look down at the wall. A small black and yellow spider is inching towards a crack. My eyes and throat are burning.

'Depends what you came for. But we've all got our reasons.'

'Yes.' Suddenly I see Michael, that last time, on my doorstep in the grey rain: *Don't try to stop me. I can make a difference there.* Thick, hot tears rise in my throat. I stumble into my room and lock the door. I fall onto my bed and sob, stuffing the pillow into my mouth so no one can hear. I cry myself into a feverish sleep.

I dream of nothing.

I wake, still in my clothes. The room is hot and bright. I drink the remains of a bottle of lukewarm water. Morag's present is still on my desk. It's no doubt an eco-friendly guide to sight-seeing in Africa, or something practical about bereavement.

Why do my hands shake as I rip the paper? But it's not a book. It's a photograph album, with a dark blue cover. On the first page is a picture of Lucy and me, at Christmas. Lucy is wearing the red cardigan I knitted for her. There's a photo of her and Morag. Clumsily I separate the stiff pages, but the rest are blank – no doubt for my adventures here. Where's Michael?

I'm about to fling the album across the room when I see the envelope, tucked under the plastic on the last page. I imagine Morag's rounded, childish writing. What's she going to say? My heart knocks as I tear the flap. But there's no letter; just a photograph I've never seen before. It shows a group of people, some wearing white coats, standing outside a low-rise building, like the ones here. There's a big, empty sky, and trees at the edge. I search the faces. My heart thuds. There he is: my son, with his colleagues, on his last project. The one he had to come back for. He's laughing in the sunlight. Perhaps he's just made a joke – everyone else is laughing, too. He looks happy.

Did Morag hide the photo in the envelope to spare me the shock of seeing it in the album? Is she saying it's up to me, what I do with it? Is she trying to show me, how happy Michael was here?

I picture her and Lucy, wrapped up against the cold, hurrying to playgroup in the dank Edinburgh morning. I think of Michael, who had to come back, just one last time.

Perhaps I'll never understand.

Kwa heri, my son.

Now I can't stop the tears and I stare at the picture, stare at his eyes, at his smile, until his features blur into the face of the person next to him, and behind him, until I can't see him any more.

Ring Out the Old

As Ed slid the Audi into the kerb, the dashboard clock hit 18:30. The numbers glowered at him in the dark. Out of habit he checked his shirt collar for Marcie's lipstick in the rear-view mirror, and was about to sniff his jacket when he stopped himself.

Through the rainy windscreen the sky exploded with crimson stars. New Year's Eve. *Ring out the old; ring in the new.* Ed's heart tripped.

Sophie was in the kitchen, her back to him, listening to the radio. She had scraped her hair into a ponytail and was wearing an old shirt over her jeans. The steamy air smelled of roasting meat. Ed's stomach did a somersault. He tapped her on the shoulder.

She jumped. 'Christ, Ed! Don't do that!'

'Sorry I'm late.' The words were out before he could stop them. He went into the hall and threw his jacket over the banister. 'The early train was cancelled,' he lied, 'then it took ages to get out of the car park.' He came back into the kitchen, and saw there were four pans on the stove. 'This looks elaborate.' Did his voice sound odd?

Sophie was reaching into a cupboard. She said something from behind the door.

'Why so much?' Ed imagined the courses, lining up like hurdles.

Sophie stood up, a packet of flour in one hand. 'It is a special occasion.'

He stared. Then he realised she meant New Year's Eve. The scene he had rehearsed formed and re-formed in his head.

'Right.' He pulled a wine bottle from the fridge and searched noisily for a glass. His heart poked his ribs.

'Guess what?' Sophie went on. 'I rang Mike, and he said they'd love to come over.'

Ed held onto the fridge door. He pictured Sophie's brother, a bear of a PE teacher with a short fuse. 'Why'd you ask them?'

'Why not? They're family.' She turned round. 'Did you want it to be just the two of us?'

He couldn't look at her. 'Yes. I mean – no. That's fine.' He sat down at the table. The thudding in his ears and chest subsided.

His thoughts had telescoped to nothing. He picked up the freesheet. The England women's football team were out to crush their opponents. The headline blurred.

Sophie was tipping salad leaves into a bowl, a ceramic kaleidoscope of red and orange.

Ed saw the colours move. He was back in a dusty Barcelona street, seven years ago. He and Sophie were standing at a market stall, Sophie haggling over the dish in her 'A' level Spanish. The stallholder's amused look had met Ed's. 'We're on our honeymoon,' he'd offered, in English. He'd wanted Sophie to stop. But the man laughed, and gave in to her bargaining. She and Ed had drinks in a smart bar with the money she'd saved. They were only wearing beach gear, and he'd kept expecting someone to throw them out.

Sophie lifted the bowl. 'Remember that day? I knew I'd beat him down in the end!' She swept a pile of cucumber slices onto the leaves.

She and her mother had organised the wedding; her aunts had done the catering. Their energy was a physical presence, solid as a wall. Ed's suggestions never seemed right.

He glanced at the clock. 'What time are they coming?'

'Seven-ish. I said we'd fit in with the baby.'

'Baby?'

'Your niece.'

Ed pictured it mewling in the corner, interrupting dinner with feeds and nappy changes. Everything would take even longer. 'Couldn't they get a babysitter?'

'Why? She's family too. Nancy. Three months old,' Sophie said. 'Try to remember.' She found a coaster and slid it under his glass.

Ed stood on the landing. The door to Sophie's office was open, revealing her neat desk, and pinboard covered with photos and bits of fabric. Her part-time work as a set designer seemed to have become full-time.

She had decorated the box room in yellow and blue. Ed knew that if he opened the door he would see the cot pieces, still in their plastic wrapping, stacked against the wall.

He presumed all the books and the other stuff was in there too. It was the only one of Sophie's projects that hadn't worked out. And now it was for the best. The few times he'd tried to start a conversation about their future, Sophie had shown no sign of hearing him. But she must have sensed that things had changed between them. It was weeks since she'd filled in the temperature chart on the kitchen wall, and told him they had to have an early night.

He slumped on the end of the bed, pushing his hands through his thinning hair. In the wardrobe mirror he glimpsed his face. His once-boyish features had acquired the look of experience. Sophie hadn't noticed.

The smell of frying garlic drifted up from the kitchen. Ed's stomach growled. He hadn't wasted his lunch hour eating. He swung his backpack onto the duvet and took out the dark blue box. On the matching lining, the silver bangle was as striking and perfect as a constellation. Ed pictured it sliding on Marcie's arm, and was skewered by longing: a physical ache, between his chest and his groin.

Impossible to remember, now, how his life used to be. A couple of days ago, he'd been Googling a Keats sonnet Marcie had mentioned, and *Searching for Love?* popped up on his screen. The bald statement was shocking. Was that how he and Marcie's paths had crossed? He'd never been unfaithful before. Marcie said it was fate. They were kindred spirits. She understood him.

Only once had he slipped up: at her place, he'd left his trousers near her easel – when he got home, he'd found a smear of green paint on the right leg. He'd tried to clean it off in the bathroom, but had only made it worse. In the end he'd put the trousers at the bottom of the wardrobe. The following week they'd reappeared, hanging up in a dry-cleaning bag.

Ed thought later that, if Sophie had asked, he could have said an artist was painting a mural in the office, and he must have brushed against a paint tin. That was mostly true.

*

His mobile lay on the duvet. If he rang Marcie now, he knew what she would ask. He would have to say, *No, not yet. But I will. Tonight.*

With a jolt, Ed realised he was both hostage and negotiator.

He should pack a bag. But what if Sophie came up and found it? He would have to come back for his things.

His chinos were ironed and folded over the bedroom chair; the olive linen shirt Sophie had given him for Christmas was on a hanger on the wardrobe door. Ed changed out of his suit and went downstairs.

In the kitchen, Sophie was pouring herself fizzy water. She rarely started drinking before guests arrived. She was so bloody sensible. Ed couldn't remember the last time he'd seen her drunk.

He refilled his wine glass and followed her into the hall. 'Do I need to do anything?'

She turned on her way up the stairs and smiled. 'No, everything's under control. Can you just check the music?'

In the sitting room, anonymous jazz was seeping from the iPod. Ed sat on the leather sofa, in the glow of the floor lamp, and stared at the fake fur rug. It felt like being trapped in a furniture showroom. Marcie's flat was full of mis-matched furniture, and half-finished paintings, and there were scented sticks and candles everywhere. And heaps of cushions, unfortunately covered in cat hairs which made him sneeze. The cats would have to go.

There was a new photograph on the bookshelf. Ed picked it up: him and Sophie, four years ago, in Arizona. They'd hired a Buick, and put the top down, and cruised the empty road under a sky as wide as the ocean. He'd loved the simplicity of it, the movement from A to B. Even Sophie had temporarily forgotten her list of places to visit. He couldn't remember now which town this was, but she'd asked a woman with orange hair to take their photo in a diner parking lot. The car gleamed in the sun. They stood either side of it, tanned and smiling.

A rush of sadness swept through him. He put the photo back, face down.

He drained his glass. He'd slip away after dinner. He'd book an Uber, and tell it to wait at the end of the road. How easy would that be, on New Year's Eve? They'd probably all be booked; or people would just take them.

No. Better to go now, before Mike and Helen arrived, and come back tomorrow. Then he and Sophie could talk, face to face. He stood up.

'They're here!' Sophie called. The doorbell chimed.

Ed went to the door. Under the ghostly streetlight Mike was bending into the car. A bulging overnight bag had been left on the step. Ed lifted it, and staggered under its weight into the hall.

When he turned round, Mike and Helen were coming up the path, Mike swinging the baby in a carry-seat.

'Ed! How's life at the management coalface?' Mike put the baby down and pumped Ed's hand.

Ed was surprised how much roast lamb he could eat, once he concentrated on the food. Sophie had always been a good cook. His wine glass was permanently full. Through the haze of the evening he hung on to the idea of Marcie, solid and real. He'd texted her from the bathroom to say he'd be there by midnight. She hadn't replied yet.

New Year. A new start. He realised he was clenching his fists.

Across the table Sophie was laughing with Mike, their blonde heads together. Ed pushed away his half-eaten trifle. Sophie would come to understand. Marcie said that on some level Sophie already knew: she'd be relieved to hear the truth. Once everything had settled down, they could still be friends.

Maybe not with Mike and Helen, though.

'Here's to New Year resolutions – for making and breaking!' Helen chinked glasses with her sister-in-law.

'I make them, Ed breaks them,' said Sophie. She gave him an odd smile.

The baby started to grizzle, and Mike picked her up and held her on his chest. Her hands plucked at his shirt.

'Let Ed have a go!' trilled Helen. Her nose was shining, her glasses askew.

'No, really, it's all right,' he protested, but Mike was already out of his seat, making his way round the table like an Oscar winner heading for the podium.

He held the baby out. 'Hello, Uncle Ed!'

Ed had no option but to take the squirming bundle. He propped her against his shoulder, like the others had. Surreptitiously, he patted the phone in his pocket. He needed to call or text Marcie. He had drunk a lot of wine. His head was as light as a balloon.

The baby scrabbled against him. Without thinking he put his finger into her hand, and her grip closed on him. She gazed up, and in her doll's eyes he saw steely determination.

Sophie's voice came from far away. 'I've – we've – got some news.' She looked serious.

Ed's heart began to race. How the hell had she found out? Typical of Sophie to plan a showdown when he was too drunk to defend himself. He needed to get rid of the baby, but nobody came to take her and he couldn't think how to ask.

'Sorry Ed –' Sophie turned to him '– I should have told you first, but – with Mike and Helen coming over – with it being New Year, it seems right.' She smiled, and looked so dreamy and unlike herself that for an instant Ed thought she was drunk. Had she been drinking much? It felt important to remember, but the more he tried the more the idea slid away. The roaring in his head threatened to burst out of his mouth.

Sophie stood up. 'I wanted it to be a surprise.'

Ed wanted to stick his fingers in his ears, but he had no free hand. 'A surprise?' he heard himself say.

'You're so slooooow!' Sophie dragged the word out. 'Do I need to spell it out? D – A – D!'

'Dead?' Ed's brain refused to work.

Above the noise of Mike's booming laugh, Ed heard the letters again.

Everyone was talking at once. A cork popped.

A thump on his back made Ed shudder. 'Congratulations, mate!' Someone burst into tears.

Helen swayed towards him, and slopped a winey kiss on his cheek. 'That's fantastic!'

Ed clutched the baby as the room whirled. 'How –' he began. Mike guffawed, but Ed pushed on, 'How d'you know? Are you sure?'

'Course she is!' Mike seemed to be shouting.

'That's why I waited, you idiot.' Sophie came over and hugged him. 'I'm absolutely sure. Twelve weeks.' She patted her belly.

'Oh, Ed!' Helen giggled. 'Didn't you suspect anything?'

'He's in his own little world,' Sophie said.

'You should have told me first.' Was that his voice?

'Come on mate! She's telling you now!' Mike slapped him on the back again, harder this time, and Ed felt a hot bubble well up in his throat. He stared at the top of the baby's head as she wriggled against his shirt.

'Nearly midnight! New Year countdown!' Helen threw her arms round Mike's neck, and they stumbled out of the door. A chorus of bagpipes wailed from the TV.

Sophie walked to the window. Now Ed could see the thickening at her waist. She drew back the curtains and snapped off the lights. In the dark glass, Ed saw his reflection: a lumpy silhouette. He felt his limbs turning to lead, his arms holding the weight of the baby against his heart. In the distance, fireworks burst silently. Sophie came to sit next to him.

I'm leaving you. That's what he should have said.

In his head he was already gone, out in the damp night air, hurrying to meet Marcie by the bridge where she always waited. She was wearing the cashmere wrap he'd bought her for her birthday: the tiny hairs stroked his chin when he bent to kiss her. He hugged her to him, and all around fireworks exploded. They stood together in the dark. She put her fingers to his cheek and wiped the tears that were sliding down his face.

'You big softie.' Sophie gave him a tissue, and took the baby. 'I knew you had no idea.'

Ed wiped his eyes with the back of his hand.

'What I've always wanted,' Sophie said. 'It'll be wonderful.'

He looked up, but she was talking to the baby.

Ed stared at the window. In the black pane, for an instant, he saw Marcie's face.

In his pocket, his phone began to ring.

Paradise Acre

My pa's a hunter. He's got a cool jacket from the military, full of pockets for wire and bait. And boots with thick soles, good for sneaking up on things.

The soles are made out of special bark. They get sewed on with thread from vines that grow in the forest. The forest comes nearly up to our plot, but Pa keeps it back. With the other men he cuts the trees down with an axe. Then Ma and the women pull the bark off with their fingers. Their nails break and oftentimes their fingers bleed.

They take the bark to the river where there's a waterfall. Some days, if you look hard, there's a rainbow, which Pastor Adam says surely means a Blessing. He stands on the bank and talks in his old-timer's voice about the pure river and the water of life and waves his big white hands about. The little 'uns run in and out of the water while the mothers smash that bark to Kingdom Come with big old stones. When it's dried in the sun they stitch it to the soles of the hunters' boots.

Now I'm into double figures Pa says I'll get my own boots. Then I can go hunting too. For now my job is tending the goats or fishing with the other boys. Some of 'em are taller than me but I'm the best at catching things, like him. I get the bait on the hook and cast the line while the others are still fighting over the worm can. And I don't never rip my skin.

The men hunt all the livelong year. But the mothers only make shoes and boots in summer, because standing in that river in winter would surely be a Tribulation. In winter they work in the kitchen and the store room. If all my outdoor jobs are done, I help Ma stir the wide pans of apples and pears and tip them into glass jars. When I push the small white bodies down with the back of the spoon, they look like they're drowning.

Sometimes I just have to take a tiny bite. That's when I get the back of the hot spoon on my arm. I never even yell.

*

My pa used to say I was overly fond of books. But it's true to tell we ain't got too many here, in Paradise Acre. In actual fact we've only got one. It's big and thick, with a pattern on the front that you can feel if you run your finger over it: up, down, across, back. That is surely the only book we need, Pa says.

On Sundays, after we've been to Gathering and eaten our special dinner with meat, he takes the book down off the shelf. Ma gives him his pipe and baccy. He gets out a pinch of the little dry worms and pushes them into his pipe and lights it, and the flame jumps up. 'Burning like the sinners in Hell,' he says, and stares at me, and my little brother sitting on my ma's lap. Then he opens the book. The pages are so thin I can see the shape of his fingers through them. He reads out about the wicked, and wrath of God, and fiery flames. When he's not looking, Ma covers my brother's ears. In those stories people wail and burn. Pa puffs on his pipe and I close my eyes and breathe in the smoke. I imagine the fire licking at my toes, and me running to the river to cool them.

I can run real fast.

At the end he says, 'Amen,' and we all say it and he puts the book back on the shelf.

One time, the pattern on the front of the book was gold

– like the gold that men sweated and died for, so that women could sit around all day wearing it on their fingers and in their ears, Pa says.

When he talks like that, in his stone-hard voice, Ma puts her head down. She makes her hands go like river weed, tangled up, one over the other.

And Pa says to me, 'That means she agrees.'

We had to sell our gold before we come here. Ma couldn't get the small hoops out of her ears, so Pa made her sit on the chair in the kitchen while he pulled them out. She tried to push him away, which was darn stupid and made everything worse and all. He had to find his rope and tie some big knots. My legs hurt, 'cause I was sitting so still and the floor was hard. But not as much as my chest and my throat hurt, from hearing her scream and knowing not to cry. Blood ran down her neck, and got on her blouse.

It turned out the earrings were no good, and Pa couldn't sell them for much, so he took her ring as well. That came off easier, 'cause her fingers had gotten thin.

Then it was night and we locked up the farm and put everything in the truck. Me and my brother lay on the mattress in the back, and I watched the stars but I couldn't see the ones I knew. We bumped down the track and I wondered if anyone'd know we'd gone. The only person I could call to mind was Mister Lee, who came by now and then to buy our corn. I tried not to feel the shivers in my belly, and the lump in my throat like old bread. When I woke up it was still dark. Pa drove all another day and night and we were here.

We are Self Sufficient now, he says. It is surely a Different World.

But some things are the same.

Summer's the best time, because the hunting's good and there's plenty to eat. The men get fish, and sometimes birds, or a forest pig. The pig comes back upside down, carried on a pole, legs tied front and back. I like looking at its strange small feet. Pa says they're like a town lady's, wearing shoes.

When he gets back from a hunt, he always shows me what he's caught. He comes up from the clearing to the back of the yard and shouts, 'Cody!' and I stop what I'm doing – throwing bones for the dogs, or pulling up ironweed – and I make my feet get there real quick. Pa puts his sack on the table, and I can see the shapes. Sometimes one's still twitching and squirming and I think it'll jump right out, like my heart could from under my shirt.

I stand next to him and close my eyes. He smells like blood, and the Lord's good earth. I hold out my right hand, and he takes it in his hard fingers. Then he pushes my hand into the scratchy sack, and I have to guess what's in there. If it's smooth and slimy, I find the fin and say, 'Catfish.' Just as easy if it's a small furry body, with a tail like a whip.

I don't like it if I feel feathers. I keep my hand still. I check the beak and the tail: it's easy to go mixing up a crow with a jay. Then I say, 'Good shot, Pa!'

Ma never says, 'Well done.'

If he's caught a rabbit or a squirrel he skins it right there, and his knife flashes at us through the fur. He throws the bare little body in a bucket, and picks up the skin and brings it close to my face. It's still warm, and red underneath. He rubs it on my arms, then my cheek. It smells like all the sadness in the world. I stand as still as I can, pushing my feet into the floor.

Pa says hunters never run away. If that's true, I thought, why have we come here, so far from where we used to live? But when I asked him he got real angry and said that was Other People, Other People had driven him to it. Then he said, 'like your Ma' but she can't drive. At our old place he wouldn't let her near the truck, 'cause she's got No Darn Idea.

Pa says before I can go hunting I need to be a better shot. He's made me a bow and shortened some arrows. He says I learn fast because I am a Chip Off the Old Block. That made me think of something lost. First time I tried, I missed the squirrel he'd hung up in the tree, but I got it on the third go. Next time, make it the first, he said.

My little brother can't be no hunter because Pa says he's a girl. His sickness makes him look pale and cough all the time, and he wakes Ma up in the night. When she says she's tired, Pa says she should have blood in her veins instead of ice. He rolls his eyes at me and we laugh.

*

Now Pa goes hunting at night because he says he can't stay in this house no more, because what does she expect him to do?

When he sits in his chair after supper and pulls on his boots, Ma cries. I tell her to stop being a silly woman and Pa smiles at me. I get his jacket off the hook by the door, and he gives me a special penny from his pocket.

When he's gone, I take it up to my room and feel under my bed for my treasure box. It's made of wood and it smells of Pa's pipe. I put the penny in there, alongside my lucky stones and the rat's skull I found behind the log store. Then I drag the chair across the floor and wedge it under the door handle. I feel sick. I take off my shirt. My fingers are fumbly and I can't slip the buttons. I close my eyes, and feel under my arm for the edge of the bandage. I took it from the medicine cupboard, but Ma didn't notice. I hold my breath, and unwind the fabric, slowly, slowly. I dare to look. It's okay. I prod, and poke, and check – nothing. Not even a tiny swelling. I bite my fist, to stop myself yelling with joy. I take a few deep breaths, really breathe. Then I rewind the bandage, round and round. Just a bit tighter.

I climb into bed and pull the blankets up. When I hear Ma coming to say goodnight, I pretend I'm asleep. I feel her icy breath and keep my eyes screwed shut. I hear her whispering and singing to my brother. And I push myself down into sleep, hard as I can.

But it don't always work.

When Pa comes back from hunting at night he smells like a new squirrel skin. He don't hardly catch nothing these days. The animals must all be hiding. I hear him grunt, and throw his sack down. I go right under the blankets and close my eyes. His footsteps are so soft, so quiet – he's good at being quiet, even though he's big. The nights he don't catch nothing his footsteps are quicker. He goes to his room first, to check if Ma and my brother are asleep. I lie still as a log.

Sometimes Pa has the stick that he takes when he goes hunting: it goes tap-tap, tap-tap, on the floor. I shrink in my bed and screw my eyes up tight and I think about my other night-time Pa, who is a real hunter. He goes into the forest when there's hardly any moon, and he's brave and strong. He traps animals that are too stupid to hear him, or see him, even though they're used to being out at night and he ain't. He's had to learn how to creep and prowl, which makes him even cleverer.

I think about the moon shining through the branches, and the leaves all silvery in the moonlight, and my pa's fingers pulling the bow string back, setting the arrow on the bow string like he showed me, and when all the covers are back I keep my eyes closed real tight and pretend I'm in the forest, the green and blessed forest or perhaps I'm by the waterfall playing and splashing in the sun, like one of God's own children, by the pure river of the water of life and the drops are clear and clean and sparkling and I can feel them on my skin, now they're running down my face.

My pa is a hunter and he prowls at night.

He says it's our secret.

Magpie

On the day in April that Ben's headship is confirmed, two blackbirds appear in the back garden. Madeleine, who has forgotten the bird facts Ben used to tell her, doesn't at first understand what they're doing. But she knows frantic activity when she sees it.

The male hurries across the narrow lawn, or swoops past the window to perch on the fence, his tail up. The dull-coloured female forages in the flower bed, her beak stuffed with scraps. When Madeleine realises they are building a nest, their shared purpose makes her anxious. She can't help watching them, her attention wandering from the proof pages she's correcting.

Curious about the nest, she ventures outside in the cold wind, and catches sight of her reflection in the French window. In her tracksuit bottoms and baggy sweater, she looks like the no-hope contestant on a daytime TV show.

Ben has an evening meeting. Standing at the sink, scraping the brown skin of her scrambled egg supper from the milk pan, Madeleine sees the female bird, still busy in the fading light. Feeling only slightly foolish she says into the window pane, 'Watch out, girl! When the chicks come along, you'll be stuck on the nest!' She can't resist banging on the glass in warning, and the bird takes off, complaining.

But her words make her feel a fraud. She got what she wanted. It's just that now there's too much time to think.

Madeleine's on the phone to her old friend when her mobile buzzes with a text. Ben's been delayed: is staying over with a colleague.

'How many times now?' Clare asks.

'I trust my husband,' Madeleine says, aware of sounding priggish. A small, icy hand grips her heart.

'You don't have to confront him.' Clare sounds exasperated. 'Just investigate. You're not devious enough.'

'You don't know how devious I am.' She didn't mean to say that.

*

They celebrate Ben's promotion a few evenings later, at their favourite Italian. Madeleine has dug out the faithful tunic dress that hides the bulges from her desk-bound days, and made up her eyes and mouth.

She breaks off a piece of ciabatta. The words she needs won't come. 'I wonder how the twins are getting on this term,' she tries.

'The twins are getting on with their lives,' Ben says. His slim fingers dunk bread in a small puddle of olive oil. He's barely put on weight over the years. He's ten years older than Madeleine but his thick hair is only now starting to grey.

'The house is always so quiet after the holidays.'

'You could go back to work,' he says. 'There are never enough teachers.'

Madeleine pictures the proof pages littering her desk, and the regular – if small – sums that appear on the joint account statements. She tries to smile. 'But I do work. And you always said, "Never go back". Remember?'

He shrugs, half-smiles. 'Did I?'

It wasn't just me, she wants to say. She used to sense a bubble of complicity, surrounding them. But now she feels a tear in the skin; another world, pushing in. She can't stop a surge of panic.

Into her head flashes an image of the nesting birds. His old interest. As soon she says the words they feel desperate, but she can't stop.

'Their nest's in the wrong place,' she persists. 'It's on the ivy, too close to the house. They'll abandon the chicks. Or a cat will get them.'

Ben looks up from his osso buco. 'They always build in stupid places.' He cuts the meat carefully. 'They're known for it.'

Madeleine is horrified to feel her eyes fill with tears. She forces down a forkful of risotto. She wants to ask if pairs mate for life, but everything means something else. She wants to press, to prod: to say, *Do you ever think about those days?* But she can't find the words. And if she did, something would shatter.

Ben laughs. 'You need to get out more, as the girls would say.'

She hears his boredom, and tries to sound defiant. 'Maybe I do.'

'That's definitely a home-worker's dress.'

In bed, he pulls her to him. But Madeleine sees his unwillingness, his wish to be somewhere else.

'I'm not really in the mood.' She moves away, and sits on the edge of the mattress.

'Perhaps it's your hormones.' Ben lies on his back, staring at the ceiling.

She waits a beat. 'What are you thinking?'

'Nothing,' he says. 'Why don't you make an appointment with the GP?' He turns over to go to sleep.

Who is she? Madeleine wants to ask. *Is she young?*

*

The next morning, Ben leaves the house early.

He's always taught in girls' schools. Boys are too disruptive, he says. Now Madeleine thinks he didn't want to be reminded. Promotion has pushed him up the management structure: he comes home late, three or four nights a week. There's a weekend course in the offing. He's volunteered for a staff/ student committee, looking at ways to fundraise.

These are the facts, he says. Her facts seem to lose their certainty around Ben. He says a lifetime of teaching history has given him a highly developed sense of what's relevant.

Perhaps it's her. It's hard to remember, nearly twenty years later, where she began and ended. Her memories slip and slide, although the undercurrent is still there, the anxiety she thought had faded. As if it has lain dormant all this time, only to erupt into the now-empty house, catching her unawares. Taking her breath away.

Before she starts work Madeleine does her domestic tidying and sorting, although there's little to do now. It's a hangover from when the girls lived at home – the vain attempt to subdue the tidal wave of tasks that threatened to overwhelm her.

In the bathroom, she stares into the mirror and grimaces, touching the fine, criss-crossed lines that bloom beside her eyes. She pushes her fingers back and up, making the skin taut, and views her younger self.

Without warning she's back in the staff room, with its battered chairs and lingering scent of cigarettes; golden September light falling through the high windows. The feeling that anything is possible.

Ben introduced himself on her first day. 'Allow me to show you the ropes,' he said. His dark hair was a little too long, his jacket well cut. She heard one of the women laugh theatrically, and felt flattered. Without hesitating he took her arm and guided her round the large, square room, pointing out the outsized timetable pinned to the wall, favourite chairs that must never be taken.

Someone muttered something she couldn't catch.

When he asked her to supper at his home, it never occurred to her not to go. She was surprised to meet his wife: he had said they lived separate lives. Ben called Madeleine 'My new colleague': said she was 'fresh from teacher training – and all alone in a strange town.' Madeleine was glad she'd dressed carefully, in a silk shirt and velvet skirt. His wife made little effort with her appearance.

Later that term, as if to clear the way for their adventure, he found a better job and handed in his notice. His timing was perfect.

They were adults: not responsible for anyone else's happiness. Madeleine avoided the staff room though. She knew her colleagues thought her as immature as the students. She didn't expect them to understand. She briefly considered buying herself a cheap ring, then realised that would change nothing.

But she had to be sure. She sensed he needed that extra push. And how can she regret the girls?

When they're home from uni, they argue – with each other and with her – and the house resonates with slammed doors. Madeleine seems to have lost all her powers of persuasion.

She wonders if they absorbed something, some tension, in the womb. But she was so careful when she was pregnant. She kept calm, held her breath. She waited him out. In the end, she was rewarded.

When the twins arrived, Ben liked his new status as the only man in the house. Madeleine dared to relax.

'A rose among thorns,' said his mother, up from Kent. 'Fancy you producing girls!' She ignored Madeleine. 'I believe in keeping in touch, for the children's sake,' she said.

Don't do it for my sake, Madeleine wanted to say.

Ben was involved with the girls when they were small –

bottle feeds, bedtime stories, kite-flying in the park – although sometimes Madeleine caught him studying them, in a distant way, and felt a twinge of doubt.

But he gave them whatever they wanted. She presumed he'd been fair: the financial arrangements were none of her business. Everything was done differently in those days. And having twins made it all more difficult. The house just wasn't big enough for visitors.

*

Outside the window, the April garden is still half asleep. The cold spring has delayed the blossoms. Daffodils waver in the flower beds, which are full of the dead leaves that Madeleine meant to sweep up last autumn.

The blackbirds peck in the borders, hop across the garden, heads down. Madeleine watches them flying backwards and forwards, worms dangling from their beaks, and thinks of the girls in their high chairs.

When they were small, she never left them with anyone. She was unnerved by how strongly she felt about that and put it down to maternal instinct, always tinged with fear.

But this fear is different. Some women, she has read, never notice anything. In her experience, one or two are surprisingly slow on the uptake. But Madeleine knows the signs. She doesn't want to feel this understanding, splitting her head like an atom; exposing the dark, dirty inside.

On a shelf in Ben's office – the box room – she finds the book she knew was there. She takes it down and blows dust off the top. The spine is broken, the pages bent. She should put it back. She thumbs through it, glancing at the bright photographs and familiar names; remembering trips to out-of-the-way heaths and cliff tops. She had been so delighted by his unlikely interest.

On some pages are his scribbled notes. Hearing the excitement in his words makes her cry.

It's a short step from the shelf to his jacket, on the back of the chair. Her stomach twists but she carries on. She hears Clare's voice: '*Just investigate.*' She goes through the pockets methodically and, sure she's missed something, starts again. She searches the desk drawers, looks through his spare briefcase, his papers.

She should know what to look for. She can find nothing.

She imagines the blackbirds' nest: sturdy and strong, holding a clutch of eggs, blue-green and speckled. She pictures the thin shell shattering, the soft, damp body unfurling.

When she went into labour, he came to the hospital with her. Then she knew she had won.

*

The afternoon sun slants across the papers on her desk. Madeleine has managed to push through the dull end-of-year summary of a charity's good works.

The noise takes her by surprise: the blackbirds are chak-chak-chakking, shrill and loud. It's a few moments before she spots them, one on the patio, the other on the lawn. They are both frantic, squawking.

Perched on top of the ivy-covered wall beside the house is a large bird: a young magpie, its slim body agile, head cocked to one side.

Madeleine watches, transfixed. The magpie hops delicately along the bricks. The blackbirds run towards it, flapping and squawking, and it backs off. It soon returns.

She is half-out of her chair, leaning into the window.

Before she can move, the magpie jumps down, onto the ivy. It scrabbles against the leaves, wings wide, searching for the nest. Its awkward flapping and struggling, where before was only grace, is raw desire, revealed and shocking. The blackbirds shriek, helpless, on the lawn, on the fence, but they come no nearer.

The magpie dips its head.

Madeleine bangs on the window and the intruder flies away, across the garden, a small shape dangling from its beak. It hops under a shrub, pinning its prize to the soil with one claw and pecking at it.

She unlocks the back door and rushes out into the cold wind. The magpie flies off. Under the shrub the chick lies on the soil. Its wings are half-feathered, blue-black; its thin-skinned, bulging belly is bare. Madeleine scoops the bird onto her palm, and its claws wave feebly. The eyes are closed, and bleeding. Its chest moves softly. She holds the chick, stroking its head. When it is completely still, she replaces the body on the soil and goes back into the house, feeling the loss inside her, a small, fluttering heart.

An hour or so later, the blackbirds' shrieking starts up again. Madeleine feels her stomach lurch. The magpie is back, sitting on the fence. She bangs on the window and it flies off.

For the rest of the afternoon, as the garden slips into shadow, she's poised at her desk, ready to strike the glass.

At five o'clock her mobile goes. Madeleine listens to Ben's message. She tries to picture him in his office at school, but can't. She looks out. The magpie is back.

The bird cocks its head at the window, and stares at Madeleine. In that pitiless eye she sees reflected her own, searching for the weak spot, the way in.

Madeleine runs upstairs for her old winter coat. She hurries back down, and in the garden shed finds a chair, and the broom. She sets the chair a few feet from the blackbirds' nest, but not so near as to scare them. It's cold. The breeze makes the daffodils nod and sway, and blows dead leaves across the grass. She wraps the coat round her and grips the broom, waving it whenever the magpie comes near. This works, for a while. But the blackbirds are confused by her presence, and take fright when she hisses at the magpie, so she has to move further back.

The intruder seems to sense she's powerless. The bird hardly bothers to fly away, just lifts its wings and half-runs a few yards. Then it perches, watching, waiting for Madeleine to give up.

Another magpie appears, on the ridge of next-door's roof.

They're working together.

Now Madeleine can't suppress the memory: the scent of cooking; wild flowers in a jar. The gift – the book that revealed how well she knew him – calmly handed over, under the other woman's puzzled gaze. Laughing with him, later, over the inedible meal that was laid out.

The sense of something unstoppable: already begun.

Two small, dark-haired boys, brought in to say goodnight.

Madeleine sits upright in the chair, and grips the broom. The magpies watch from the top of the fence.

She can stay out here all night, if she has to.

Your Own Tropical Hideaway

Ten minutes to kill before the evening ferry. The beach bar veranda's deserted, but there are people inside. Below me, the jetty pokes its finger into the black water.

Pole position for spotting the boat.

I can't help checking my watch, but the hands haven't moved. My new Rolex – dead as a dodo. Another thing to sort out when I get home.

Like an addict, I dig the resort brochure from my bag and flip through the pages again. The glossy shots of white sandy beaches and swanky villas still promise, 'Your own tropical hideaway!' What a con. No holiday reps anywhere, either.

'Everything has to be actioned on the mainland, sir,' said the moron on the helpline when I called. The heat was searing. I hopped from one foot to another on the broken tiles by the pool. 'This place is a fucking dump,' I yelled into the phone. 'You'll be hearing from me!' The guy was still squeaking when I pressed *End Call*. Then the signal went. I turned to see the cleaner staring at me, rake in hand, while he dragged leaves through the dirty water.

*

Across the Straits, the city lights wink and tease. Alicia's there, somewhere.

She was right behind me at the port. I heard the flap of her sandals. I turned around as she was hoisting her backpack over her shoulder, pushing a strand of blonde hair behind one ear. I've gone over the image so often it's starting to feel like a dream.

I tap out another text. *On the ferry back tonight. Get a hotel. I'll come to you.* I've sent it so many times I don't bother adding kisses. *Send.* It joins the line of green boxes. *Not Delivered.* One must have got through.

She's smart. She'll be waiting in a chic hotel room, champagne on ice.

I stand and stretch, feel my old life leave me like a shed skin.

'Enjoying the view?' A middle-aged man leans over from the next table. 'Nick Riley. Pleased to meet you.'

Where did he come from? 'Steve Mortimer.' Our palms slide.

'Welcome to our little piece of paradise.' Nick indicates the empty seat at his table. 'Won't you join me?'

'Thanks. I'm about to leave.' I nod at the sea. 'Just waiting for the boat.'

Nick pushes the chair towards me. 'You can wait just as well here.' His voice has a transatlantic twang. I feel like I've heard it before. 'Beer, Steve?'

'No, really – I'm fine.'

'Don't make me drink alone.' He raises his hand and a waiter sidles over. Within minutes the man returns, and with nicotine-stained fingers deposits two dark bottles on the table. 'Cheers!' Nick chinks his beer against mine.

I take a swig. It's warm and flat. What did I expect?

'Business trip or pleasure, Steve?'

The way Nick sits forward, with that concerned expression, reminds me of the woman D.I. 'I'm sorry for your loss, Steve,' she kept saying. I didn't like her using my first name.

'Pleasure. Supposedly.' My first proper holiday with Alicia.

'Great! Seen the sights?'

'I did the island tour bus, this afternoon.' The crappy

minibus bumped along a track from one hell-hole village to the next. 'Village' was an overstatement. Each place was a handful of ruined shacks, surrounded by burned forest. There were only two other tourists, both on their own: a bloke who looked around my age, possibly American, judging from the naff shirt; and an older woman, definitely European, short and lumpy-looking. At least there were no ankle-biters. It must be one of those places that are adults-only.

I tried a couple of glances at my fellow travellers, but neither made eye contact. They stared out in silence, presumably searching for the same ancient temples and tropical forest as I was.

I shrug. 'I guess climate change is affecting everywhere?'
Nick looks puzzled.
'It's just – the guidebook doesn't say wildfires are a problem.'
'Maybe you got the wrong book.'
On the beach, moonlight catches a shovel, stuck at an angle. I look away.
Nick loosens his tie. 'Travelling alone, Steve?'
'Yes. I mean, no. I'm heading back to the mainland, to meet my – friend.'
'Yeah?'
'She missed the ferry over. Unfortunately.'
'Shame.'
With his round face and thick grey hair, Nick looks like an overgrown schoolboy. I picture him getting the class loser in a headlock in the school toilets. 'Know this place well?'
'Sure.'
'It's a relief to find someone who speaks English.'
He smiles. 'What's your business, Steve?'
'Insurance.' I sip my beer. It's still terrible. 'You?'
'Human resources.'
'A touchy-feely type, eh?' I don't know why I said that, but it makes him laugh.

The waiter appears with a plate of steak and fries for Nick. My mouth waters. My last meal was the Welcome Pack from a machine at Reception: stale steamed buns and a carton of warm orange juice.

Nick gabbles at the man. The waiter glances at me and wanders away.

'You've mastered the lingo, then.'

'It's not that tricky, once you get used to it.' He cuts his steak into pieces. Blood runs on the plate. 'What led you into insurance?'

The sea is empty and still under the moon. It almost looks pretty, now I'm leaving. 'I've always liked numbers. Calculations. They do what they're supposed to do.' I preferred them to people, Sue always said.

'Is that all it comes down to?'

'What?'

'Life.' Nick looks up from his plate. 'Just a series of calculations?'

Christ, a bar-room philosopher. 'Of course not. But when you're trying to work out probabilities'–

– 'of nasty things happening?'

'It makes sense to anticipate – maybe avoid them.'

He spears a chunk of meat. 'People here see it differently.'

'Do they?' The smell of his dinner is distracting. From nowhere comes the memory of Sue, when we were first married, cooking steak every Friday night. I feel my throat tighten.

'Karma. What goes around comes around.' Grease glistens on Nick's chin. 'They'd say you were trying to cheat destiny.'

He'll be chanting *Hare Krishna* next. 'Haven't they heard of free will?'

Nick grins, that odd smile that makes him look familiar. 'They have this belief – it's sweet, really – that life gives you clues, if you choose to see them.'

It's time he chose to piss off. 'So you're living the life of Riley, here?'

'You got it.'

Something niggles at the back of my brain, but I can't get hold of it. 'Insurance is just about risk. That's all.'

'How do you calculate that?'

Is he humouring me? 'With databases – computer programmes. To analyse behaviour.'

'Whether you'll crash your car or burn your house down.'

The waiter returns and puts a bowl of noodles and a pair of chopsticks in front of me.

'I didn't –'

'On me,' Nick says. 'You've had a bad day. Least I can do.'

'Well, thanks.'

'The cost – the value – of a life,' he continues. 'How can you put a price on that?'

I battle with the chopsticks. 'Everything has a price.'

'Odd, isn't it – a life's only worth money when it ends?'

'I've never thought about it.'

'Really?'

The place is filling up. It's obviously popular with the silver surfer brigade. The punters, in their pastel leisure wear, are gathered in a clump at the end of the bar. A woman screams, and I jump – but she seems to be laughing. Men's voices rumble. It feels like a weird, suburban golf club, with an undercurrent of something about to kick off. Alicia would freak at it. Longing for her swamps me like a wave.

Nick leans in. 'What about the money?'

'What?'

'Do they pay up quickly, when someone dies?'

Not quickly enough, in my experience. I push the noodles around with the chopsticks. 'It depends.'

'On what?'

'On – the circumstances.'

'And if someone just disappears…' Nick raises his eyebrows. 'Presumably – it's trickier. Investigations, and so on.'

I didn't say anything while the police searched our house. I was in shock, of course. The D.I. found the note with my carefully written sentences setting out Sue's plans for her new life. I tried to look surprised, but thoughtful. 'She's been acting oddly,' I said. 'I should have seen it coming.' 'Don't blame yourself,' said the inspector.

I grasp a sliver of meat and get it to my lips. 'Do we have to talk about business?'

'Just interested, Steve. You must know the tricks of the trade.'

'There are no tricks of the trade.'

'Sorry.' Nick laughs. 'I mean, you must know all about – risk analysis.' The way he says it makes it sound illegal.

'I'm not an expert, no.'

'That's odd.' He smiles. 'You sure have taken one hell of a risk.'

Did he just say that? I push the bowl away. 'Thanks for dinner. Time I made a move.'

Nick indicates the beach. 'See the ferry yet?'

'I'll wait down on the jetty. I don't want to be late for – my friend.'

'Relax.' He spreads his hands expansively. 'You're among friends here.'

The noise from the bar swells towards us, a menacing roar. 'They're nothing to do with me.'

'That's where you're wrong. You got plenty in common.'

'What?'

'You saw something.' Nick smiles. 'You had to have it.'

'Enough philosophy, please.'

'But some people just don't get it. They make everything worse.'

A prickle at the back of my neck. 'Think I'll get some fresh air.'

'And by then it's too late.' Nick shakes his head sadly. 'The collision's inevitable – like trains on the same track.' He's too close, his beery breath hot on my face. Shreds of meat are caught in his teeth. 'Smash!'

Sue's soft flesh, under my thumbs. The odd, gargling noise from her throat.

'She was so damned annoying.' Nick goes back to his plate and swipes a piece of steak.

'I don't know what you mean.' Why am I whispering?

'On and on, all the time.' His voice changes, to a high monotone. *'You're such a cliché! She's half your age.'*

How did he do that?

His expression is kind, concerned. 'After a while it wears you down.'

In my mind's eye is the lonely line of trees. The scrape of a spade. The thump and patter of earth on plastic wrapping. 'I've no idea what you're talking about.'

'I think you do.'

I stare out at the empty sea. The distant shore glimmers. Alicia, where are you?

'It wasn't your fault,' Nick says. 'You can't be held responsible.'

Bile rises in my throat.

'Luck. Opportunity,' he goes on. 'Why should some have it and not others? No one could blame you for taking yours.'

'It wasn't like that.' It was so quick. One minute, Sue's face was in mine, her mouth working, spewing complaints: the soundtrack of our 15-year marriage. The next, she was slumped on the kitchen floor.

Nick looks up. 'How was it, then?'

Everything shrank. Came down to nothing but that place on the tiles. The bundle lying there. I watched myself as if I was someone else. How had it happened?

I didn't mean to do it.

The practicalities were the worst. I was unprepared for the weight. Sue was small, didn't even reach my shoulder. But she was as un-cooperative in death as in life. Her arms wouldn't stay crossed over her chest; her feet kept catching on the hall rug.

If only I could turn the clock back.

'I'm off.' I stand up. 'If you're some kind of wannabe private eye, you're wasting your time.'

'You did a professional job there, Steve.' Nick smiles. 'Ready for a new start, huh?'

'Goodbye.'

His hand is on my arm. 'You're safe here.'

I shake him off. 'Safe?'

'No extradition treaty, my friend.'

'I'm going.' I reach for my bag. 'The ferry'll be here soon.' I glance at my watch and remember again that it's stopped.

'Nice watch.'

'It's broken. It must be a fake.'

'When did it stop?'

I angle it under the light. 'Noon.'

'Where were you then?'

'What's it to you?'

Nick shrugs. 'Just interested, that's all.'

'At the port, if you must know. On my way here.'

'Of course.'

The chaos of the dock, in the blinding sun. Heat, pulsing from the concrete. Behind me, Alicia, calling. What was she saying?

I pull my ferry ticket from my pocket. 'At least I've got a return.'

'You have?'

The paper rectangle is stiff and crinkled, the details blurred. 'How did it get wet?'

'Come on, Steve.'

'What?'

'Remember the port?'

My US dollars got us through the crowd – the usual beggars

and no-hopers. 'We had to run to make the ferry.' There were shouts behind me, but I didn't look round. 'It was every man for himself.'

'It always is.'

I remember elbows, in my ribs. A jolt – something hard, against my ankle. 'Ah. I must have tripped, on the gangplank. Knocked myself out.'

Nick smiles.

'When I came round, I was in the bar, on the ferry.' I was lying on a bench. It was gloomy and cool. I was glad to be out of the sun. I checked my pockets. There was nothing missing. I looked round for Alicia, but no one had seen her. 'Next thing I knew, we were docking here.'

'You caught a different ferry.'

'No, I didn't.' I want to thump him. 'This is the island. The famous resort. You said it was.'

'Did I?'

'I'm leaving.'

'Oh dear, Steve.' Nick takes the ferry ticket from my hand. 'I thought you understood.' He crumples the dried paper over the table. Shreds land in the blood from his steak.

'You bastard!' I'm on my feet, my hands round his neck. His skin is cold and rubbery.

A blow to my chest. I hit the floorboards with a thud.

Nick looks down at me and straightens his collar. 'That won't work with me, Steve.'

I sit up slowly. This can't be happening. I fumble to get my mobile out of my pocket. Alicia will tell me to stop dragging my feet and get out. There'll be a boatman somewhere. People in these places are always desperate for money. I punch the buttons.

Nothing.

'Not much of a swimmer are you, Steve?'

I remember cold, oily water in my ears and in my mouth. 'Did I fall in?'

Nick nods.

The weight of seawater, in my chest.

'It's deeper than it looks, by the dock.'

'Well, I must have a guardian angel. Someone pulled me out.' I can't help smiling. 'They must have held me under the arms and dragged me.'

The image changes into Sue's body, trussed in black plastic. The rustling sound it made as I slid it into the hole.

My heart bangs against my ribs. 'It was an accident. I made a mistake. That's all.'

'You're here now,' Nick says. 'Everything's all right.'

'I'm not staying.' I struggle to my feet. Below the veranda, dark water stretches in all directions. Waves hiss onto the sand.

'You can't leave.' Nick grins. 'This is it, Steve.'

'Someone'll take me.' It's a relief to get away from him and jump down the steps. 'Anyone!'

I run down the beach, heading for the sea.

Across the Straits the port lights wink, promising everything.

In the Blood

From her bed by the parlour window, the girl watches the prairie. In the distance a dark funnel links land and sky. Her fingers grip the sill and the draught slides over her nails, bitten to the quick.

Behind her in the gloom her parents hulk in their chairs by the hearth. The wind chases the last wisps of smoke off the kindling.

From overhead comes a thud, and the sound of something heavy, rolling across the floor.

The daughter tries to picture the upstairs rooms. But she can remember only criss-crossed lengths of wood, and the jerking movements of her father's arms, shirt sleeves rolled to the elbow as he hammered nails, his curses falling on her small head like stones.

And a feeling, deep inside her, of something taken away.

A door bangs, insistently.

'You said you'd fixed everything.' The old woman grasps the bellows, and wheezes them over the dying coals.

'It's your fault,' the old man complains. 'You didn't let me finish the job.' He glances at the girl.

The daughter clenches her fists. Her long, black hair is bound with dirty ribbons; her body covered by a stiff dress. The room's unspoken words prod and poke her: sometimes she finds bruises on her skin.

She slides her feet under the bed, past her work boots, and finds the slippers she left there, a long time ago.

'I'll check the fastenings.' She hardly recognises her own voice.

'You will not.' The old man tries to get up, but falls back in his chair.

The old woman raises her walking stick. 'You up to something, missy?'

The girl dodges them and heads for the door, past the cooking pots and buckets. 'I'll come straight back.'

Above the wind's howl she hears another noise, and her blood quickens.

In the corner of the room is a rusted metal pole. Grasping it as if it's another's hand, the girl opens the door to the hall. The staircase leads up into the dark.

The two old people stare at the cracked flagstones and the blackened fire irons.

Both know what remains unsaid. *It was for her own good.* But how ungrateful she is! And look what's become of them. The old woman puts her hand to her face, and feels the parchment there. When the old man buckles his belt, he sees the bones beneath his soft, yellowy skin.

With the pole in her right hand, the daughter steps on to the first tread.

The stairs shake as the wind tugs at the house, pushing its fingers into small, dark spaces. The girl wants to cover her ears with her hands. Her chest is as tight as a pulled thread; her sweat slides on the metal. She can see only the outline of the next step. Half-way up, she wants to turn and skedaddle. Only the thought of her life downstairs keeps her going – and the echo of a feeling, which she cannot name.

She reaches the landing, and the wind drops. The sound she

heard earlier remains: fainter now, but unmistakeable. A child's cry.

The girl catches her breath. Daylight leaks through gaps between plaster and wood. As she remembered, the three doors are boarded with planks. The sound is coming from behind the nearest door. She puts her shoulder to the wood. With a loud crack, it gives way.

She falls forward, her gaze searching the space; but there's no child here. The crying has stopped.

With a jolt the daughter sees the high, old bed. Her stomach twists; she wants to back away. In the corner is the small bed and the tall shelves. She anticipates the weight of bound leather in her hands, the skin of paper under her fingers. She remembers losing herself in the glint of spilled treasure on a stone floor, the sound of waves against a wooden prow.

Dusty light slants through the wooden frame.

The girl runs her hand along the empty shelves, gathering balls of dust. Something settles in her chest. She recalls a dark figure; shadows, moving on the wall. She always called it a dream.

She has to sit down. She reaches to smooth the crumpled bedcovers, and recognises the imprint of a child's body.

Someone else is here: a little woman, bold as Rumpelstiltskin, wrapped in a cloak, her hair wild round her head.

Before the daughter can speak, the woman grabs the pole and sticks it in the middle of the floor, where it fixes itself and turns. Its core unravels, and the dusty room is filled with rippling stripes.

'Take one!' shouts the woman. 'Hold on!'

The girl plucks at the flying ribbons but misses each time. On the fourth or fifth go, she pulls a sliver of satin out of the whirling air and holds on to it with both hands. She feels her feet, in their unworn slippers, leave the ground. Before her eyes, the room becomes a kaleidoscope of pink and purple, silver and orange. She feels another hand holding onto the ribbon, and sees her young self, beside her.

Now she hears music: strong, booming notes, as deep as the ocean floor; high, bright chimes, like water in a forest. Soft, quiet ripples, like the underside of leaves. All these pictures are in the daughter's head. Her smaller self turns to her, offering her hand shyly; and the daughter sees the raw, bitten fingers.

The little woman is dancing on the spot and singing, and the two sisters (but they are even closer than sisters) are spinning round the room. The sister who has come from downstairs has a vague memory, as she feels the blood pump through her veins and her younger self slip effortlessly under her skin: the sense of two desiccated old people, sitting either side of a dying fire. But the peach-golden, marbled-pink light is dazzling, and the excitement of finding her sister – whom she has missed for so long – has addled her brain.

The air hums. The window pane becomes a spider's web. With a deafening crack the glass breaks, and the hurricane roars in and sucks the daughters out: over the prairie, towards the scarlet-streaked horizon, and into a moon-filled night.

In the parlour, the old woman has given up banging on the ceiling with her stick: her arms are tired, and she can hear nothing above the howling of the wind. She and her husband stare at the lifeless hearth, wondering if they can look each other in the eye.

Deep in the coals a spark glows. The old woman reaches for the poker but, before she can agitate the kindling, a red coal pops and falls out. She jabs at it, flicking it against the old man's trousers. He yowls as the fabric catches and burns. He kicks the coal at the old woman, and it lands, smouldering, in her lap.

She flaps her apron, sending smoke into her eyes; fanning the flames that lick her skirt. 'Now look what you've done!' she shouts, smoke in her throat. 'You stupid old man!'

'You started it!'

The old woman gets to her feet and swings the poker at her husband. But the effort unbalances her. She staggers onto him, and they both fall into the fire.

They push and shove each other, but neither can climb out. Flames roast their boots and gobble their hair. Their thick clothes turn to blackened shreds. The last drops of fat bubble in their limbs; skin cracks; thin veins shrivel, and their blood cooks.

*

Many years later – it might be the next century, or the next millennium – a dark-haired girl arrives, on horseback. She's searching for stories. She's never found a story she doesn't want, although some are hard to live with. She's heard tales, in boarding houses and inns, of a family that lived here.

She's come a long way. On her journey she's had to fend for herself; but she has a quick brain and a quick tongue, which has sometimes got her into trouble but mostly got her out of it.

She has her own riddle to solve, and is almost all the way to solving it, but she doesn't know that, yet. She loves the roar of a hurricane. She knows how to lay and light an old-fashioned fire, and she bites her nails down to the quick. But the question that torments her is why the men in her life are hard-hearted and cruel, with flint for eyes, and why the women have knives for tongues.

The light is fading when the girl reaches the prairie. She urges her horse forward until they come upon a huddle of ruins. The horse puts his head down between upturned bricks, to sniff out something to eat. The girl dismounts and, using her crop, pokes about in the bones of a house. The structure has long since rotted in the prairie sun, and under the watching moon.

The girl walks through the shell of the building, striding like

Gulliver over small ramparts and mounds, which must once have been walls. She shades her eyes and looks around, and wonders how any family survived here.

She turns to get back on her horse and something catches the toe of her boot. She bends, and picks up an unmistakeably human skull. It weighs almost nothing. Cracked, grey, marked by fire, the bone has been picked clean.

Hollow sockets stare at her, and the girl pictures eyes, cold as a handful of ash. She wants to look away, but she grips the open jaw and rubs her thumbs over the dome.

Dread creeps up behind her. The girl feels a chill move down the back of her head. It claws at her shoulders, and slides down her spine. She struggles to stay upright.

She understands what happened here.

The story is trying to get into her bones, into her blood. She feels it moving through her, searching for a place to settle. In a clamour of voices it wails, *Things were different then. It never did us any harm.*

The girl stands still, and feels the story twist in her veins. But it can find nowhere to hide, nowhere to grow.

At last, her blood flows, and her limbs soften. The story has gone. All that's left is what she's always known, what is in her core.

There's a lightness between her hands. Looking down, she sees the skull has turned to ash.

She spreads her fingers wide, and the grey dust streams out.

The Ishtar Pin

M ahmoud pushes away the heavy blanket, his heart thumping hard. He stares into the dark, listening for the rattle of gunfire.

Slowly his nightmare recedes.

Panicky old fool.

The radio newsreader was calm, yesterday, announcing the curfew: 'a safety precaution due to planned military action'. He mentioned rebel forces; a town in a distant province. Mahmoud pictured smoking rubble and dazed, crying children, and felt the familiar weary anger.

After ten years, the world's attention has moved on to other wars, and a new, invisible enemy that can't be bombed or shot. Yet in the ruins of his country, the big players and their proxies still slug it out. Mahmoud can no longer count the relatives and friends he's lost. Somehow, his own small family has survived. Life goes on.

His back aches from the thin mattress. No more sleep for him. Does the president lie awake at night? Mahmoud met the young man once, at a palace function, shortly after he'd succeeded his wily old father. The reluctant heir was tall, pale, his handshake soft. He promised a new beginning. He spoke with a lisp.

Mahmoud takes his torch, and sweeps the beam over the

stone walls. He pictures the slaves who dug this room out of the palace foundations, centuries ago: anonymous men, conquered in battle. Did they still believe in what they had fought for? Or were they just glad to be alive? They left no trace: not even ancient graffiti. He imagines leaving his own: *Mahmoud Hassan, 25 March 2021.* The stone is rough and cool. He could no sooner deface it than knife his own heart.

'I swear you care more for old stones than people, Baba,' Amir said, years ago. They were at home. The television was on; Mahmoud had turned the sound down. The barbarians had dynamited an ancient temple at the edge of the desert; red clouds billowed as the pillars fell.

'That's our heritage,' Mahmoud said, trying not to rise to his son's bait. 'Ancient buildings and artefacts can't be replaced.' He caught Noor's warning look, and felt a flicker of annoyance with his wife. 'Remember coming to the museum when you were young, Amir? You liked the basement hiding place.'

The teenager watched the screen. 'They've got the world's attention now. The Koran says –'

Mahmoud bristled. 'What those monsters do isn't religion. That's intimidation.'

*

Which monsters are on the loose now? And where are they?

Mahmoud switches the radio on. Nothing. He puts the machine to his ear and turns the volume up; moves the dial. Not even a crackle of static. When did he last replace the batteries? He checks his phone, but there's no signal down here. Last night he called Noor from his office upstairs. She was preparing dinner. Mahmoud repeated the radio announcer's words – 'a precaution'. Noor wanted him home. He heard the fear in her voice.

Noor. Longing for her almost overwhelms him. A pulse starts at the side of his head. *Keep calm.*

He finds a match, which sparks at his third attempt. The dry, desert air feels far away. He lights the small stove, measures and spoons coffee as if it's powdered gold. Coffee should never be drunk alone, Noor always says.

But he's not alone.

He opens a cabinet. The door creaks, and he wants to say, 'Shhh,' as if to a child. The hinges need oiling. Like his own.

The silver cloak pin gleams in the torchlight. Noor's favourite piece: one of the first artefacts he brought down to safety. The head, a bright blue bead of lapis lazuli, is surrounded by a gold, eight-pointed star – the symbol of Ishtar, goddess of war and love. The story of her descent into the underworld, to capture her sister's lands, explains the seasons: the turning of the year.

Noor came down here with him, once, years ago, when he started the job. She touched the cold walls and said she felt like Ishtar, imprisoned underground.

'But her husband took her place,' Mahmoud said.

'As her hostage! He had no choice.' Noor's indignation made her eyebrows almost vanish into her hijab. Mahmoud felt as reprimanded as one of her students.

He smiled. 'Fierce Ishtar. Perhaps the passions of love and war are not so different.'

'There is no pity in those stories,' Noor said. 'Come on. You can release me from captivity now.'

He extracted a kiss as payment.

They emerged into the spring sunshine of the courtyard, the lemon trees bright with blossom.

'Look,' Mahmoud said. 'New life begins.' That was the inscription he had chosen for her wedding ring.

It was a late marriage for him; he couldn't believe his luck.

*

He turns the cloak pin on his palm. It was made centuries ago, in Afghanistan. Discovered in a distant valley, the pin caused international debate. In those days Mahmoud was invited to speak at conferences, in countries that now are closed to him.

The air in the small room is stale. Standing on the ladder, Mahmoud opens the trapdoor. Above is the same murky darkness, but he can make out the end of the passage, and the pile of wooden cases he and Hussein stacked in front of the door. Behind it, four flights of steps lead up to the entrance, shuttered and locked a lifetime ago. Perhaps, before too long, it will open again.

Footsteps, on the back stairs. It must be Hussein, coming to tell him it's safe to leave.

Mahmoud folds the blanket into a lopsided square. He hopes the place doesn't smell.

Torchlight pools by the trapdoor, and falls into the room.

There is a pair of heavy black boots on the ladder.

Mahmoud's heart stutters.

A young man jumps to the ground and straightens up. He brushes down his camouflage trousers. A rifle is slung across his front.

'Amir!' Mahmoud goes to embrace his son. They come together awkwardly, the gun pushing between them.

Amir gives the greeting; Mahmoud replies.

Mahmoud can't think. 'What are you doing here?'

'I've come to find you.' Amir smiles.

His face is thin, his trousers gathered under his belt. Even his boots are too big. He looks round at the neat piles of stone tablets, the packing cases and full cabinets.

Mahmoud feels embarrassed, as if he's been caught stealing. He takes a cup and pours coffee into it. Liquid spills on his hand, and he's pleased to feel it burn. It is some reality, in this strange dream.

He passes the cup to his son. 'I couldn't get home last night. The radio said the rebels…' Is Amir one of them?

'And you wanted to protect your treasures.'

They protect me, Mahmoud wants to say. Instead, he blurts, 'Is that army uniform?'

Amir grins. 'What do you think?'

Whose side are you on, Mahmoud wants to ask. *Am I in danger?* He pushes the thought away. 'I was about to leave.' He sounds ridiculous – a late-staying guest at a party. 'I'll tell your mother you are well. Have you seen her?'

He hears his words running on. He's playing for time; but why? To find his son under the dirt and camouflage? To work out what this young man wants?

'Hiding away down here.' Amir knocks a cabinet and the torch on top wobbles, sending jagged light across the ceiling.

'You'll break something if you don't sit down,' Mahmoud says. 'Surely that's not what you've come for?'

Amir looks into a display case of clay statuettes. His hand hovers over the lock.

Mahmoud wants to stop him. 'Your new job. The security firm – was it true?'

'You don't need to worry about that.'

'Have you seen your mother?'

Amir nods.

Mahmoud feels clumsy, as if, in this strange dance, only his son knows the steps. How did he win arguments with the teenage Amir? 'What are you fighting for?'

'So many questions!'

Images of trigger-happy young men swarm in Mahmoud's head: factions who fight in the rubble of cities; shifting alliances. Is his son part of that chaos? 'Sometimes it's hard to know who's fighting for what.'

'Sometimes it's easy.' Amir moves and light glances off the gun. His fingers brush it as if for luck.

Mahmoud imagines those fingers squeezing the trigger. 'Where are you living?'

'Here and there.'

Mahmoud knows, from TV footage, how drones seek out body heat. He's seen the grainy images of small, white figures and silent explosions. Without warning his heart aches for his son.

Amir picks up the radio and turns it on. He holds it to his ear and puts it down again. 'No wonder you don't know.'

'Know what?' Mahmoud feels old; slow. 'You mean – the rebels? Haven't the city walls kept them out?' He realises 'them' includes his son.

Amir shakes his head. 'Still putting your faith in old stones.'

'The walls have fallen?'

'It won't be long.'

Mahmoud has a sudden memory of walking along the walls at dusk with Noor when they were first married. They watched the swifts swooping and diving. She was fascinated by the birds' speed; how they fed on the wing. He heard her passion for her subject and loved her even more.

He has to get home. 'Where are they? The – others?' He takes out his phone. Of course. No signal.

'There's still time, if you come with me now.'

'What about all this?' But Mahmoud knows. 'It will be destroyed.'

'Not by me.'

'But – stolen, yes? Or – smashed, to prove a point. That culture and history is worthless. Knowledge is nothing.' Mahmoud hates his voice. He can't find the right tone.

Amir wipes his face with his sleeve. 'If you come with me, you'll be safe.'

'Safe?'

'No one knows I'm here.'

'Didn't they send you? That would be their way.'

'Who is "they"?'

'Your commanders. Superiors. Whatever you call them. Or are you all the same? Equals in some mad brotherhood?'

Amir frowns. 'What are you trying to prove?'

'Surely it is you and your friends who are in the business of proving things.'

The young man turns away. 'You think Mama would wish this for you?'

'Why must you involve her?'

Amir reaches into a cardboard box and takes out an object wrapped in newspaper. 'She never shared your obsession with these dead things.' He rips the paper to reveal a clay cylinder, a few inches high. Around its edge, delicately carved, barefoot men carry armfuls of wheat. He slips the piece inside his jacket.

'Some dead things are useful, then?' Mahmoud knows that artefacts are sold to international buyers. He picks up the Ishtar pin. 'You should be grateful to me. I have kept all this safe. Perhaps I should have taken a hammer to it myself.'

Amir shrugs.

For an instant, Mahmoud glimpses uncertainty and regret. The boy in the soldier's clothes. The child, fascinated by the ancient engravings, who ran his fingers over them, tracing the script.

Mahmoud points to a stack of clay tablets. 'They discovered the stars. They named them. They discovered mathematics. Your tanks and weapons – none of that would be possible. Your rockets and mortars.' He can't stop his voice rising. 'What will your legacy be?'

'Save your breath.'

'You've been brainwashed.'

'Because I care more about people than – all this?' Amir takes a tablet from the pile against the wall. The rest fall into each other with a crack, sending fragments to the floor in a shower of dust.

Mahmoud resists the urge to right the pieces. 'Once it was dangerous to be a soldier. These days it's more dangerous to be a civilian.'

'What would you know about being a soldier?'

'You are right, of course.' Sadness, and anger, at the loss of the life he had wanted for his son, wells up in Mahmoud. 'At least your mother knows you are alive.'

A shadow moves behind Amir's eyes.

'What?'

Amir takes something from his pocket, and places it on Mahmoud's palm.

The gold ring is scratched and slightly flattened.

The air goes from Mahmoud's chest. He stares at the ring. Blood has crusted and dried on the metal, making a terrible joke of the inscription: *New life begins.*

Amir is by the ladder. 'You must come now.'

'What happened?' Mahmoud whispers. 'She is injured?'

Amir shakes his head.

'What happened?' Mahmoud's thoughts are stuck.

'We came under attack. In the eastern suburbs.' Amir's voice is flat. 'In our advance.'

'Your advance?' The pompous military term bludgeons Mahmoud's brain. But he has to listen. If he hears everything, there will be a fact he can grasp to show Amir that he's wrong. That this cold, soldier's talk has no place between them. 'What advance? What are you talking about?'

'There's no more time,' Amir says. 'We must leave, now.'

'Where is she?'

'I came to help you.' The young man moves into the light from the torch. His eyes glisten. 'Why must you make everything so difficult? We've all had to make sacrifices.'

Mahmoud is on his feet, his arm swinging. From nowhere comes an image: of his own hand, gripping the teenage Amir's skinny shoulders, his other fist raised, ready to strike. His son's shocked, panicked face.

Amir pushes him away.

Loud, jagged sobs force their way out of Mahmoud's chest.

He can't stop the terrible pictures unspooling in his head. 'Noor. Oh, Noor.' He slips the ring onto his little finger. 'There must be – where's her hand? You must have found her hand?' What a question.

Amir doesn't reply.

Mahmoud turns the ring on his finger. The flattened metal resists. With a flash of memory that fells him he sees Noor on their wedding day, and her smile as he slid the ring on for her.

It must have been quick. *Insh'Allah* it was quick.

Bargaining with the gods.

He is no different from the ancient people, after all. But Noor was right. The gods are pitiless.

Noor. Her name means 'light'. He's always thought how well it suits her.

Amir steps on to the ladder. Mahmoud stares, bewildered. He needs to know all the details of this man's appearance, this stranger, who holds the key to such horror. Can this really be his son?

Surely in a moment he will turn, and apologise, and hug his father? They will go home to Noor, and all this will be a bad dream.

Amir stops. 'We're fighting for our country. For our people.'

Mahmoud finds his voice. 'You are not fighting for me.'

Amir climbs the rungs, his thin back moving easily through the narrow hatch.

From the distance comes the thump of a mortar. The building shakes.

Mahmoud sinks to the floor. His chest is being crushed in a vice.

Something hard is digging into his palm: the Ishtar pin. He tests it against his finger and watches the bead of blood.

Proof

I'm walking so quickly I'm level with the van before I realise. My chest pinches and I slow down. I can't see the number plate, but it's definitely his. In the May sunlight the blue spray job looks even crappier. If I went round the front, I'd see the wing dent where he hit the wall the night he left.

It's parked outside a gone-to-seed Victorian three-storey. There's a basement too, with a mouldy window that looks like it hasn't been opened in years. There'll be plenty of work: new windows, kitchen, bathroom; maybe knocking down walls and ripping out chimneys. Then all the decorating. There'd have to be a deposit for materials. And the bill settled in full, within seven days. I used to insist on that.

But insisting only got me so far.

He always ended up working Saturdays, because the job was over-running, and the customer threatening not to pay. And on Sundays he wanted to tile the bathroom, or sand the stairs, or change the kitchen cupboards.

'We should have bought shares in these,' I used to say, as I slashed the top of another microwaveable TV dinner.

*

As I pass the van, the barking starts. What a surprise. He always got what he wanted. I go round the back and peer in. Standing on a blanket, surrounded by old paint tins and lengths of wood, is a scrappy little terrier, dirty white, missing an eye. Obviously been in a few fights.

When it sees me, the pathetic little dog leaps up and growls. There's manky, stretched skin where its right eye should be. It doesn't look very lovable.

'Just shut up, for Christ's sake!' I press my nose to the glass. 'Stop going on!' It throws itself around, snarling and yapping, defending its tatty territory.

No worries, I'm off.

Why do I turn, and glance at the windscreen?

Now I can't help myself. I kick the tyre, which makes the dog even angrier.

I know how you feel, I want to say.

I'm always the first one in the office.

I leave the answering machine on, and sit at my desk. The archive shelves crowd in: rows of legal textbooks and folders, bursting with documents. All those words; all those voices. Who said what, to whom? Was the crime intentional? Accidental? *Here's the evidence, Your Honour. Any mitigating circumstances?*

Sometimes the wrong people get off scot-free. When does No turn into Yes? Never slide into Maybe? How do you know when someone's lying?

He said we'd always agreed on it.

I said things change.

He said No meant No.

I wander round and open the blinds, turn on the shredder and the air-con, and check the levels in the water cooler. I mark off another day on the Year Planner. At the top of the 'Live Cases' board, I rub out yesterday's date, and write in today's. But my fingers are wobbly. I have to do it twice. I can feel my eyes tearing up. I sit down quickly.

'Jane is the backbone of our admin team,' my last appraisal said. 'Always willing to cover for colleagues on leave.'

I'm fine once they've left. It's the weeks before that I can't stand. First the coy hints, then the endless discussions about cravings and clothes. All too soon, they're back, full of smug smiles and fake complaints, and moaning about lack of sleep. After a few minutes of it I have to get up and go to the Ladies.

Why did I keep a photo? Incriminating evidence, as our briefs would say. My fingers find it in my drawer, underneath a pile of recycled envelopes.

It's the seafront, at Brighton, two years ago. A bright spring day. His birthday. I thought it would be the perfect surprise. But my timing's always been a bit dodgy.

We could get to the coast in a couple of hours, the van rattling, motorway slipping by. We were off on an adventure; we were Bonnie and Clyde, we were invincible.

He always had to have music, on his phone. He played Springsteen. We were rolling down the highway, and the blacktop was melting, even though I didn't know what blacktop was, and it was never that hot. In Springsteen-land it was always summer.

But the van kept breaking down. And the middle safety belt didn't work.

'When are you going to get this fixed?' I used to say every time I got in, pulling out the loop that hung down the back of the seat between us.

'I'll get round to it.' He was always fiddling with the music when he should have been concentrating on the road. 'What's the problem? These two work fine.'

We'd just parked up, and were walking along the prom. He stopped and leaned on the railings, looking down over the beach. He was only wearing jeans and his old grey hoodie, and the wind was messing his hair, but he grinned at me, and my heart squeezed. I had my camera. I wanted a photo of him. I don't know if he didn't hear me, or thought I'd already taken it, but he turned away at the wrong time.

The photo shows the back of his head. It's a good reminder.

I waited until we got to the pub. I thought it might be better somewhere contained. A cosy corner, just the two of us. Afterwards I wondered if I should have told him when we were walking on the beach, so the wind whipped our words away, so I didn't have to see the look on his face.

I knew how it'd happened. I just couldn't believe it. Bank Holiday weekend, and the GP's closed. I'd meant to find the duty chemist but I kept forgetting.

I saw something on-line the other day, on a chat: someone said women these days are too ambitious; we want everything. We're making men nervous, undermining their confidence, wanting the same as them at work. At home, we're putting them under too much pressure to have the perfect relationship.

But I didn't want everything.

He said he'd come with me but I wanted to go alone. Funnily enough I got my own way over that. I was pretty sure I knew what would happen. I just never thought I'd be doing it.

It was a largeish room, where you had to wait. Three rows of chairs, all facing forward. Pale walls. Net curtains that could have done with a wash. No one crying, luckily. I noticed an older woman, who'd brought a friend with her. The teenager along from me was definitely with her mum. She went in ahead of me, then came out again, and they sat whispering over a list of pros and cons. That's what the counsellor had suggested doing, if I had any doubts.

I didn't need a list. If I chose one, I had to lose the other. And it was still early; it was going to be straightforward.

Except it wasn't. There were signs of deterioration, the lovely doctor said. It might just be me; how I was made. It might be to do with my age. I needed to be aware of it, for the future.

That was the bit I couldn't forget.

For a few weeks he insisted we went out on a Sunday: walks and pub lunches, or to the cinema if it was raining.

One overcast afternoon we were dragging up a hill towards an old church. The walks book said there was a great view from the graveyard at the top. Ahead of us was an older couple, with a light brown dog which kept circling them, looping backwards and forwards. It ran up to us, sniffing round our legs, and jumped up. I stood still, waiting for it to stop. But he bent down to it; patted its head, stroked its back. He laughed, and let it lick his hand. I watched its slobbering pink tongue on his fingers and I felt my eyes fill. I wanted to kick the stupid animal.

After it ran off, he said, 'Maybe that's what we need.'

'I don't want a dog,' I said.

Three months later, he was in such a hurry to leave he drove the van into the front wall.

'There's no one else,' he said, 'there's only you.' It was just that we wanted different things.

Even though I'd tried to want what he wanted.

I believed him. I always did.

But I didn't see what was staring me in the face.

*

I look at the photo again – really look at it, this time: at the back of his head, turned away. Already gone.

99

I cross the room and carefully line the photo up on top of the shredder. Then I feed it into the machine.

Sometimes No turns into Yes; sometimes it turns into Maybe. Nothing stays the same forever.

And people can be wrong – even lovely doctors.

I sit at my desk, remembering my morning; why I was walking so quickly, so confidently into the new day. I find my phone in my handbag. I start to tap out a text, but that's not what I want. I choose the phone icon instead and listen to the ringing tone. I'm about to press *End* when the ringing stops.

'Hi, love. Everything okay?'

Because it hasn't been. Because for some women it will always be harder than for others.

Your voice always makes me smile. 'Yes. Yes, I'm fine.'

I am.

It doesn't matter any more: the van with the dent; the barking dog; even the little blue and red checked car-seat, strapped in the front.

I can prod my heart, and it doesn't even twinge.

'I just wanted to tell you.' I fiddle with my wedding ring.

'Yeah?'

'Today – I – it's the first morning I haven't been sick.'

'Hey!' I hear your delight. 'That's brilliant, Janey! Great! That's a good sign.'

I sit back in the chair, feel my body relax. 'Yes.' I smile. 'Yes, it is.'

A Thousand Grains

The rider is Liu Qiang. Despite his woollen gloves, his fingers are cold. He grips the handlebars and circles his bicycle again, beyond the reach of the street light. The Beijing air seeps through his padded jacket, chilling his bones.

Is this how death would feel? Last week Liu went with his work unit comrades to pay their respects at the Great Leader's mausoleum in Tian an Men. Three years after his death, the Great Leader's embalmed body was swollen and yellow, his skin like wax. But it was him. The old man has really gone.

And now a new year with the luckiest of numbers has begun. 1980. Everything will be different.

Liu pats his breast pocket, feeling the outline of his papers. If any Public Security comrades appear, he has his story ready: he had to get out of the house, away from his wife and son. You know how it is, comrade. A man needs a little peace. A former Red Guard will be believed. His heart beats hard through the layers of his clothes.

Hallo. I am very pleased to make your acquaintance. The sentence goes round in his head. This is the language – as slippery and full of hisses as a bucket of snakes – that he longs for: as a starving man dreams of rice. The universities have only recently re-opened; he has not been chosen to study English.

But in the spirit of the new Paramount Leader Deng Xiaoping, Liu is making changes.

He watches the road. The two English girls are late. When he invited them he spoke slowly, in his simplest Mandarin. He thought they might laugh. Confusingly, they often do. But clever Ka-Lin understood straight away, pushing her glasses up her pointed nose in excitement. She explained to Zhu-Li. Then Ka-Lin got out her dictionary and found the word for *adventure*. They practised saying it in Mandarin: *mao xian.* They didn't notice that one of the meanings is 'risk'. As if Liu was the one who needed to understand, Zhu-Li wrote the characters out, over and over again, in a lumpy line.

Liu thinks of his father's writing, the lines and dashes as beautiful as music, that in the chaos of recent years he has had to forget. The curves and sweeps became black squares – Big Character slogans, daubed on posters and walls: 'Rebellion is just!' Liu remembers with unease the crunch of spectacles under his shoe.

The girls' writing is poor. He wonders about their education at the Foreign Languages Institute. When he heard that English students had arrived there, he knew he had to meet them. He plucked up his courage – and it was easy, to cycle past the guard house after dark in a crowd of students and whisper, 'Hallo' to a tall, light-haired girl standing there. Luckily for him it was the soft-hearted Ka-Lin. She introduced him to Zhu-Li, who looked at him suspiciously.

The girls are nineteen, ten years younger than Liu. At their age he was working in the countryside, digging the frozen earth to plant cabbages with an old peasant couple whose one-room home he shared. In the evenings he read to them from the Great Leader's thoughts, ignoring his hands full of cuts and their mocking laughter.

When he returned to the city he met Han Mei at a rally. Two years ago she produced Pangpang. Under the new policy they can have no more children. It is hope for his son's future, too, that is tangled up in Liu Qiang's plan.

He finds it hard to concentrate on his work at the East Wind bicycle factory, but none of his comrades has accused him of having a Bad Attitude. Nor has he been summoned to a Self-Criticism Meeting, where he would have to explain his lack of enthusiasm for fitting spokes into iron rims. On the production line he smiles to himself when he imagines living in the West: in a big house with three cars, like all Westerners.

The shadows ripple, becoming two bulky outlines. Could they be police? Liu holds his breath. Now the lamplight shows the gleam of new bicycles and the dark fur collars of expensive coats. The girls have understood his instruction to push their hats down and their collars up. But in between their faces are pale.

He whistles and sets off along the street. If the girls are stopped he will go on ahead. They would be escorted to the main road and warned not to be out after dark again.

Liu turns left and right, then doubles back into the *hu-tongs*. The single-storey buildings are dark. Here and there a light shows behind a blind. He cycles past his courtyard and turns back. Before he reaches his house he stops and signals to the girls to walk.

In the small room lit by a fluorescent strip, Han Mei sets the special chopsticks on the table and tastes the seasoning in the pork offal soup. Her hand wobbles and a scalding drip lands on her chin. She re-arranges the plate of fried tofu and the mutton, and with a spoon pushes the boiled peanuts into a bigger heap. She tries not to think of the ration coupons she's used. In the queue this afternoon old Mrs Zhang said loudly, 'So much food for one family, comrade?' Quick as a whip, Han Mei replied, 'I suppose you've forgotten how much a hungry husband and a growing son can eat?' That shut the old witch up. Her husband,

Teacher Zhang, hasn't been seen since he was arrested four years ago for being a counter-revolutionary.

On the bench seat against the wall, Pangpang is quiet, his head drooping on his chest. Han Mei nudges him awake. She knows that these Foreign Friends, as they must now be called, will be impressed with her son. She tries to picture the students. Her husband said they want to see how worker-comrades live. 'Let them find out from someone else,' said Han Mei. Her friend has stood next to foreign students on the bus. They smell of milk. Like babies.

The sound of the latch, a rush of cold air. Han Mei feels her chest tighten.

Liu is first through the door. He nods at her, full of self-importance. Behind him are two dark figures. Han Mei can't help staring. Foreign Devils, right here in her house! She straightens her jacket, glad she has mended the rip in the padding.

Like visiting Party comrades, the girls look round, as if they are checking up on her. They have big noses, just as her friend said, and round eyes; although the taller girl's are hidden by glasses. They are wearing expensive cotton shoes, and it's true: their feet are as big as men's.

When they introduce themselves, Han Mei wants to laugh. 'What kind of names are those?' she says to Liu, behind her hand.

'Don't be stupid.' He fusses with a chair. 'Their teachers made them up.'

Stung, she waits for the girls to praise her cooking; but Liu gets in the way, waving his arms about like an actor in the Beijing Opera. Squashed at the small table, she thinks of a work unit meeting, or a Self-Denunciation session. She puts her arm round her son.

'*Chi ba, chi ba.* Eat!' Liu spoons rice into the students' bowls.

Han Mei studies the visitors. Even with her glasses, the light-haired girl, Ka-Lin, is better looking than the dark-haired one, but they are both so white they could be actors in face paint. Their hair is curly: does it grow like that? Now that permed hair is allowed, she has hers done regularly at the hairdressers on the corner. When Liu said he didn't like it she pretended not to care – why should a revolutionary woman worry what her husband thinks?

Until he started going out on a Tuesday evening and coming back late.

When she confronted him his story was so strange it had to be true. She could hardly speak. 'Meeting Foreign Devils? You'll lose your job!'

But Liu just smiled. 'I'm getting a better job.' He spoke slowly, as if she wouldn't understand. 'Interpreter with a Trade Delegation.'

'Those jobs are only for high-ups!'

'My work unit will put my name forward,' he said. 'The students say my English is very good.' Before she could ask anything else he added, 'Think of the presents I'll bring back from England.'

Since then, whenever she is bored working the sewing machine at the Number Five underwear factory, Han Mei imagines her husband, smart in his Party uniform, returning from a foreign trip with a new plastic suitcase. Inside are toys for Pangpang, and shoes with a heel for her. Perhaps even a radio. Of course there are obstacles to overcome – one of them, these Foreign Devils coming here tonight. But as Liu always says, *a thousand grains of sand build a tower.*

'Do they speak Mandarin?' Han Mei asks.

'They speak Mandarin to me and I speak English to them,' Liu says proudly. He leans over the table and makes strange hissing noises. The girls smile and say something about the weather. Their pronunciation is terrible.

Han Mei pictures an official car, waiting at the end of the alleyway, its blue paint and chrome trim gleaming. She sees Liu climbing into it and waving to her before he pulls the curtains closed and sets off for the airport.

The girls open their backpacks, and Han Mei wonders what they have brought for Pangpang from the foreigners' Friendship Store. She's often wheeled her bicycle past the store windows, studying the silk scarves and jade ornaments, but there must be toys in there too. Pangpang would be happy with a bat and ball, although that might be hard to explain to the neighbours. A picture book or some pencils would be better. He can hold a pencil now.

Smiling, the girls take out their own chopsticks.

Pushing down her disappointment Han Mei pulls Pangpang onto her lap, where he squirms and cries until she puts her little finger in his mouth. He settles in her arms and falls asleep.

The dark-haired girl tries to pick up a square of tofu. It falls to the oilcloth and she grabs it with her fingers.

'They have no manners,' says Han Mei.

Liu ignores her.

She leans back against the seat and shuts out the girls' ugly talk. The clock on the shelf says eight thirty; she is on an early shift tomorrow. Weariness pulls at her like the waves on the lake at Bei Hai where they once hired a boat before they were married. It was Liu's idea, but he couldn't row. After going in circles, Han Mei took the oars, and rowed them back to the bank.

Her head is as heavy as an iron bell. She lays Pangpang down on the bench beside her, covering him with her jacket. She folds her arms on the table and puts her head down as she was taught to do at school.

She's aware of a commotion, but she's far away: on the lake at Bei Hai.

She bumps the bank.

A prod on her arm wakes her. Liu's face is in hers. 'What do you think you're doing?'

The two girls jump up, as if they've been burned. The dark-haired one says something that makes no sense.

Han Mei sits up, confused. 'Are they going?'

'Of course not!'

Liu feels Han Mei watching him. The questions he wants to ask Ka-Lin – *how near to the airport is your house; which bus should I catch?* – will have to wait for a Tuesday evening. He's trying to keep the conversation moving. But the girls are so slow to understand. When he gets to England, and Ka-Lin introduces him to her high-up contacts, at least they'll all speak the same language.

A headache is starting at his temples. He looks round for inspiration and spots the studio photo of Pangpang taken at New Year. The little boy in his new padded jacket stares seriously into the camera.

Zhu-Li has noticed too. 'Son good picture!'

'Lucky no daughter!' Liu smiles. 'Please to tell me, how are you spent Chinese New Year?'

She looks puzzled.

'New Year,' he repeats, his neck growing hot.

'Ah! New Year,' says Ka-Lin. 'We go to Xian.' She looks at him and his heart stutters. If only he could talk to her alone.

'Xian very – beautiful,' he says, carefully. 'From Beijing long way.'

His wife looks up. 'Did she say Xian?' She's always wanted to see the old city in the west.

'We no allow travel in countryside,' Liu tells the girls. He wonders how to explain 'restrictions on internal movements', but they nod, as if they understand.

'Sorry,' says Ka-Lin.

'Xian very old city,' he says. 'You see Drum Tower? Wild Goose Pagoda?' He is surprised at the longing he feels for the ancient names: places he has seen only in photographs. He waits for Ka-Lin to translate.

But Zhu-Li says, 'We see very bad thing.' She takes a cloth from her pocket and empties her nose into it.

'Ugh.' Han Mei shudders.

Liu smiles his encouragement at Ka-Lin.

'Something at Xian, we no like,' the girl says, sadly.

Something in her manner makes him anxious. 'Hotel not good to foreign friends?'

She shakes her head.

Han Mei nudges him. 'What's wrong with that one?'

'Will you stop interrupting!'

His wife glowers at him.

'Prisoners,' says Zhu-Li, as if she has just remembered the word.

'What?' Liu tries to keep calm. Foreigners wouldn't be allowed anywhere near prisoners. The girls often use the wrong word, or the wrong tone, which changes the meaning. He has a flash of inspiration. 'Soldiers!' He laughs with relief. 'You see terracotta army!'

'No army,' says Zhu-Li. She reminds Liu of a dog he saw once in the alley, that had a rat by the tail. In fact, her long nose and small eyes make her look more like the rat. 'We see prisoners, in lorry.'

'No, not possible.' Liu smiles. He feels sick.

Ka-Lin says, 'They no have hair.'

Liu pictures shaved heads. 'No, no,' he says, laughing. 'You make mistake.' He leans over the table, finds the tastiest pieces of liver in the soup and drops them onto Ka-Lin's rice. 'This food better than Institute, yes?'

'Why do you keep talking to her?' says Han Mei.

Liu feels heat rise to his face. 'Shut up!' he hisses.

'Much people watch prisoners,' says Zhu-Li.

'Did she say prisoners?' Han Mei reaches to pull the blind down, but it's stuck.

'She's not talking to you.' Liu catches Ka-Lin's eye, willing the girl to stop this nonsense.

Instead she says, 'Prisoners have signs.'

Liu imagines the placards swinging at the men's necks as the lorry carried them towards a crowded stadium. He casts around for something to say. 'But you no good read Mandarin!'

The girls laugh. Dare he hope the subject is closed?

With gestures and odd words, the students explain: the signs at the prisoners' necks described their crimes.

'So small things.' Ka-Lin puts her finger and thumb close together.

'Thief only,' says Zhu-Li, frowning.

Liu hopes she lives far away from Ka-Lin in England. When he gets there he does not want to meet her.

'They go be kill.' Ka-Lin points an imaginary gun at her head.

Han Mei nudges him. 'What the hell is she doing?'

Liu can't look at his wife. The conversation is sliding away from him like water out of a bowl.

Zhu-Li peers at him. 'You think kill is right?'

Liu's head is a muddle of half-remembered English phrases. He knows the students hear the news on the loudspeaker at the Institute every morning: they complain that it wakes them up. He has a vision of Ka-Lin, waking up beside him. He's sure Han Mei knows what he's thinking. He feels sweat under his arms.

'At Xian you see – Bad Elements.' He drops his voice, but the words explode in his mouth.

Han Mei stares. 'What on earth are you saying?'

His wife's anger makes Liu panic. 'Stop asking silly questions!'

Zhu-Li frowns. 'Bad Elements?' Her voice is loud in the small room.

Liu glances at the door. Who's listening?

'Bad Elements!' The girl laughs. She looks at him as if he's an idiot. As if he has spent all his life believing the wrong things. Liu is transported back to the peasants' hut: explaining to the old couple the Great Leader's thoughts.

Han Mei prods him. 'What's so funny?'

'I don't know.'

'So much for you speaking English.' She sounds like his work unit comrades.

Liu wishes his wife had stayed asleep. He wants to put his head down on his arms. He stares at the oilcloth where Han Mei's special chopsticks lie, unused, and at the trail of dropped food in front of the girls; their soft, pale hands.

He sees them watching him, amused and curious – as if he should be in a cage at Beijing Zoo.

Anger rises in Liu's chest. What kind of country would this be if people who broke the law weren't punished? The students can only understand simple words. He says clearly, '*Zhong guo ren tai duo le.*'

The girls repeat: *there are too many Chinese people.*

They've understood. Relieved, Liu smiles. 'So, no matter if some die.'

Behind her glasses Ka-Lin's eyes are cold. 'State kill prisoners. State is Bad Element.'

Startled, Han Mei sits upright. 'What did she just say?'

'Nothing,' says Liu.

'You must think I'm a fool.' His wife leans across the table and wags her finger in the girls' faces. 'That's enough from you two.'

Liu pulls her back. 'Shut up, you ignorant woman.'

She shakes him off. 'Are you trying to destroy this family?'

'Now look what you've done.' Liu grabs the back of Ka-Lin's chair, but the girl is on her feet, a shocked look on her face. 'Sit, please. Stay! Please, Ka-Lin.'

'Get them out of here.' Han Mei hisses. 'Stupid Foreign Devils.'

'They don't understand.'

'But I do.' Han Mei takes Ka-Lin's coat and shoves it at the girl. 'Get lost!'

Ka-Lin heads for the door. 'Thank you! Goodbye!' Zhu-Li joins in. '*Zaijian, zaijian.*'

'Tell the silly bitches to be quiet.' Pangpang wakes up and wails. Han Mei pulls him to her. 'You're a liability, Liu Qiang! I wish I'd never married you.'

Fixing a smile on his face, Liu ushers the students out. 'And I the same, you miserable old hag!'

The door slams behind him. There's the sound of sliding metal as Han Mei slips the bolt across. Then her voice hisses through the gap: 'Don't bother coming back.'

Liu pulls his jacket collar up and his cap down. The girls follow him through the courtyard. Silently they wheel their bicycles into the lane.

He cycles in front. When the main road is in sight he turns back. Perhaps they say goodbye. Liu doesn't hear. Their silhouettes are soon swallowed by the dark.

The air is cool on his face. The rhythm of the pedals soothes him. Han Mei will have calmed down by tomorrow.

He remembers the sharp edge of frozen earth in the cabbage fields at dawn and how his torn fingertips refused to bleed. '*Hallo. I am very pleased to make your acquaintance,*' he whispers.

Off the Shelf

I'm on the graveyard shift at NicePrice and I can't stop scratching. It started as soon as I sat at the till. I'm sure it's the heat. It's the longest, hottest day of the year and the air-con's broken. Even the perky Special Offer signs look limp. *Last Chance To Buy*! More desperate than inviting.

If only my customer would hurry up. 'No plastic bags for me,' she says cheerily, pushing her glasses up her nose and tucking grey hair behind her ear. Four apples wobble onto the scanner and go rolling down the belt before I can stop them.

With my good hand, I retrieve them one by one and shove them on the scales. I resist the urge to hurl them into her recycled bag. At last I slap her receipt on the counter, and go back to rubbing my shoulders against the swivel chair. She raises an eyebrow at me. I must look like a dog with fleas.

When she's gone, I turn round to Sheila. 'Scratch my back for me?'

'Sure.' She smiles, her brown eyes searching my face. 'You all right, Cath?'

'Just heat rash.' I push my chair nearer to her.

'Scratching will only make it worse, you know.'

'Don't care. Come on.'

Her nails rake my shirt, and for a few delicious seconds the burning itch stops. Her fingertips press my skin. 'It doesn't feel like heat rash. Maybe it's chickenpox.'

That's been going round. We're in the front line here for being sneezed and coughed on. Management said if we were worried about germs, we should buy hand gel. It's in Toiletries, next to the hand soap. When I looked it had run out. I imagine red spots multiplying under my uniform. Chickenpox was about the only thing I never caught as a kid, which just confirmed my status as the playground freak.

I glance at Sheila. 'Cover for me a minute?'

'No problem.'

The Tannoy whines, *Good evening and welcome to your twenty-four-hour convenience store.* I limp to the disabled loo and lock the door. I fumble with my shirt and twist towards the low-level mirror. My pale skin is covered with the sweaty weals of heat rash but on my right shoulder blade there's a line of raised, angry-looking spots. I touch the nearest one gingerly. I can't remember what chickenpox looks like, but this is more like a wart: soft but scaly, like a prong on my hairbrush. I button my shirt up. It feels tight over my tender skin. What trick is my unreliable body playing now? I catch sight of my narrow face in the mirror. My frown lines are deeper than ever and sweat has made my light brown bob stick to my head. The bags under my eyes are bigger than the ones we're meant to charge for at the till.

Just my luck George is duty manager tonight. I find him in Frozen Food. When he sees me approaching, he bends into the cabinet, as if pizza is suddenly fascinating.

'George?' He pretends not to hear me, so I have to tap him on the shoulder.

He stands up, feigning surprise, smoothing his quiff – strangely dark for a man in his forties – and checking his flies at the same time. 'Cath! This is an unexpected pleasure! What can I do for you?'

'Can I have a word?'

'Of course, of course.' He tries to pin me against the freezer but I duck away and make for his office.

He gets there first. 'Come into my hidey-hole.' He moves the electric fan off the desk and perches on the end, his thighs bulging in his blue trousers. 'You've had second thoughts about turning me down?'

George's perennial offer to take me off the shelf: damaged goods that I am. At thirty-seven I should be glad of any interest, as my mother says. I stand by the door. 'I need to go home, George. I'm not feeling great.' My glance catches the NicePrice pens spiking out of his desk tidy.

'Sorry to hear that, Cath. Is it to do with…' he waves vaguely at me, a gesture no doubt intended to take in my withered arm and wonky hip: an accident of childbirth, apparently. Nobody's fault.

I say nothing.

'Of course, as you're part of our – er – *quota*, let's hope no one comes checking on us tonight, eh?' He chuckles.

My good hand aches to punch him. 'I'm going home, George. Okay?' I slam the door behind me.

On the way home I stop at the petrol station and buy a bottle of cheap wine. At the late-night chemist, I spend fifty quid on two tubes of stuff to nuke warts and verrucas, and calamine lotion – just in case.

I draw the curtains and switch the light on. I pour a large glass of wine, clear my cereal bowl and coffee mug off the dressing table and lay out the potions. I peel off my shirt and bra, and angle the mirrors so I can see my back. The red marks are still there. The line of warts has grown; there are bumps visible, under the skin, at the top of my left shoulder. I feel sick. I pull the top off the first tube and apply the tip of the nozzle to the nearest spot.

My hand's shaking so much it takes a few goes to hit the target. I wait for the pain: nothing happens. But the wart at the top of my right shoulder blade splits, and a shoot pokes out. As I watch, another wart explodes; then another. I retch, drop the plastic tube and tumble forwards, crying, my bad arm crumpled under me. Face squashed against the old pink carpet, I keep my eyes closed, tears squeezing out, while the skin on my back ripples and pops.

At last my back stops twitching. I sit up slowly. My blotchy face, splodged with mascara, floats in the mirror. I adjust the glass and study my shoulders. The bumps on my left shoulder blade have erupted into a line of brown warts. On my right shoulder blade, each wart has produced a tiny, pale feather.

I pick up my wine glass and tip the contents down my throat. I reach behind me and tug the longest feather, but it's stuck fast, the stalk smooth and hard, like a fingernail. If I pluck it, will another one grow? Or two? The warts look as if only cosmetic surgery would get rid of them. Can you get that on the NHS?

I've watched plenty of films where women grow wings and claws and turn into vampires. I bare my teeth: do the front ones look sharper? My hands are dry and rough, as usual, but no claws yet. The nails are still mine: short and square, in need of a manicure. Suddenly my future is clear: to live out my days as a lonely freak, leaving the house only at night, trailing tattered feathers behind me.

I wake in the stuffy air, the rustle at my back like an electric shock, prodding me to the window. I pull back the curtains. It's still dark. The balcony is a narrow oblong with a rail and a plastic chair: I've never been out there. I slide the glass open and step out. The concrete is cold under my feet.

I shake my shoulders and hear the dry whisper of feathers. I twist, and glimpse glossy layers of honey and gold, each shading silkily to the next, like the hair on shampoo ads. I feel a forgotten muscle uncoil; weight pushing on my spine. My wings open, filling the small space. Tingling spreads through my limbs, as if my veins are on fire. My feet twitch. I have to move. I drag over the chair and climb on to it, teetering above the balcony rail. What am I doing? This isn't me. When we went to Alton Towers for Sheila's hen night I ended up holding the coats. But this feels different.

The air is solid around me and slowly the pressure increases. My feet pulse with the need to push. I hold my breath. There's a tug, as if someone has fixed a cable to my shoulders and is winding it in, straightening my spine, hauling me up and off the chair. I put my right foot on the rail. I don't look down. I imagine interlocking feathers, clinging to each other and to me. My chest tightens and blood pounds in my head and ears. I close my eyes and lean forward. The muscle in my back tenses: then I hear slow, heavy flapping. The movement speeds up; and my wings lift me, carry me upwards into the night air, cool against my burning face.

I don't dare open my eyes. I let out the breath I've been holding in one huge yell. Relief at being airborne and alive makes me flap my good arm wildly and flail my legs until I nearly turn myself upside down. I gulp at the air, gasping and spluttering, trying not to swallow flies and midges. Moths fly into me, their dusty wings brushing my goosepimply skin.

Despite myself, I'm climbing higher. It's so empty up here. I fling my arm out but that upsets my balance; it's better to hold my bad arm across my breasts, and focus on the rhythm of my wings. When I dare to look down, my stomach shivers at the toy roads and shrunken houses. I fly over the reservoir, a glinting, misshapen coin in the moonlight.

I can change direction by tilting my shoulder or moving my head. I follow the main road, the lamps orange beads on a string. My legs hurt from holding them still. Ahead is an ideal landing place – an old oak. I circle it, but I can't see a way in. I go round again, my back aching. In desperation I plunge feet-first into the top, startling a family of rooks that scatters, cawing and complaining. I crash through the greenery, clutching at twigs, leaves slapping my face. A branch stops my fall. I catch my breath and rub my scratched arms.

When I pluck up the courage to set off again, it's surprisingly easy. I'm getting the hang of it. I drift over the town, grey and quiet. Along my street and past my flat, the light still showing at the window, the solitary chair propped against the balcony rail. Evidence of a different life. I head for the industrial estate. In the distance, the lights of NicePrice burn dully. I cruise over the car park, cars dotted in spaces like the last chocolates in the box. Delivery lorries are lined up at the side entrance. I make sure the front is clear, and in one smooth movement I flap through the doors and into the fluorescent lighting. The glare makes my eyes water. I fly up to the ceiling and sit on a metal roof strut, dangling my legs. I'm glad I kept my trousers on.

Sheila's at a far till, reading a magazine. My heart squeezes. I set off, keeping as close to the roof as I can, weaving in and out of Special Offer signs. I land above her.

'Pssst!' I hiss but she doesn't look up. 'Sheila!'

When she finally sees me, she shrieks and drops her magazine. 'Cath? Is that you?'

I wave from my perch. 'Look!' I shimmy and shake my feathers.

Her face crumples in amazement. 'You've got wings? How? What's it like?'

'It's a bit complicated,' I call. 'But they're fantastic!' I stretch my wings up and back, feeling the power of my muscles. 'Ow!' A stab of pain. I smell burning. I'm too near a spotlight.

Panicked, I swoop, ending up in Sweets and Biscuits. My feather tips brush Pic'n'Mix and for an instant I regret that I can't grab any. I swerve to avoid an old lady and lose my balance. My wings scrape the shelves and packets skitter and burst across the aisle.

I struggle back up to the ceiling and bat about, gasping. The old woman is calling feebly; a cleaner has spotted me and is shouting, waving his mop. I crouch on a ledge, my wings twitching. As the news spreads through the store, staff and shoppers come running, squashing into the aisle below, pushing and shoving to get a better view. A teenager points her mobile at me, taking my picture; a bald man in a grey suit is on his phone. I cross my arms over my chest.

George is heading my way, smoothing his hair furiously. With him is a tall ginger-haired guy from Security, holding a large fishing net from the summer range. They elbow their way through the spectators and Ginger waves the net around under my feet.

'It's all right!' I shout, but no one's listening. A siren screeches in the distance.

'Catherine!' George calls through cupped hands. 'Is this some sort of stunt? You're not helping the NicePrice image! This will be a disciplinary matter!'

Sheila's behind him, laughing. I catch her eye and cock my head towards the emergency exit. She gives me the thumbs up and pushes on the metal bar, opening both doors wide.

I wave at George. He's staring at my breasts. 'I'm off the shelf, George!' I yell.

I plunge off the ledge and everyone screams. I dive past him, and the tip of my right wing catches his quiff and sends it frisbeeing down the aisle. I always knew it was a toupée. I head for the doors, holding my breath, my feathers skimming the cool metal.

I'm out and away, gliding up above the car park and the grey street, into the summer dawn.

Acknowledgements

A big thank you to my family and friends for their encouragement, and interest in my writing.

I'd also like to thank writing colleagues for their generosity with constructive feedback and guidance.

For unfailing advice and support, my heartfelt thanks to my dear friend and fellow author Jo Pepper.

If you have enjoyed this book, please leave a review on Amazon or on my website: http://sarahhegarty.wordpress.com
I would love to hear from you!

About the

Paul Hardcastle has been immersed in music for over four decades. The track '19' springboarded him into fame overnight as it became No.1 in thirteen countries with multi-platinum sales. Hardcastle became Simon Fuller's first-ever artist, which gave birth to 19 Management. The rest is history.

Hardcastle went on to produce for the likes of Phil Lynott, won the Ivor Novello Award in 1986 for Best Selling International Hit of the Year, designed the Top of the Pops theme tune, 'The Wizard', and won the ASCAP Award for best score with the film *Spiceworld*. His list of television scores is also extensive. Moving into new adult contemporary music, Hardcastle has generated over thirty

No.1's, in addition to receiving major plaudits such as Smooth Jazz Artist of the Year on Billboard, Best Smooth Jazz Artist of All Time and UK Smooth Jazz Artist of the Year.

Hardcastle collaborated with **Paul Zanon** on his book. Zanon has had many books published, with the majority reaching number-one bestseller in their categories on Amazon.

The Hard Way

Paul Hardcastle with Paul Zanon

The Hard Way

Pegasus

A CIP catalogue record for this title is available from the British Library

ISBN-978-1-80468-078-0

*Pegasus is an imprint of
Pegasus Elliot MacKenzie Publishers Ltd.*
www.pegasuspublishers.com

First Published in 2024

**Pegasus
Sheraton House Castle Park
Cambridge CB3 0AX England**

Printed & Bound in Great Britain

Acknowledgements

A big thanks to everyone who took the time to share some stories about my life, including Rory Bremner, Kim Chappell, Les Cutmore, Eric Doel (Joint), Simon Fuller, Tony Gale, Paul Hardcastle Jr, Ritchie Hardcastle, Allen Kepler, Jeff Lunt, Pete Quinton, Gary Stewart (Stewpot...now Sensei), Helen Rogers, Susan Hardcastle and Mick Ward (Wardy).

A special thanks to my fantastic children Maxine, Paul Hardcastle Jr and Ritchie; my beautiful grandchildren Paul Jr, Jr and Penelope and my good friend Francesca Adriana Spiteri, who was the driving force behind me taking the leap of faith and getting my life story penned.

Finally, a few words about my ghostwriter. I was asked by my old schoolmate and football ace Tony Gale if I would say a few words about our time growing up for his autobiography and of course, I said, 'Yes.'

Galey replied, 'I'll get the writer to give you a call. His name is Paul Zanon.'

Paul gave me a call on the phone, we had a chat and I could sense he was a nice guy. He asked if I had ever considered doing a book myself and I mentioned I'd been asked before but I never went ahead with anything because I didn't ever think I would have enough to say.

He said, 'Once I've finished Tony's book, I will give you a call and maybe we can have a chat.' A few months down the line, we had a call and I invited him over to my house.

We got on very well and by the time he had left, I had changed my mind and said, 'Yes. Let's do this.' We got to work in January 2023 and from the first day, I really enjoyed thinking back on all the old memories and my journey to date. Paul is great at getting you to dig just that bit deeper and I can honestly say he made it fun to do. I was lucky to have someone who I got on with so well and it was almost like a Simon Fuller moment, where we instantly became friends. Thank you, Paul, for the mega hard work you put into this book.

Paul H.

I'd like to dedicate this book to all my fans.
You are the ones who have given me such a great life.

October 2022

I was writing Tony Gale's book, compiling a list of people to interview who might have some good anecdotes to add colour to Tony's life. Galey started with family, then the kids he grew up with on his estate in Pimlico. As he mentioned a few names, he said, 'Give Paul Hardcastle a call. We used to play football together as kids.'

I replied jokingly, 'Spelt like the guy who did Na-na-na-na-nineteen!'

Tony calmly replied, 'Yep. That's him, mate.'

A few weeks later, I caught up with Paul, who kindly shared a few stories from back in the day and towards the end of the call, we spoke about the possibility of him having his life story penned. Writing a book isn't just a case of meeting someone and agreeing to write their life story; it's like a marriage. You spend several months talking with the client, getting to know their life inside and out, so it's essential you get on.

A few months later, I had taken Tony's book over the line and Paul and I met. Well – let's just say we clicked immediately. He's the most unassuming person, generous, down to earth and his anecdotes have been a pleasure to scribe. If you thought you knew Paul Hardcastle because of '19', you'll be knocked back by the depth of the man's life either side of that one track. Enjoy the nostalgic ride as it takes you through drainpipe trousers, to flares, 80s shoulder pads and way beyond. I assure you, at some point of reading this book, you will nod your head in recognition of going down memory lane and say to yourself, 'I remember that!'

Paul Zanon

Foreword

The Unexpected

It was around the start of 1985 that I first came across the name Hardcastle. I was working for Chrysalis Music, publishing at the time, and had just signed the writers of Madonna's 'Like a Virgin'. The track was sitting at No.1 on the 12" sales chart for a little while, then I noticed it had been replaced by a record called 'Rainforest' and by someone who I didn't really know much about. His name was Paul Hardcastle.

What was quite unbelievable was that 'Rainforest' was an instrumental, but seemed to capture a lot of different audiences by way of Club, RnB, Hip Hop, etc. I wanted to know more about this guy and decided to track him down. After getting hold of his contact details, I gave him a call, explained who I was and asked him if he fancied a chat about maybe doing something for Chrysalis.

We met at the Chrysalis building in Stratford Place and straight away, I saw a young guy who I knew wanted to succeed in the music industry. I think my first words were, 'Oh. So, you're the bloke who has taken my No.1 spot!'

He laughed, then said, 'Errrrr, yeah, sorry about that!'

We talked for about an hour and I thought it would be a good idea for him to meet the record label personnel and some of the top A&R people, plus two of the managing directors. I asked him to bring any new material he might be working on and he said he had something which he couldn't describe as it was impossible to do so, which instantly did set my mind off wondering what it was.

About a week later, Paul came back and we were all in the main room at Chrysalis and everyone was expecting a kind of 'Rainforest Part II'. Oh boy – that was so far from what he was about to play us all. As he started to play the demo of this track, the room went silent, as everyone thought, *What the hell is this?* I even thought the same at first, but something told me, *Hey – this is so different, it might just change the dance world,* as it had a mega story. Also, it had this na-na-na nineteen sample, which was most probably the first track to use a sampler in this way.

Well, the meeting ended in a sort of confused state and everyone kind of said unenthusiastically, 'Let's keep in touch.' However, I asked Paul to stay along with the promotions man, Ken Grunbaum. Ken felt that it would either be a monster hit or the biggest flop that year. Then Ken left and it was just Paul and me.

Paul knew as well as I did that they thought I was mad to back a record which talked about people being killed at such a young age and this strong na-na-na nineteen sample, which highlighted that even more! I still remember saying to myself, 'Even if it's not this track, this guy will do something in the music industry.' So, I said to him shortly after Ken left the room, 'What would you say if I became your manager and left my job here?'

He just looked at me a bit strangely and said, 'What does a manager do?'

At the time, I was not a manager and replied, 'Oh. I guess I just take all the shit for you.'

He said, 'OK! Let's do it.'

Two months later, the track was a global success and reached No.1 in thirteen countries. Paul was my first client. We started out together, are still on top of our game and, most importantly, are still the best of friends.

Simon Fuller

December 1957

First large-scale nuclear power plant for peacetime use opens in Pennsylvania, USA.

Sam Cooke reaches No.1 with his single, 'You Send Me'.

CBS broadcast *The Sound of Jazz*, live, featuring a number of contemporary jazz artists, including Count Basie, Thelonious Monk and Billie Holiday.

The Soviet Union launches *Sputnik*.

Alexander R. Todd wins the Nobel Peace Prize in chemistry.

Paul Hardcastle is born on 10 December 1957.

Little Paul

I couldn't have written things like 'Low' and 'Heroes',
those particular albums, if it hadn't have been for Berlin
and the kind of atmosphere I felt there.

David Bowie

I was born at St Mary Abbots Hospital on Marloes Road, Kensington, on 10 December 1957 and grew up at 33 St George's Square in Pimlico. I suppose you're thinking, *He was born with a silver spoon in his mouth*, because that's a multimillion-pound property in a very affluent Central London location. The truth is, one of my strongest childhood memories was living in poverty.

As a family, we never went short of anything and there was always food on the table, but nothing was ever flash. It certainly wasn't steak suppers and we didn't wear brand names or any of the latest gear. My nan was the housekeeper for the place in St George's Square and she somehow managed to get us all in the basement to live rent-free. Not even sure if the owner, Mr Vernon, was aware of that. I didn't know at the time, but a guy called Major Walter Clopton Wingfield used to live there years before my parents were even born and it turns out he was one of the pioneers of lawn tennis. There's now a blue plaque outside the building in recognition of him.

The basement we lived in hadn't been done up in forever. It was a bit dark and grotty, not particularly colourful, but at least there was a little yard out back to get some natural light. The highlights of the inside were a big fireplace where we'd make toast and an old dial telephone with the number VIC1960 (with VIC denoting the region, Victoria). The most vivid memory of the outside of the house was a newspaper seller on the corner who used to call out, *'Evenin' news and Standard.'*

Despite my grandmother being a grey-haired old lady who always wore an apron, she was the gaffer. I have fond memories of her in the basement drinking a glass of Guinness every day with her friends Maureen and Eddie, putting the world to rights and my nan suddenly breaking into a chorus of 'Underneath the Arches' by the Crazy Gang, as everyone would start singing along. Back then, Guinness, like Lucozade, was advertised in chemists for its health benefits, which was always a great cover-up for adults when a child asked what they were doing with a glass of the black stuff. I always used to think, though, *Why does she keep singing this bloody song?* It wasn't until a few decades later that I realised the relevance of it and also how massive the Crazy Gang was.

As far as growing up in Pimlico goes, there was always loads to do in the local area, but Battersea Funfair is where all the action happened. We were always skint, so we used to squeeze through the wire turnstile and bunk in.

Then, when we were inside, we used to do our best to get a few quid so we could go on the rides.

There was that machine where you'd throw a penny in and it would land on loads of other pennies on this shelf and it would move backwards and forwards, making you think the coins at the edge were all about to collapse and come your way. They never did, though! If you bumped it, an alarm would go off, so the trick was to slowly push some of the silver foil paper you'd get in a fag box in there and that would help push everything forward. If you went home with ten pence, you were rich.

The other thing we did was get grubby with the Waltzer. People used to lose money out of their pockets as they were spinning around and it would go through the cracks in the floor. The platform with the spinning cars was about eighteen inches off the ground and me and a mate would crawl underneath and hoover up what everyone had lost. However, it was quite scary under there, as literally a few inches above your head, these cars were spinning about, with the floor bouncing up and down, making you think, *This better not collapse.* It was worth it, though, as we found half crowns, shillings, sixpence pieces, thrupenny bits, albeit, the money didn't travel very far as we'd crawl back out and spend it on whatever we fancied at the funfair, like the Helter Skelter.

I went to Churchill Gardens Primary School in Ranelagh Gardens, which was just a short walk away from where we lived and started playing football when I was about five or six. Then, when I got a little older, I went on to hang around with some guys from Bessborough Gardens Estate down the road. We had our own little pitch and we'd play against Tachbrook Estate, with both teams taking it really seriously. Famed footballer Tony Gale played for Tachbrook, as did the late DJ Steve Walsh, who was a goalie. I was a striker, well, more of a goal poacher, but if the ball came anywhere near me, there was a very good chance I'd score. Tony stood out a mile with his talent and unsurprisingly had a glittering career, but funnily enough, I went on to have a record label with Steve called Total Control. More about that later.

My mum, Joyce, worked in Sainsbury's in Victoria Street and did her shifts while we were at school at Churchill Gardens, which was only a short walk down the road for me and my sister Sue, who's a couple of years younger than me. Mum's work was stable, whereas my dad, Louis, was always out and about getting work in the entertainment field, coming and going, working out different ways to generate money. As a result, apart from memories of being pretty poor, the other childhood memory that stood out for me was not being in one place for very long. From as young as I can remember, my dad taught me a few chords on the guitar and he also taught me how to play the drums. Then, from the age of five or six, I was on the road with him, playing gigs, which consequently meant our family was constantly relocating.

In 1963, we moved to Berlin, where flyers were going up all around the centre saying, *Die Sensation in Berlin: Little Paul and Louie.* I really enjoyed Berlin and the adventure we had there for the next two years. We lived in a flat right across the road from Berlin's largest and most famous department store called KaDaWe, just down the road from The Kaiser Wilhelm Memorial Church, also known as *The Bombed Church*.

One thing I did enjoy in KaDeWe was the sweet shop, but as a six-year-old, I couldn't get enough. So, on one occasion, I hatched a plan to get some extras. I said to my four-year-old sister, Sue, 'There's sweets there. You can go in and get some for us.' She picked them up and walked out, not realising she'd nicked them and the guy inside came running out. I spoke enough German to say something like, 'I'm really sorry. She's very young and didn't realise she had to pay.'

The guy knew and half smiled, then said to her, 'You can't take them.' She still had one in her hand and he saw it and let her have it, which meant the plan kind of backfired because she got a sweet and I didn't!

As far as the music goes, we were performing two to three times per week for about an hour each time, usually at around eight p.m. Most of the performance was me in my little yellow suit alongside my dad, where we used to cover songs from bands like The Beatles and generally anything that was well known at the time, then my dad would tell jokes in between sets. I'd then come back on and do something with him and finally, he'd finish with something like playing 'Danny Boy' on the trumpet or a solo tap dance. My dad was a really good tap dancer. I'm talking very, very good. He used to show me a few of his moves and he'd say something like, 'When we get to this bit of the song, we'll do this routine and then copy me.' We had a bit of practice, but it wasn't like hours of rehearsals; otherwise, that wouldn't have been fun. Same went with the singing.

Despite my dad being born at Rampayne Street in Pimlico, he had quite a cosmopolitan background. His dad was half Cuban, but he had lived in the US and had American citizenship. Then he came back to the UK, met my grandmother and started a family there. Then, when my dad was six months old, they moved to Philadelphia and my dad gained American citizenship over the coming years. After a stint in the US Marines, he was honourably discharged, at which point my dad came back to the UK, met my mum and stayed here. As a result of him being both a UK and US passport holder, this gave us wider marketing traction in Germany.

Venues varied from restaurants to small music halls, where we'd get between a hundred to two hundred people attending each night, but with my dad being an American citizen, this got us into lots of American army bases, where we'd play for the GI's. In fact, I remember doing my first TV show when I was about seven, albeit for a regional channel and I still have the original pen they gave me for appearing on it. It said AFTV on it (Armed Forces TV) and had a little old-school multi-lens film camera engraved on the front of it.

Compared to an average six-year-old who was probably asleep at that time, I was up on stage, which genuinely wasn't a problem for me. We'd get home a couple of hours later, have some food and I'd be in bed about ten p.m. and always had a good sleep. Incredibly, I didn't go to school in Berlin. Can you imagine that these days? Two years without school. For me, though, it felt normal to be doing what I was doing and I guess I was getting a different sort of schooling through life experiences and picking up a new language. I can still count to one hundred in German and still remember the basics, like, *Can you help me?* and *Two beers, please!* Also, as opposed to reading about history, I was remembering it through experiences. For example, when Kennedy was assassinated in November 1963, I remember hearing my mum shouting in the flat in Berlin, 'Oh my God', then she started crying. As for the Berlin Wall, I was actually seeing it instead of being given a book or being told about it in a class. The wall had only been put up a couple of years before and a lot of it was still being transformed from a wall of barbed wire to concrete and electrified fences when we were there. My first memory of seeing it was from the back of a taxi after the driver had made a wrong turn. As he went down the street, there was this massive wall in front of us and he said, *Scheisse. Berliner Mauer,* which translates as, *Oh shit. The Berlin Wall,* which was quickly followed by a U-turn and a different route.

My dad performed with the likes of Danny Kaye, Duke Ellington, Dizzy Gillespie, Flannagan and Allan, Gracie Fields and Max Miller, amongst others. When we were in Berlin, the Count Basie Band was there and it wasn't a case of me hanging out with them, more that I was with my dad and when he was with them, I'd also meet them. I crossed paths with so many musicians during those years, but as a six-year-old, I wasn't taking it all in. However, one person I do remember who said to my dad, 'He's crazily good for his age', was Madelaine Bell, who sang for Blue Mink at the time.

The gigs were all organised through an agency, so it wasn't like busking, but we can't have been paid a lot because we didn't live a lavish life. For my dad, though, it wasn't just about the money; it was doing what he loved to do, which is something I started to understand far more as I got older. Funnily enough, my dad was performing with his dad from about the age of six and was travelling to the likes of Paris, Vegas and Berlin. It looks like I inherited the pattern, but at the time, I never asked him much about anything because I was a little kid having fun and once we finished the gigs, I'd probably play with my new Thunderbirds toy or something like that.

Coincidentally, after a couple of great years in Berlin, we also went to Paris and lived there for about three months by the Champs Elysees in a little bed- and breakfast-type flat. I remember every morning there used to be a funfair in the middle of it and I'd constantly be going in my dad's pockets to get some change and say, 'I'm going across to the funfair.'

And my parents would smile and say, 'Have fun.' As I ran off to go on the rides before even waiting for their approval.

After Paris, we headed to Denmark for a couple of months, where I have fond memories of going to the Tivoli Gardens in Copenhagen, which is one of the oldest amusement parks in the world, dating back to the mid-1800s. The window at the hotel we were staying at opened onto the Gardens, so I used to crawl out and be right in the middle of the rides and all the fun, which was an amazing thing for a little kid.

After Denmark, we hopped around a lot of places in England for about a month each time, like Sheffield, Newcastle and Leicester. The biggest gig we ever did was in a place called Greasbrough, near Rotherham, which is near to Sheffield. There was only one venue there at the time and about one thousand people turned up that night from the region, which, bearing in mind the population of Greasbrough is about two thousand, that was a pretty good turnout. When I came off stage, loads of people wanted to have a chat with me because I guess I was novel being so young.

I might have been popular on the stage, but that wasn't always the case off it. I wouldn't say I was a mischievous kid; let's just say I enjoyed being adventurous and pushing the limits, mostly of other people's patience. On one occasion, when I was about nine, we were at a scrapyard which backed onto the accommodation we were staying at up in Yorkshire. My dad had a Humber Super Snipe car, which they'd stopped producing at that point and we were down the scrapyard as he was looking for a part. While he was talking to the scrap merchant, I got a bit bored, got out of the car and started looking around at things. Then I spotted this vehicle at the top of this mound of scrap cars, which were stacked one on top of the other and I went and sat in it. For some reason, I thought it was a good idea to release the handbrake and the car started rolling forward. Because I was so young, I didn't think about pulling the handbrake back up and instead opened the door and tried to stop by holding on to it, which was silly as I could have got run over. By now, it had gone past the point of no return and me being a skinny little youngster, I couldn't stop it and had to let it go and watch it go down the scrapyard. My family were at the bottom of the hill in the Humber as I looked at this scrap car on a collision course straight for them. The only reason it didn't whack into them was because there was this massive lorry axel on the ground in front of them and the car smashed into that. Although the car was scrap, the body was in good shape and people would come in and buy panels or components from cars, which were cheaper than going down the car dealers. So, when I had this collision, it damaged a few panels and smashed a few lights, so my dad had to pay the guy a few bob to keep him sweet. I got quite a telling off for that one.

We also lived in Cardiff on and off for a couple of years at 85 Corporation Road, Grangetown and this time, I even went to school at Grangetown Primary. We were there in 1966 and I distinctly remember watching the telly when England won the World Cup. Another memory which was a little more savoury was winkle picking. We'd go down the beach and collect them, then we'd get a pin, pull them out and eat them, which I thought was disgusting. That's until I tried a whelk, which was like eating phlegm.

By about ten years old, I became fed up of constantly being on the move and I said to my dad that I didn't want to be on the road any more and just wanted to go out and play with kids my age, doing what ten or eleven-year-olds did. He was really disappointed, but I remember him telling my brother-in-law at a later date that he was happy I made that decision and had my childhood because the music trade is full of strange people. He made the comparison of Michael Jackson, of a kid who missed his childhood and then lost the plot later in life. As a ten-year-old, I didn't understand that part of it, but I could certainly vouch for witnessing the damage the industry could have on individuals a few years down the line.

By now, our base was now more consistently back at 33 St George's Square, Pimlico. Although my dad was still on the road, my parents weren't split up; it was just a case of he would go where the work was, come back and go again.

**

Although I wasn't touring with my dad any more, old habits die hard and I'd be tapping on the desk at Churchill

Gardens School with my hands, which drove the teachers crazy, but my mates loved it. My favourite was drumming to the beat of *Hawaii Five-O*, which had just come out at the time.

My mate Gary Stewart is one of my best friends from Churchill Gardens School, whom I've known since I was eight. There was always a school bully in the class and when he joined the school, I said to him, 'Watch out for him. He'll get you after class.' We'd watch each other's backs, but the irony is that Gary is now a seventh Dan in karate and certainly doesn't need to watch his back anymore, albeit I was the one who soon gained a reputation of having no fear. In Gary's words, *When we were kids on the council estate, if there was a wall you had to jump off or a gap you had to jump over, Paul would be the first one to try and do it and the rest would follow.* Very true, although that crazy streak did get me in a lot of bother down the line.

His dad, Rocky Dzidzornu, was one of the first African percussionists to play with a supergroup when he started to play with the Rolling Stones. He did percussion on tracks like 'Sympathy for the Devil', 'Wild Horses' and all those really good Stones tunes, but he also played with Stevie Wonder, Herbie Hancock, Ginger Baker and Chaka Khan, to name a few. Gary's brother, Reg, also went on to become a great percussionist and still plays with the likes of Level 42.

With both our dads being musicians, we instantly had something in common and me and Gary became really good friends straight away. He even came and saw me perform live at my last gig with my dad at RAF Mildenhall, Suffolk and he was knocked back by the fact that there was a guy on drums and I took over from him and finished the set.

Me and Gary were always having drumming competitions on the desk, using a rolled-up Beano or Dandy as our drumsticks, as the other kids would be cheering us on. It was like the first ever *Pop Idol*. Gary was really good and I genuinely believe he could have become a musician. One day, we were disturbing the class, tapping on the desks to whichever theme tune we'd decided, when suddenly I spotted the door open and realised it was the headmistress, Miss Fox. I thought, *Oh shit.* I stopped, but Gary hadn't seen her and was really going for it. She walked over and stood in front of him and shouted, 'Steeeewaart! What are you doing?'

Me and Gary got into so much trouble for being noisy that when we got to secondary school, they split us up. Gary was supposed to go to the same school as me at Rutherford, but they made him go to a school called Henry Compton in Fulham instead. Around this time, our family was getting ready to move out of the area, which meant me and Gary lost touch for a while, but thankfully, we reconnected a few years later.

As for myself, what did the future hold? Perhaps a glittering academic career?

September 1969

Jackie Stewart wins his first Formula 1 World Driver's Championship.

Scooby Doo debuts on CBS, USA.

The Beatles release the *Abbey Road* album.

Butch Cassidy and the Sundance Kid premieres in Connecticut.

Paul Hardcastle moves to East London.

Hoxton

There was a teacher at our school who thought he was the world's best drummer and he said to Paul a number of times, 'You're a waste of space. You'll never get anywhere in life. You'll never achieve anything.' It's one of those moments in life I look back and think. Ha! Ya bastard. You got that one wrong, didn't ya? Paul never let things go to his head. He's just better behaved now than when he was a kid. Was I surprised he became famous in music? No. Not at all.

Eric Doel

Back then, my money didn't last very long. Whatever I earned, I spent it just as fast. I used to go round the corner to a place called the Golden Goose, which was an arcade right across the road from the Victoria Palace and drop all my coins into whichever machine took my fancy.

Apart from cleaning out the backyard in Pimlico for my nan for half a crown every week, my first job was just by Victoria, where I used to sell chestnuts on the corner, next to the train station. It was a family-run business with about four young kids, two older brothers and the mum and dad, who were in charge of this chestnut firepit. I would take over for a couple of hours for two bob, putting these chestnuts on the fire for sixpence a bag, but I also used to eat quite a few of them. Round the corner was a café and I remember hearing this track by Matthews Southern Comfort called 'Woodstock' and the guitar riff caught my attention. I thought, *Cor blimey. I like that music.* Every time I'd go in there with my mates, I'd pop a shilling in the jukebox and play that song. After a while, I'd spent so much it occurred to me that I could have bought the single. Around this time, ma and my sister, Sue were sharing a little portable red record player we'd been given for Christmas and the first single I bought to play on it was, unsurprisingly, 'Woodstock'. Sue, on the other hand, asked me to buy her 'Paranoid', by Black Sabbath, which was quite a hard-hitting track for a nine-year-old. The B side to 'Paranoid' was a track called, 'The Wizard', which influenced me naming a track seventeen years down the line.

One of my last memories of Pimlico was watching Neil Armstrong land on the moon in July 1969. One of the tenants at St George's Sq in Pimlico had a cine projector and when my dad found out he had the footage that he'd recorded from the television, he took me up with him to watch it.

Autumn 1969, I was eleven and my nan was coming to the end of her tenure as housekeeper at the St George's Square house. We moved to No.13 Kempton House in this old block of council flats on an estate in Hoxton, which was three floors high and situated just off the roundabout by Hoxton Street and Pitfield Street. That was the only place that was feasible for us at the time and it was a bit of a culture shock going from a very rich and affluent area to Hoxton, which was famous for The Krays and Lenny McLean. Funnily enough, I met Lenny when I was about seventeen. I was out with my mate Gary Hoy, who knew him and we went to a pub called The Swan in Whitechapel where Lenny was working on the door and I was knocked back by how massive he was. Gary said, 'All right, Lenny!'

Len replied, 'All right, boy. This guy with you?'

He said, 'Yeah. This is my mate, Paul.'

Len looked me up and down and then said in that growly voice. 'All right, son.'

Although Hoxton was a pretty tough place, I really liked it and there were some real characters on the estate, like the boxer Sylvester Mittee, who lived in the next block of flats. The funny thing is, it's all turned around now. Pimlico has gone down a bit and there's a lot of trouble on the streets there, whereas Hoxton has become a very trendy, gentrified area.

The man landing on the moon might have been one of my last memories of Pimlico, but for my sister Sue, one of her lasting memories of Pimlico was me getting her to take part in one of my pranks, which nearly fatally backfired on me. What happened was, we were crossing the road and I told her to run but gave her a little shove. A car suddenly appeared out of nowhere and everyone, including myself, thought she'd been hit by the car as she fell to the floor.

There was a big fuss outside our house and an ambulance was called as loads of people crowded around, but thankfully, she only had a few cuts and grazes. I felt so guilty about that and still do. What nobody realised at the time was that she actually she tripped over the kerb, fell over and never even made contact with the car. Either way, that gave everyone a proper fright.

Then, when we got to Hoxton, I got Sue involved in something else, but thankfully, this time, it wasn't as painful. I was always looking for ideas to make money but was constantly changing jobs. Shortly after getting to Hoxton, I took on a paper round, but not long after, I decided I'd had enough and asked Sue to pick up the round for me, which wasn't a great idea for a young girl on her own, early in the dark of the morning. She did it a couple of times and then jacked it in.

It didn't take me long to make new friends in the local area and at school, there was a few new boys who joined our year. One was Eric Doel, who I'm still friends with to this very day. We were in the same class, had very similar interests in music, both supported Chelsea FC and the friendship basically grew from there.

Eric's parents lived in a few places during our time at Rutherford School. One was Harley Street and the other was Park Square West, which was the address of Sir Richard Baylis, who was the Queen's personal physician at the time. Very posh. Although we both lived at mega addresses with important heritage, we also had similar circumstances in so much, as my nan was a housekeeper at our place and his mum was a receptionist in Harley Street and a housekeeper at Park Square West.

I visited both of Eric's addresses and his mum would always take the piss out of me because she said I looked a bit on the scruffy side and apparently, I never used to wash the back of my neck. In my defence, I couldn't actually see the back of my neck and at that age, we'd always be wrestling, pretend fighting or playing football. So yeah, we got dirty. I used to do a great impression of Eric's mum, who had a thick West Country accent. When she'd had enough of us, that was it; we were out. There was no gently, gently about it. She'd say, 'Eric. Your mates are going home.' And minutes later, we'd be out the door and heading back.

We used to hang around a lot together and if I wasn't at his place, he'd be over my way. The very first time he came up to the flat, mum cooked us eggs and chips for tea and I passed Eric this bottle, which he thought was tomato ketchup. He splashed it about like anything and then as he tucked into the food, it took his head off while I sat there pissing myself laughing. That was Eric's introduction to Tabasco sauce.

By the age of thirteen, we were both working in Marylebone Street at wine merchants, which was the posh name for off licences. I worked on one side of the high street for Gough Brothers and Eric worked on the other side for Peter Dominic. We used to do deliveries on these old heavy metal trade bikes with the baskets at the front and at the weekends, they'd let us borrow them. Of course, we never drove them sensibly and we'd take turns to sit in the basket and then drive them down the road, narrowly missing some really expensive cars.

The other perk of the wine shops was Thursday nights. We used to put all the crap and empty boxes out for the rubbish collection early the next morning, but we'd also put a few extra bits into the boxes. Eric used to put in a bottle of gin and I would have chucked in something like a few mint Aero bars, which had just come out at the time. Then, later that night, we'd go through the boxes and take our bits home. At the time, my wages were pennies and my manager kind of knew I was taking a few bars home and didn't mind.

Although I stepped away from performing with my dad, he was still very much doing his music, but he also had jobs to supplement his income. One of the things he did was a clothing distribution and delivery job in a transit van, which he used to bring home after he'd done the drop-offs. I was about fourteen and at the bottom of the flats, there was a lot of space, so I used to take the keys and get in the transit and drive around the flats. Then, one day, a police car pulled in and dragged me out and they said, 'You're too young to be driving this.'

I replied, 'It's private property.' I then shouted up to the flat, 'DAAAAAAAD.' My dad came down and always had my back.

He said, 'OK, he's driving it and maybe he shouldn't be, but as he said, it's private property.'

The police gave me the keys back and said, 'It may be private property, but don't get in the habit because if you do have an accident, you'll be in big trouble.' Then they left. Of course, if I would have hit someone, I would have been up shit street, but at fourteen you don't think about things like that or insurance. Silly, really. Although that was the last time I drove that transit, it didn't stop me from driving underage or without a license, which, again, wasn't sensible.

Something else I used to do back then, which also didn't get local approval, was playing Hawkwind full blast through my speakers, which were placed out on the window ledge, just above where I'd sprayed my initials, PH, onto the brickwork. My mum said she could hear the music a quarter of a mile away from the pub and would come home shouting, 'Paul. Turn that down! You're embarrassing me.' The track I used to play was 'Sonic Attack' and the lyrics were very controversial at the time, talking about the need for bodies to come to orgasm simultaneously in the event of a sonic attack.

As you can imagine, it didn't go down well with the locals, but I just thought they were all being difficult and didn't appreciate good music.

A lifelong passion of mine has been buying old cars and bikes and then doing them up. I used to love buying second-hand bike frames and making a functioning bike from them, but I became fascinated with motorcycles from about fourteen. I swapped my push bike for a Honda C50 and even though I wasn't old enough to drive it, I still used to thrash it around the flats. I absolutely loved that bike and even when it had a flat tyre, I'd still ride it because, at that age, that's all I thought about, even if it did get me in a bit of trouble.

The top speed on that Honda C50 was slightly faster than a snail and it looked a proper old man's bike with these moulded plastic leg shields at the front. In London, it was best known as the Cabbie's bike, which they'd do The Knowledge on. I used to charge the kids in my area 50p to have a ride on the Honda for a couple of hundred yards and they loved it. My mate Eric was quite keen on this bike and said, 'Why don't we take it out somewhere?'

I said, 'Why not.' We went to this common in Dalston and ended up getting chased by the Old Bill. We were flat out on this thing, doing about 20mph and we came to this place where we could just about fit under this really low bridge. We slowly went under, lost the Old Bill, then we called my old man on a payphone and he came and picked us up in his van and chucked me, Eric and the bike in the back. Close call.

As far as school goes, a lot was happening back then, but mainly outside of the school gates. We had another good mate called Tom Malone, who lived in Ladbroke Grove and we used to bunk off school, then head to Tom's house to play records and stuff like that. There was a guy next door to him called Jan Radwan Kujolewski and Jan introduced me to a German rock band called Amon Düül II, which I'd never heard of before at that point. At the time, we were mainly listening to tracks like

'Frankenstein' by Edgar Winter band and Black Sabbath, but we'd also go down the record shop on the Edgware Road and that's the first time I heard 'Meddle' by Pink Floyd and also a track called 'Run Run Run', by Jo Jo Gunne.

With the three of us living in different parts of London, we'd sometimes get tired of walking around and we'd hail a cab down, even though we were broke. I'm ashamed to admit it, but on occasions, we'd ask the cabbie to stop on the way somewhere and then do a runner. Poor old Tom wasn't as quick as us and a couple of times got caught and received a slap. We also did the same with buses because they were open at the back, which meant you could jump on and off as long as the ticket collector was far enough away from you.

The only time we did enjoy going to school was when we knew we'd be straight out soon after. In May 1972, I was only fourteen and the famous school strikes were in action, which were all about getting rid of a load of things, including corporal punishment and school uniforms. However, all we really cared about at that age was having a laugh and just joining in. At Rutherford, there was a guy called Steve Finch who was the student union rep and he organised these strikes, which became quite famous in London and we had the TV and press at our school for weeks. Finchy would shout, 'Enough of this crap.' And we'd all pile out of school.

There were a couple of occasions we did these marches up to Westminster and on the way up, we stopped off at other schools and gathered up more kids. We went past Sarah Siddon's school further down the road from us in Paddington, then Quintin Kynaston up near the vale and everyone kept joining in. The strikes went on for about four or five days and we loved them. For us, it was just an excuse to bunk off and walk miles through London with loads of other kids, laughing and having fun while TV reporters asked you questions.

Our French teacher was a right old battle-axe who had a face like a sack full of spanners and when she saw us in the likes of the Evening Standard jumping over school fences and stuff like that, she'd pull out the papers and shout, 'What is this?' And really lay into us for our behaviour. We'd start laughing because there was nothing, she could do because pretty much the whole school was out.

My other big passion outside of school at the time was live music and in early 1973, everyone was talking about going to see Status Quo at The Rainbow in Finsbury Park, which was *the* music venue to go at the time. About six of us decided we would get tickets to watch Quo on 6 April 1973 and even though I'd never heard of them before, that night they were playing alongside a really good band called Byzantium, who were one of the first bands to use an electric violin.

The rest of the guys turned up on time and went inside, apart from Eric, who waited for me because I was running late. Eric hung around, waited ages for me, then thought I wasn't going to turn up and decided to sell his ticket. Then

42

about ten minutes later I showed up and he said, 'Oh shit.' Eric then came up with a plan. He roughed up all his clothes, went round the stage door at the back and knocked on the door. This bouncer comes out and Eric said all desperate, 'Sorry, mate. I've been rolled over and had my ticket nicked off me. I don't know what to do.'

This geezer said, 'Go and get yourself a cup of tea, settle down and come back in an hour.' Eric went back in an hour and the guy let him in for free!

It was the first rock concert I'd ever been to and I remember looking at the other people doing the head-banging thing with the long hair, thinking, *What the fuck are they doing?* What a gig, though. When we came out of there, we were deaf for about twelve hours.

***

Everyone had motorbikes when I was living in Hoxton and being a year younger than them in terms of being able to legally drive, I became very impatient and frustrated as all my mates were going off somewhere and I couldn't. So, when I was fifteen, I acted like an idiot and lied about my age and said I was born in 1956 and sent my licence off a year before I was allowed to drive a moped. Unfortunately, I got sussed out because I stupidly let someone have a go on the bike who didn't have a licence and who couldn't drive it properly. He got done by the police; then, when they found out the owner (myself) was underage, I also got done. So, before I'd even had my licence, I had all these charges against my name, including making a false declaration for obtaining insurance and a driving licence, which had me in court answering all sorts of questions. Then there was driving underage, without licence and aiding and abetting an unlicensed driver to drive a motorbike. I didn't think about any of that and just thought I was being clever; however, after standing up in court and paying a load of fines, I didn't think I was so clever then.

As opposed to motorbikes, school, unfortunately, wasn't for me. Rutherford wasn't the best of schools and was rough as fuck, but it still had the likes of actors Phil Daniels and Gary Crowley as students, whereas I was crap and finished school about nine months before I should have and didn't come away with a single qualification. Here's what happened. I had a gold Yamaha FS1E, which everyone called a Fizzie and it was one of the first mopeds that was made to look like a motorbike. Apart from the looks, everybody wanted one because you could give someone a proper back-seater because it had the long seat as opposed to most mopeds, which had a small seat and it did about 45mph as opposed to mopeds, which did about 30mph flat out. I'd drive it from Hoxton to Edgware Road to where the school was and I'd give my mates back-seaters around the place and do wheelies at dinner time. The headmaster got to know about it and said, 'If you bring that bike back again, don't bother coming to school again.' Well, that gave me the reason I was looking for to leave school and I didn't go back.

When I got home, I told my mum and she was fine with what I'd done, although I didn't really give her the whole picture. She said, 'Oh, OK.' A couple of seconds later, she then said, 'I thought you had to be sixteen before you left school?'

I said, 'The school said I don't have to go back if I don't want to.' I just selectively missed out on the bit where they said, 'If you bring the motorcycle with you, don't come back.'

There was never really anything at school for me. I could write, I could read, I could add up and do all the things that were beneficial to me in life and I had a bit of an interest in history and geography, but I was only really interested in games, so I could play football. I got on the school team and was a pretty good striker, but that's about as far as my school accolades go. I left Rutherford School and went straight out and got a job as a dispatch rider in Moorgate for £11 per week for a printing company and they paid my petrol, which was about 40p a gallon. I was as happy as a sandboy.

At the time, unemployment was starting to go through the roof; however, as a dispatch rider, it didn't really seem to affect me because I loved motorcycles and took on jobs that other people didn't want to do, like six p.m., on a Friday evening across town with a package and I didn't care if I got soaked. I was one of the top earners in the company and I'd be delivering everything from documents for solicitors to someone giving the nod to a proof in the printing trade. I'd have to wait until they gave an answer, whereas nowadays, they'd just e-mail the client straight away and wouldn't need dispatch riders. Through the nature of the work, I'd also drop stuff off to the odd celebrity. I was once asked to drop off a package to a flash studio boat in Putney addressed to a certain Pete Townsend. When I handed over the parcel, I joked, 'Is this for *the* Pete Townsend.

The guy said, 'Yeah, yeah.'

Although I didn't meet Pete, I couldn't wait to tell my mates.

By the age of sixteen, I'd joined a few motorbike clubs and after work, they'd come around on their bikes to call for me. The flat had sash windows and because we were only a couple of floors up, they'd shout to me and I'd pull up the window and shout back, 'I'm coming down.' I'd then go out and there would be about fifteen of them revving away in the yard at the bottom of the block of flats, where I'd join them and we'd head off to somewhere like the 59 Club in Hackney, which was a club where bikers hung out.

Eager to drive a more powerful motorcycle, I bought a Kawasaki triple 250 when I was sixteen, but I wasn't allowed to drive it until I was seventeen. Having already been in trouble with the police for underage driving, I resisted the temptation and waited up until midnight on the day of my seventeenth, just so I could legally get on the road and ride for an hour. Even though it was freezing and it had been snowing, I didn't give a shit. That's how obsessed I was with motorbikes. One of the first people I took for a ride on it was Eric. I turned up at his house in Harley Street late one evening and said, 'Jump on. I'll take you for a spin.' I put him on the back and we sped through the streets of London. When I dropped him back, he said, 'Thanks for that. I really enjoyed it.' However, years later he admitted, 'I was crapping myself!'

***

Being the adult I was now, I started to make adult decisions, such as getting tattoos and earrings, albeit not with the most hygienic of practices. Shortly after leaving school at the age of sixteen, I was around a friend's house in Haggerston, East London. He says, 'Why don't you get a tattoo?'

I said, 'Because I don't really want one.'

He didn't give up and said, 'I can do it for you. It will save you the hassle of going down to a shop and having it done, plus it will look cool. You sure you don't want one?'

I said, 'Errr, yeah, OK.'

We looked through this book and there was a design with a skull and crossbones, with the crossbones being pistons. Being a motorbike rider that caught my attention. He then drew the design on a bit of paper, wet it, put it on my skin to get the transfer and then started to dig my arm out with a sowing needle and some Indian ink. No buzzing machinery or any of that game; it was like a sowing machine going tap, tap, tap on my skin with this needle.

It took about two hours to finish and to my horror, my arm came up like a balloon. In the meantime, my mate was well happy with it and wrapped it in clingfilm with a big smile on his face. Me and scabs don't get on and where there was supposed to be fire behind the tattoo image, I picked off that part and the fire never happened. Fair play to my mate, though, because it did take shape after a while, albeit it now looks like an image of the Pyrenees mountains.

My earring was done a few months later by an old girlfriend, Leslie Agonbar, who's sadly no longer with us. I was about seventeen and again round Haggerston and she asked me, 'Why don't you get an earring?'

Like with the tattoo, I replied, 'I don't want a bloody earing!'

She said, 'I think it would be really cool.' She somehow convinced me and her anaesthetic was her holding two-pence pieces with my earlobe in between and squeezing them as tightly as she could, trying to make the ear go numb. Then she shoved a thick needle through it, put the earring through and said, 'There you go. It's done.'

I said, 'That fucking hurt! And it's bleeding!'

She laughed and said, 'Don't worry about that! It will stop.' As it was dripping all over my jeans. However, tattoos and earrings were the least of my worries moving into my late teens, as my passion for motorbikes started to intensify.

My first love was a girl called Julie Ann Dean. You'll see a photo booth picture of us in this book, which was taken in Lowestoft and to my knowledge, this is the only photo I have of myself at nineteen years old. Julie Ann, unfortunately, passed away in her early 30s, but she'd kept the picture for years and her mum gave it to me at her funeral and said, 'She will have wanted you to have this.' That's something I'll never forget because it was so poignant. Something else I'll never forget about Julie Ann was her prediction. Around the time of that photo, she said I would kill myself on my bike and three months later, she was almost right.

September 1978

Last broadcast of *Columbo* starring Peter Falk on NBC

Jimmy Connors beats Björn Borg to become the first player to win the US Open on three different surfaces.

'Three Times a Lady' by The Commodores was No.1

Twenty-three Ford plants close across Britain due to strikes.

Paul Hardcastle collides with a car at 90mph on a motorcycle.

Fuelled Injection

'To hell with safety. All I want to do is race.

James Hunt

The mid to late 1970s were fun times for me. I've got great memories of clubbing all over the place and dancing to tracks like 'Dancer', by Gino Soccio, 'Everybody Have A Good Time Right Now', by Archie Bell and the Drills, *That Lady,* by The Isley Brothers and 'Jungle Boogie', by Kool and The Gang, which has one of the best bass lines ever. We'd go to the Lyceum in Central London, Goldmine in Canvey Island, Zero 6 in Southend, the Hammersmith Palais, The Tottenham Royal, you name it. I used to love dancing and I wasn't too bad, if I may say so, even though I'll admit that I body popped poorly and I could never get on my head when breakdancing. Sadly, most of these places have been demolished many years ago. However, the last part of that decade was also my most dangerous.

July 1978, I was out with a couple of mates in this Ford Escort van. The van actually belonged to one of my mates, but I was driving it and we were on our way back from a scrapyard in Rye House after getting something for his car. There we were driving through the Essex countryside and just before we got to Epping, I decided to drive through this field to take a shortcut. It was a bit muddy and thought it would be fun to do a bit of rally driving. As we were flying around this field, doing doughnuts, all of a sudden, we heard *BANG*. There were three of us in the van. One was in the passenger seat to the left and one of my mates was sitting behind me and he could see the panel of the van was indented just behind me. He said, 'That was a fucking shotgun!' The reason he knew that sound is because he'd witnessed his dad being murdered at his front door with a shotgun and that sound was engrained in his head.

My dad was livid and wanted to go around there, but I wouldn't tell him where it happened because, firstly, I was partly to blame in terms of cutting through the field and also, I didn't want my dad going around to see some nutter with a shotgun. That was a close call, but unfortunately, I wasn't so lucky a couple of months later.

I used to go to Brands Hatch on my bike and through my passion for the sport, I met Eddie Kidd in 1978. He was always around places like Stoke Newington, whereas me and my mates were more Hoxton based. I got to know him a bit as a bike rider and then I used to go and watch him practising driving cars on two wheels and things like that. In fact, I've still got some old cine film somewhere that I took, when he was practising. He used to calculate distances, wind factors and all that, whereas I'd race anyone in what was uncalculated madness. I once tried to jump five cars up in Tottenham and I fell off and that was a tiny fraction of what this guy had achieved. He cleared fourteen double-decker buses when he was nineteen, which was not far off 200ft.

Then, a few years later, I bumped into him in Stringfellows at some event for someone's birthday party and he said to my future wife, as he pointed at me, 'See him? He's a fucking nutcase on the bike.' Coming from a motorbike hero of mine who had all the records, I took that as a big compliment. Bearing in mind what he did for a living when he made the comment.

I thought he was joking and said, 'Have you been drinking?'

He said, 'When I jump, I just jump; I know there's no other cars or bikes in my way. When you race, you don't worry about a car pulling out, whereas I do!' Absolutely lovely guy, a good-looking bloke and he was actually looking to get into the music business if it hadn't of been for his last near-fatal crash.

Back to 1978. I had a Bang and Olufsen music system, which cost me a fortune, but I traded that in, along with my Ford Cortina, for a Triumph Stag and the second night I had it, I smashed it to pieces. I was driving down the road talking to my girlfriend, not paying attention, when all of a sudden, my mate in front stopped because some guy had jumped off a bus and run across the road. That was that. The car was a write-off and I felt sick as a dog, not for being involved in an accident, but because I'd wrecked my beloved Stag. That crash in the Triumph wasn't my first and it certainly wasn't my last. However, the next one came with far greater consequences.

Everyone who used to race their bikes would always meet at Whipps Cross café, right across the road from the hospital. As a motorcycle rider, I didn't have any fears and would race anywhere and against anyone. I was skinny, never used to use the clutch to change gears and never assessed the speed I was going in relation to oncoming traffic. My aim was to come first at all costs. I never got beaten and I genuinely thought that's where my career was going to be. Everyone used to say I would have a bad accident, but I never believed it. Why would I?

On 19 September 1978, I'd been to work, which at this point was as a delivery driver in a car. There were always about eight or ten of us who used to meet all the time and we'd often say, 'What shall we do tonight?' Most of the time, it was, 'Let's go to Whipps.' On this night, we got there and hung out a few hours. Then, on our way back, there were some traffic lights at a place called the Bakers Arms, which is on the border of Leytonstone and Walthamstow. Across the road were about three or four guys on motorbikes and they were looking over. Me, being the idiot that I was, decided to turn around and joined them at the lights. I was on a Yamaha RD400, but it was ported, which means they drilled out the exhaust ports to improve airflow and ultimately made it almost as fast as a 750cc. It would get to 100mph really quickly from a standing start.

There I am lined up with these other motorbikes with a mate on the back of my bike and we're all looking at each other left and right, waiting for the lights to change. Next thing, they go green and I get ahead of everyone. There was a bend as you were going around by a place called Shernhall Street going up to Whipps Cross from Leyton High Road – it wasn't a blind bend, but I was doing about 90mph and was clear of the pack. There was a garage on the left and I saw this car slightly pulling out and I thought, *He's seen us. He won't pull out.* I have to be very honest, though; I've never knocked anyone off a bike before, but I can see why they get knocked off if they're going fast. This guy must have thought, *They're just coming along, I've got loads of time* but probably didn't realise the speed I was going. He's pulled out and by the time he has, *BANG*, I went straight into his front wing by the bonnet. At the moment of impact, I thought, *Holy shit. You fucking idiot. What have you done?* I'm flying through the air at this point and it's true what they say as my life was literally flashing in front of my eyes, as I was thinking about my mum and all sorts of stuff in literally a couple of seconds.

My bike pushed the engine of that Ford Cortina about three inches into the bodywork, which shows how fast I went into it. I went flying over the top and forward into mid-air about 100ft down the road. When I hit the ground, I was rolling, rolling, rolling until I finally stopped. Me and my mate both hit our heads multiple times and without a doubt, our helmets saved our lives. There was a massive crack on my helmet, but at that moment, all I remember thinking was, *Oh my God. I'm in so much pain. What the fuck have you done?*

This guy came over and tried to console me and I grabbed him by the head, screaming, 'Help, help.' What had happened was, I thought the handlebars had gone through my leg and I was lying there holding onto one of the bars. However, when I looked down, it was actually my femur bone, which had gone clean through my jeans and was sticking out of my leg. That's what I was holding onto. I let out an almighty scream.

As I was there looking at my leg with all this blood gushing out, the ambulance turned up and one of the paramedics ran over and gave me gas and air. No disrespect to the ambulance guy, but when you've got a compound fracture, I felt he should have given me something a little bit stronger. They asked if I'd been drinking and I told them I hadn't, which was true, and the next thing I remember clearly was being up in the hospital as they were cutting my jeans off and me asking them to knock me out cold. They told me they couldn't until they checked out my vitals. I was on this trolley and was so desperate that I thought, *If I can get to the end of this trolley, fall off it and hit my head, maybe that would knock me out,* because this pain was something I'd never experienced before.

When we got to the hospital, me and my mate were screaming in agony in beds next to each other and the doctor came over to my mate and said, 'Yes, you have a broken leg, but your friend's injuries are far worse.'

I thought, *Great! Just what I needed to hear.*

Dr Jeremiah was the orthopaedic surgeon and didn't say much. He just got on with it all. The leg is made up from the tibia, fibula and femur and all three had sustained compound fractures, which not only meant the bones were broken but that they'd all broken through the skin at the time of impact. Also, the femoral artery was cut, which is the biggest artery to provide blood to the lower body.

The first op was over eight hours and they gave me six pints of blood. When I woke up the next morning looking down, I thought, *I guess it wasn't a bad dream then.* The doctors told me that if I hadn't of been near the hospital, I probably wouldn't have made it.

Over the next couple of months, I had to have a load more operations, but I was desperate to get out of the hospital and kept complaining that I was all right and wanted to go home. They put a bivalve cast on my leg, which is a cast with a split down both sides, which allows room for swelling and they said, 'We're going to give you a shot of Valium because the doctor is going to take the cast off and have a look at how the leg is.'

When the doctor arrived, I said, 'I'm ready to leave. It's not that painful now.' The doctor pulled off the bivalve cast, got hold of my tibia and fibula and gave them a squeeze at the area they'd been broken and I screamed, 'Ahhhhhh. Put the cast back on!'

Back then, you could smoke in hospitals and planes and at the time, I was a forty-a-day smoker. However, I was in hospital for the next couple of months in traction, bored out of my head, which meant I smoked around sixty a day. When I finally did come out, I was in plaster for four months and my mum had bought me a TV for my room, because she thought I was going to be staying indoors for quite a while. She was right.

A few weeks after coming out, while cooped up in my room, I was given a copy of *Superbike* magazine, February 1979 edition, and there was this two-page spread about motorcycle accidents. There was a guy going around with a medic who was getting called out to different accidents and in the article, he talked about the nature of the accidents and how serious they were. There was no mention of those involved in the accidents, but it showed a photo of my crash helmet and the remains of my bike, which is when I knew they had definitely been to the scene of my accident. The article was called, *Heads You Lose,* with a subtitle of *Finding out the Truth About Helmets – The Hard Way.*

The femur started to mend, but unfortunately, the tibia and fibula bones never healed up and they had to take bone off my left hip and graft it into the leg. That procedure of scraping the bone was as painful as the bone shooting out through the skin. In the morning, the nurse said, 'You've got to get up and start walking on that leg.'

I had a big row with her and asked, 'How am I supposed to get up with this excruciating pain?' She shrugged her shoulders.

It took me about eighteen months to get back to normal, which, in all honestly, was never normal again because the left leg never healed properly and is about half an inch shorter than the right one. If you're reading this and like racing, do it on a circuit and with all the gear on. I had a wake-up call I almost didn't wake up from. Don't be that person.

Being a mature and sensible twenty-two-year-old, I got nicked in 1979 for driving with my leg cast on after I'd had the bone graft. On this particular day, I was driving fast and erratically in my purple Ford Cortina, which I called the Purple Prowler. I was on the inside lane and pulled away quickly from the lights to overtake the car next to me, but the problem was I had to use my hand to push the top of the plaster, which came up to the top of my hip, to get my leg to push the clutch down. I probably should have traded the Cortina in for an automatic.

Anyway. I got pulled up by this copper who told me I was speeding and all the rest of it. I stupidly said, 'I couldn't have been speeding because I've got a plaster on my leg.'

He told me to get out of the car, looked at me and said laughing, 'You can't be in control of the car with that thing on!' I stood there deadpan-faced. He wrote all these things down and started being patronising, so I told him what I thought of him, none of which helped me.

I had the gall shortly after to go down to Leyton police station and asked to see the sergeant. I intentionally parked close to the station so they could see me walking in and out. The sergeant came out and told me that his constable nicked me for so and so and then I said, 'Do I not look like I'm in control?' I then did an award-winning bit of acting and walked with no apparent issues. The truth was, my leg was killing me, but they dropped all the charges.

Motorbikes and cars became a lifetime passion for me. I'm not proud to say it, but within the first couple of years after that accident, I clocked up about sixty motorbike and car driving convictions and amassed twenty-seven endorsements on my licence. I even got banned. I got done about five times for not having L plates on the bike and for other things like driving on the pavement, speeding and bald tyres (twice). I also had a crash because I had no front brake, because my lever had snapped, which meant I was only using the back brake. What happened was I was coming back from Holborn and it was right in front of Holborn police station on a wet night. There was a cop car on the side and I came along. I saw the car, hit the back brake and went skidding across the road right in front of this car. At first, they were all sympathetic and they helped to pick the bike up. Then he said, 'How does the front brake work?'

I replied all innocent, 'It must have snapped off.' This was true…but it happened a week before. They looked around for the brake lever, but I obviously knew they weren't going to find anything. I got done for driving a vehicle where means of stopping were not adequate. Fair enough.

***

After the accident, my whole plan of being a motorbike racer changed. I realised there must have been less painful ways of making a living. During those four months in hospital, I was listening to the radio all the time and, at one point was listening to Radio Invicta and heard them announcing, Steve Walsh, the DJ. I wondered, *Surely that can't be the same Steve I grew up with and went to school with?* I started to think about what I used to do with my dad when I was young and thought, *Maybe you can get into music?* About three months after coming out of hospital, I swapped a video recorder I had for a mini-Korg synthesiser and had no idea how important that swap was going to influence my future.

July 1979

Sony introduces the Walkman.

Bjorn Borg beats Roscoe Tanner for his fourth consecutive Wimbledon title.

Sebastian Coe sets record time for the mile – 3 mins 48.95 secs.

Voyager 2 flies past Jupiter.

Comedian Kevin Hart was born.

Paul Hardcastle works in a Hi-Fi shop.

Musical Stowaway

"When I was growing up there was a product made by Sony called the Sony Walkman – a rage, everyone had to have one. Well, you don't hear about the Walkman anymore."

Kevin B. Rollins

I was really keen on video cameras back in the 70s. If you go on YouTube and type in *Hoxton in the 70s,* you'll see me with my mates doing all kinds of stupid things on motorbikes, like wheelies, or me driving down the road with my mate standing on my shoulders. That was all done on my Cine 8 camera, but I was always thinking ahead to the next best thing, which had sound and better-quality video. What I didn't realise was that the skills, passion and knowledge I picked up using cine cameras were soon going to help me get a job.

I went for an interview in the summer of 1979 at a place called Pontons, which was at No.55 Sloane Square, Central London and the manager asked me about my knowledge of video cameras and Hi-Fi's. I went into great detail about this cine camera I had and also my knowledge of music technology, TVs and radios and he said, 'You know a lot more than I do. Would you like to start today?'

I said, 'Yeah!' I didn't get any commission or anything like that, but I enjoyed talking to people and it was a social job.'

Soon after I joined, the very first Sony Walkman came out, which for the first six months was actually called a Sony Stowaway in the UK and was known as the Soundabout in America. It was a great bit of kit and it came with this demo tape that buzzed the music from right to left in the earphones. I've still got the demo cassette, which was done by some Japanese guy and it was an instrumental to 'Diamonds Are Forever' but speeded up. People were blown away by the whole stereo side of it and despite the unit costing £99, which was six weeks of my salary, everyone who listened to that demo bought one.

The Sony Walkman, to an extent, revolutionised the way we listened to music. It was only slightly bigger than the cassette itself, had small headphones, you could listen to a choice of your music whilst on the move either walking, jogging or down the gym and you could put the whole thing into a handbag or pocket. I sold so many of them, it was unreal, but it's just a shame I wasn't on commission back then, especially as people were coming in and buying up to five or six at a time. For me, though, what really revolutionised it was the sound because there was nothing out there back then that could match it.

At the time, everyone used to hit record and play on their cassette player while listening to the Top 40 on the radio. The quality was shit and as much as you tried to time it, you'd always get a little bit of the DJ talking at the beginning and the end; however, you did have a copy of your favourite songs on a cassette. I also started mixing stuff together with two cassette decks and a third to record it onto. I didn't share what I made; it was more for me in my car. Everybody did it at the time and as a result, a campaign was started called, 'Home Taping is killing Music…and it's illegal.' That was the start of when people were using double deck cassette players, copying albums and giving them away. It wasn't like nowadays, where you could send someone an exact quality copy in high resolution; it was a case of bouncing the album off a cassette for about an hour and once you'd done that, the whole quality went haywire. Either way, that cassette could go in your Walkman.

Pontons was located in a very rich part of London, just next to Belgravia, so the customers who came into the shop had serious cash and would casually buy a couple of TVs with their Walkmans and not batter an eyelid. The likes of Lord and Lady Beecham from *Beecham Powders* and lots of actors would come in, including Diana Rigg from *The Avengers*, Paul Angelis from *The Sweeney* and *Honour Blackman,* better known as *Pussy Galore.* In fact, I went to the Beecham's house in Eaton Square to install a TV because Pontons used to do TV rentals as well. All you had to do was plug it in, pop the aerial in, turn it on and tune it in. How difficult was that? I used to take about an hour and a half to bunk off to install these tellys, which only took about fifteen minutes to set up.

Despite extensively touring with my dad, I wasn't actually a massive fan of music. It wasn't until I came out of the hospital and got that mini-Korg that I started teaching myself how to play it. It was a monophonic synthesiser that only allowed you to play one note at a time, as opposed to a polyphonic, which allowed you to play multiple notes simultaneously.

In 1980, we moved from Hoxton to a council flat in Hackney at No.5 Shellness Road, just by Clapton. Around this time, I reconnected with my old schoolmate Gary Stewart, whom I'd lost touch with after they forced us to go to different secondary schools. I decided to call him out of the blue, asked what he was up to and then asked him to come over and see our new flat and see mum and dad, who always liked Gary.

At the time, I'd just started to learn how to play the synthesiser one note at a time and when Gary came over, we had an impromptu jamming session playing on buckets and pots and pans from the kitchen. I popped microphones underneath everything, put towels all around them for sound insulation and we started banging away. Gary hadn't seen my dad for about ten years at this point and when he walked in, as we were mid-flow, it him took a moment to recognise Gary. The second the penny dropped, he started screaming with joy and gave him a big hug.

Jamming with Gary was great and I managed to convince him to get a drum kit, with the intention of starting a band together. He said, 'Yes!' all enthusiastically, then went home to his missus and said, 'I'm buying a drumkit.'

She said, 'No you fucking ain't.' That was that.

Gary still says to this very day, 'I could have been a popstar by now!'

***

I used to listen to Deep Purple and Black Sabbath, but Hawkwind was my favourite. I would go and see them live and would be straight down the shops whenever an album or single of theirs was released. In fact, around this time, I had a Mk III Cortina and stuck a poster of *Warrior on The Edge of Time* on the boot and I'd only ever play Hawkwind in the car, to my mates delight.

There were a number of companies making synths at the time, including Roland, Casio and Yamaha, but the Korg 700S held a special place in my heart because the keyboard player from Hawkwind, Simon House, used to play one. There was a music shop on Charring Cross Road called Macari's and in the early 1970s, I was in there looking around when I saw the Korg. I hit this key and it made a great noise. Then there was this switch which said, *Traveller*. When I moved, it made this whistling swishing sound, which sounded like a gust of wind. I was like, 'Woooow.'

I ended up going there every Saturday and used to take my mates in there sometimes and say, 'Check this out…'

They'd say, 'That sounds good, Paul.' Even though it probably didn't. I used to drive the guy in the shop crazy and after a while, he would always kick me out. But I'd always go back the week after.

Then, in early 1981, I decided I wanted to own that Korg. There was a mate who lived a few doors down from me in Hackney who I used to hang around with and he had this Korg 700S. I couldn't afford to buy one, so I asked him, 'Do you fancy swapping that synth for my video camera?'

He said, 'All right then.' He couldn't play the Korg, but neither could I; however, I just wanted to have some fun with it. It also meant I no longer had to worry about the guy in Macari's looking at me playing around on the one in his shop.

After fiddling about with the Korg 700S, I found that I was able to make the sound of the start of Hawkwind's 'Silver Machine,' and also had some fun playing along to Sister Sledge's, 'He's The Greatest Dancer' and 'It Seems to Hang On,' by Ashford and Simpson. I'd play the cassettes, then add stuff by playing notes over it.

Not long after getting the 700S, I bought this tiny little Korg drum machine, which was just a little block with a few buttons on it. At the time, musically, I was fairly limited in terms of what I'd done and what I had to work with due to the 700S being monophonic, but I was able to create chords with what I had by recording onto multiple cassette players. Let's say I held down C-Minor and then hit record; I now had a C note on one cassette. Then I'd take that tape out and when I played it, all you were getting was a C, but I was there now playing an E-Flat and recording that to another cassette recorder. I now had two notes I could play at the same time, which I then recorded onto another cassette whilst also holding down the F key. From there, I record it back onto the other cassette player with the F now and all of a sudden, I've got a chord on one cassette. I then added a bassline and by the time you got to the end, with all the times I'd bounced it from one cassette to another, the hiss, crackle and sound was terrible. It sounded like a frying pan in a chip shop, but the funny thing is though, that actually added character. You even find modern-day musicians adding some hiss and crackles to their tracks to give a retro feel. I didn't care, though, because I had a chord. I then added something else to it and these tapes kept building and building. You could just about make out what was happening with what I was trying to do and within about six weeks, I'd come up with little melodies and ideas. I was relentless in trying to get something that sounded unique.

At the time, I was going out with a girl called Teresa and we got a place together in Leytonstone, which we shared with my mum and dad. This was our first adventure of getting out of flats and buying a house. My mum paid the downstairs and we paid the upstairs. My routine was quite standard. I used to get up at six-thirty a.m. and drive to Sloane Square in my Mk IV Ford Cortina because I hated the tube, whereas now I'd never drive into London. As soon as you came out of my house, which was on Grove

Green Road, there was a traffic jam which went on for about three miles towards Stratford. It used to take me about an hour and a half to get to Sloane Square from Leytonstone; then, I'd do my shift and drive home in the rush hour at about five-thirty p.m. I'd get home to Leytonstone about seven-thirty p.m., work in the studio until about two a.m., then get up again at six-thirty a.m. It was like the hamster wheel.

I say studio but it was actually just a small room on the ground floor of this terraced house. Was it properly soundproofed? No. Absolutely nothing. It was a very small room, so there was less echo. I did, however, have one neighbour who complained about the noise all the time, understandably. At this point, I was totally focused on making music, which was unique and that room gave me the space to do that. There were a few trees at the back of the house in this small garden and we had birds there. I recorded the sounds of them chirping away for the start of a track called *AM* by sticking a microphone out of the window and hitting the record button at about four a.m., just to get those sounds.

After about three months of experimenting with sounds and messing around on this Korg, I was reading Melody Maker and there was an advert which said, '*Keyboard player wanted for new funk band.*' I laughed and thought, *What's the worst that could happen?*

September 1981

Fuel stations start selling fuel by the litre.

The first episode of *Only Fools* and *Horses* is aired on BBC television.

Vauxhall Motors launches the Mk II Cavalier.

Ford announces discontinuing the Cortina and replacing it with the Sierra.

The Smurfs first broadcast in America.

Simon and Garfunkel reunite for a concert in Central Park, NYC.

Paul Hardcastle has his first gig with Direct Drive.

Two Crates of Holstein

Direct Drive are the latest self-contained band from London to find their way onto vinyl with the release of their first 12" single via Charlie Gillett's 'Oval' label. They are a six-piece band...and I think that the boys could well have a real future once they get some experience behind them...I, for one, predict that they will be one of 'THE' UK bands to watch in 1982!

Blues & Soul Magazine, January 1982

There were a lot of changes from the late 1970s to the early 1980s. Flares started to go out of fashion, as did long collars and massive sideburns. Wimpy bars were still around, thankfully, but if you wanted to be cool, you'd be wearing Ben Sherman, Levi's jeans, a pair of Brogue's or loafers, or massive disco shoes with Cuban Heels. The early 80s also highlighted some massive shifts in my own personal timeline.

I often get asked if I was tutored in any instruments or perhaps had music lessons of any sort, but apart from being on the road with my dad for five years as *Little Paul*, the answer is no. However, there might have been something in the blood.

My dad was a multi-talented musician and dancer, my mum was in the Tiller Girls, but it was the generation above them who were well-known across Britain at the time. My nan's name was Eliza Gray and her brother, my great uncle Eddie, who was better known as Monsewer Eddie Gray (with an intentional misspelling of monsieur) from the very famous comedy group, The Crazy Gang. My dad always used to tell me Eddie was a good juggler, but it wasn't until I saw a clip of him years later that I realised just how talented he was.

Their records included 'Underneath the Arches,' and 'They were Strollin,' and between 1935 and 1960, they performed fifteen times on stage at places like The Palladium and the Victoria Palace, not to mention they also made five films. My nan used to tell me about Eddie all the time, saying what a funny guy he was, but also a great multi-talented entertainer. Eddie, one of nine kids, was also born in Pimlico and him and his brother Danny became apprentices to a juggling troupe when he was about eight or nine. Looks like being on the road from a young age certainly passed down the generations.

However, when I answered that advert in Melody Maker magazine, I genuinely wasn't expecting them to respond to someone with only a few months of experience. The band used to be called Ritual and it was a nine-piece band with a brass section, but then it fell apart for whatever reasons. However, Robert Williams, the guitarist; Mick Ward, the bass player; Pete Quinton, the drummer; and Mick Hammond, known as Bones, who was the charismatic percussionist and frontman, decided to continue the band.

They hired a good vocalist in Derek Green and they were using different keyboard players for different things, but they thought it would be a good idea to get someone in permanently. They started auditioning for people the old-fashioned way, where they hired a rehearsal studio and got different keyboard players along to try out. After about two or three times, they weren't getting anywhere and it kind of got a bit boring and a bit of a chore, so they thought, *Why don't we just audition the next set of keyboard players round at somebody's house?* That's when they started auditioning people at Bones' place.

They got different keyboard players along, asking them to bring some representation of their work in the form of a recording and then they'd have a chat with them to gauge their personality and their style of play. I answered the advert and went along to Bones' flat and when I arrived, they were chatting with someone else who'd just auditioned.

I'd only been playing the Korg for about six weeks and I go up to this audition and there's a guy in there before me who was brilliant. I was so close to just walking out because I didn't want to be embarrassed. Thankfully, I didn't have to play; I just brought a tape of a track called 'Time Machine', played them some other ideas I had and we had a chat to see how we all got on. They asked, 'What equipment do you use?'

I replied, 'I've got a Korg 700S.'

One of them replied with a confused look on his face and said, 'But that's only monophonic.'

I then told them how I created the music and despite all the crackling and hiss, I think they respected that.

Then they asked, 'Did you write that all yourself?'

I replied, 'No. I just made it up.'

They started pissing themselves laughing while I was wondering seriously faced what was going on. Then the penny suddenly dropped! I thought they were referring to me having physically written something down, which I hadn't, whereas they were just checking that it was my music.

Pete has never let me forget about that to this very day and always says, 'If the programme *This is Your Life* was still going, that would be the intro line to you walking on stage.'

In all honesty, though, I thought they were pissing me about because I didn't really know any chords and was quite limited with musical ability. I knew I had a good ear and was already very confident in programming, but I thought I was out of my depth. They asked me to go out of the room for a bit and about minute later, they called me back in. They said, 'Would you like to join the band?'

I said, 'Why would you want me to join my band when you've just had some guy in there who's a classically trained pianist? Also, I've heard some of the demo tapes of other people you've spoken to and they're really good.'

They said, 'Because we can hear you've got the vibe in what you do and we believe you'd fit into the direction we're going. Do you want to join or not?'

I said, 'Errr, yeah!' I was really chuffed, but really shocked.

They were looking for a new sound and I guess I had something to bring to the table in terms of my music and the way I approached getting a track together. For example, there are classically trained musicians that might say something like, *You should never put a D Minor next to a so and so*, then I'd be thinking, *OK. But I wonder what it sounds like?* I'd try it and next thing, I'd be like, *Hold on a minute. That sounds bloody good.* I've never gone by the book. There are musicians out there who are twenty times better than me, but I wouldn't say they could write better melodies than me. A few years later, melodies like 'Rainforest' had people thinking, *How come that did so well? I could do that.*

I'd say, 'Yeah? It is easy to make a track, but to make one that lots of people remember is another story. What many people try to do is show someone how fast they can play because that's what they've been practising. All that shows is that you've been practising scales instead of writing songs.'

I became good friends with the Direct Drive guitarist Robert because I used to give him a lift home, as he lived in Hackney, not far from me. Robert was a fountain of knowledge and I gained a lot of experience from him. He was not only an absolutely lovely guy but a rock-solid rhythm guitarist and he gave me some great advice from the very beginning when he said, 'Writing is about making music, not writing dialogue.' As a drummer, you've got to be in sync with the rhythm player and as much as Pete would like to tell you they were always right in the grove, they weren't! Every time we used to start this track called 'Time's Running Out,' it would start off with me making some weird windy sort of noise on my synthesiser and then all of a sudden Pete would start playing the drums and every single time, Bones would start in the wrong place, which would put the song out. Pete would be there rolling his eyes, like, *Here we go again.* The look on his face used to crack us up. Robert sadly died in 2022, but the old crew came together for his funeral and we gave him a good send-off. RIP mate.

I thought 'Time Machine,' sounded awful, because it was only something I'd been mucking about with, however, the band said, 'This is really good. We should record it.' That was my first opportunity to be on a record. The other side was called 'Don't Depend on Me.'

I swapped the Korg 700S for a Korg Delta shortly after joining Direct Drive, which allowed me to do polyphonic chords, string sounds and loads of other stuff. It saved me hours than having to record, add, record, add. Then, not long after that, I bought a Fender Rhodes, which was also a polyphonic keyboard. At the time, many bands were using Fender Rhodes because it gave it that mellow sound and for myself, that was a big step up from my Korgs, albeit I had to teach myself chords. One thing about the Fender – it was a great bit of kit, but I never realised how bloody heavy it was until I had to start lugging it to venues.

Back then, I used to trade in stuff all the time, as I was always looking to upgrade or expand my music equipment. Between wheeling and dealing, I was able to buy a tape machine and a mixer before eventually swapping some kit for a Korg Lambda. However, my main ambition after that was to get a Prophet 5, which was about £2,500, roughly two grand more than the Lambda. I remember seeing the band Freeez and Andy Stennett played the Prophet in the band and I thought it sounded great. I was on a mission to get one and about three months after joining Direct Drive, I achieved my goal.

From the time I joined, we spent a lot of time practising under a record shop just by Kennington underground station. However, our first-ever recordings were done at the First Light studio in Penge, where we created and recorded three or four tracks that we'd written between us. Then, after about three months, we had our first gig at The Cricketers pub, which no longer exists, right by the cricket ground in Oval. That night in September 1981, I was the most inexperienced and scared member of the band. I never ever had stage fright as a nipper, but that night, I was bricking it. Maybe it's because when I was a kid, we used to do a lot of cover tracks, whereas we wrote our own material in Direct Drive and that meant we were putting ourselves out there because we were not doing tracks that people would immediately know and get into. They were either going to like us or hate us. From the band's perspective, it was a case of, *Can we perform it as well as we know we can on the night?*

I was so nervous for that first gig that I tried to talk my way out of it, so much so that I even considered saying I didn't feel well. I said to Mick Ward, 'I don't want to do it.'

Mick replied, 'Paul. You're the best keyboard player I've ever played with and I doubt I will play with a better one. You've got this, mate.'

On reflection, I think he was spinning me a load of bullshit, but it must have worked because I said, 'Oh fuck it. Let's do it.' I just needed a kick up the arse, but I was still bloody nervous though.

At the time, there was a really good band called Deep Feeling, who I used to go and see with my motorbike mates at a massive pub in Leytonstone called The Green Man. There was a guy in the band who had a synth and I remember going up to him once at halftime and asking him to give me a little demo of it. I was really impressed. Well, two of them were at the Cricketers that night and I when I spotted them, I thought, *Shit. I'm nervous enough as it is. They're going to think we're crap.* Thankfully, I never got to speak with them.

I went up and said on the microphone, 'We've only been together three months and if it sounds a bit bad...' and all that. If I was worried about not sounding the part, I also had grounds for being concerned about not looking the part. Up in the city, you had all the yuppies with their gigantic mobile phones, Filofaxes, long-tanned coloured cashmere overcoats and Golf GTi convertibles, whereas there was me sitting on two empty crates of Holstein beer because the venue didn't have a stool. I sat behind this keyboard, trying to stay as low as I could and doing my best to not make eye contact with anyone in the crowd. Despite being really nervous, there were no fluffs from anyone that night and we never hit a bad note. The gig went down really well and we ended up playing at that venue a number of times. My mates Arthur, Twink and Boo, along with a few others from Hoxton, came to support me and we finished the night off going for a few beers after.

We went under the name Splash for that first gig as we were trying to come up with band names before eventually going with Direct Drive. I think it was Robert who came up with the name, which was a no-brainer. The rationale behind the name didn't have any hidden meaning; it was more a reflection of the technology, as in direct drive turntables, which were state of the art, rather than the old ones, which were belt driven. Splash was a bit limp in comparison and got binned.

In the coming months, we started gigging at a number of places, including The Walmer Castle near the Elephant and Castle, Goldsmith Tavern in New Cross and a few gigs up the Old Kent Road, including the Thomas A Beckett pub, which was famous at the time for having a boxing gym above it, with some of the biggest names training there, like Frank Bruno. We went down really well there and I remember someone coming up to us afterwards who was a bit of a shady character and he asked us if we wanted to be managed and we said we didn't.

He said, 'I'll manage you and paint your name all around Trafalgar Square.' We all looked at each other like, *Not sure we fancy that*, then made a swift exit. We also played a gig at the staff club in St George's Hospital in Tooting, which I probably think was due to the fact Pete was going out with a nurse who used to work there at the time.

By now, we'd also accidentally developed something we called 'The Riot', which we played towards the end of the night. Basically, it was a case of anything goes and we all went mad, totally unrehearsed. Pete would start off with a drumbeat; I would get every crazy sound I could muster from my Prophet 5 synthesiser. Rob was doing what he did best on guitar and it always went down a storm. Without a doubt, that was our favourite track of the night.

***

The band wasn't a hobby, but because we weren't earning enough money to survive, I guess we were what you'd have called semi-professional but always aiming to be professional. As a result, we were all ducking and diving doing temporary jobs to pay the bills and the mortgage.

When I joined Direct Drive, I still had my job at Pontons selling Hi-Fi's because we were only doing a gig roughly every ten days and were rehearsing once a week.

However, after a couple of months, I quit the job and was then reliant on what I could get from music, which wasn't a lot. My manager at Pontons told me, 'Nothing will come of that. You'll be back here in a month.' I had loads of people telling me that sort of thing, but I didn't give a shit. I just knew that if I wanted to make a go of this properly, nothing was going to stop me. I had some savings and some money from the compensation from the accident, plus I didn't have massive outgoings and wasn't a flamboyant spender, so getting by wasn't too hard. However, the fact remained that we needed to start generating some serious cash from the music because the money we were earning would literally last me a couple of months.

All was not lost from the gigs, though, because we had enough in the kitty to be able to go to the First Light studio and record our first three tracks, which only cost us around £350. The technology we were using back then, by today's standards, was ancient. Unless you went into a professional studio, where they used large reel-to-reel, you were using cassettes. Simple as that. I'd saved up enough money to buy a thing called a TEAC 144 Portastudio, which meant it had four tracks on a cassette so we could adjust the levels. It was almost like a miniature recording studio, which enabled us to make good-quality recordings. That first small demo album acted as our calling card to get us in with a record label. However, we now needed to find someone who would take us on.

We each had cassettes of the demo and we came up with a list of record labels and apportioned them out between us of who to approach. One of the labels was Oval Records in Clapham, which was close to where Pete lived, so he dropped the demo through the letterbox of their basement entrance with a covering letter and didn't even knock, ring the bell, or wait for an answer. He simply dropped it off and drove away straight after. Why didn't we ring them up? Who knows. The guy in charge there was Charlie Gillett and he said at a later date, 'I heard something come through the letterbox and came rushing out to find out who had left it, by which stage nobody was there.' Either way, the music on the tape excited Charlie's interest and he was impressed with how we were able to do the cassettes so cheap as they were such good quality. We reached an agreement that he would release it for us and we'd go fifty/fifty on the royalties.

Soon after, we started getting radio play, which meant that shop sales started to increase. We did do a few appearances around clubs, but it wasn't like before, where all we did was pubs and clubs for income. Robbie Vincent and Greg Edwards were the two most influential DJs at the time and they were the ones that supported new English dance music, or Brit-Funk, as they called it. The first time I heard 'Time Machine' on the radio, it was played by Robbie Vincent, on BBC Radio London and I was in my car driving. I was looking at the radio, saying, 'No way!' and veered off into the side of this lady's car.

I came out of the car and said, 'That was my fault. Here's my details for the insurance. I'm happy to sign something right now to say something to that effect. I have to be bloody honest with you – I've just heard my record on the radio and simply wasn't paying enough attention.'

She smiled and said, 'I've heard some crazy excuses before, but that beats them all.'

I said, 'It's true though! Why do you think I'm smiling after crashing into you!'

That made her look at me a bit strange. It didn't do my no-claims bonus any favours, but I thought, *Never mind that, I'll put in an insurance claim. You're on the radio!* When I went to the pub that night, people were coming up to me saying, 'We heard 'Time Machine' on the radio today.' I felt absolutely brilliant. What a rush.

***

About a year after joining Direct Drive, I started to have thoughts about doing something different. When you have six guys with different ideas, arguments start. It was one of those things that I had new ideas and there's no way I could make them work having six people to ask each time. Also, some of the band were umming and ahing about Charlie putting the records out and I said, to Charlie, 'If the band don't want to go with you, I'm always open to doing something.' That's when me and Derek Green formed First Light. When I left the band, I wanted to do it the right way. We met down at Oval Records and Pete and

Mick were fine, as was Robert, but Bones had the hump. Thankfully, we all remained mates, even though we went our separate ways.

Helen Rogers replaced Derek in Direct Drive and they used a few different keyboard players, but sometimes, when they didn't have a keyboard player for a gig, they'd give me a call and of course, I'd play with them. We had some fun nights, but there's one particular outing that does stand out. They'd booked a gig up in Manchester at the PSV Club, which later became the Hacienda and they needed a favour as they were short of a keyboard player. Even though there wasn't a lot of money in it for me and I knew it was a long trip, I agreed. I brought my Prophet 5 along, which I'd modified a bit, putting a little joystick on it to manipulate the machine to my own style. I didn't have the Prophet 5 in the case, as I thought it would be all right to pop it into the back of the van balanced on top all the gear.

At the time, they had this long-wheelbase Ford Transit van that had a reconditioned engine, which I'd actually picked up for the band when I was with them. It was an old meat van and it took a couple of days of intense cleaning to get rid of the smell. I drove it for a bit and because we were running late for this gig, I had this van going off the clock. Everyone was saying, 'This ain't funny, Paul. Slow down!' Then, Alvin, our official driver, took over.

Shortly after, I said to everyone, 'Can you smell that?' Next thing, the van filled up with smoke, Alvin chucked on the brakes and my Prophet-5 went flying.

It turns out the van blew a gasket on us and we limped into a service station, where we pushed it into an area where we could park. We opened up the back of the van and the Prophet-5 fell out onto the floor and broke the joystick. We ended up walking to somewhere to find a transit van hire place and although it was a short wheelbase, we somehow managed to get all the gear in it. I took over the driving again and we went all the way to Manchester in record time, as I drove like a madman. We arrived just about in time to make it to the PSV, which looked like a rundown council hall and the promoter was there standing outside.

We all jumped out and the first thing he said to us was, 'There are no people. The gig's off.' He expected us to get back in the van and drive back empty-handed, but instead, we held him upside down and got what we were owed. We ended up having a game of football in the car park and then drove back to London. Life on the road ain't always so glamorous, but you have some fun on the way. As far as that van goes, it never worked again after that trip and stayed outside Mick's flat for about eighteen months until he somehow managed to convince someone to buy it.

In the meantime, I was already looking at the next road of my personal journey in music.

December 1982

Chris Evert-Lloyd beats Martina Navratilova to win her
first Australian title.

TIME's Man of the Year is a computer.

UK release the film *Gandhi*.

Gibraltar gains a pedestrian link to Spain.

Paul Hardcastle and Derek Green form First Light.

First Flight

As both a part of Direct Drive and on their own as First Light, Derek Green and Paul Hardcastle have impressed me as musicians of an extremely high calibre and have already shown maturity and awareness beyond their years. ...A.M. is full of all the energy and sparkle that we have come to expect from the duo. An instrumental that gives Paul the opportunity to show what a versatile performer he is and it's amazing to consider he is self-taught and only over the last couple of years at that. (Rating 9/10)

Justin Lubbock, Blues & Soul Magazine, Reviews First Light.

I had a good relationship with Charlie Gillett from the beginning and he was almost like an informal mentor. For me, he was one of the most competent people to talk about anything relating to the music industry, because he always spoke sense and he was the person who really drilled the importance of a good, memorable chorus in a song into my head. He managed Ian Dury and the Blockheads, which used to be Kilburn and the High Roads, discovered a number of new artists such as Lene Lovich and even wrote a book entitled, *Making Tracks: Atlantic Records and the growth of a multi-billion-dollar industry.* He was a very, very wise man and when we signed with him, it felt right. We called the band First Light simply after the recording studio in Penge and for no other reason than we liked the name.

At a time when British dance music was coming out from under the jazz-funk umbrella and trying some new grooves, Charlie heard the promise in First Light's uninhibited, upbeat approach and even took a punt with a sizeable advance against sales of our first album with First Light. I'd originally asked Roger Ames, who was head at Polygram, if they could give me an advance so I could get a better recorder and they said no, then Charlie said, 'I think we can help out here.' Charlie gave me the money to buy a TEAC 8-track recorder, which was about five grand, which shows the confidence he had in us.

The demos started getting better and we did one in particular which Charlie said, 'We should really record it properly.' So we hired a 24-track studio and I totally fucked it up. We lost the complete feel of the track and the excitement of when you first do something.

Charlie said, 'It's not as good as the demo.'

I said, 'It's got to be because it's got more stuff on it.'

He replied, 'But it's lost the vibe.' It took me about five years to understand what he meant, but at the start, I thought he was nuts. What I hadn't realised was that I'd produced the hell out of it. A demo can often sound better than when it's re-recorded and that was a good lesson in my I thinking of, *The more that's in it, surely means the better it's going to be?* Far from it. We re-recorded it, but we never released it and went on to something different.

We released our debut single in June 1982, which was 'Don't be Mistaken,' and an update of America's early 70s anthem 'A Horse with No Name' on the B side. Then, five months later, in November, came 'Sixteen Minutes of First Light,' which was a 12" single that also included 'A.M.,' and 'I Don't Care', co-written with Derek. 'A.M.' was particularly appreciated by the general public and one of my first interviews was with Pete Tong in Praed Street, Paddington, for Blues and Soul after he'd got to hear a couple of tracks. The Record Mirror also wrote in December 1982, *Paul and Derek come to notice via a single called* 'A.M.,' *heating feet on dance floors all over the country.* Especially in London. 'A.M.' got us known and got to No.1 on a couple of funk charts, which was actually my first No.1.

And as far as the track 'I Don't Care' goes, that was the first ever national TV appearance I was featured on, by way of Channel 4. There was me, Derek and a couple of backing singers, with nobody allowed to mime it. The programme was called *The Switch* and there I was doing keyboard and this little bit of slapping on the bass guitar, which was popular at the time. It's where you use your thumb to slap down hard on the strings to add a percussive sound. I taught myself how to do that and I've still got the marks and callouses on my thumb. I only knew about ten notes, but I could keep it in time pretty well rhythmically.

However, at one point, as I turned around, my hand came off the bass and hit the keyboard, which was quite funny. Well, funny for everyone watching live television, apart from me, as it really stung and I had to act like nothing happened.

First Light was classified as a Brit funk band, which basically meant it was danceable and funky. You had all the imports from America and there weren't that many Brit bands offering what they did. You had Central Line, Level 42, Freeez (which had Bluey, who went on to form Incognito) and bands like that and it was almost like First Light was our interpretation of what was coming out of America.

Me and Derek did a couple more records together and then in 1983, we went back and saw Roger Ames, who wanted us to do this ballad called 'Explain The Reasons,' and introduced us to this guy at London Records called Steve Levine. Steve had just produced Culture Club's 'Do You Really Want To Hurt Me?' And was obviously a big name in music, but I think he made our track too pop because we were getting known in the clubs by then. However, Steve did teach me a great deal. In 1983, I did some instrumental work for him for a few of his artists like Celena Duncan and Leesha Paradise, then in 1984, I did some work for him for the Beach Boys overdubbing the hi-hat. Funnily enough, the studio we recorded Explain The Reasons at, was called Red Bus and it was right by my old school, Rutherford, just off Bell Street.

We then did a track called 'Wish You Were Here,' by the producer Bob Carter, who had done Junior Giscombe's hit 'Mamma Used to Say' and 'You're Lying,' by Linx. Steve did a good job on 'Wish You Were Here,' but we were becoming a bit of a dance band and I decided to embrace my passion and did this track called '*Daybreak*' in my mum's front room.

The band was basically just me and Derek, with myself doing all the instrumentals and Derek on vocals. Derek had a great falsetto voice like Phil Bailey, who sang with Phil Collins, but it couldn't have been great for Derek to have been in a band where some of the tracks were purely instrumental. After about eighteen months of First Light, me and Derek had naturally started to go in different directions. He was thinking of more vocal stuff, which made sense, because he was the vocalist, whereas I was being more experimental with instrumentals and hiring in singers as and when I needed to. I said, 'This is good what we're doing, but I've got different ideas.' That's when we went our separate ways by mutual consent, but we remained mates after.

After we split, I started getting records out under the brand name of Paul Hardcastle and all I thought about was music every single day. I'll be the first to admit that my relationship with my girlfriend at the time, Teresa, broke down because every spare hour I had I dedicated to my music, which ultimately meant we'd be lucky to see each other for an hour each day. That naturally and sadly made us grow apart. I basically wanted to succeed at any cost and that, unfortunately, meant the cost of my girlfriend.

The only tiny salvation I was able to offer a few months down the line was from some kind of pension policy we'd taken out together. When we split up, it worked out that there was a payment for about six grand payable, which, in essence, should have been split down the middle. I called her up and said, 'This payment has come through. You have it.'

She replied, 'But we both paid into it equally, though.'

Teresa had helped me buy a car when I was struggling to make ends meet and I said, 'It's the least I can do. It's all yours.'

There was also another issue I needed to iron out with her. In the coming year, one of the major tabloids said I had been seeing someone for about a year, which would have meant I was doing the dirties behind Teresa's back. I assured her that I'd only been seeing my new girlfriend for a few months, which she appreciated. I think!

I was with Teresa for about two and a half years and I carried on with my work in search of that big breakthrough. Was it all worth it, though?

January 1985

The first mobile phone network is launched by Vodafone.

'Born in the USA.' peaks at No.9.

The Sinclair C5 is launched.

Oxford University refused to give the UK Prime Minister, Margaret Thatcher, an honorary degree.

Britain's House of Lords debate first televised.

Paul Hardcastle knocks Madonna off the No.1 chart position in America.

Chart Toppler

New styles are entering the mainstream and with them new artists who bring fresh vitality to the turntable, to video and to the concert stage…Paul Hardcastle's 'Rainforest' is an unusual jazz and hip-hop instrumental that's already sold more than two hundred thousand, 12" singles on the independent Profile label.

New York Post, 8 January 1985

One night in 1982, I was at the Lyceum and I heard someone shout, 'Curly!' Which is what a lot of people used to call me when I grew up in Pimlico. It was my old mate, Steve Walsh.

He then says, 'I saw your name on the back of a record cover and wanted to check. Are you in a band called Direct Drive?'

I said, 'Yeah.' I then said, 'Who you out with tonight?'

And he replied, 'I'm resident DJ here.' We hadn't seen each other for about twelve or thirteen years and by total coincidence, we were now both working in the music trade. We kept in touch after that and it became a regular thing that I'd go out with him to his Saturday night radio show in Guildford and then we'd go onto a club after.

Then, in 1984, we decided to create a record label together. We wanted a company name that reflected the fact that we were leaving people and organisations that had too much control and management over our music careers. I stuck my fingers in my ears and said, 'Let's call it Total Control. I don't want to listen to record companies any more.' That's how me and Walshy created our label and the logo for Total Control on our records was a cartoon drawing of a person with their fingers in their ears. Our mindset was, if we went with our ideas and they worked, then great, but if they didn't, then at least we wouldn't be looking over our shoulders in resentment, wondering, *What if?*

In 1984, we released two singles, a remake of D-Train's, 'You're the One for Me,' then 'AM' and 'Daybreak,' which was quickly followed by 'Guilty.' Running our own label brought us to street level – literally. Me and Walshy got 'You're the One for Me' to No.41 without any help, but I do wonder if it could have got in the Top 40 using a distribution company instead of driving around in my Ford Cortina to record shops in and around London saying, *Have a listen to this.* That said, I still enjoyed that face-to-face interaction and building up a rapport with the shops.

After 'You're the One for Me,' we went through a company called IDS (Independent Distribution Service) for 'AM Daybreak' and 'Guilty.' The way it worked was that we paid for the copies ourselves and they were distributed. Creating the copies cost us about 50p each and we were charging a couple of quid, which, even after IDS took their cut, meant me and Steve made a nice profit.

We ended up selling three thousand copies, which was massively surprising as we thought we'd sell a few hundred tops. Every place we went, people were buying no less than twenty-five. City Sounds took one hundred and fifty, Shack Attack took about the same and then I took it to a place called Sergeant Peppers. He asked, 'How many copies do you have left?

I said, 'I've got about three hundred left in the car.'

He replied, 'I'll have them.' Job done. Unfortunately, neither *Guilty*, nor *You're One for Me*, broke into the top 40 which was a real shame. A major factor was BBC Radio One's refusal to play what they termed as *new-fangled dance music*.

One of the big reasons why me and Walshy clicked was because we were very different characters. He didn't really know anything about the music business, but he knew how to get a crowd going better than anyone I've ever seen and everyone who knew him still says that about him now. Walshy could take a dead crowd and using the simplest techniques, he'd bring them to life. He would just say something like, 'Right, you lot. You're all looking a bit down. Let me ask you a question. Who's from London?' and straight away, the crowd would erupt.

Then he'd say, 'Let's see if you can really get into this one,' and he'd play something like *Ain't No Stoppin Us Now*, by McFadden and Whitehead and everyone would dance to it. Once, we went across to Holland and back on a boat and he was the DJ. In the club part, there weren't that many people on it and all of a sudden, he said to everyone in there, 'Right then. Go and get your friends, because I've got something special. They don't want to miss this.'

I was there in the capacity of First Light with Derek and there were also some other Brit funk bands. Steve asked us if we had any promo copies of our music to give away and we all said, 'Yeah.' Well, the hall started filling up and me and Derek did the PA as we were giving away 12" records. Walshy turned it around from what was a sinking ship to a hovercraft.

Walshy was also one of the best salesmen I've ever heard and had loads of front to go with it. Many labels would only speak to either agents or managers and at the time, he didn't have either. I went up to his flat once and I've walked in on him pretending that he was his own manager on a phone call. He's given me the shhhhh sign with his finger over his lips as he then says to the person on the phone, 'Yeah. I'm sure Steve would like to play that. What sort of dates are you looking at, as I'll need to check with him. Also, what sort of money are we talking about?' He was such a blagger, but he was such a nice guy and always got the job done. He lived in a council block and his address was 32 Parsons House, but instead, he called it Suite 32, Parsons House, which is where all our correspondence for Total Control was sent to.

Total Control lasted about two years and we did a handful of records, but me and Walshy started to fall out a bit and it made sense to step away from the record label and salvage the friendship because, at the end of the day, he was a really good friend to me. I'd let Walshy do the business side of things, which was a mistake as he had no business acumen and he'd spend whatever we had before looking at the outgoings. We had tax to pay and things like that and all of a sudden, he'd say, 'My accountant has told me that we've got so and so bills to pay and we don't have enough money.' I'd never really touched the money, but I started to think, *If I start going into this, we're going to get into a ruck.* We also owed some money on publishing to Charlie Gillett and stuff like that and he'd be asking if I could call Charlie and waive this and that. It wasn't tons of money and we got everything sorted out, but I knew long-term it was best we went our separate ways in music. In fact, after Total Control, we not only remained friends but became better friends.

On the whole, business and friendship don't tend to work and that's where a manager comes in handy. If you go in with a record and they say the track is a pile of crap, they wouldn't really say that to my face, but they'd say that to my manager and it would be his job to water it down a bit and say, 'I don't think they're really into this type of thing.' And then I wouldn't blow my lid. That's a manager's job, to be the in-between man and with friends.

Unfortunately and very sadly, Walshy had a really bad car accident in Ibiza in July 1988 and ended up smashing his femur bone in a very similar way to myself. However, due to being so overweight, he died from a heart attack a few days later while they were doing the operation. He was only twenty-nine. The sad thing is he phoned me up the night before he had the operation and asked me, 'Curly. I'll be all right, won't I?'

I said, 'I'm sure you will, mate.'

Then, the next morning, around nine a.m., which was a Sunday, I received a call from his manager, Martin Levitt. 'Paul.'

I replied, 'Hello Martin.' But then straight away, in a micro-second, my brain clicked as I thought, *Why's he calling at this time on a Sunday morning? He's been in the hospital with Walshy. He's died.* Before he could reply to my hello.

I said, 'He's dead, isn't he?'

He didn't even ask me how I knew; he just replied, 'Yes.'

There were so many people at his funeral at Kensal Green that you couldn't get into the hall and the service itself will be remembered by many just for the music. As the coffin started moving towards the crematorium oven, one of his tracks comes on and the lyrics starts with Walshy's voice singing, 'Here we go, here we go, here we go, here we go, here we go.' People weren't really listening to the lyrics, but I was there thinking, *This is spooky and surreal,* as he disappeared behind the curtains! RIP, Walshy... and cheers for the memories.

***

Back to 1984. It took a few years for the insurance money of my motorbike accident to fully come to fruition and the reason I got ten grand from it was because they said I'd need special shoes for the rest of my life because one leg was about half an inch shorter than the other. I would have got more, but they said about forty percent of the accident was my fault because I was going too fast. It also didn't help that there was an off-duty copper who said I was going no less than 80mph at the time of impact. As for the special shoes, I never bought them. Instead, I was happy to limp a bit and once the money fully landed in my account, I went out and bought a twenty-four-track reel-to-reel mixer made by Aces. It was very reasonably priced, but to me at the time, it was expensive because I didn't have a great deal of cash. However, the tracks I ended up recording on it meant that it paid itself back pretty quickly.

I was in the process of signing for Chrysalis Records' emerging label, Cooltempo when another opportunity came my way. Steve Walsh's nearest record shop, Bluebird Records, was just off the Edgware Road and was owned by a guy called Billy Russell. Steve said to me, 'I've been in the shop and Billy asked if you'd be interested in doing four tracks for a body-popping video that they're making for Bluebird and sending to America.'

I said, 'Yeah, yeah.' I agreed to write the music but hadn't anticipated a single release. It came out under the album cover name of *Zero One* with *Profile*, which was owned by a guy called Cory Robbins in America, who had just started working with Run DMC and the album was licensed by Billy at Bluebird in the UK.

I managed to record the start of 'Rainforest' on the 24-track and then took it to the Sound Suite in Camden, which became my go-to studio for a number of years. It was a small place, quite cheap and I got on really well with the tape guy, Alvin Clark. It was a great learning curve being around Alvin as he'd teach me about sounds that would clash and the different frequencies in relation to all the instruments, making sure they don't clash. For example – you might need to cut out some of the guitar, perhaps take the middle frequencies out and then the voice will have room to breathe in that frequency. Otherwise, it would be a big cacophony of everything trying to fight to make this sound. It's like paints. You can get loads which are all nearly the same colour, but how do you differentiate them? You might need to take out some of the white and make it a much darker grey Pantone. I also didn't realise all this stuff with equalisation, but now it's easier because you can see everything on screen and you can move things around quickly if something's rumbling too much because on screen, it will give you a good idea of where it's rumbling.

Now I had a demo of 'Rainforest', I needed to find a record label. I decided to take the track to Roger Ames from Polygram Records, whom I'd previously approached to take on First Light, mainly because Roger was a massive name and had worked with the likes of Tears for Fears and brought a lot of clout to the table. I headed over to their Hanover Square office towards the end of 1983 and he also had Pete Tong in the meeting. I played them the track and Roger said, 'Where's the vocals?'

I said, 'There ain't no vocals. It's called an instrumental.' I think Pete liked it, but Roger had said his piece and with Pete having his label through Roger, maybe didn't want to rock the boat.

I then decided to give a copy of 'Rainforest' to Billy Russell at Bluebird to listen to and he said to Steve Walsh, 'This is going to be a big record. Let's give it a try.'

Steve also said to me, 'I agree with Billy. Every time I go out and DJ, I'm being asked to play 'Rainforest' by Paul Hardcastle.' The track got to No.1 in the Club chart but unfortunately peaked at the graveyard position of No.41 again in the UK's pop chart.

At the time, all the reps would be out giving merchandise to the radio stations and taking them out to flash dinners and sports events, trying to get their record in the pop chart. That's what I was competing against when I was at No.41 and didn't have the money to buy leather jackets and stuff to give away to the record shops. However, all was not lost as Billy was looking beyond the UK scene. Although I didn't think it would sell, he proved me wrong. That was the benefit of being with an experienced record label because they can gauge the market accurately and have better experience with potential sales projections. The other bonus of signing with Bluebird was the advance they gave me. By this stage of my life, I hadn't had any big holidays or anything like that, but that changed when I was given an eight-grand advance from Bluebird, which enabled me to buy a blue Ford Escort XR3i convertible, which was a massive deal for me.

As far as Polygram goes, a bit further down the line, after 'Rainforest' started blowing up in America, I received a call from Pete Tong asking, 'Can we have the track? We're doing the best dance hits compilations and Roger would like it to be on there.'

I was a bit of an idiot and said, 'Now he wants it! Well, he can't. He didn't want the track before because he didn't think it would sell without vocals and it wouldn't amount to anything.' I was annoyed that he'd turned it down and although I lost money by saying no, I stuck to my principles.

After First Light dissolved, I wanted to build up a pool of in-house writers, artists and producers and maintain a high quality of sound. Kevin Henry used to be lead singer of Push, which, incidentally, my old mate Gary Stewart's brother, Reg, also played in, doing percussion.

I said to Kevin, 'Would you like to do some vocals for some stuff I'm doing?' That's when I started working with Kevin on and off for the next couple of years. He's a great vocalist, talented guy and lovely bloke. We got on very well.

One memorable track we did for Profile Records was called, 'Eat Your Heart Out.' I asked Cooltempo to send us to New York for about a week to mix the track and it just so happened RUN DMC were in the same studio recording. I remember hearing them playing back their chorus for 'Walk this Way,' and I thought, *That sounds wicked. Rap with rock.*

New York was a real buzz because it was the first time I'd ever been there, but I initially struggled to get into most places serving alcohol. I was a very young-looking twenty-four-year-old and even though the law was twenty-one to drink booze, you needed to present ID, even if you looked as old as Father Christmas. As a result, I was turned away from the Limelight Club. Straight after that, I carried my passport on me everywhere. It's funny, though, because a track involving age was going to prove pivotal in my career in the coming months.

(May 1985 Prequel)
November 1984

Prince opens his Purple Rain tour.

Nightmare on Elm Street premieres in the US.

McDonald's sells its fifty millionth burger.

Eight hundred Miners cease striking in the UK.

British Telecom shares go on sale, with two million
people buying.

Paul Hardcastle watches *Vietnam Requiem*.

Timing is Everything

I'd never met anyone so completely focused on succeeding but not on any terms. He wanted to succeed, but doing something that came out of him. Therefore, when he did eventually succeed, it was a totally legitimate expression of the person he was. The fact that it [19] was a brilliantly inventive record was a bonus. He was always going to do it somehow.

It was that combination of a brilliant idea, a novelty because nobody had played anything quite this way but with a very danceable rhythm. This paradox of dancing to a record that was reporting very serious material about the Vietnam War.

This was very much a D.I.Y. record. He came up with the ideas himself and he did mix it in a professional studio, but it was a small, inexpensive place, not some grand studio that people have in their mind when they think of commercial studios. He was in every way the forerunner all studio-based people who followed in their droves, including Fat Boy Slim. He was a pioneer.

Charlie Gillett, *Single Luck* Television Programme

Looking back, the mid-80s was a nostalgic overload. Breakdancing was all the rage; wrestling on both sides of the pond was huge with the likes of Hulk Hogan in the US and Big Daddy and Giant Haystacks in the UK and everyone seemed to be doing Jane Fonda workouts. I was watching the video but not taking part. Then, if you fancied some decent telly, all you had to do was tune in at five thirty p.m. on a Saturday and you'd be treated to either the *A-Team, Knight Rider, CHIPS, Airwolf,* etc. I watched them all and what I couldn't watch, I'd record onto a video cassette and play them back the day after with my remote control, which wasn't so remote because it had a wire which went right the way across the room, which acted like a trip wire. Back then, it was almost a status symbol to have countless shelves and racks of music and video cassettes of Betamax or VHS videos, vinyl records and C90 music cassettes. Then, let's not forget a decent Hi-Fi stack in a glass cabinet. And if you wanted to make noise on the move, you had a ghetto blaster which needed about twenty massive batteries to keep it going.

On the big screen, Mr Miyagi and Daniel-san had everyone doing the crane kick; Eddie Murphy's laugh became a hit with *Beverly Hills Cop* and Brat Pack movies like *The Breakfast Club* provided the ultimate feel-good factor. Luminous colours were in and everyone was wearing big shoulder pads, oversized T-shirts and baggy trousers, which worked for me because I was so skinny back then and it helped to cover up how small I was.

At home, you'd kill hours and hours playing on a Binatone computer console, a Commodore 64, a Sinclair ZX Spectrum, Vic 20, or maybe tried your luck with the Rubix Cube, which, for the records, I hated. I tried it once and gave up after a minute. Then, when you decided to head out and wanted to be cool, you had a watch with a calculator (usually bought with Green Shield Stamps) and if you wanted to get some attention down the nightclubs, you'd be splashing on some Tabac, Taboo, Hai Karate, Old Spice, Brut or Denim. The good old days.

Towards the end of November 1984, I was working on a number of projects, including 'Rainforest', but I had a moment as an unknowing visionary that was about to change my life. I was at home in Leytonstone reading the paper and I saw there was a programme called *Vietnam Requiem* coming on Channel 4, which had originally come out in 1982 on the American network ABC. I taped it on my Betamax video recorder and then watched it later that day with absolutely no idea the influence it would have on me.

The programme was about forty-five minutes long and focused on a small number of American soldiers, talking about the effects of that war while focusing on the average age of the soldiers being sent out to Vietnam. They went into great detail talking about death and PTSD; however, what really grabbed me was a line which talked about the average age of the kids being sent out to the war. *In World War Two, the average age of the combat soldier was twenty-six. In Vietnam, he was nineteen.* I was only twenty-five at the time and thought, *What would I have been doing at nineteen years of age? I was probably out clubbing and stuff.* I wondered what it would have been like in some jungle dodging incoming bullets, grenades, bombs and all the things that go on with war. There was a big difference between my life in comparison to theirs. I also thought it was strange that nineteen-year-olds were allowed to go into a combat zone but were not seen as mature enough to have a drink until they were twenty-one in America.

The timing of the record was perfect because, around this time, I wanted to make a concerted effort to deliver more electro and hip-hop because I felt there was a gap in the market for that kind of music. There were a number of tracks about Vietnam which danced around the subject area or delivered the message with softer lyrics, music and instrumentals, whereas I wanted this track to be the total opposite and become the ultimate attention grabber.

From me recording the television programme onto a Betamax video cassette, it then went into a quarter-inch tape, then into my Emulator II, which was one of the first sampling synthesisers. The problem was I could only get two seconds of sampling at a time in the machine, whereas nowadays, you can get hours. I started mucking around with some rhythms and then started trying to put some samples of the commentary from the Vietnam Requiem programme into the Emulator.

The next morning, I sat there with a cup of tea on the ground floor of the house in Leytonstone and listened to what I'd done. I thought, *That actually sounds quite good.* However, there was still something missing. There was no chorus. I thought – *what's the hook?* The answer was that these kids were so young. *In Vietnam, he was nineteen.*

I tapped the sample, *In Vietnam, he was nineteen,* a few times on the keyboard with one finger, focusing on the number nineteen. As *Na-na-na-na-na nineteen* came out, I thought, *Fucking eureka! That's it. That's the chorus.* The other word I played with was *Destruction*, or *D-d-d-destruction*, as it was on the track. However, it was the two-second sample of '19', which told a story of the Vietnam War. I added some bass and sound effects on my Prophet 5 and one acoustic effect, which was a bell recorded backwards which accompanied the lyrics, *You're eighteen years old and you're wearing someone's brains on your shirt because they got their head blown off right next to you.*

I left it for about an hour and went and had some tea, then came back and had another listen and thought, *I need to add something to the chorus.* That's when I wrote the lyrics,

'All those who remember the war,
They won't forget what they've seen,
Destruction of men in their prime,
Whose average age was nineteen.

Over the next week, I asked someone to get me a vocalist to sing the lyrics and it just so happened it was my friend Lloyd's sister that I used to go to school with, but I never found that out until about fifteen years later. Her name was Janice Hoyte and I got her to sing the lyrics, which put some icing on the cake and then added these big orchestra stabs to make it sound more dynamic. That's basically how the track happened.

About a week later, I went over to see the Direct Drive guys who were preparing for a gig at a club in New Cross later that night and said, 'I've got a new track which I'm looking to release soon. I just need to find a record label that is interested. Do you want to listen to it?' At this stage, it was just a demo and more of an idea, but certainly nothing like the finished article. However, it gave a feel of where the track was going.

Pete said, 'Play it through the PA system.' I popped it on and when the track finished, there was a stunned silence from the band.

I thought, *Oh shit.*

Pete said, 'This is either going to be absolutely massive, or it's going to be a complete dud. It's a track where there can be no middle ground.'

As the year ended, a few things happened. I released my first track for Chrysalis Records' Cooltempo. The track was, 'Eat Your Heart Out' which featured vocals by Kevin Henry and topped out at No.59. In chart terms, it was like I was invisible in the UK. I even called up Gallup once when I was at No.41 for the second time and asked, 'Have you got something against dance music?' However, all was not lost because across the Atlantic something was stirring.

Profile Records had been pushing 'Rainforest' out to urban radio in America and in the first week of January 1985, the track hit No.4 on the Billboard Hot 100. Soon after, 'King Tut' was released, which hit the top 40. I also met my future wife, Dolores, on New Year's Eve 1984. Life was good and everything else was now a bonus.

In 1965, Vietnam seemed like just another foreign war,
but it wasn't
It was different in many ways, as so were those who did
the fighting
In World War II, the average age of the combat soldier
was twenty-six
In Vietnam, he was nineteen
In in in in in in in Vietnam, he was nineteen
In in in in in in in Vietnam, he was nineteen
In Vietnam, he was nineteen
N-n-n-n-nineteen
The heaviest fighting of the past two weeks
Continued today twenty-five miles northwest of Saigon
I really wasn't sure what was going on
N-n-n-n-nineteen, nineteen
N-nineteen, nineteen
In Vietnam, the combat soldier typically served a twelve-
month tour of duty.
But was exposed to hostile fire almost every day
N-n-n-n-nineteen
N-n-n-n-nineteen nineteen
In Saigon, a US military spokesman said today

*More than seven hundred enemy troops were killed last
week*
In that sensitive border area
In all of South Vietnam
*The enemy lost a total of two thousand six hundred
eighty-nine soldiers*
All those who remember the war
They won't forget what they've seen
Destruction of men in their prime
Whose average age was nineteen
D-d-d-d-d-destruction
D-d-d-d-d-destruction
According to a Veteran's Administration study
*Half of the Vietnam combat veterans suffered from what
psychiatrists call*
Post-traumatic stress disorder
Many vets complain of alienation, rage, or guilt
Some succumb to suicidal thoughts
Eight to ten years after coming home
Almost eight-hundred-thousand men
Are still fighting the Vietnam War
None of them received a hero's welcome
Nineteen
S-S-S-S-Saigon
Nineteen, n-n-n-n-n-ninteenN-n-n-n-n-ninteen
Nineteen n-n-n-n-n-ninteenN-n-n-n-n-ninteen, nineteen
Purple Heart, Saigon.

May 1985

Bradford City football club experiences the worst fire in English football history.

Michael Jordan named NBA Rookie of the Year.

Scientists of the British Antarctic Survey discovered the ozone hole.

Dire Straits, *Brothers in Arms* album is released and becomes the first CD to sell over one million copies.

Film premiere of the latest James Bond movie, *A View to a Kill.*

Britain agreed to return Hong Kong in 1997.

Paul Hardcastle releases a track originally entitled 'Vietnam'.

19

*I was working for Chrysalis Records and Simon Fuller –
whose 19 Entertainment would later launch the Spice
Girls – was a very young A&R (artists and repertoire)
guy, but we just got on. He wanted me to sit in on a
meeting. Right at the end, Paul said: "Oh, did you see
that documentary about Vietnam last week? I taped it and
have been messing about with it." He played us a very
rough version of 19. When I heard that N-n-n-nineteen
hook, I had a What the heck? Moment.
These were the early days of spoken-word sampling: the
general public had never heard anything like it. One of
the first people to get behind 19 was Tony Blackburn on
his Radio London show. He played it and the public went
mad for it. Not only did 19 sound unlike anything else on
the radio, it also told a story. But because it wasn't a
performance song with a band standing there, it needed a
video. So, I edited one from the documentary.
Our legal department had a nightmare getting clearance
for the samples; there were no precedents for something
like this. We ended up having to pay Peter Thomas, the
narrator, royalties. Paul was off doing more mixes of the
song to keep the interest in it high, too – and the public
wanted every version. It was amazing.*

At the time, Madonna's 'Like a Virgin', was out and was produced by Warner Brothers, but with Chrysalis involvement. Unbeknown to me, I'd pushed Madonna off the No.1 spot in America on their 12" sales chart with 'Rainforest' and Chrysalis obviously thought, 'Who the fuck is this guy who's knocked our award-winning artist off the top spot?' I was soon to receive a call that would change the rest of my life.

From the time I watched Vietnam Requiem to the time I had a demo track ready, was about two weeks. Then, about three weeks later, in early January 1985, I got a call out of the blue from a twenty-three-year-old A&R guy called Simon. I didn't know who he was and until 'Rainforest', he didn't know who I was.

He said, 'Hi. Is that Paul?'

I said, 'Yeah. Who's that?'

He replied, 'My name's Simon Fuller and I work for the publishing department of Chrysalis. Congratulations on reaching No.1 on the 12" sales chart. This 'Rainforest' track is absolutely blowing up in America.'

I'm thinking, *How's that possible? It tanked out at No.41 in the UK pop charts.* To me, it was a nice little melody over a dancey backing track, which had everybody popping to it, but never in my wildest dreams did I think it

118

had the legs to take out Madonna. You also have to remember I was a complete nobody at this point. Simon continued. 'I have to tell you; I signed the writers of that track by Madonna!' Then we both laughed. I liked his tone and the way he spoke and then he said, 'We'd like you to come over and meet us at Chrysalis. Maybe we could work together. Also, if you have anything else in the pipeline, bring that with you.'

I said, 'Sounds good. I'm working on something at the moment, which is very different. You may like it, then again, maybe not. I'll bring it over.'

A couple of days later, I went over to their office at Stratford Place, Central London and walked into a room where there were about fifteen people, including Simon, Roy Eldridge, Stuart Slater, Ken Grunbaum, who was head of promotions at Chrysalis, Chris Wright and Doug Darcy. Basically, all the big wigs that made the decisions. I only had a few chats with Chris, but he seemed like a nice enough guy and just let the hierarchy do their jobs. Between Chris Wright and Doug Ellis, they created the name of the company – Chris-Ellis…Chrysalis.

They didn't know much about me at all and they asked, 'what other stuff do you do?'

I told them, 'I've got a track called 'King Tut', which is a bit like 'Rainforest' and is in the chart in America at the moment.'

They then asked, 'And after that?'

I replied, 'I'm working on one song which is very different to what has previously been heard.'

They said, 'Really? Can you play us a bit?'

I said, 'Sure. I've got the demo right here. The track is called *Vietnam*.'

At the time, electro-dance music and anything politically charged was a no-no, with the likes of Radio 1 not even considering touching dance music, so you can imagine how quickly everyone started rolling their eyes and wanted to get out of the room after I'd played the demo. They thought I was crazy. As if a record with death and destruction was going to get any play. I never considered scrapping it, even though a few people at the label said, 'Are you sure you want this track to go out as your first release on a major label?' which, in a roundabout way, was saying, 'Don't do it!'

As everyone left the room, you had that whole thing of, 'Thank you very much. We'll be in contact soon,' and all that crap, which made me doubt myself for about twenty seconds, then I thought, *Bollocks to them. I'm doing it no matter what anyone says and if it's not with them, it will be with someone else.* That was also a great lesson for the future for me not listen to anyone and go with my passion.

The only two left in the room were Ken and Simon, who were both on the same wavelength. We get chatting and about twenty minutes into this conversation, Simon said, 'I'm not sure if these guys get it. It's a great track and great idea. The industry needs something different and this could be it.'

Ken, similar to my old mate Pete from Direct Drive said, 'I'm not sure if I get it, to be honest. It's either going to be one of the biggest records of the year, or it will drop like a lead balloon.'

Ken left the room, then me and Simon got talking. That's when he asked, 'What about I leave my job and become your manager?'

I replied, 'What does a manager do?'

He replied, 'I just take all the shit for you.'

I thought, *He's honest and funny and we got on very well.*

I replied, 'OK. Let's do it!' From that day onwards, Simon became my manager and we developed a lifelong friendship far beyond business. I never had a contract with Simon; it was based on trust and a handshake. I was his first-ever artist and consequently, he named his company, '19 Management'. He has gone on to become the biggest and most successful manager in the world, with clients such as The Spice Girls and Annie Lennox, not to mention being the creator of *Pop Idol* and *American Idol*.

Despite the naysayers, Chrysalis signed me up and gave me an advance for my first album, entitled *Paul Hardcastle,* which included the tracks '19' and 'Rainforest'. I bought a new telly and a Sony Video Hi8 recorder, which was one of the first smallish cameras, not like the big VHS ones, which weighed a ton and you needed to be a bodybuilder to carry it around. I remember being in a cab and seeing it in a shop in Tottenham Court Road, then asking the cab driver to stop, as I jumped out, ran into the shop and bought it. I was also aware that I might not get another advance like that for a while, perhaps never again, as I had no idea what the future held or how well the track or album would do.

The intention was to release the *track* as quickly as possible in February 1985. That was the plan until Debbie Cochran, who was in charge of sales at Chrysalis, came up with a better plan and said we should delay it until the beginning of May to coincide with the tenth anniversary of the end of the Vietnam War. I wasn't so clued up, but Simon was and had a meeting with the powers that be and had it put back until May. What a difference that made. We also had a name change of the track. I'd originally called it 'Vietnam', but Simon pointed out the chorus hook is what everyone will remember and he tentatively suggested calling it '19', which turned out to be a great suggestion. The News at Ten said, *It's the tenth anniversary of the Vietnam War and this has inspired a record by a young man called Paul Hardcastle. Controversial or not, it looks likely to be a big hit.*

It snowballed really quickly from there. Even the people in the room who thought the track was crap now thought it was great. The music and entertainment industry can be a very fickle business. With the track in place, we now needed a video really quickly, which is when we called the producers who made the original programme and asked them to create a video for the track.

Chrysalis were producing music which people could dance to, most of it feel-good tracks and there's me talking about nineteen-year-olds having their heads blown off or being covered in brains from someone else's head who'd been shot or blown up next to them. As a result, the video came with a *Warning. This video contains...* blah, blah, blah, which left many with a look of bemusement and shock and horror on their faces because of the message it conveyed and also by chucking war in their faces and the realities that came with it. I remember going to Chrysalis to see the video and seeing three journalists coming out crying. I thought, *Wow. What have we created here.*

Ken asked me to do something for the B side, just in case the A side tanked, which I did. The track was called 'Fly By Night', but it wasn't needed because '19' far from tanked. At the time, Charlie Gillet was a DJ at Capital Radio and they had received a 12" white label copy as advanced promotion. When he played it, someone else who was a daytime DJ heard it and played it the next day. The next DJ who heard it did the same thing and it was like passing a baton in a relay. After each DJ heard the track, they wanted to play it and we soon started getting calls from all around the world saying they wanted the record.

Shortly after '19' was released, I headed over to LA with Simon to make a video for the 'King Tut' track. When we boarded that plane at Heathrow, Simon said to the stewardess, 'This is Paul Hardcastle. You might not know him, but he's going places. He's just gone in at No.4 in the chart today.' We recorded 'King Tut' with Profile Records, then after four days we headed back to Chrysalis head office in London, swiftly followed by a trip to Newcastle the morning after to do some interviews for television and radio, including Metro, which was like Capital Radio to London.

Going in at No.4 was almost unheard of at the time. No.3 was 'Tears for Fears', 'Everybody Wants to Rule the World'; in second place was 'USA for Africa', 'We Are the World' and No.1 was Phyllis Nelson with 'Move Closer'. However, we now had that big hurdle of selling a crazy amount of records to climb higher for the week after. The chart came in at different times of the day, which meant it could be ten a.m., midday or one p.m. After having done our media commitments in Newcastle, we flew back to Heathrow in the morning with no concrete news about the chart. The fact is, Chrysalis had been given the chart position, but because we were in the air, we had no way of finding out.

When we landed in London, there was a guy called Mike, who worked in promotions and he phoned up Chrysalis on a pay phone at Heathrow to find out the chart position. We were looking over in anticipation, then after about ten seconds, I saw this massive smile come across his face and he looked over at me and put his index finger up to say, 'No.1.' That's a moment I'll never forget. We stayed at the top spot for five weeks in the UK and within a matter of weeks from its release, we were No.1 in thirteen different countries. The track eventually sold over eight million copies worldwide and I think it became a hit because it was so different. It talked about a very touchy subject of war and was right in people's faces instead of trying to be cute about it.

I was obviously over the moon with the success but was also very happy for everyone who had helped me arrive in the position. For Simon, as a first-time manager, having a No.1 record that sold millions of copies in a matter of weeks with his first artist, enabled him to get into an office and also gave him the money to help set him up. It didn't make him rich; it made him comfortable. From there on, his reputation grew and the rest is history.

When I got home, my answerphone was full up with some lovely messages congratulating me, telling me they were proud of me. All sorts of people, from school friends, ex-girlfriends, old band members and even my next-door neighbour, whom I'd known for about seven years, came knocking on my door asking for my autograph, which I was a bit taken aback by. One of my fondest memories was going into Barclays bank where my mum worked and she was very proud to show me off to all her friends and colleagues. Same as my dad.

My life changed very, very quickly. As I said, the track was No.1 in the pop charts in thirteen countries. However, America was not one of them. The LA Times wrote on 8 June 1985, *As soon as 19 began getting airplay, it became the target of attack on two fronts. In this country, some listeners argued that the mix of message and disco music trivialises the Vietnam veterans' situation, while liberal observers in Britain maintained that the record glorifies the wrong victims of the war.*

The only reason it didn't get to No.1 in America is because they based their chart on two things– radio play and sales. About five or six radio stations took the track the wrong way and some DJs thought it was anti-America, so they wouldn't play it. However, sales-wise, it should have been No.1 on their pop chart for at least three weeks. Charlie told me, 'You must be so frustrated because these people (the DJs) have got it wrong.' What the American press selectively failed to report at the time was that I had some fantastic letters from Vietnam veterans. Around two thousand, in fact. The Vietnam vets also informed me in the coming years that they used '19' on their annual march through Washington.

I even received a letter from the editor of The Wall Street Journal thanking me for making the record. I received thousands of letters from the general public in America and the big question they had was, 'Why and how has a young Brit got involved in this?' I didn't know everything about the Vietnam War apart from what I'd seen on *Vietnam Requiem* and the fact that these soldiers were very young, got spat at when they came home and many became homeless. Hence, 'None of them received a hero's welcome.'

Many said to me, 'Thank you for keeping our name alive.'

***

Of the thirteen countries where the track was No.1, I'd only ever visited three of them, which were Germany, France and the UK, not to mention all the other countries where the track broke into the Top 10. It soon became obvious that people didn't care where the music came from in order to play it in their country. I could have been a frog on heat from another planet and they would have still turned up.

We soon remade the track in five other languages, which included Spanish, German, French, Italian and Japanese. Alvin Clark from the Sound Suite Studios in Camden (who we called Jeff by now because he looked a bit like Jeff Beck) was a massive help with the remixes. We got famous newscasters and people off the TV to do the voiceovers for each country and had to have translators to check the words were in the right place and had the same meaning. At the time, it was fun, but I'd never do anything like that again because it was a long, laborious task. It's the only track I've ever done in other languages, but it worked because it sold a lot of records in their own countries. Funnily enough though, the English version sold more in France than the French version, as it did in Germany also.

As sales kept going through the roof, Michael Hurll, the producer at Top of the Pops, kept saying, 'Do you not think you could do something on the show?'

I sat down with Simon and said, 'Let's be honest. I can do interviews until they're coming out of my head, but trying to do the track live will look rubbish. I'm not featured in the video; I don't sing and as they say, *It's all in the mix.* It's just going to be me there tapping on a keyboard, which will look crap. There's no point.'

Harold Faltermeyer did the Axel F tune from *Beverly Hills Cop* in 1985 live on stage on Top of The Pops and it went down like a lead balloon. It would have been the same for me. Simon agreed. A keyboard player tapping away is boring to look at as opposed to a drummer, guitarist, or vocalist. That's why I was already working on loads of other tracks before '19' because I knew I wouldn't need to allocate that time to go on stage.

About a week after '19' took over the No.1 spot on the pop charts, Duran Duran released their film track, 'A View to A Kill'. This is where I really started to appreciate the value of the whole remixing thing. You have to remember I'd come out of nowhere and you've got possibly the biggest band in the world at the time, who have a single from the latest James Bond movie. That should have obliterated me. I thought, *Let's add some vocals and some new documentary footage and play around with it. What's the worst that can happen?* I did the first mix of '19', then I did the Destruction mix, which had different words to it, but it was still under the same catalogue number. About another one hundred and fifty-thousand people went out and bought it and that kept me above Duran Duran. Every time we released a new mix, we also did a new video, which I worked on with Ken Grunbaum. Some of the times it was just about changing all the colours and starting it off in a different place, that sort of thing, but on the fourth week of being No.1, Ken said, 'We can't hold this place much longer because the film is coming out.'

I thought, *The only thing a remix is supposed to do is enhance the track. Fuck it. Get back in the studio and start enhancing.* I did '19 The Final Story', which rocketed again, because people knew it was the last mix (for that moment!) and boom, the sales rocketed again and they couldn't overtake me. Each week, a different edit went on Top of the Pops and Duran Duran ended up staying at No.2 for three weeks before sliding down the charts.

After five weeks at No.1 in the UK, The Crowd released their charity record for the Bradford stadium fire, which was a rerecording of 'You'll Never Walk Alone' and they knocked me off the top. I was happier that track knocked me off than Duran Duran because it served a good purpose for the victims of a horrible disaster.

Although 19's time at the top had run its course in the UK, it was still holding top spot in a number of countries, not to mention provided a comical opportunity that arose a couple of months down the line.

August 1985

David Gower scores his 5000th run in Test cricket.

Michael Jackson buys ATV Music for $47.5 million.

The first UK lung transplant carried out in Harefield hospital.

The Sinclair C5 ceases production after seven months.

Rory Bremner does a spoof of '19'.

Frank Hitachi

It was an unforgettable summer because I was breaking into comedy and suddenly had this top 20 hit and Paul was incredibly supportive and generous to let us do it, which is quite rare because he could have easily been very protective and said no about this record which mattered so much to him. Instead, he let us come in and take the piss with this inspired nonsense. I'm so grateful to Paul.

Rory Bremner

At the time, I'd never met Rory, although I knew of him and had seen him on telly as he was already making waves on the impressions and stand-up circuit, even though he'd only left university the year before. He was on the Wogan shows that they were doing in those days and was also doing stuff for Capital Radio with John Sachs, son of Andrew Sachs, who was Manuel in Fawlty Towers. John was a DJ on Capital and his show, Sachs in the Afternoon, had a massive following. Rory had done the voiceovers for various jingles and one-liners at Capital, when one day, an idea popped into his head and he told John about it. John was immediately on board and said, 'Let's do this.' That's when they approached me with the request to make The Commentators, 'Na-Na-Na-Nineteen Not Out.'

The track was based on the England cricket team's terrible performance against the West Indies the previous summer in 1984, but in all honesty, I didn't know much about cricket and still don't, if truth be told. The record company said, 'It's going to look really bad if you've just made one of the most serious records and then you're making fun of it.'

I said, 'Listen. If I can't take the piss out of myself, I'll stop doing music. Let's just have a bit of fun.'

We hooked up Rory with Charlie Gillett and next thing he knew, he was in a studio with John Langdon, Simon's brother Kim and Charlie overseeing them. I'd said a quick hello to Rory at the beginning, but I was mainly behind the glass while they were getting on with it. Kim was a top-established comedy writer, having written with Lenny Henry for a great deal of his career and he wrote loads for Jasper Carrott's show and Ben Elton. It was a culmination of Kim's writing, Rory's thoughts and John Langdon's stuff in the studio that led to the track evolving, with lyrics like,

'They fought the most disastrous series in test history.

In 1984, the test series against the West Indies seemed like just another runner. But it wasn't, it was different in many ways. And so were those who did the batting. In 1933, the England captain's average was 35. In 1984, it was nineteen. Na-Na-Na-Nineteen, Nineteen.'

It was Charlie's idea to call them 'The Commentators', as opposed to doing it under Rory's own name because he envisaged them doing a few more tracks due to one of Rory's strengths being able to do numerous impressions of sports commentators. Unfortunately, that never happened and Rory still regrets that they didn't do the follow-up of a cricket version of MC Hammer's 'You Can't Touch This,' calling it MCC Hammer, showing endless footage of England players unable to get a bat on the delivery from these fast bowlers. I did all the backing track, used different chords, baseline, all that kind of stuff, but kept it sounding similar to '19'. It was a pop record, but the intention was always to make it as funny as possible.

Rory had never recorded a track before and the studio director was getting a little bit frustrated and starting to say, 'We need to get this right soon; otherwise, we won't be able to do it.' Rory had autocue, but he really had to go into sixth gear and nail it on the fourth and last take, which he did.

Once I had Rory's voice sorted, I called Helen Rogers and asked if she could do the backing vocals and she agreed to sing lines like,

'All those who've forgotten the score
They still remember the team
Destruction, they got bodyline
The captains name was Jardine.'

I got on with Helen really well and over the years, we've had so much fun being involved in so many diverse projects and sessions. What made this one a little bit more memorable was that Helen was eight months pregnant. As it was a cricket song, when Rory was being interviewed, he kept making comments about Helen's up-and-coming 'delivery'.

Once the track had been recorded, we did the Wogan Show and also Top of the Pops, which was funny. With Helen being so heavily pregnant, she had to sit down and wear a white cricket umpire's coat to cover her bump up. She still teases her son to this day that the first time he was on TV was on Top of the Pops before he was even born.

As far as Rory goes, this was his first experience of the world of A&R, record promoting, ending up on Top of the Pops and all the rest of it. He absolutely loved it and really got into it. He dug out his old Wellingtonian cricket sweater, pads and stuff like that and despite the song being complicated because he had to jump between all kinds of different commentators singing and interjecting in the dialogue, he did brilliantly. Rory was absolutely made up when he got a call from his agent who said, 'We made it in the top 20! The track hit No.13 on the pop charts.'

Very few people actually knew that I was involved in the track due to me intentionally keeping a low profile. If you look up the record, it will be under an alias of Frank Hitachi, simply because I'd done about fifteen remixes of the track at this point and didn't want to plonk my name all over it because I thought people would be bored of hearing another version of the track. Most importantly, though, I didn't want to take away the focus from Rory.

Within literally a few months of '19', Simon had relocated and re-established himself. He moved to a one-room office in Putney on Disraeli Road with Terry Hall as his secretary, which had a desk for each of them and two '19' posters on the wall. That was it. I could just about squeeze into the room with the both of them there, but that didn't matter because there was always such a good vibe whenever I went over. By the time of the Rory Bremner record, Simon had become a very astute business manager, making great moves for his clients but still protecting them by brokering the right deals, like the one he did with Chrysalis for me. However – one thing we can't always accurately predict or protect people from is the knock-on effects of fame. That's a lesson I had to learn by myself.

Time Jump – November 1971

Play Misty for Me premieres in America.

Billy Joel releases *Cold Spring Harbor* album.

Spaghetti Junction interchange was opened in
Birmingham, UK.

Paul Hardcastle unknowingly stars in a Marc Bolan film.

Cost of Fame

"I honestly feel it could all end tomorrow. Not just the
band thing – I mean life."

Marc Bolan

Would I have imagined the success that followed '19'? Not
really. Did it change my life? Immensely.

The speed it all happened was frightening and I had a
lot of those 'Really?' moments. I remember going to the
massive HMV on Bond Street to do promo, which was
very close to Chrysalis office on Stratford Place and not
everyone recognised me when I walked in, which was
great as I was able to stand back to an extent and watch
this madness unfold. What struck me was how many
copies of '19' I saw on every single rack and people
walking past me picking them up nonstop and joining
these crazy long queues to pay. As I made my way to the
table to start the signing, one of the HMV staff said to me,
'Do you know you're outselling Frankie Goes to
Hollywood?' I thought he was taking the piss, but that
quickly changed as this queue of people waiting to get
their copy of '19' signed kept getting longer and longer
until I couldn't see the end of it. I wish I had my video

camera with me to have filmed from the moment I walked in because that was a moment I'd never forget.

As the record sold more and more in the coming weeks, I started getting invited to countless parties, some of which were face-showing exercises, some were networking and others just a chance to drink loads of champagne. One time at Stringfellows, me and the drummer, John Keeble, out of Spandau, had a disagreement. We got into this conversation about why I didn't use real drums in my music and I said something like, 'Because I want it to be in time.' I was trying to be semi-funny, but it obviously didn't go down too well. I wasn't trying to be a dick because I agree with a lot of what John was saying in terms of live drumming, but '19' would not have suited a live drummer because it needed that mechanical side of things in terms of delivery. Simon was there and his head dropped, but you could see him sniggering.

It couldn't have been easy for my girlfriend Dolores because every time we'd go out, people would constantly come up to me. I probably could have done a little bit better when we were out and I maybe should have introduced her to people more when that happened, but when it was people from the industry who you might be making or producing a record with, I kind of got into business mode. In the first three months that followed '19', the energy was incredible and I'd go to the opening of a letter, especially to anyone who had helped me out along the way, such as Simon, Tony Blackburn and Walshy.

When the track first hit the scene, Blackburn said, 'I predict this could be a No.1.' He was always giving me airtime when he could.

In return, I'd attend anything he asked me to, like the Radio London Soul Night Out, which was with Steve Walsh, then, when Walshy asked, 'Paul. Can you come on stage at the Lyceum and say hello to everyone?'

I instantly said, 'Yeah! No problem.'

Then it was, 'Paul. Can you cut the ribbon our new supermarket?'

'Yeah! Of course.' These are the people who smacked me up to No.1 and they're going to be the people turning up to these events. I made myself available, no matter what.

At the time, Simon's dad was a headmaster at a school in East Sussex and I was asked to go down to the school to meet the kids at this big school fete and do a little speech. We drove down to Hastings in two really nice cars with chauffeurs which Simon had hired. One with Simon and my mate Pete inside and I was in the other with my dog, Rocky, the rottweiler, who would later feature in the video 'The Wizard.' There we were, getting close to this school, going down these country lanes and we hit a little traffic jam. Pete's looked back and saw I was standing in the car through the sunroof bit, with half of my body out. As Pete was laughing, I then thought it would be a sensible thing to climb out and stand on top of the car with a bottle of champagne in my hand. God knows what Rocky was thinking.

As the car came to a standstill, I jumped off, still holding the champagne and walked down the road with Rocky, with a load of parked cars looking at us, thinking, *Who's this idiot?* Simon didn't mind my antics, but he wasn't happy that I brought Rocky because his hair was left all over the car and he had to have it professionally cleaned after.

***

There's an old saying, *Where there's a hit, there's a writ.* Whatever you do in life, when people get wind of the fact you're making a few quid, you'll always find people looking for a cut. There are some who I was more than delighted that they'd made a few quid off the success of my music because they'd supported me even before the money had initially come in, such as Simon or Charlie Gillett.

After I'd split up with Derek and First Light came to an end, Charlie still remained my publisher as we had a six-year contract. I didn't begrudge Charlie one bit getting his cut of the royalties because he always had the faith in me long before I was earning any big money and he handed me an advance for the TEAC 8-track recorder to reel in the early days with no guarantee he'd ever make that money back. I do, however, think he got his money back for that advance about a hundred times over because he went onto publish 'Rainforest' and '19', which made him a nice box of cash. If I had borrowed the money for the 8-track, I may have been a hell of a lot richer, but he took the risk and my music may very well have never made the advance back and it would have been purely him who would have been out of pocket. Same as Simon and paying him his percentage. They both worked really hard in terms of paving my career and making it as good as possible, but most importantly, they believed in me. However, there were a whole bunch of others who suddenly surfaced which came from a different angle.

The whole suing thing is typical, but if '19' hadn't been a multi-platinum hit, nobody would have bothered. When it comes to sampling, it's quite simple. As everyone now knows, every time you use someone's material or they use your material, there's a cost involved. Otherwise, you leave yourself open to be sued. How much you pay depends on how long the sample is, how often it is played and who it belongs to.

As the numbers stacked up, I had Mike Oldfield weighing in because he felt there was one bit in the riff that sounded like his track 'Tubular Bells', which he based on the first three notes. We had a musicologist who came down and said, 'This is just the way Paul writes.'

My barrister said, 'The track is doing really well at the moment. You don't need this hanging over your head. Just give him a percentage.' In the end, we settled out of court.

The other person was Peter Thomas, the narrator from *Vietnam Requiem*. Chrysalis lawyers had dealt with all the legal stuff with '19' beforehand but obviously hadn't gone through it thoroughly enough because Peter had a point where his legal people said, 'You never agreed for it to be on a record.' He had a smart lawyer to have spotted that loophole because he became a rich man off that and ended up getting an extra three per cent.

Their angle was, 'The track could destroy Peter's career.' What a load of bollocks. I knew I was going to be doing more albums, so I agreed to it. On the first album, I took off the riff, which Mike Oldfield wasn't happy about and also took Peter Thomas off. I got Clarke Peters, who's a very well-known actor with a great voice, to become the voice on the album version of '19'.

Everybody wanted a piece of the pie. We used a sample of one of the guys from Sound Suite in Camden screaming and even he was joking that he was going to sue because his voice sounded like a woman screaming by the time we'd finished with it.

However, I'd be a complete hypocrite though if I didn't say I cash in on opportunities that came my way. Many years later, U2 were doing a gig and Bono made a reference to some lad who looked nineteen and said, 'Na-na-na-nineteen.' Just once. One of my advisors gave me a call to let me know and I ended up getting over ten grand for it.

***

As I've mentioned before, the music industry can be very fickle and when fame hit, that really surfaced. Here's an example. Back in early 1985, I was living in Leytonstone with my girlfriend and we were thinking of buying somewhere a bit bigger. We looked at places that were out of our reach, one in particular on The Avenue in Wanstead. When we walked into the estate agency, the guy in there hardly even looked up. As he was reading some magazines, he said, 'Here's a leaflet on the place.' I asked about mortgages and he was very dismissive.

He said, 'I'd go and find yourself a mortgage broker.' He completely blanked us.

Over the next six weeks, '19' came out and I said to my girlfriend, 'I wonder if that house is still available?' At this point, I didn't know if I could afford it because I had no idea about the net royalties from '19', but we walked back to the same estate agent and talk about dickheads and hypocrisy. As I've walked in, the same guy has looked up, then done a double-take. He quickly jumped up out of his seat and said, 'Are you Paul Hardcastle?'

I said, 'Yeah.'

He said, all jolly with a big smile on his face, 'Please take a seat! Can I get you a drink? Tea, coffee, water?'

I replied, 'You know, I'm the same bloke that you neigh on kicked out six weeks ago.'

He starts to backtrack and grovel, saying, 'I'm really sorry. I was so busy that day.'

The excuses were pitiful. 'Had too much to drink, the cat died.' Whatever.

Jumping forward about eighteen months, we needed to move again because I was using one of the bedrooms for my own working space, which kept my girlfriend up because I worked through the night. Basically, the house was too small. It probably also didn't help that I'd leap out of bed with an idea in the middle of the night and then started recorded it, but that was my job. Either way, I knew it was time to move again.

One day, in 1987, I was out for a drive in the countryside near Ongar and saw somewhere that was half finished. It said outside, 'Viewing via appointment only.'

I turned the car around and drove into the driveway and this guy said, 'Did you not see the sign? Appointment only.'

I said, 'I'm really sorry, I just thought, while I'm here, I could take a little look?'

He said, 'No.'

His son just happened to come to the back door and he's looked at me with a look of shock, his eyes wide open. By now, his dad had disappeared and the son had run off to find him. A minute later, the dad says, 'Well, errrrr, as you've come out this far, you're more than welcome to take a look around if you think you might be interested.' It had a massive garden, which enabled me to build a studio at the back and it looked perfect. However, I had no idea of my financial situation at that point and called my accountant.

I asked, 'Would I be able to afford this mortgage?'

He asked Simon to send him over the sales figures and he came back to me and said, 'Yes, you can take on this mortgage.' I went back in, bought the house and still live in it to this very day.

When I bought the place in Wanstead back in 1985, I told the estate agent, please don't say who's bought the place, but a week later, it was in the Wanstead Gazette on the front page. *Paul Hardcastle moves to so and so place.* I asked the same when I bought the place in 1987 and again, the guy who showed me around ignored me. As a result, every fan from the local area was knocking on the door. After that, that's when I decided I wasn't a fan of fame. You simply can't turn it off. Your life changes beyond all recognition. You are no longer you. You're everyone's. The goldfish bowl syndrome as I call it. I remember going to a Michael Jackson concert and I tried to disguise myself with glasses and a hat and this guy in the queue next to me said, 'If you're trying to disguise yourself, Hardcastle, you need to do fucking better than that!'

However, many people weren't as bold as that. Instead, they would just stare at you. I wish people would just come up and say, 'Paul. Can you sign this', or whatever? But most of the time, they just stared, then looked away. I developed a second sense after a while and I'd go out to a restaurant and just from the walk from the door to the table, I'd already worked out who was going to stare and who was going to come over and ask for something. It's like a double take, then their head goes back down and all of a sudden, they have a chat and tell the other person and their head turns.

Once, I was in Iceland supermarket doing a bit of shopping and the manager started following me and then he started talking to the staff and pointing over to me. It got to a stage when I saw his badge, which said *Jason* on it and I thought, *This is getting boring now.*

So, I went up to him and said, 'Jason! How you doing, mate? Haven't seen you in ages. Where have you been?' He almost fell over, but in the meantime, the other staff were well impressed with him, although he looked uncomfortable as hell and bemused. I just wanted to break that uncomfortable silence and mooching about.

On the flip side of the coin, you had fans who were far from silent, especially when everyone else was. Having teenage kids banging on my door at three a.m., asking for autographs while body popping outside became a regular thing for the next year. And you know what? I was happy to go out and sign what they wanted and felt a big debt of gratitude to everyone who bought it. What was I going to do? Come out of the house telling them all to fuck off? No. Having a load of people body popping in the middle of the night and asking for autographs was the ultimate compliment. It was a sincere pleasure. Albeit, in the daytime, it would have been nicer!

***

Turning kids away would have made me the biggest hypocrite because I did exactly the same at that age. I'm a massive Marc Bolan fan and I can reel off all his lyrics if you asked me to. I used to go to school in Edgware Road and Marc Bolan lived in a house just by Maida Vale in

Clarendon Gardens. At the time, I had that job working in Gough Brothers off-licence on the Marylebone Road, while my mate Eric worked across the road at Peter Dominic. We used to do drop-off deliveries of wine and spirits to people on these pushbikes with the metal baskets at the front of them, which was like the Deliveroo of the 1970s. The perk of the job was that we were allowed to keep the bikes at the weekend, which meant me and Eric would be pedalling all over town.

One day, towards the end of 1971, we're on these bikes and I said to Eric, 'Let's go and see if Bolan's around,' as we were both massive fans. At the time, one of our other mates, whose dad was a policeman, used to have a flat a few minutes away from where Bolan used to live and he would quite often spot him in the mornings. There would be girls hiding in Bolan's dustbins, trying to nick anything whatsoever that he might have made contact with.

For me, just to get a glimpse of the guy was a big thing. We went over about one p.m. and we noticed this van turning up outside his house. As it stopped, we noticed it was the whole T-Rex band, minus Bolan. Next thing, they loaded it up with kit and then Marc came out and got in his white Rolls Royce, number plate TOF262, with his wife June behind the wheel. He couldn't drive it because he'd never learnt to drive and had no intention to because he was worried, he'd die in a car accident. How's that for a premonition? Anyway – everyone took off and we followed them. We went from Maida Vale right down the

Edgware Road to Marble Arch through all this rush hour traffic, which helped; otherwise, we couldn't have kept up on our push bikes. Eventually, the car pulled up into Tachbrook Street, round the corner from the area I grew up and we kept on following until next thing they stopped, about a quarter of a mile from where I was brought up in St George's Square.

Bolan and his missus got out and went down in this basement and they all started practising in this rehearsal room. They were rehearsing for a gig, but we couldn't hear anything because the room was all padded. Mickey Finn, who played the congas, had his motorbike parked outside on the ground floor level. After a bit, Eric went over to it and thought, *I'll have a sit down on that.* He'd literally parked his arse on it and Mickey came out and grabbed him by his collars, telling him in no uncertain terms to piss off. Then, about an hour later, Bolan came out with a little cine camera and as he was walking up the stairs, he started filming us. There were about twenty people outside by now and as he came out, we were all hanging over the railing and looking down. He films for a few seconds and then, bang, he was gone. We waited around for about an hour longer, hoping he would come out again, but it eventually fizzled out and we made our own way home.

At the time, we all thought his camera episode was just a gimmick and he was just having a laugh, but that changed when we went to see Born to Boogie at Clapton Pond Cinema in Hackney about a year later. As the credits went past quickly at the end of the film, all of a sudden, the screen split into little screens showing different people at the same time shot through a cine camera. I had one of those moments of, *That looked like me. It couldn't have been though, could it?*

At the time, me and Eric had both bought the same cameras from Cooks in Praed Street, which cost us about eight quid. It was known as a fixed focus cine with no zoom capability. We used to take our cameras to school and had these staged fights in the playground, which used to very often get out of hand and we'd have to call a stop to them. Then, when the teachers found out what we were playing at, they took our cameras away. Back to Born to Boogie. About a week later, I had an idea to watch the film again but to bring my cine camera into the cinema in the hope I could film the bit at the end, but unfortunately, it was too fuzzy. It was only when the DVD came out and I saw the film about twenty years later that I spotted myself with my black tank top on and my curly hair waving to Marc Bolan. I was finally able to say, 'Yes! It knew it was me!'

Eric, on the other hand, wasn't as excited. In his own words, 'I got filmed and Paul got filmed, but Paul got about three seconds in the film and I got bugger all.' However, my next track's title was far from being about bugger all. It was all about the money.

October 1985

Alain Prost wins his first Formula One World Championship.

Lynette Woodward becomes the first woman to be chosen for the Harlem Globetrotters.

Little Richard is seriously injured in a car accident in Los Angeles.

Intel introduces 32-bit 80386 microcomputer chip.

Production of the Peugeot 309 begins at the Ryton car factory.

Paul Hardcastle makes Just for Money with Lord Laurence Olivier and Bob Hoskins.

12-Incher

Paul Hardcastle has pulled off an artistic coup by persuading Lord Laurence Olivier to perform on his new single.

The London Standard, 16 October 1985

My recording studio at home originally started with a pair of cassette decks, but by 1985, it was now made up of a twenty-four-track Aces desk, a Yamaha R1000 reverb unit, a Roland TR808 for drums and a load of synthesisers, including a Roland Jupiter 8, Mini Moog, Emulator II, a Linn and the Prophet-5, which I still have. Once I had the tracks in decent shape, I'd take them down to the Sound Suite studios in Camden, which is exactly what happened with my next tune.

After '19', I wanted to do a track which had an edge to it and to give people a reason to talk about it. However, like '19', I wanted people to be able to dance to it and appreciate the story at the same time. Everyone was giving me advice and my head was exploding. I must have tried twenty different ideas and in the end, I thought, *What interests me?* I was fascinated with *The Great Train Robbery* in terms of the plot and how they actioned it, but it was also an event the public knew at the time and has since gone on to become firmly ingrained in British folklore. It was technically the perfect crime because the notes they stole were on their way to being incinerated, which meant they couldn't be traced. To do that under the noses of the authorities generated them a lot of respect by many people, not for the crime, but how it was masterminded. Another point of interest to me was *The St Valentine's Day Massacre* and I thought the two crimes were a good contrast because one was a bloodbath and the other was pretty much claret free, apart from the poor train driver, Jack Mills, who got hit over the head with a metal bar and suffered major head injuries.

I went and saw Simon and said, 'My next track is going to be about *The Great Train Robbery* and *The St Valentine's Day Massacre.*' He looked at me a bit strangely, but after we talked it through, he liked the idea, but we both agreed we needed someone on it that was going to make the newspapers go, *Fucking 'ell.*

I said, 'I need someone to open it up. A narrator with a very well-known British voice, but a massive name in entertainment that will generate loads of press.'

I think he was even kidding himself when he said, 'What about Laurence Olivier?' As crazy a suggestion as it was, somehow, he managed to track him down.

I didn't know much about Lord Olivier, but I read up on him and he was supposed to be our best-ever actor in the UK. He was a huge name. I went to his house in Chelsea for the first talk and it was his daughter, Julie Kate, who told him about '19', because he'd never heard about it and understandably so. Why would an eighty-year-old man have an interest in a pop chart? Julie Kate was a big fan of the track and she convinced her dad that he should be on the Just for Money single.

Simon called me up the day after and said, 'Have a guess what?'

I said, 'Go on.'

He replied, 'Laurence Oliver has agreed to be on the record.' To say I was happy was an understatement. Lord Olivier wasn't cheap, but it wasn't about the money for him because he'd got to a stage in his life where he was only picking a handful of projects to engage in and ones which he saw the merits in. Thankfully, he thought this was one of them, which said a lot, especially as he'd never been on a record before.

The first time we went to meet Lord Laurence to record, we had to change the date and venue because he wasn't very well and we couldn't get him up the stairs to the studio because they didn't have a lift. Then, one day, we both happened to be near Newcastle and that's where we managed to record him. The whole experience was so surreal. He told us some great stories, like when he was working with Marylyn Munroe and one of her boobs half came out as he was talking and she went, 'Sorry, people.'

Everybody turned to her and said, 'We never noticed,' because everyone was listening to Laurence. That shows the presence of the man!

Now, I wanted Bob Hoskins to be in it. Bob had done films like *The Long Good Friday*, which was actually the film that made me think he'd be great for this video. Simon contacted Bob and then I managed to have a chat with him at his house, which, again, was very surreal. I said, 'Bob. We're doing a track about *The Great Train Robbery* and *The St Valentine's Day Massacre.* A gangster sort of record.'

He said with that growly Cockney voice, 'What do you need? Do you want real gangsters in it?'

I said, 'No. I want you.'

He says, 'What do you want me to do?'

I said, 'We've got a script and I'd really like you to take a look at it.'

Simon's brother, Kim, helped to write the lyrics for this track and Bob said, 'Let me hear something and then I'll decide.'

Bob only lived about five minutes away from the studios in Camden, which was handy and he liked the idea of the track and how it sounded, then agreed to do it. At the time of recording, he was filming Mona Lisa with Michael Caine. He would run over once he'd finished there and then come over to record the track after.

After one take, we took a break in a pub just near the studios and as we walked in, the glare we received was something else. I was well known in 1985 because of '19', but his face was much more recognisable than mine with his resume of films. So, there we are in this pub and people started coming over and everyone was actually really nice and civilised. We were only there for about half an hour and we did loads of autograph signing, then headed back to the studio.

About three weeks after recording the record, we shot the video at an old, disused warehouse in Battersea. Bob played quite serious acting roles and we wanted to make him a bit of a lighter character for the video and even managed to put a joker's hat on him when we were filming up in south London, albeit it took some encouragement. He wasn't in the mood for it initially, but after half a bottle of whiskey and a few cigars, he was buzzing. At the end of the video, you'll see him laughing. That's why!

We had a lot of fun making the video. In one of the outtakes, one of the guys got his line wrong and said, 'We're going to Spain in a villa.'

Bob goes, 'Eh? What you going to do? Row the fucking thing there?'

There's another one where Laurence says, 'I'm a bit uncomfortable. Would you mind if I undo my trousers? Don't worry, ladies, it's not going anywhere. I'm just bloated.' Everyone was rolling about in laughter.

We also had Alan Talbot in the video through Bob, who was a really lovely man and had starred in everything from television series such as *Grange Hill to London's Burning*, right the way through to massive films like *007, The Living Daylights* and loads of Bob's films like *The Long Good Friday*. Ed O'Ross was another big name in the video and was also an incredibly nice guy. Again, I got to meet him through Bob. We were looking for someone to play the part of a mobster and Bob said, 'Do you know Ed O'Ross?

I said, 'I don't think so.'

He replied, 'What? He was in *The Cotton Club, Lethal Weapon, The Pope of Greenwich Village* and loads more. He'd be brilliant.'

Ed happened to be over in the UK and through Bob, was able to fit us in for the filming, which worked like a dream. He had a great laugh, but the biggest thing he was excited about was meeting Lord Olivier. When he saw Larry, he was like a little kid. After *Just for Money*, Ed went on to be in some massive movies like *Full Metal Jacket and Red Heat* and is still active to this day.

That video cost about £200,000, which was a hell of a lot of money, but it was worth it. On the record, I was using a sampler, tapping away at a rhythmic sound, which I managed to marry up with the video to make it look and sound like gunfire. There was a sequence where we had these cartoon gangsters, which were all hand-drawn and were being shot at. As the shots were fired, the gangsters were breakdancing to dodging bullets, in time with the tempo. However, the main reason for the high cost was that I wanted everything to be as authentic as possible. I had old Jaguar cars and original vintage bank notes from the time period, which we hired from some guy. If you watch the video, you'll see us counting out all the ten bob notes, the old pound notes and fivers. When we were packing up, I asked the guy that owned them if I could keep an old pound note and he said, 'Go on. Take one. You've paid enough to borrow them. Have one on the house as a memento.' I've still got it.

We also bought the rights to use some of the black and white films of the great train robbery, as I wanted to show the train coming down from Glasgow. My intention was also to include some footage from the police broadcasts, but apparently, you are not allowed to use them for about a hundred years after they're made. The only other snag was a bit of red tape from the BBC. They didn't like the bullets and breakdancing bit, so I had to cut it out for them. I left it in for everyone else, though and not a single person complained. In fact, the video won an award from Creative Circles and I ended up on MTV Live in the UK, CNN and Entertainment Tonight in America to promote the track. So, it can't have been that bad.

Bob Hospkins was great in terms of promotions. He went to all the top DJs and in only a way Bob could, he asked them to play the track. He approached the likes of Janice Long, Mike Reed, Gary Davies, Peter Powell, Simon Bates and Steve Right. At the time, Steve was famous for his show, *Steve Right in the Afternoon,* and Bob made a parody of Steve and said to him, 'Steve. If you still want to be around in the Afternoons for your show, make sure you play this record, or else, I'll be round to find ya.'

At the time, Tony Blackburn was massive on Radio London and he used to make this joke and say, 'We've got a new twelve-incher.'

Bob Hoskins spoke to Tony and said, 'Tony Blackburn. I'm on Paul Hardcastle's latest record. If you want to keep your twelve-incher, you better play it, my son.' Well, Tony kept up his end of the bargain and the track ironically reached number 19 on the charts. As it goes, that famous number was about to be part of my immediate future again, but from a different angle.

Timeline for December 1985

Out of Africa, with Meryl Streep and Harrison Ford, premieres in Los Angeles.

Michel Platini wins Ballon d'Or.

IBM DOS Version 3.2 is released.

Poet Robert Graves dies at ninety years of age.

Comic Relief is launched in the UK.

Paul Hardcastle produces a track for Phil Lynott.

The Ace with the Bass

If you're going to re-mix a track — somebody else's track — I, think you should make sure that it is as different as possible. There's no point in just whipping the faders up and down. That doesn't mean anything. Similarly, just elongating a drum break or putting in twenty handclaps instead of eight doesn't do anything for the track. The only thing a re-mix should do is enhance the song itself. Putting a bass drum through an AMS for the re-mix isn't important if the bass drum doesn't mean anything in the context of the track.

Paul Hardcastle – International Musician magazine, November 1985

In amongst all the madness of '19', in November 1985, I got married to Dolores, who was coincidentally nineteen at the time. The ceremony was at Langtons in Hornchurch and all the paparazzi were there clicking away on their cameras throughout. Simon was my best man and did a funny and entertaining speech, albeit I suspect his brother Kim did have a lot of input in writing it! I didn't have a stag do because I firstly didn't have the time and secondly couldn't be arsed. The honeymoon in Paris was nice, but all a bit rushed due to my commitments and the number of opportunities which were coming my way at the time, mainly a lot of remixes.

The first remix I did, 'Now That We've Found Love', by Third World, was before I'd done '19', on Chris Blackwell's Island Records label. This guy called Adrian, who used to be my promo man at Chrysalis, asked, 'Would you remix it?' They'd had some top people like Francois Kevorkian mixing for them and after he played me some of the other remixes that had been done.

I said, 'They're bloody good. Why do you need me?'

They said, 'Because they're not different. They've broken the track down, put some percussion in and called it a remix.'

I thought, *All right. I'll give it a bash.*

I asked them to get me a copy of the 24" master and I wiped it all, apart from the lead vocal. When I remade the backing track, I could hear the spill of the record he was singing to and I basically played the LinnDrum to the spill of that. I got the timing down, added a bass drum, keyboard, bongos and snare, cut something here and there and then started putting these backing vocals in, which I got Helen Rogers to sing. It became a totally different record. When I went back to Island Records, I was worried I might have gone too far, just like '19', but when I put it on, everyone was dancing around the studio and they loved it.

They said, 'That's what we wanted!'

Adrian put his thumb up and I was like, 'Phew!'

1985, I also released remixes of the 'Silent Underdog' and an electrofunk update of 'Papa's Got a Brand New Pigbag' under Kaz Records.

I'd watched this film called *The Evil Dead* and there are these kids that turn into demons and there's this woman in the house who says, 'Weeeee're gonna get yooooou,' in a spooky voice. I used that for the start of the PigBag record. Then, me and Steve had a request from Billy Russell if we'd do a remix of a track for a band called the Frank Chickens, which was made up of two Japanese ladies. We did the remix, but I'm not sure if it ever even came out.

As word got around, the two years surrounding '19' turned out to be a massive time of remixes for me. Dave Robinson from Stiff Records approached me to remix four Ian Dury tracks. 'Hit Me With Your Rhythm Stick' (by Ian Dury and The Blockheads), 'Wake Up and Make Love to Me,' 'Sex and Drugs and Rock & Roll,' which I funked up because it was never a funky track and 'Reasons to Be Cheerful.' Ian actually came down to the studio to hear '*Hit Me With Your Rhythm Stick*,' not to spy on me, but just to say hello.

I asked him, 'What do you think?'

He replied, 'I like it. I won't have to hit you with a stick now.'

It's nice when you get people's blessings. Barry White is another example a few years later. I did the Mammoth mix of 'Never Gonna Give You Up' and I got on a call with Bazza and he said with that deep voice, 'Hiiii

162

Paul. Love what you did with the remix.' Then he went into greater detail about the changes I made. I was blown away by what a kind and genuine person he was.

I said, 'I've listened to your stuff a lot and you don't change chords just for fun. Yours is a groove and you get in that groove and stick with it.'

He replied, 'You keep the groove, Paul. You keep the groove, man.'

I also remixed 'Let's Go Together,' and 'Oh, What A Feeling,' for Change, which was Luther Vandross's band, a track for Don Snow from the band Squeeze, George McCrae, 'Rock Your Baby,' 'Love Won't be Denied,' by Len Boone, 'Love Take-Over,' by Five Star, 'World Domination,' by the Belle Stars and 'Money Go Round,' by the Style Council.

I was asked to do a remix of a track for Frankie Beverly and Maze, which I rejected. I was really buzzing about being asked to do it, but Frankie Beverly wanted to be there while I was doing it and I said, 'No. I don't work like that. You won't get the best out of me by someone constantly looking over my shoulder.'

Someone in Blues in Soul magazine said something like, 'Who does Paul Hardcastle think he is, not wanting to work with Frankie Beverly?' I wasn't looking to make history.

I wrote back and said, 'This is how I work. Paul Weller and Barry White were happy for me not to be there.' I then gave a few more examples and explained how well all those tracks had done. There was then a flood of letters from the general public backing me up. I didn't write my letter to get that response from everyone, but it was encouraging how many people understood that I wasn't being a prima donna.

I had to turn down a number of great opportunities at the time, mainly due to not having the capacity. For example, I was asked to mix the B-side of Live Aid but turned it down due to being in America and delivering to a hectic schedule. That was a massively missed opportunity because the track was No.1 all over the world; however, at the end of the day, it was the A-side that mattered and made a difference and whatever I did for the B-side would have just been an add-on. I was very flattered that they thought of me, though.

Another one I was asked to produce was the 'Pet Shop Boys', 'West End Girls.' Simon was asked by their manager if I wanted to do it, but I was producing a funk band called LW5 and there were some other things that I was doing, like finishing the Paul Hardcastle album and consequently, I just didn't have the time. Don't get me wrong, Simon said it was going to do well and it did, but it was just bad timing for me.

Let me give you an insight into the intricacies of producing with this example. After recording the first Direct Drive track, at the end of a session, we were just about to mix the record and I noticed that the faders were at the top. Derek Green wanted his vocals louder, Mick wanted his bass louder, Robert wasn't too fussed, Bones said he couldn't hear the congas and I wanted my side up as well. Pete was the only one who was happy because his Hi-hat was louder than anything. Basically, there was no control! Thankfully, the guy we were renting the studio from told us how it should be and we all listened. When you're a producer, you are there to get the right engineer to tell the vocalist, 'That's good, but we can do it better like this…'

Basically, everything apart from being the artist to make the track sound right. It's a big, hands-on responsibility. If you look at mega producers like Quincy Jones and what they bring to the table, it's absolutely priceless. There are a lot of artists out there who wouldn't be where they are now without great producers. However, there were a couple of tracks I didn't pass on, which just so happened to be with artists who were massive idols of mine. Here's how those opportunities came about.

Simon called one day and said, 'I've just had a call about remixing a track.'

I said, 'Simon. You know I'm flat out. I want to crack on with my album and I want to stop remixing for a while. I'm not interested.'

He replied, 'You might be with this one.'

I said, 'Nope. Absolutely not. I'm not remixing at the moment.'

He then said, almost taking the piss in that 'Can I speak?' sort of tone.

I said, 'Go on. I hope you know I'll say no straight after, though.'

He says, 'D-Train.'

I said, 'Fuckin 'ell! Yes!' The original track came out in 1982 and was my favourite record of the 80s and it still sounds so great. When I first heard it, I thought, *Thats how I should be making music.* The remix I did became a hit and I ended up on Top of the Pops with D-Train, which was the first time I performed live on the show.

Then, a few months later, in September 1985, Simon called me again. At the time, he worked in partnership with a guy called Chris Morrison, who looked after bands like Blur and Simon said, 'Would you like to produce Phil Lynott? He wants you to produce one of his records.'

I said, 'Of course!' although I initially thought he was winding me up. Turns out he wasn't. I grew up listening to Thin Lizzy when I was at school, so it was almost odd to hear, *Would you produce Phil?* Simon pre-warned me that some people got on with Phil in the studio and others didn't. I knew if I didn't give it a go, I'd be an idiot and regret it for the rest of my life.

I went and met him at the Chrysalis office and we got on like a house on fire. I spoke with him about his music career, his gold disks, guitarists he'd used like Gary Moore and stuff like that, which was so great. However, I was nervous at the prospect of working with someone who I idolised as a schoolkid and was thinking, *How am I supposed to be telling this guy what to do?*

He told me in his thick Irish accent, 'I fucking love what you've done with that '19' record. You're at the top of your game right now, so you can certainly help me.' That put me at ease.

Phil wrote a record that was coincidentally called, 'Nineteen,' but nothing like mine. It was about bad boys and the lyrics included lines like, *You want it mean? I'm bad, I'm nineteen.* He played me the demo and it was rock. Because I liked rock, I wasn't out of my depth. We soon booked the Roundhouse studios in Camden to record it and I had this idea that I wanted a motorbike sound included in the track. The problem was we didn't have a motorbike; however, across the road was a motorbike shop.

Me and Phil went over there and the guy at the shop said, 'Ah, Mr Hardcastle! Who's your friend?' Phil was miles more famous than me and this guy dug him out a bit.

In the end, Phil said, 'All right. So, you're not impressed with who I am, but I don't care. Can you lend us a fucking bike, or what?'

The guy said, 'Yeeeeah, no problem.'

We get it back to the recording studio and Phil decides to jump on and starts revving the crap out of this thing in the recording booth. I was outside in the control room as I wanted to hear what it sounded like. I only wanted him to rev it about three or four times and he kept revving and revving until I started to realise the room was filling up with smoke. I shouted, 'Phil, no, no, no. That's enough. Stop!' In the meantime, all the smoke alarms have gone off and everyone is starting to cough from the fumes. Everyone had to evacuate for at least an hour because of the carbon monoxide.

Finally, we got a good recording a couple of hours later from the bike, then we took it back and said our thank yous. I wanted to do something special with the noise and decided to put it in the sampler and slowed it right down. I then started to manually enter this sample on the keyboard myself in time with the tempo of the drums. The only way you can describe the noise is like a machine gun. A motorbike, once revved, goes, brrrrm, brrrrm, which is like the equivalent noise of tens of bullets per second being fired. Then imagine that sample is slowed down and it's bah, bah, bah, bah, bah and I can play that single note at the speed and pitch I want in relation to the record. Phil's listened and gone, 'I fucking love that.'

He went out to the toilet at one point and I thought, *I've got to go and pick up his bass guitar.* It was the one with the mirror on it that I'd seen years and years before. I can play the bass a bit, just from being self-taught and I got the engineer to record a little sample of something I was trying out, which was me slapping the bass for about fifteen seconds. As the engineer was playing it back, Phil returned and I said to him, 'I hope you don't mind, but I wanted to try this idea out on the bass for the track, but if you don't like it, we can erase it.'

He listened to it and said, 'We're leaving that in there. It sounds fucking great. That's going on the track.'

I was actually worried he was going to say, 'You cheeky bastard. Who said you could mess around with my bass?' but he was great and I kept pinching myself to be working with one of the best rock stars in the world.

Not long after, I went over to his lovely house in Kew to do a photoshoot and there was a huge cardboard cut-out of him that you could see through the front window as you walked up the driveway. The photo they used in the shoot is the picture you'll see in an article The Mirror did with me in 2015 and it's also my Facebook header. After the shoot, he showed me around and he had this beautiful jukebox in his house and I said, 'That's stunning.' He started to give me the history about it and how much he treasured the piece.

He knew I'd just got married and about a week later, these two massive bouncer-type-looking blokes turned up at my house in a lorry and they said, 'Are you Paul Hardcastle?'

I've said, 'Errrr. Yeah.'

They said, 'We've got something here for you from Phil Lynott.'

I've said, 'Oh. OK.'

He'd sent the jukebox as a wedding present and also sent my wife some flowers. The note which came with the flowers for my wife said, 'Sorry for keeping him out so long at night!'

And there was another card to myself which said, 'From your big brother, Phil.'

The music industry brings many challenges and stresses and going from being a kid from a poor household to selling Hi-Fi's and then not having to worry about the bills in a matter of weeks is not as glamorous as it sounds. Also, I wasn't in a band where the attention and fame can kind of be diluted and spread among you. It all fell down on me and that's not something I was prepared for. In all honesty, how much can you realistically prepare yourself for something like that until it actually happens? For many, it spirals very quickly to drugs and alcohol and goes off the rails at an intense rate. Getting married and having a child so early on helped centre me and kept my feet on the ground. Meeting Phil Lynott was an education in itself, though. At the time, he knew he wasn't very well and realised just how precious life was. Taking drugs probably had something to do with that and he really drilled home to me about steering clear of the gear. He explained what it had done to him and how everything you have can disappear in a heartbeat by getting involved in that scene. He was so right. I just want to clarify something. The Mirror article was well written and it was the whole centre page of the paper, but there's a headline of, *Junkie pal Phil Lynott saved me from turning to drugs.* I never said that and would never be disrespectful to anyone with a cheap shot like that. That kind of spoilt the article for me.

Phil sadly died on 4 January 1986 due to drug-related issues. He was only thirty-six. I was at home when Simon called me to give me the news and I was absolutely devastated. He was such a nice guy and was especially nice to me. Unfortunately, I couldn't attend the funeral because I was overseas, but I did send flowers with a note. *Dear Phil. So glad I got to meet you, but so sad it was only for such a short while. Your brother, Paul Hardcastle.*

That was a crazy sequence of events in 1985. '19' came out, I bought a house, got married, made a track with Lord Olivier and Bob Hoskins and produced a track for

Phil Lynott, who then gave me his jukebox and died about three weeks after. That year was like driving in the fast lane flat out without looking at the rear-view mirror. Maybe 1986 would be more relaxed?

Nipper Paul – 18 months old

Two years old and already getting a taste
for bikes

Paul Hardcastle with Paul Jr on the back,
similar ages...with the help of Dave Leonard

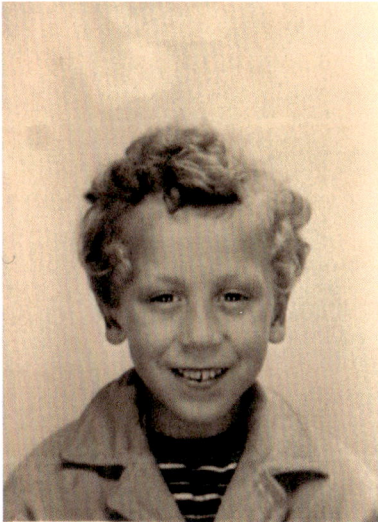

Little Paul

1963 Little Paul and dad in Berlin

Me and Dad busting moves

July 1978 Being Shot at

Bike madness early 1970's

More bike madness

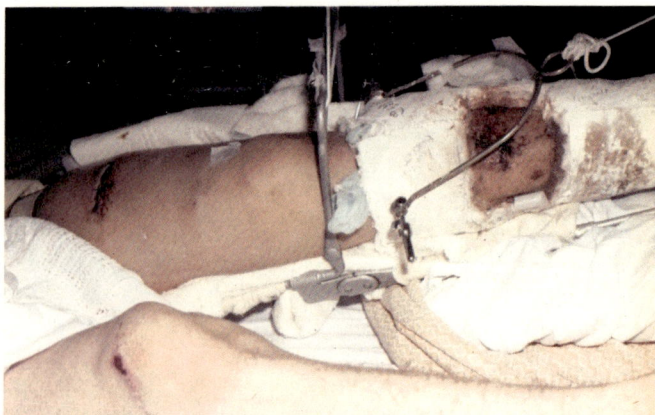

Sept 1978 Four months in hospital after motorcycle accident

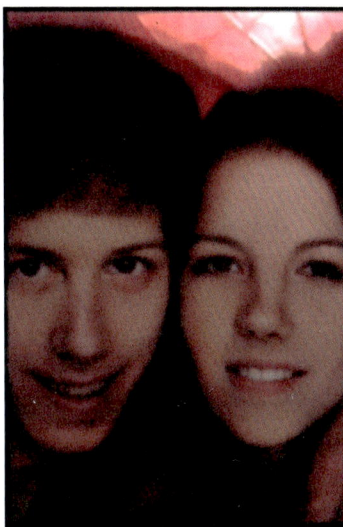

With my first serious girlfriend Julie
Ann Dean

With Direct Drive, crammed into a phone box. Circa 1981

Shortly after 19 exploded. With Simon Fuller & the Chrysalis crew

1989 - A room full of equipment, which would now hardly take up one desk space

The day you hear you've won International Hit of the Year.
Notice Rocky celebrating in the back seat...

Performing live on Top of the Pops with D
Train

With Bob Hoskins filming 'Just For Money'

With the legend, Lord Laurence Olivier, filming 'Just for Money'

The legendary Synclavier, which revolutionised my
working practice

With the legend, Phil Lynott

Sharing time with football royalty,
Gianfranco Zola, during my stint at
Chelsea FC

With Simon Fuller at his mums birthday
Lifelong friendship

Best smooth Jazz Artist of all time

Bikes I rebuilt - Photo © Mark KehoeKen Rake
Gallery

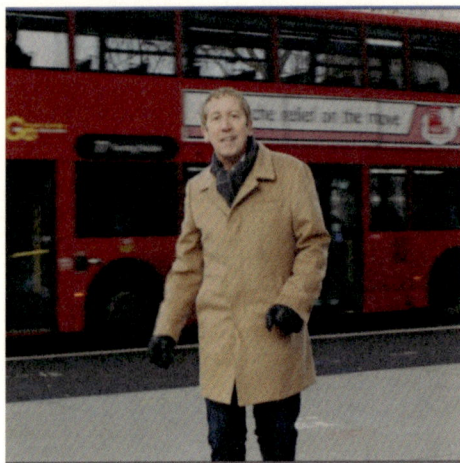

Filming dementia - charity video for the Utley
Foundation

Ritchie and Fuller in LA,
Sept 2023

2023 - With my ghostwriter, Paul Zanon. We had some fun getting the book together

April 1986

Clint Eastwood becomes Mayor of Carmel, California.

IBM produces the first megabit chip.

Crocodile Dundee premieres in Australia.

Explosion at Chernobyl nuclear power plant.

Sir Clive Sinclair sells the right of ZX Spectrum to
AMSTRAD.

'The Wizard' is the new theme tune to *Top of the Pops*.

Plastic Rotating Demon

A 1970s pop musician transported through time to a modern recording studio would probably feel like a 1940s Spitfire pilot suddenly finding himself on the flight deck of the space shuttle. The ultimate pop music machine will be a powerful computer that does everything – synthesises voices and musical instruments, processes the sounds and records it. The closest yet is New England Digital's Direct-to-Disk add-on for its Synclavier audio system.

Ralph Denyer Interviews Paul Hardcastle for the Times
28 December 1986

After *Just For Money*, towards the end of 1985, I released my Album *Paul Hardcastle,* which featured ten tracks, including '19', 'Rainforest' and 'King Tut'. There was also a track called 'Don't Waste My Time'.

I'd originally written this backing track for Lenny Henry called 'The Essential Crucial Well Hard, Remix', and in the middle of the 12" version, he does this really good comedy sketch and starts talking about the police and his fictional pirate DJ character, Delbert Wilkins.

However, the track took a different route when someone suggested, 'That would be great if you had a proper artist singing through it.' I'd always wanted to work with Carol Kenyon after hearing her sing 'Temptation', for Heaven 17 and I managed to track her down. We agreed to meet at the studio.

On the day itself, I was writing the lyrics in the back of the cab on the way there. I arrived before her and I started going through the lyrics for the track, reading it over and singing it to myself when Carol turned up.

I said, 'Can you give me half an hour, please?'

She said, 'No problem.' Thirty minutes later, she came back in, sang the track and killed it stone dead. What an incredible voice.

The track was very different, mainly because it had vocals, a good song and different track format to anything else I'd done before. The promo for 'Don't Waste My Time,' started almost immediately and we soon ended up performing live on Wogan, which was a great experience. Terry was a very nice guy and extremely hospitable. After the show, there was a green room and he asked me, 'What gave you the idea to write '19'?' By now, I was on autopilot with the answer.

I also went on Razzmatazz with Rod Hull and Emu, which was a kid's television show in the 1980s. There was a birthday party and I was in charge of bringing the cake in. I'm on national telly and am wearing this party wig and a beard as a disguise, when next thing, Rod Hull says,

'Hold on a minute. You're not just a person bringing in the cake. You're Paul Hardcastle, aren't you?'

Emu pulls the beard off my face and then Rod says, 'You've got a new video coming out soon. What's it called?'

I replied, 'Don't waste my time.' Emu went for my face and really whacked into my nose. He had my eyes streaming and it bloody hurt!

I did loads of stuff like Video and Chips with presenters Sonya Saul, Mick Brown and Mick Sharp and towards the end of 1985, we promoted the track on a TV show in Amsterdam. At the time, I was pretty popular in Holland because it was the place where I had the longest No.1 for '19' in the pop charts, which was sixteen weeks. I got to meet Errol Brown from Hot Chocolate and then someone introduced me to Will Smith and Jazzy Jeff, who were really just known as being a rapper and a DJ back then. He introduced him as *Will Smith* because the *Fresh Prince* didn't come out for about another five years at that point and it turns out he was a big fan of 'Rainforest'. I don't want to come across as big-headed, but at the time, he was a bit in awe of me when I was introduced as Paul Hardcastle. He said, 'You made that "Rainforest" track!' Then, a couple of years later, they used a sample of '19' on their album, *Rock the House.* Obviously, the roles got reversed pretty quickly and he went on to mega-stardom, whereas I'm like a minnow compared to him now but at the time, he was really happy to meet me like I would be to meet him now. As people, they were very polite and I respect Will a lot, as he's good at what he does.

'Don't Waste My Time' got to No.8 in the UK and reached the Top 20 in about ten other countries. I still used Lenny on the remix a few months later and he also recorded a bespoke telephone answering message for my landline, which was brilliant. *What's happening, guy? This is Delbert Wilkins here talking to you on Paul Hardcastle's answering machine. Isn't it wicked? Yeaaaah. Listen, right – Paul's not in at the moment coz he's a busy dude. But if you really, really want to speak to him and you're not here to waste his time, then call back and he'll try his best to get back to you. See you in a bit.*

As opposed to '19', I didn't mind performing this one live on Top of the Pops and me and Carol even had a basic synchronised dance routine, which was fun. She was singing while I was playing the key-tar. However, it was what happened straight after the performance that I remember the most. Soon after stepping off the stage, this guy came over to me, extended his hand and said, 'Hi, I'm Michael. I really liked '19.'' I thought he was a cameraman.

I said, 'Thank you. That's very kind.'

He then said, 'I also really enjoyed what you've just performed and I have a question for you. Would you be interested in writing a new theme for Top of the Pops?'

It turned out to be Michael Hurll who produced the show. I obviously said, 'Yes!' Swiftly followed by, 'How long do I have to do this?'

He replied, 'As quick as possible.' Ironically, Phil Lynott had co-written the previous Top of the Pops theme tune with Midge Ure, which was called Yellow Pearl.

I phoned Fuller and said, 'I've been asked to do the next Top of the Pops theme tune.

He said, 'Bullshit.'

I said, 'You won't say that tomorrow, matey!' Next morning, he got the call from Michael's secretary to discuss terms.

As luck would have it, I'd just bought this thing called a Synclavier, which was the best bit of kit in the recording industry at the time, albeit it was far from compact. I'd been pre-warned of its size when I ordered it and explained to them that I lived in a small house and that they wouldn't be able to get it through the front door and up the stairs. They asked for other options and I explained I had a small first-floor balcony, not thinking it was going to be a big operation.

Well, they arrived at about ten a.m. for what was a twofold delivery. The first lump of equipment was the direct to disk sixteen-track, which was the first piece of machinery that recorded directly-to-disks and it was twice the size of the Synclavier itself, which for the records was the size of a Portaloo.

This crane turns up and I was thinking, *Wait for the neighbours to start moaning as they start to say, what the fuck is going on here?* The Avenue was and still is, one of the nicest roads in Wanstead, but by now, they knew about my music and had thankfully started to become quite supportive, which was handy because the crane and delivery people were there for quite a while. Then, the lorry turned up with the actual Synclavier itself. It took about half an hour just to get each unit from the lorry hoisted up by the crane to the first-floor balcony, but then came the next stage of installation.

I was as excited as hell and couldn't wait to get into it, but it took a while to set it up because of all the wiring. I'd bought a new desk in a very small bedroom and had to knock a hole through into the bathroom to get part of the Synclavier in and the balance of the equipment went into another room.

The guy who sold me the Synclavier was there on the day of the delivery and he was great because he really knew what he was talking about. However, I think he expected it to work. He turned up with four people and they stayed for a while and got it to work. They also had a wiring guy who stayed for about three days for all the electrical outputs. There were something like five hundred cables, each going to different channels into a patch bay, which meant you didn't have to get behind the unit, similar to a telephone system back in the day. It was cutting-edge technology, whereas now I look back at it, the size and all the complexities and think, *That's crazy*.

I had my Sony Hi8 video recorder and decided to film the whole delivery, which is a great bit of nostalgia to revisit almost forty years later. I loved my video cameras and still do. I recorded all my kid's birthdays from as young as they could speak until they were fully grown adults and they'd say, 'Hi. It's my birthday and I'm three years old.'

Then the year after, 'Hi. It's my birthday and I'm four years old.' Etc. I also had every Christmas of them running down the stairs on Christmas day. When you put all the clips together, year after year, it makes for great viewing, but I've got so much footage you would need a couple of lifetimes to watch it.

Back to the Synclavier. When you looked at an album in those days and it said it was digital, it was bullshit. It was digital tape and not direct to disk. Synclavier's direct-to-disk system was the first in the world to ever record straight to hard drive and I was the only one to have one in 1985 because it came straight out of the R&D department from New England Digital. As for the Synclavier, there were only about five in the country who had one because they were a ridiculous price. Sting, Trevor Horn from Frankie Goes to Hollywood, George Michael, me and Benny Anderson had one. I only found out about Benny because I knew the guy that repaired them and once, after finishing off at my place, he said, 'Right. I'm off to repair Benny's now.'

I said, 'Benny who?'

He replied, 'Anderson. The guy from ABBA.'

The original '19' was all recorded analogue on my twenty-four-track tape machine as I didn't have the Synclavier then. Looking back, it was really tedious. You'd get to the end of a song and sometimes you'd run out of tracks. Let's just say you had eight lots of backing vocals by one person, eight by another, then another four more for harmonies; that's twenty tracks, which left us with four to spare. What we had to do was bounce the mix off to a one-inch tape, which you mastered on to. Then, we would wipe everything that had filled up the twenty tracks. What you'd do is play the track and maybe leave one chorus from the twenty-four-track just to make sure it's in sync. Then you would put a chinagraph pencil mark on it and you'd look for it to come around and as soon as it did, you'd put it into record mode and hope that you got it in time. You couldn't drag it slightly back, but on average, it would take about half a dozen times to mix these things in.

The Synclavier cost me £250,000 but it got rid of all the issues I had with the cassettes and the quality was incredible. I wouldn't have been able to afford the down payment on a Synclavier without '19', but I was also aware that I genuinely could have bought a decent house with what that thing cost back then. However, even with that price tag, it wasn't just a case of ordering one and get cracking. You had to be vetted by the CIA to get a Synclavier as certain parts used, such as the red-light switches, were the same as a B-52 Bomber and you could still see if they were on or off in the sunlight. Also, if I ever had any affiliation with communism, I wouldn't have been able to buy a Synclavier. Apparently, in the wrong hands, a person could take parts out of the machine and put them to improper use. That's why the CIA vetted everyone who bought one and they also had the right to conduct an onsite inspection at any point after purchase to make sure you weren't going to be the next bad guy from a Bond movie.

The crazy thing is, in comparison to a modern-day smartphone, it had a fraction of the capability in terms of memory and speed. A Synclavier could hold about thirty-two tracks digitally, with instant playback and I got an extra 4MB of RAM for free, which might not sound a lot, especially as my iPhone at the time of writing has 32GB of RAM, which is eight thousand times more. Crazy now when you think a phone can hold thousands of tracks and we've got access to millions through the cloud; however, that 4MB back then cost $14,000 and you could quickly zap that up when recording. The other issue was the density you recorded at. Let's say human hearing is supposed to be up to 20,000Hz, maximum. A CD is 44,100Hz, over double what we can hear. My Synclavier recorded at 196,000Hz and you couldn't tell the difference between that and 20,000Hz apart from it using up loads more memory and the fact that I'm not a dog. Thankfully, you could record at lower Hz; otherwise, you'd use up all the disk space too quickly.

I've always worked much better at pace. If I've got an idea in my head, I want to get it down quickly, or the vibe can go quickly.

At the time, people were saying to me, 'You're paying that much for a fucking keyboard?' But at that time, all I wanted to do was live in the studio, make the best music, mix the best tracks and do it at my own speed. The

Synclavier was the only bit of kit which allowed me to do everything.

Apart from the cost, the other consideration when buying a Synclavier, as I mentioned earlier, was the size. Even a couple of years after buying it, when I'd set up a big studio at the back of my garden, it still became cramped with the amount of gear I had to record tracks with. I had loads of keyboards and a giant stack of about twenty synthesisers, but without a keyboard because, I was able to play them all through MIDI (Musical Instrument Digital Interface) through the Synclavier. Then there was my effects rack, which had more synthesisers and did everything from guitar effects to delays, four JBL speakers and the iconic Winchester disks, which were recording from the Synclavier. Now add in two massive memory racks which came with the Synclavier, which were both the size of 6ft high fridge freezers. You had 60MB of disk space but could only access 40MB out of it because of the software. It ran at the same speed as something like an old Sinclair ZX Spectrum, but because of the hardware I had, it was very quick, even for today's standards, because the RAM took over, which meant you didn't need a fast processor.

The problem with alpha versions of anything is that they will always have snags and my direct-to-disk had loads. It came with four thick instruction manuals and a load of video cassette tutorials, but none of that was any help. In the end, they sent an engineer called Ted from New England Digital, who came all the way from America and ended up staying at my house for a month trying to get the Synclavier to a point where it was functionally reliable. Unfortunately, every time it was fixed, it would break down again. There was something wrong with it constantly overheating because it used tons of power at any one time due to having about twenty fans at the back amongst loads of other technology. It sounded like a 747 when you turned it on.

They made the Synclavier operate at 110V in America, which meant it needed a converter in the UK. It kept blowing up the normal yellow voltage converters you would see on building sites and each time they were fixed, they still kept blowing up. They must have given me about half a dozen of these converters and in the end, it took them weeks to build me one which could take the power this thing was drawing.

While they were trying to fix it, they paid for me to hire a digital Mitsubishi tape recorder, but in the end, they had to admit defeat and take the sixteen-track back. They gave me the smaller eight-track version, which meant I was only using one of the massive storage boxes and I saved myself a lot of money downsizing. Unsurprisingly, soon after my experience, they stopped making the sixteen-track.

The first thing I did on the Synclavier was 'The Wizard,' for Top of the Pops. I had a vision for the track and as my son Paul Jr says, 'You're the heat-seeking missile.' Once I've latched onto something, I really do go for it. When Michael Hurll asked me to do the track as quickly as possible, I stayed up for two days solid. The adrenaline was pumping and I looked at the clock in the middle of the night, thinking, *Who cares? You won't get this opportunity every day to make the Top of The Pops theme tune.* Michael Hurll was very happy and it ended up being the theme tune for the next five years. However, it wasn't a smooth ride getting the track airtime.

A few months later, the theme tune was released as a record, but it was a slow start. The plugger, who is the person who markets the track to be featured on radio and TV, came back from Radio 1 and told Michael that they were not interested in playing the record. The problem then was that all the other stations, like Capital, weren't going to start to play a BBC track, which meant 'The Wizard' wouldn't receive any airtime.

Michael said to me, 'They're not going to play my record?'

I love the way he said, 'My', showing his faith and trust in the track. He went nuts. Back then, you had a midweek position and because we weren't getting any airplay, it was around No.80. That was all because the BBC didn't want to play it, which was crazy, especially as it was the theme tune for a BBC show.

The main reason was due to a number of actors and actresses from Eastenders at the time who were releasing records. You had Nick Berry, Letitia Dean and Paul Medford, to mention a few. As a result, nobody knew about 'The Wizard' because it had intentionally been given a swerve by the BBC. What Michael Hurll then did showed the power of the man. He took them to war and got what he wanted. We went from not being in the charts to being something like No.31 within a few days, which was a huge leap and eventually getting as high as No.15.

Little bit of trivia about the front cover of 'The Wizard' single. It basically had the Top of the Pops branding on the front with the tagline of *Paul Hardcastle –The Wizard The Theme from Top of the Pops* and a photo of me on the back with two floating synthesisers. However, the original photoshoot was with me, coloured green, looking like Obi-Wan Kenobi from Star Wars in front of a massive synthesiser in the background, which Hans Zimmer kindly had leant me. It was a bit more mystical and had more of the wizard vibe about it, but unfortunately, it got binned because they were trying to get as much financial and marketing traction as possible, which was far better achieved with the Top of The Pops logo on the front. The Zimmer synth photo didn't stand out, whereas the other one was instantly recognisable and, in all honesty, made total commercial sense. However, all was not lost as they did use the old green photo as part of the front cover of my *Nineteen and Beyond: 1984-1988* album, which Chrysalis released in 2023.

***

There's a number of people who said to me at the time, 'Why are you doing music for television? Surely, you'd get much more money doing more singles?' Yes, 'The

Wizard' wasn't going to recoup the investment of the Synclavier on its own, but I knew that piece of equipment would eventually pay for itself. After 'The Wizard,' I had a number of TV shows approaching me to do their themes tunes, all generating income at the same time, such as *Watchdog, The Clothes Show, Saturday Night Live, Wildlife on One, the Late Late Breakfast Show, Think Holiday and Supersense.*

I was getting £90 a minute for TV shows. So, let's take Top of the Pops. You got thirty seconds intro and thirty seconds outro. However, where the money was made was all the chart rundowns. Two minutes on one part, a minute on the other. I was generating about £500 or £600 every time the show was aired and my tune was used for a good few years. Same went with the others, which were being aired on the likes of BBC1 and other major terrestrial channels. It turned out to be a nice little earner in the background, although I did have a few little battles along the way.

You'll always find some really strange people, mainly in A&R, who just want to find things wrong with anything. Otherwise, it shows they haven't contributed to the making of the track and that's certainly something I learned during the process of making 'Just For Money'. In fact, that's why I don't like the track without watching the video; it's because of the way I was forced to change things. Watching the film and looking at Bob and Lord Larry and stuff like that, it's a bloody good video, but as a track, I listen to it and can hear it's basically everyone else's ideas.

Simon Fuller could see I was a bit annoyed by the whole thing because it was my first record since '19' and I was trying to please the record company.

They were saying, 'Don't put that in it, do it this way, put this in instead, blah, blah, blah.'

Simon said, 'After this, you've got to go with what you want to do.'

I did, however, manage to put my little trademark in there once though. There's a bit where it goes, '…they died for money.' And I put, 'D-d-d-d-d-died for money.'

Unfortunately, I encountered similar issues with the television guys when it came to the adverts for the next two or three years. When I did the music for Watchdog, there was a bit where a baby went up towards a pan of boiling water and I put the sound of a baby crying in the background for a split second to add authenticity and a little fear factor. Well, they came back to me and said, 'It's a bit too much.'

I thought, *'It's a programme about things that could happen and the consequences! What did they want when a kid got scolded by a burning pan? A lullaby?'* In the end, they kept the sound of the kid screaming.

I had another one where they came back to me and said, 'It's good, but we think it needs more bass.'

I listened to it and thought, *'The bass is great as it is.'* So, I sent the exact track back a week later and said, 'What do you think now?'

They said, 'That's much better. Sounds great now.' I kid you not. Then, another time, I was doing effects for some advert to do with a spritzer or something like that. I was throwing all these effects at the advert and they kept saying, 'More effects. We need more effects.' I've added fire engines, bombs, Daffy Duck and anything you can imagine and took it back to them.

They said, 'We can't hear anything now. It's all effects.' Grrr.

It wasn't all doom and gloom, though and I had a lot of fun doing scores for television. When I was given the brief for the BBC's programme Supersense, which was narrated by John Sachs, they asked me to make something nobody else had heard before but not to go too crazy with it. Supersense was a pioneering show because it was the first time they'd used tiny cameras on top of a bird flying and they would go right inside ant's nests and that sort of thing. I knew I had to do something unique.

I'm quite experimental and similar to Pink Floyd; I'll put anything on a record. Gilmour has a track on the album Meddle, which has a dog howling to him and that gave me the idea to do something similar for Supersense, using just animal sounds. The BBC gave me a few ideas, then I asked for all the wildlife sounds they had and made up the tune. When I went over to present it, I said, 'I've got something here and you might tell me I'm off my tree, but have a listen. Before I start, just bear in mind there are no human voices in it. I've used the sounds from your BBC sound library and where the frog makes a burping sound, I've stretched it out for the bass drum. Then there was a rattlesnake, which I used as the snare and a bird tweeting, which was like a high hat.' They raised their eyebrows and didn't seem impressed with what I was telling them, then I played it and they all looked at each other and said, 'My God. That's brilliant. That's exactly what we want. Don't touch it.' The BBC loved it and the score won an award. I also did the follow-up series, which was called Lifesense, where I did something similar, added a few things to make it stand out, but also integrated people's voices this time.

The last nature programme I did was called Giants, which came out in the late 90s and looked at prehistoric creatures. I had to make the sound of a monitor lizard munching on this smaller prey, crunching through its bones, so I decided to use the sound of ice cracking. I got that sample from a mate who was working on a documentary in Alaska. I then used the sound of a monitor lizard and reversed it, which made it sound a like a dinosaur, which was quite appropriate because they look prehistoric.

Back to 'The Wizard'. I had some fun with the 12" version of the track. At the time, I thought, *I could do with a voiceover, but who would make a good wizard for this track?* I was a massive fan of the programme Catweazle and thought that Geoffrey Bayldon would be ideal. Similar to Lord Laurence and Bob Hoskins, I'd mention to Simon Fuller, who I'd like to use in a track and he'd hunt them down. Then, like a bounty hunter, he'd always make contact with them. This was no different.

Geoffrey came over to my house in Wanstead and he was such a nice person. We had a chat and of course, I told him I used to watch Catweazle and absolutely loved it. I tried to resist asking him too many questions, but I did ask him about his magical frog, Touchwood! In terms of the track, I'd written this little script out of what I thought a wizard would say. It was something like,

Darkness and light
I bid you collide
Turn day into night
Where forests have died
Rekindle the spirits
Awaken by ten
To emerge from this cauldron
Alive again.

He said, 'Yeah. That works.' After finishing the track.

I said, 'While you're here, could you say something that could fit into the record in your wizard persona.'

He said, 'No problem.'

Off the cuff he said, '*Buy this rotating plastic demon, or I will curse ye till the end of time!*' which ended up on the end of the extended mix. That was genius from him. We recorded it about two or three times, had a cup of tea, then Geoffrey left. That was the last I ever saw of him. Such a nice man.

The next few weeks were perhaps not wizardry, but certainly possessed elements of magic to them and without a doubt, ranked up there as incredible experiences.

May 1986

Top Gun with Tom Cruise premieres.

Bobby Ewing comes back from the dead on the hit TV show Dallas.

The Mask of Orpheus premieres in London.

Talbot cars cease to be made by Peugeot in France and Britain.

Paul Hardcastle plays live at the Montreux Rock Festival.

Swiss Roll...And Rock

*I began my career with infantile dreams of becoming a
composer.*

Ivor Novello

A couple of months after getting married, I decided I
wanted to fly on Concorde as it was something I'd dreamt
of doing but never thought I'd be in a position to afford it.
What happened was, me and my wife were going on a
holiday to Miami and I said, 'Before all this goes away in
six months' time and I start getting old, I want to make sure
I have a bit of fun with it. I want to go on Concorde.'

One of the first things that struck me about Concorde
was its size. Compared to a jumbo jet where you'd got, say,
ten seats across, it was only four in a row. Two seats, a
narrow aisle and then another two seats. However, you
didn't travel on Concorde for comfort; it was about the
speed, the altitude and exclusivity. Also, apart from the
cost, flying Concorde was literally the high life. We were
flying at sixty thousand feet, about twenty-five thousand
feet higher than regular commercial airlines, which meant
you could see the shape of the earth, but incredibly,
without turbulence.

The speed was something else. We were cruising at Mach 2, at 1,350mph, which, again, was about 800mph faster than a 747, covering a mile every three seconds. On the way back to London from Miami, they stopped for fuel at Washington. However, they didn't put much in the tank because they were going to fill it up in Heathrow. When we took off from Washington, it was crazy and I felt really, really dizzy because we had taken off like a rocket.

I said to the stewardess, 'What's going on? We seem to be going a lot faster than when we took off from Miami. I don't feel great.'

She replied, 'We get used to that. With less fuel, it's a lot lighter and that means we're flying a hell of a lot faster!' After taking off, they then had to shut off the afterburners because of the noise, but as we kept rising in altitude, they came back on as the plane started to fly towards supersonic. They made an announcement saying how fast we were going and as we approached 750mph, they made another announcement to say we were about to break the sound barrier. Minus the fuel now, I was expecting it to be something like Captain Kirk in *Star Trek*, whoosh, but I didn't feel a thing. I just looked at the speed, going from 730mph to 1,000mph, really quickly and the last I remember, it went up to 1,440mph, which I recorded on my video. What a great experience.

I even got to go into the tiny little cockpit and film the inside while we were flying, which you'd never get the chance to do these days since 9/11. What I found incredible on landing was that most of the people left all the goodies they'd been given because they were probably flying Concorde all the time and their company was picking up the tab, whereas I came from a poor background and found it hard to fathom. There were things like wallets, silver photo frames and folders with all the facts about Concorde, but also my favourite part, the electronics. As we were walking off the plane, I looked down at the empty seats and saw all these headphones, which were Sennheiser.

I thought I'd try my luck and asked the stewardess, 'Can I take a few of these if they've been left?'

She said, 'Help yourself.' Not just that, she even gave me a bottle of champagne to pop into my bag! I left with about fifteen pairs of those headphones and I've still got a couple! The rest I gave out to friends and family.

1986 provided me with some massive memories and experiences and the most memorable was becoming a father for the first time. My daughter Maxine was born on 28 April 1986, which was, without a doubt, the most amazing thing to have ever happened to me at that point in my life. Irrespective of the family she was born into and Simon Fuller as her godfather, she would show the world of music what an incredible talent she is in her own right.

On my own music front, it was all going on. I had the first DAT (Digital audio tape) in my Jaguar XJS, which Kenwood kindly decked out for me. It included three amps and sounded incredible. However, you can't beat live music. After I left Direct Drive, I still kept in touch with the guys and if I was available, I'd help them if they were short of keyboard player and they'd often reciprocate. As

I started to make music, which involved me being live on stage, I needed someone to mime the guitars or drums and that's when I'd call in my good mate Pete Quinton to help out. We had some great times gigging on Top of the Pops, with Pete doing the drumming for the remix of 'You're The One For Me,' by D-Train and 'Don't Waste my Time,' but one of the most memorable came in May 1986.

About a week after Michael Hurll asked me to write the Top of the Pops tune, he asked me if I wanted to take part in something much bigger. 'Paul. Do you fancy going to Montreux?'

I said, 'Yeeaaah!' Michael organised all that and I'm very grateful for the many opportunities he gave me during that period. I liked Michael, but a lot of people feared him because he could be quite blunt sometimes. I remember, once on Top of the Pops, the audience was really flat and not making it look like it was a party.

He came down and said to them, 'If you lot don't liven up, you can all go and I'll bring some other people in.' All of a sudden, they're screaming and shouting like it was the best show ever.

For me, it was a massive honour to have been invited to perform live at the Montreux Rock Festival in Geneva, Switzerland. There were some massive names taking part, such as Electric Light Orchestra (ELO), Thompson Twins, Spandau Ballet, Roger Daltrey, Elvis Costello, Culture Club, Patti Labelle, Joe Jackson, Bryan Adams, Big Country, Eurythmics and A-HA. I was on after Queen, then had Genesis after me, which was crazy looking back.

The festival itself was manic and you didn't get the chance to mingle that much, but I did get the chance to speak to Brian May quickly. However, the one I really wanted to speak with was Phil Collins, which I managed to do.

I went over and said, 'Hi Phil. I'm Paul.'

He replied, 'I know who you are.'

He then said, 'I've read a few interviews where you've mentioned who your favourite artists are and who you appreciate and I noticed I was in the mix. Thank you for that.'

I was bowled over by how down-to-earth he was. Phil then introduced me to the band, which was a big thing for me as I was a Genesis fan. I got to speak with the likes of Mike Rutherford and Tony Banks, which was all a bit surreal.

We performed three tracks and Simon Fuller went out the front and recorded the whole thing on his video. We came out to 'Don't Waste My Time,' with Carol Kenyon, then '19' *and* we finished with 'Foolin' Yourself' with Kevin Henry, which is a proper dance track and had the crowds jumping around. In addition to myself, Carol and Kevin, there was also Pete, three backing singers who used to be in the group Hot Gossip and a couple of dancers.

Performing '19' at Montreux was actually the first time I'd ever performed the track live and would be one of only two live performances like that in my lifetime. I say the performance was live, but it was more semi-live. A lot of the drum patterns were going through drum machines because a drummer would need four arms and three legs to have done that on his own live, but Pete did a great job of miming the drums, similar to what they did on Top of the Pops. In all fairness, it was a really well-put-together performance. We walked out on stage without doing any pre-concert rehearsals and just performed on this massive stage to a huge crowd, which was so much fun.

A few months later me and Walshy did a track for charity called 'Give, Give, Give,' for Disco Aid. Here's how that came about. Walshy had been inspired by the charity tracks, 'Do They Know It's Christmas?' by Band-Aid and 'We Are The World,' in the US, which had both come out a few months earlier. He decided to contact Steve Macintosh from the pop-funk band The Cool Notes to create a record which would raise funds and awareness for multiple sclerosis.

I was asked to produce the song, Steve Mac wrote it and we had some massive names who agreed to take part, including Hazell Dean, Mel and Kim, ASWAD, Jackie Graham, Tony Blackburn, Lenny Henry, Chris Amoo, Edwin Starr, Odyssey, Hazell Dean, Sheila Fergusson from The Three Degrees and Kenny G. About thirty years down the line, me and Kenny G ended up working together again, but at this point, he hadn't really had any major success. Kenny G was over here doing some gigs with his band, G Force and we got him to come into the studio and do a solo on the track which I was producing. It turned out that I was the first person to do something with him over here with that record. That was all before he blew up with

Songbird and then obviously, he became mega and the best-selling instrumentalist.

***

I was never one for craving the media, but I often found myself in the headlines after a track or an event had happened in my life, usually with some spin on '19' by the tabloids. For example, when Maxine was born a few days later, the headline was, *It's Na-na-na-Nappy time for Paul.* Also, around that time, I decided to buy a Lotus Esprit and I went out for a spin and put my foot down to see what it could do. As the turbo kicked in and the exhausts were roaring, I just so happened to be going past an unmarked police car and all of a sudden, I saw the blue flashing lights in the rearview and the sirens blaring. The day after, the headline was, *Paul Hardcastle nicked for doing, Na-na-na-ninety.*

On the subject of cars, I'd always been a massive fan of Ferrari but never thought I'd own one. That all changed after a chance encounter with my one of my Pink Floyd idols. Here's what happened. I was in Nice, down the south of France and I was standing at the counter of the Beach Regency Hotel and I looked over and I thought, *Fucking hell. It's David Gilmour.* He looked back and nodded to me and I looked behind me to check the nod was intended for me, but there was nobody there. I was over the moon that Gilmour had acknowledged me.

I walked over and said, 'Hi Dave. How are you?'

He replied, 'I'm very good, Paul. How are you?'

I thought, *Wow! He knows my name.* It was another Phil Lynott moment.

He asked what I was doing in Nice and I explained a family holiday and he then said, 'We're playing tonight if you want to come to the show?'

I replied, 'Yeah!'

He said, 'Leave it with me. I'll sort you out with some tickets and some backstage passes.' I went back to the family and spoke at a million miles an hour, mumbling about my chance encounter with Gilmour and they looked at me like I was on drugs.

After the gig in Perpignan, I went to the after party at the Beach Regency Hotel and I was chatting to the drummer, Nick Mason, who had a number of Ferraris, including a 250 GTO, which is now worth more than $35million. At this point of my life, I felt that I'd work my arse off for years, but especially the last twelve months, between '19' and all the remixes and I thought, *I'd like a Ferrari.* I looked over the balcony as we were chatting and I saw this 328 GTS and I thought to myself, *That is the nicest car I've ever seen.* I wasn't going out and spending five grand on a suit every weekend and doing all the things that pop stars do, like hiring private jets, limos and all that sort of stuff. In fact, while people were going to all the posh restaurants, I was working and saving. I wanted something to say, 'That's a reason why you're in the recording studio.' Some people bought artwork, but I couldn't tell you the difference between a Monet and a money. However, one thing I did know was my cars and motorcycles. That's when I thought, *I'm gonna get that Ferrari.*

The problem was that the Ferrari 328 had just come out and there weren't any available. However, Nick Mason knew a car dealer called Nick Lancaster, who knew someone who had bought it just to resell it. Mason calls over Lancaster and his wife Jane and Nick said, 'Paul's looking for a 328. Can you help?'

He replied, 'I've got one, but it's top dollar because it's only got six hundred miles on it and it's in mint condition.' I knew it wasn't going to go down in value because they only made about seven thousand of them and rather than wait a couple of years, I paid about fifteen grand over the asking price, which was a hell of a lot of money. However, if my career ended the following week, I knew I could still make money on it.

Meeting Dave Gilmour was immense, but my musical highlight of 1986, recognition-wise, was winning an Ivor Novello award for my achievements the year before. I was actually nominated for three Novello awards, which were Best Contemporary Song, Best Selling International Hit of the Year and Best Selling *A* Side. In 1985, I had the fourth bestselling song in the UK with '19', behind Madonna's, 'Into the Groove,' Elaine Paige and Barbara Dickson's, 'I Know Him so Well' and Jennifer Rush's, 'The Power of Love.' However, on the international stage, I was number one. I ended up winning International Hit of 1985, with Duran Duran's, 'View to a Kill' and 'Tears for Fears'

'Shout' trailing as runners-up. Benny Andersson from Abba presented me the award at the Grosvenor House Hotel and I was also very happy that Simon also received one.

If there's one thing nobody can accuse me of, it is trying new things. My next track certainly ticked that box.

June 1988

Steffi Graf wins the French Women's Open.

Bloodsport, with Jean-Claude Van Damme, premieres in Germany.

Microsoft releases MS-DOS 4.0.

Eighty thousand people attend music concert in honour of Nelson Mandela.

US President Ronald Reagan visits the UK.

Paul Hardcastle releases the album, *No Winners*.

Radio-Active

No Winners is a good example of how modern studio technology allows the application of a cut-and-paste technique, enabling any kind of effect, noise, or piece of dialogue to be spliced into the musical fabric of a song. It heightens the potential for a pop composition to take on an abstract journalistic form, where the artists organises material into a kind of drama-documentary collage you can dance to… As such, the Nuclear side of No Winners inhibits a territory that has become familiar to the pop world since Band-Aid, where the great and perilous issues facing the earth are addressed as humanitarian matters rather than questions of power relationships and vested interest.

Dave Hill, June 1988, The Independent

The year after Montreux, I produced a track for Johnny Logan, who had just won the 1987 Eurovision Song Contest. Johnny was looked after by Chris Morrison, who was Simon's business partner and they said, 'Would you like to do something with him?' I didn't really know Johnny, simply because I don't really watch the Eurovision, but I went and met him and he was a really nice guy. I also got to hear some of his other stuff and thought, *This guy can certainly sing,* but it wasn't my sort of thing. I was thinking of an appropriate cover to produce and said, 'What about 'I'm not in Love', by 10cc?' Everyone was in agreement and he sang it brilliantly.

My mother-in-law at the time, Maria, an absolutely lovely woman, listened to the record and said how good she thought Johnny was and how good the track sounded. Knowing she was a fan of Johnny, I decided to give her a little surprise. I got him to come over to my house, which is not far from where she used to live and I took him around there. As she answered the door, I said, 'Hello Maria. I've got someone who wants to see you.'

She sees who's standing next to me and says with a big smile, 'It's Johnny Logan!' He made a real fuss of her, which was lovely to see. That was one of the first tracks I did on the Synclavier after 'The Wizard.'

I also wrote and produced a track for Sinitta. Here's how that came about. Simon Cowell got in touch with Fuller and then he called me and said, 'Cowell's working with Sinitta and he wants to do a few tracks. Could you come up with something a bit like 'Rainforest' because he's a big fan of the track? However, he'd like vocals on the top of it.'

That's what I did and 'If I let You Go' was one of the tracks on the album I produced in 1987. Sinitta's got a lovely voice, but some of her previous stuff up to that point, like 'So Macho,' hadn't done her justice. I got a lot of people saying to me, 'I didn't realise what a soulful voice she has until I heard that track. She can really sing.' Sinitta's a really nice person, with genuine talent and we recently had a chat about doing something in the not-too-distant future.

A couple of months after the Johnny track, I was reading something about the Cuban Missile Crisis of 1962 and I saw comments from Robert MacNamara, the then US Secretary of Defence, saying, 'As I left the Whitehouse and walked through the garden to my car, to return to the Pentagon on that beautiful evening, I feared I might not live to see another Saturday night.'

In 1962, there were about five thousand warheads and I started to think, *What would happen if today (in 1987) the same situation happened, with fifty thousand warheads?* I didn't give it another thought until the year after when I was coincidentally contacted by a man called Dr Jeremy Leggett.

Jeremy was from Imperial College in London and he explained how they were trying to make people aware of the number of nuclear warheads being made and the lack of awareness of this worldwide. He asked me if I would help to spread the word and said, 'If you do agree to help with this, I'll get the college behind us and I'll ask your record company if they will let me take you to Washington to meet the top people out there.'

I spoke with Simon and said, 'I think this might be my next project.'

He replied, 'If that's what you want to do, go for it.'

I called Jeremy back and said, 'I'm in.' Next thing I was on Concorde on my way to Washington with Simon.

Funnily enough, one of the first people I bumped into on the plane was Sir David Frost, who didn't recognise me at first. I introduced myself and told him that I was a big fan of his and he said, 'The Vietnam track, right? We've had you on one of our music channels, I believe?'

I said, 'That's right!' I couldn't have been more chuffed that he recognised me.

In Washington, we stayed with these people from the Freedom of Information Act, who were good friends with Sir Rudolf Peierls, who prophesized that nuclear fission was possible. I was interested to know how a golf ball-sized piece of plutonium could make such a massive explosion and I wanted to know more about nuclear fission and neutron bombs. I asked them all, but it was Sir Rudolf who explained the facts and theories with clarity.

I stayed at Rear Admiral Eugene Carroll and Rear-Admiral Gene Laroque's houses in Washington and ironically, at the time of writing, Laroque was a nuclear advisor at the Pentagon. Despite everyone talking about how close the Cuban Missile Crisis was to fully kicking off, Carroll explained how the US had nine times the amount of nuclear weapons compared to Russia. Carroll was basically trying to say how the media were playing it all up because there was no way Russia would have flexed their muscles being outweighed by that ratio. That comes from someone who had been bang in the middle of the Cuban Missile Crisis on a ship which was part of the blockade that was ready to launch nuclear missiles. At the time, there were more than enough bombs to blow the world up, so what was the point of building even more bombs? That's the message they were trying to get across and that was kind of my brief in terms of making the track.

I ended up spending two months in Washington being briefed by Carroll, LaRocque and a number of others and between us, we put in fifteen months of research to get the album together. *No Winners* was not intended to take a political stance, merely pointing out the obvious that if anyone decides to start a nuclear war, there genuinely will be no winners. The primary aim was to help people understand the situation that had unfolded since Hiroshima, which inspired the track on the album '40 Years,' which referred to what had happened about forty years previously.

The album originally started as an instrumental, but then I decided that vocals would help complement what I was trying to achieve. If you watch the '40 Years' video, you'll see me as the front man, singing and dancing in a proper 80s leather outfit. I highly recommend you don't watch it! I've always preferred being in the background and as invisible as I can be, but for this track, it was an experiment, really. I knew I wasn't Luther Vandross; it was all about the message the song gave out. There's one line on it which says, *One large warhead is more destructive than all the explosions made in World War II.* If someone was able to walk away with that fact, then it was worth it. However, I also realised that if I was going to have other tracks with vocals on the album, I'd need someone with a great voice and that's when I brought Helen Rogers on board.

There was another little lady who was also involved in the album, who not only spoke on it but featured on the front cover. It was my two-year-old daughter, Maxine. I needed the face of a child crying on the cover and I felt really bad saying this, but I had to make Max cry for the photo. I think I had to tell her that I wasn't going to give her something that I'd promised, whether it was a toy or favourite food, because I really needed her to look the part for the album cover.

Once the photos were done, I said, 'I was only joking.' Then I made it up to her straight away and gave her everything I promised and some, but I got what I needed for the cover! Max was also featured on the '40 Years' track.

The album itself was a mishmash of people saying different things and expressing their opinions, including a sample of Paul Newman talking about bombs, which he'd done for an advertising company. I asked if I could use his voice from the ad and they agreed. Paul sounded great on it and he said,

Without testing in the 1950s, there would be no hydrogen bomb,

Without testing in the 60s, there would be no nuclear weapons,

Without testing in the 70s, there would be no neutron bomb,

By stopping testing now, neither we nor the Soviet Union will be able to build nuclear-powered lasers to be able to extend our battlefield into space.

However, my favourite quote from the album narrated by Mark Peters is, *We will become victims of our own genius.*

Shortly after the release of '40 Years', I had about half a dozen of these guys from the Freedom of Information Act at the V&A museum in London for the launch. The press who attended were amazed that they were sitting next to scientists who'd been involved in designing some of these nuclear bombs.

It seems ironic that after the release of the album, Gorbachov and Reagan signed a deal to massively cut production of nuclear warheads. I'm not saying the album stopped nuclear proliferation, but it all added to that melting pot of making a contribution in the right direction. The big guns involved with the album certainly saw the merits in *No Winners,* and it's worth taking a minute to read their comments below, which were on the album sleeve.

For sixteen years, I justified my intense devotion to the design and promotion of nuclear warheads on the grounds that their existence was making the war unthinkable. In 1965, while working in the Pentagon as the war in Vietnam intensified, I was forced to admit that we, the nuclear weaponeers, had not stopped war but were instead threatening the existence of humanity. I did a complete about-face, for reasons that will be clear to anyone who listens to this record and have since devoted myself to pressing for worldwide abolition of all weapons of mass destruction.

Dr Theodore Taylor was a top nuclear weapons designer at Los Alamos in the 1950s and early 1960s.

The present nuclear arsenals are enormously too large. The time for large-scale nuclear disarmament is long overdue. We could feasibly reduce our nuclear warheads to ten per cent of current levels by the year 2,000. And we must agree on a ban on nuclear testing with the Soviets. Because of the silo-killing capabilities of many of the current weapons – some of them described on this record – because of the destabilising weapons designs which are on the drawing boards for the future, this process of disarmament MUST happen in the next two decades. We are living through a crucial time in human history.

Dr Hugh De Witt. Worked for thirty years as a physicist in the largest American weapons design industry, the Lawrence Livermore Laboratory.

We cannot; we must not let the nuclear arms race reach its finishing line. As Albert Einstein said before he died, If we are to avoid that fate, then we must radically change the way we think. Paul Hardcastle believes that music can help to change the way people think. I have watched him at work researching and consulting with scientists and military men – during the long process of compiling this album. He has summed up the full range of threats which nuclear weapons pose to the survival of humankind. Too many people believe that because nuclear weapons might have kept a form of peace for forty years, we will need them forever. Nobody who listens to this album will ever be able to accept that dangerous idea again.

Dr Jeremy Leggett. Scientist at Imperial College, London and director of the Verification Technology Information Centre. With his colleagues, he researches ways of ensuring that states who sign disarmament treaties will not be able to cheat.

All over the world, on land and at sea, are thousands of so-called tactical nuclear weapons. They are war-fighting weapons. Every day, the nuclear nations practice for a war with these bombs, missiles, torpedoes, depth charges, landmines and artillery shells. These weapons are the hair-trigger for a nuclear war. A war which, as Paul Hardcastle says, will have no winners.

Rear-Admiral Gene Laroque – (US Navy Retd) commanded warships and task forces during his thirty-one years in the US Navy. He became a senior planner in the Pentagon for nuclear strategy.

Based on thirty-seven years of military experience, I know believe – as this album points out – that humanity is heading for disaster. The myth for nearly twenty years now has been that the Soviets could – or would – roll over Europe if there were no American nuclear weapons. This is simply not true. Some world leaders are saying, in effect, that we're not safe without nuclear weapons: that we're going to have to learn to live with them because it is the only way in which we can be safe. *This addiction to nuclear weapons is a fatal concept. If we have to live with them indefinitely, each side with thousands of warheads aimed at the other side, the first failure of that relationship will be fatal. And there is nothing more certain in this world than that at some place, at some time, through human error, computer error, mechanical error, irrational acts or miscalculations, there will be a failure and we will have a nuclear war. The short-sighted response we can't afford, for our own safety, to start getting rid of nuclear weapons is absolutely false and must be rejected by thinking people everywhere.*

Rear-Admiral Eugene J. Carroll (US Navy Retd). Former director of US military operations for forces in Europe and the Middle East in 1979. His responsibilities included the safety, security and readiness of all the six thousand US weapons then in Europe.

The A side of *No Winners* was covering very serious and dark detail about nuclear war and I felt I'd said as much as I could on that side of the album. I then decided to make the B side more upbeat for the soul and dancey fans, which included a remix of 'The Wizard' and a track called 'Walk in the Night', where you'll see me acting as a music conductor with a baton motioning to a bunch of animals.

What happened was I'd seen something similar to it on the television and I thought that could be fun. I got to the studio and they had this big extravagant John Paul Gaultier suit ready for me to wear. This was one of the first tracks I used Helen Rogers as a session singer and she was absolutely brilliant. However, she was a bit bamboozled by the technology because she had been used to working with the old analogue reel-to-reel tape system. Back then, when you were in the studio and wanted to go back and rerecord a bit of vocal, you had to wait for the tape to rewind. So, there we were at my studio working on this track and I stopped and said, 'Let's redo part of that vocal.'

Helen stopped and I said, 'Hel. What you waiting for?'

She said, 'I'm waiting for the tape to rewind.'

I said, 'What tape? We're at the point to record.'

She replied, 'Oh wow. Just like that!'

It was called random access, which is where the term RAM comes from (random access memory) when talking about technology. That track got me a lot of recognition with the soul crowd and to an extent, it brought them back towards me. 'Don't Waste My Time', wasn't totally off the soul scale, but 'Just for Money' and 'The Wizard' definitely were.

I had good fun making 'Walk in the Night', but I did have a few people give negative feedback about the video. One of the people from the record label said, 'The music is good, but I don't agree with the video. I remember watching it back and thinking, *Here we go. He's just sticking his oar in*, but after a few weeks, I started to reflect and thought, *Yeah. He's right,* because although the majority of footage involved wild animals, there were some clips of animals in caged environments and others performing tricks, which I would have refused to do now as I have a great love for animals and believe they should be in their natural habitat and treated correctly.

From jungle to acid. Despite investing a lot of time into *No Winners,* I was still making new music and being the experimentalist I am, it didn't always follow suit to my previous stuff. Same year, I was talking about nuclear bombs; I also did an Acid album, which I made in about thirty-six hours. At the time, the Acid scene was massive and I did this mix, which was really awful, but it sold fifty thousand albums and one of the bands on the album was called ELLiS.D.

Before the year was up, '19' was sampled by Rob Hubbard in a Commodore 64 game called Boot Camp and I did the TV advertising with him. It was a classic game and I still have an original in its box. Then, in 1989, I sampled something equally destructive as nuclear fission with Simon Fuller. Back then, I enjoyed the odd glass of champagne, but I wasn't a big drinker. Instead, you'd find me with a pint of Coca-Cola while my mates would be sinking lager or bitter. For years, I'd been saying to Simon that he needed to see Pink Floyd live and in July 1989, we managed to see them at Docklands Arena. He loved it.

As we were coming back from the concert, we stopped at an Indian restaurant and Simon had a Kingfisher lager. He said, 'This is a nice beer, but you wouldn't know because you don't drink.'

Then I thought, *Let me have a taste of it.*

I thought, *Mmm. I'll have one of those.* That was it. That's how I became a lager drinker. Fuller got me onto beer!

Thankfully, I never felt the shockwaves from a nuclear bomb; however, in the next couple of years, I did feel seismic shakes and the direction of my new music certainly made some noise.

April 1991

US minimum wage goes from $3.80 to $4.35.

Evander Holyfield beats George Foreman in the world heavyweight title bout.

Intel releases the i486 microprocessor.

Graham Greene dies, aged eighty-six.

Paul Hardcastle signs with Motown Records.

Shhhhhhhh...

Paul Hardcastle, despite his low profile of late, has been a busy man.

Paul Ireson, Sound on Sound Magazine, September 1991

Towards the end of the 1980s, there was a new guy who was head of A&R at Chrysalis Records and he wasn't crazy on the sort of stuff I was doing, which was more popular in America.

I said to Simon, 'We've had a good run, but I'd like to change labels and be somewhere where the people are positive.'

Simon agreed, went to Chrysalis and did a deal on the onus that they'd get an override on the next two albums. However, they had to be nationally distributed albums, otherwise, I could have gone to my local corner shop and asked them to sell ten copies and that would have gotten me out of the contract. One album was First Light and the other was called Sound Syndicate.

I banged out these albums for Chrysalis in less than six months and everyone was happy. It all worked well because I wasn't a frontman, whereas if I'd been a vocalist, there's no way they would have allowed it. Whilst doing those albums and for the coming months after, I still made a number of records under different names, which included a few tracks that received gold disks. I was also doing music under the name of Deff Boyz, which was a massive hit around Europe, even though nobody knew it was me and I was also LFO and Silent Underdog. I can't mention which other tracks and albums I did because I was, in essence, invisible due to overlapping with my Chrysalis contract.

The highlight of 1990 was on 27 August, when my first son, Paul Jr, was born. He would develop into one of the best saxophonists I know and we'd have the pleasure of topping the charts down the line with a genre of music I was on the cusp of breaking into. However, the five years that followed '19' were crazy busy, to say the least. From making tracks to producing, remixing, singing and making scores for television, nobody really knew what I was about and I still don't know myself! Despite enjoying my time in the pop charts, 'Rainforest' was the foundation of so much of my passion and I wanted to go back to that sort of music again. That pretty much marked the start of the next part of my career.

By this stage, I'd signed with JVC in Japan a couple of years before and things were going well out there for me, but I'd not signed to their American side of the company yet. In the meantime, Motown Records came in with an offer and it all moved pretty quickly. Here's what happened. We had a few tracks on the radio at the time, like 'Voodoo Chile' and 'Living for You' and we started to get a bit of momentum with the up-and-coming album, *Kiss the Sky*, with Jaki Graham. That's when a guy called Mervyn Lyn, who worked at Motown in London, got in touch and asked if we could meet and also if I could send him a few more tracks, which I did. Shortly after the meeting, he said, 'I'm going to send this to the bosses in America.'

Mervyn contacts Motown America and sends them the music. Shortly after, in early 1991, I got a call from a guy called Steve McKeever, who was one of the very senior guys at Motown. Steve said, 'I've heard a couple of your tracks from the album and I liked what I heard. I'm coming to London soon and I'm interested in signing you to our label. Would you like to meet for dinner?' I was blown away that this guy from one of the most famous record labels on the planet said that and I obviously said yes about meeting up.

A few days later, he arrived in London and I went and met him in the West End at some nice restaurant where he had booked a table. I was obviously over the moon, but I had to tell them that they had to cut out Japan and Southeast Asia in the deal because JVC was already doing it over there. That basically meant that Motown had it for the rest of the world. He said, 'No problem.' We chatted a bit more; I agreed to send him some more of my music and shortly after, we signed contracts. What a privilege to be on the Motown label.

Signing to Motown, to an extent, also cemented my working association with Jaki Graham for the album. I'd left Chrysalis by then and I always thought Jaki was a really good singer. I invited her down to chat about the *Kiss the Sky* album. There were ten tracks and the target audience was soul.

Jaki's husband, Tony Ormsby, was a lovely bloke and also happened to be the brother of Brendan, who used to play for Aston Villa. Tony would come down and we'd have a really good laugh, but he wouldn't interfere with her career. Me and Jaki got on really well, but unfortunately, she had this guy who came on board about six months down the line after we started working together. I don't know who he was, but he was just an idiot.

One day, I got a call from him and he said, 'Jaki deserves some writing credits on the album.'

I replied, 'How did you work that one out?'

He said, 'Well, she was there singing them.'

I then said, 'OK. But what exactly did she write in terms of the lyrics or music themselves?'

He said, 'No, but she was singing them.'

I then said, 'Do you know the difference between publishing and recording? Also – do you know the difference between writing and singing?'

I felt sorry for Tony because he was stuck in the middle and it nearly ended up going to court. Jaki wasn't a writer; she was a great singer; in the same way, I wasn't a singer. It was such a shame because she's a lovely woman and after that episode happened, we drifted and never worked together again. We parted ways after *Kiss the Sky,* but we could have easily done another album. I just felt uneasy after that and when I work with someone, I have to be good friends with them and have a laugh. That was no longer possible.

Jaki and I going our separate ways wasn't great, but I came to terms with it pretty quickly. Unfortunately, some things aren't as easy to brush over. The same year *Kiss the Sky* came out, my mum was dealt a horrible hand. I distinctly remember the day my mum came home after coming back from the doctor. She was living at Grove Green Road in Leytonstone and she said, 'The doctors said that I've got cancer.' It wasn't that I ignored what she said, but I told a few people and when I mentioned cancer, their faces dropped, whereas I was like, *She'll be fine!* simply because I was totally ignorant about the disease.

It turns out she had cancer of the oesophagus and they wanted to operate. I went up to the hospital after the operation and I thought she was going to be groggy, but she was sitting up in bed and totally with it. I thought, *That's brilliant. You look great,* but she then said, 'They didn't do the operation.'

I thought, *That's obviously a great sign that she's healthy enough and that she doesn't need the op.*

Then the specialist came over and said, 'There's nothing we can do to help your mum.'

Again, I just thought, *She won't be very well for the rest of her life,* but it was far more serious than that. He then said, 'She's got about four months. That's when the reality hit.

She soon started losing a hell of a lot of weight and within a few months, I remember going to the hospital thinking, *In a day or two, I'm not going to have a mum.* Within about four months of the diagnosis, she was dead. She was only sixty and I'm so glad that she got to see me do well because she was always so supportive of everything I did and I've never met a prouder parent. And let's not forget, she let me take over her front room to get all my music equipment in!

I went on to release a track called, 'You May be Gone', which was all about her and featured my daughter Maxine and my niece Hayley, who were saying bye to their nan. There were also backing vocals from Helen Rogers and lead vocals from Steve Menzies, who's a great singer. Here are some of the lyrics.

Then came the news
It cut like a knife
It was the coldest day of my life
It seemed that time was not on your side
Your right to live had been denied.

You may be gone
But you'll never be forgotten
You may be gone
But I still think about you often

RIP, Mum.

I had already produced music for the Sound Syndicate album, which was like a combination of house, synth-pop and adult contemporary, but when I started the *Jazzmasters*, the intention was for the music to be more along the lines of a cross between 'Rainforest' and 'King Tut'. I decided to try something which was sax-led with Gary Barnacle, who used to play with Level 42 but had also done a great job on my earlier track, 'Walk in the Night.'

I wanted vocals that would complement the music perfectly and approached Helen Rogers. At the time, Helen was taking a break from music and was doing a course at university. Then I called her out of the blue, telling her I had this new project, which would involve co-writing with her if she came on board. After a little chat, I asked if she'd like to come over and listen to what I had and despite being up to her ears in studies, she came over.

After I played a few minutes, she said, 'Wow. That's lovely.' I think she was taken in by the fact that it was something I wanted to do instead of following a market trend, but it was also something that really suited her voice.

Helen then said, 'Let me take away a couple of backing tracks to see if I can write something over it and see how it works.' Shortly after, we got cracking with recording. I ended up working with Helen on five of the

Jazzmasters albums and five of the Hardcastle series and I'm so glad I did.

A number of people said, 'This is different from Paul, but it's great.' However, you can't keep everyone happy.

I once had someone say to me, 'How have you got the name *Jazzmasters*? You don't play jazz.'

I replied, 'It's just a name and there are many different takes on the jazz genre. I've never pretended to be a jazz purist. What are you going to do if you see a stone coming down the hill? Accuse it of trying to be Mick Jagger?'

He laughed and accepted that. Starting *Jazzmasters* was ideal for the time of my life because it provided a different vibe and it wasn't as crazy as before because I wasn't promoting one big blockbuster track. Also, the timing after Motown was ideal.

I'd signed to Motown about six months before I started the *Jazzmasters*. However, they'd just signed 'Boyz 2 Men' and they were their main priority. A few of the tracks on my album did really well, but we didn't get that much of a look in, understandably. At the time, 'Boyz 2 Men' were smashing the whole world to pieces and we sort of got lost in the mix, which I didn't blame them for one little bit. If you've got a group which is going to sell twenty million records and I'm going to sell five hundred thousand, it's obvious where you need to dedicate your time to.

In my contract, Motown had only signed *Kiss the Sky*, which meant *Jazzmasters* made me eligible to go elsewhere. The question now was, *Where?*

September 1993

Noureddine Morceli breaks the mile world record in three minutes 44:39 seconds.

Steffi Graf wins her fifteenth Grand Slam singles title.

'I'd Do Anything for Love' (But I won't do that), (sung by Meatloaf) is released.

Television series Frasier premieres on NBC.

Ford ceases production of the Orion car in the UK.

Paul Hardcastle receives a letter from President Bill Clinton.

I'll not forget the moment back, I think, in 1991–92 when I received a call from Allen Kepler from Broadcast Architecture and programmer of J-Wave radio in Japan informing me about a new album project that he thought I might be interested in. At the time, I was acting Director of National Promotion for JVC Music in Los Angeles and Allen proceeded to tell me about this thing called The Jazzmasters. First question he asked was, "Do you know of Paul Hardcastle?" I had to think for a minute and as I paused to think, he mentioned 'Rainforest' and '19' which brought the name into complete focus. Who didn't know who that was? He proceeded to tell me about this exciting new project and how it already found its way to a few major market radio stations, namely KKSF in San Francisco and CD 101 in New York City. I asked him to send me a copy of the project so that I could hear what was going on. When it arrived in the mail, I dug into it immediately and to my surprise, it was a new sound that was completely different to anything that was going on in the genre at the time. It was all about the songs and what they had to say over instrumentation. I could immediately see why this thing was causing such a stir where it had been spun off of the Japanese import. It took weeks of standing up on my soapbox at the record label, refusing to accept anything less than signing him to a recording contract in the States. After making enough noise to wear them down, we made it official and signed Paul to a long-term recording contract and put out Jazzmasters 1.

In my thirty-eight-year career, to this day, I've not experienced anything like it, before or after. The buzz on this record was so strong and the word had gotten to other stations wanting to get on board and where it was getting played, it was blowing out at retail. We were fielding calls from across the country asking what this thing was and how to get it. Absolutely crazy. This was the beginning of a total resurgence of Paul's career and on a differing plain than ever before. What we have managed to do in the ensuing years has been nothing short of incredible. I've lost count of the number of No.1's s we've had together. I know it's well north of 20. We currently hold the Billboard record for the longest-running No.1 single, Walking to Freedom in the chart's history at sixteen consecutive weeks. Also, for the Most Added Single ever for the same, picking up all but two of the Radio & Records reporting stations in the first week and if my memory serves me correctly, it was somewhere in the range of thirty-four of thirty-six stations. In our storied history together now over thirty years, we have accomplished so much and Paul truly has no peers. He has now and has always had his own definitive sound that, to this day, no one has duplicated nor even tried to. What a blessing it has been for me in my music business life to be a part of a movement that changed the genre and to ride the Hardcastle train. What working with Paul and his music did for my career I can't put a price on, but it took a passionate little independent music promoter from the small to the big time in short order and opened

241

the gates of amazing future success for me. We accomplished so many historic things over the last three decades and I was/am so blessed to have played a small part in it.'

Jeff Lunt

What You Doing for the Next Month?

There's no denying the fact that over the last decade, Hardcastle has grown to become one of the premier producers in Britain, if not Europe, as he has managed to rack up hit after hit.

Terry Muggleton, BRE Magazine, 30 July 1993

By the early 90s, I decided to concentrate on the Japanese and American markets because the music I was now making was not having much of an impact on the rave scene, which was big in the UK at the time. Funnily enough, though, I'd actually recorded a few rave-type dance cuts a couple of years before, which sold very well, but I quickly got bored doing that sort of music. I've always been about chasing the passion of what I do and if the money comes with that, then great; if not, I'm still content to have made music, which I take a lot of pride in.

Although I'd been recording music for the *Jazzmasters* since 1990, I didn't actually release the ten-track album until the end of 1992. The first ever track I did to start this new sound off with *Jazzmasters* was called 'Lost Summer'. Just to say, don't get that mixed up with 'Lost Summer' from the *No Winners* album of 1988 when

243

I was with Chrysalis. I just happened to like the name and decided to use the title again for the *Jazzmasters*. I put the success of that track down to 'Rainforest' because it was basically a slowed-down version with sax. That was done on the Synclavier and sounds like it could have been done today because the quality was that good.

At the time, the two main distributors in the entertainment industry were Lasgo and Windsong. They would take, say, five hundred albums from you at a reduced price and then send them all over the world. 'Lost Summer' was doing well in Japan and a man called Allen Kepler heard about it, which became a game changer.

Back then, Allen was programming several hours of new adult contemporary (NAC) music for Tokyo's No.1 rated station, J-WAVE 81.3FM. While his duties were to deliver NAC programming from the US, he always liked keeping up with other popular songs on the radio station to see what might also fit into their program titled *AZ WAVE*. Each week, the J-WAVE programming team would send their *Tokio HOT 100* chart and one particular week, Allen was looking and noticed that the No.1 song on their pop-oriented chart was called 'Lost Summer', and was from an album called *The Jazzmasters*.

Allen figured, 'Hey, this might be good for us.' He then emailed his counterpart at J-WAVE and asked him if he might connect him with the record label to find out who was behind the album.

Allen was also head of Broadcast Architecture and his company would go around to different cities all around the world testing records. They would have say eight hundred people in an auditorium and they all had these slider buttons as the records played. They would then move the slider controls either up or down to show how much they liked the record. Allen was also working with radio stations in New York City, Chicago, San Francisco, Dallas and Los Angeles and, off his own back, decided to test 'Lost Summer' in America and against a load of other tracks, it won by a wide margin. If you are trying to get the record out in the marketplace and the feedback says it tested ninety percent positive, it gives the radio producers something to think about.

In the meantime, Allen's counterpart found out that the *Jazzmasters* album was produced by myself and the guys at J-Wave somehow got my number. Allen called me and said, 'I've got your *Jazzmasters* album and it's tested brilliantly here in America. If you could send me over five or six copies, I'll send them to all the main radio stations.' He sent them to New York, Washington, Dallas, Atlanta, LA and Chicago, all of which were massive coverage for me. Allen became a good friend and without him, I would never have gotten into the American market the way I did. In fact, over thirty years later, I'm still very good friends with him.

At the time, I was still only signed with JVC Japan, but with this data in hand, I decided to ask the head guy in Tokyo, Takashi, if he could pass me the number of the person I could speak to for JVC America, as I wanted global reach with the album. Shortly after, I was speaking to JVC America's A&R guy, Jeff Lunt, who was an absolutely lovely man and he said, 'We also had the data from Allen and we loved *The Jazzmasters*. We have to get you to come over and we can sit down and talk.' That's how I signed up for JVC America.

They were great from day one. They knew what they were doing and the niche I worked in, which helps when you are looking to market a client specifically to the target audience. Jeff was really in the know, which is why I went on to work with him for such a long time. He made a massive success of the first *Jazzmasters* album, for which I was and still am very grateful.

I'd say *The Jazzmasters* was my first big step into shifting into new adult contemporary (NAC) and similar, which was also an opportunity for me to show that I was a versatile artist. On 16 December 1992, *The Post* backed this up by writing an article entitled, *The Sky's not the limit for Paul!* They added, *Paul is concentrating his efforts on the lucrative markets of America and Japan. One of Paul's new projects – a jazz album appropriately released under the name Jazzmasters – is already riding high in the land of the rising sun.*

With all eyes on me, the pressure was on to deliver the goods and walk the walk.

***

A few months after Jazzmasters was released, JVC asked me to do a month-long promotional tour of America and

Japan in the summer of 1993, with them covering all my expenses as I went around all the radio stations. Of course, I said, 'Yes.' However, as the date for departure got closer, the reality struck me, *I'm going on my own for a month. That's going to be boring.* That's when I asked my old mate, Les Cutmore, to come along.

I'd like to take a few moments to tell you more about Les because there's a lovely poetic twist in the tale that comes with this story involving his future after this particular trip. Les is a couple of years younger than me and I first met him back in 1973 when I was fifteen. I was friends with his brother and I'd earned myself a bit of a name of being a lunatic on a motorbike, along with about four or five bikers where Les used to live in Haggerston. Then, one day, Les thought, *I've been warned not to go on the back of this guy's bike, but let's see if he's as crazy as everyone thinks.*

We got talking and he said, 'Any chance of a back-seater?'

I said, 'Yeah. Sure, no problem.' He was wearing a T-shirt, so I asked him to get a jacket on and I found him a helmet.

We went up the road and within about three seconds, Les almost fell off the back of the bike because the front wheel was close to vertical as we were doing about 40mph on this wheelie. Les grabbed me around the waist for dear life because a fraction of a second later and, he would have fallen off. I then put the front of the bike back down and he nervously laughed. We started going down some roads at serious speed and I turned to Les and asked, 'You OK, mate?' He didn't want to show his fear and said all upbeat, 'Yeah! Yeah! Love it!' I knew Les was testing me, so I thought, *Time to ramp this up another notch.*

Where Les used to live on Queensbridge Road in Haggerston, there was a humpback bridge that went across the canal and it went up at a really sharp angle. There we were, doing 80mph down this main road as Les was thinking, *He'll slow down for this,* but no, I pulled the throttle back even more. We took off and must have caught about thirty yards of air as Les was seconds away from bringing up his breakfast. When we got back, Les got off and said with a nervous laugh, 'Yeah. Thanks for that. I need to get back now.' That started our friendship.

We lost contact for a about three or four years because I'd moved and was deep into my music and we'd kind of gone our separate ways. However, he'd been following my success along the way with 'Rainforest' and '19'. Then, one day in 1985, he turned up at my house and said, 'How you doing?' I was delighted to see him. We had a good catch-up, exchanged numbers and kept in regular contact from then on.

Les worked with his dad in scrap, removing old equipment from telephone exchanges, where there were lots of precious metals in things like phones and cables. At the time, I was building my studio and I used to ask him get me cable because everything was analogue back then and his dad said, 'Yeah. Give him what he wants.' First time I asked Les, he came around with his van and two massive racks, which were worth about £250 back then and the old GPO patch bays, which would have also cost a fortune. Les made no fuss, but I was very appreciative of his help and friendship.

Roll the clock forward to the summer of 1993 and I've called Les with a random question. 'What you doing for the next month?'

He's said, 'Not a lot. Why's that?'

I replied, 'Do you fancy coming to America and then across to Japan?'

He said, 'I'm not sure if I can afford that.'

I said, 'No. You're my manager. You've got to come. It won't cost you a penny.'

He's gone, 'Eh? What you talking about, manager?'

I then said, 'JVC want me to do a tour promoting my Jazzmasters album and I'd like you to come as my manager – but you won't really be my manager. I just don't want to go on my own!'

He laughed, then said, 'But I don't know anything about music.'

I said, 'Basically. Just come over, stand around, meet the guys at the label and be support for me. Come on, Les. We'll have a right laugh!'

He said, 'For someone who's been pulling scrap out of places, to now going across the other side of the world and be your pretend manager – this is very different! Why not. Let's do it.'

Now I'd asked Les to come along. I phoned up Denny Stilwell from JVC in America and asked, 'You've obviously booked my manager in as well?' Basically blagging it.

He replied, 'No. You never mentioned anything about a manager.'

I replied, 'Every artist has a manager.'

He said, 'What would happen if we said we can't pay for that person?'

I replied, 'I won't be coming.' If my records had sold next to nothing, I wouldn't have been so cocky and they would have most likely said, 'Cool. Don't come. We don't give a shit.' But having become their biggest-selling artist on their label with *Jazzmasters*, I was confident in their response.

Denny said, 'No problem. We'll cover his costs.'

Shortly after, we left London, Heathrow and headed out to America. When we arrived in LA, it took me a while to realise we'd landed, as I was a bit phased by the time difference, which didn't help with me not sleeping on the plane due to my fear of flying. They were eight hours behind and the flight was eleven hours, which kind of meant we'd only lost three hours in real-time. My body clock was all over the place.

On arrival in America, *Jazzmasters* was No.1 in the NAC charts and was the bestselling independently distributed record in the country. Me and Les headed over to the JVC offices and started off on visiting twenty cities in twenty-three days, which was gruelling but also great fun. To see all these American fans attend signings was impressive. Every single city we went to, people had my records and I made sure I signed every vinyl, cassette, CD and piece of memorabilia they had because I was very appreciative of each and every person's support. Some radio stations really rolled the carpet out, such as Raleigh on the East Coast, which hired a really nice boat to go out on the lake and it was *Have dinner with Hardcastle* type of thing. They pulled out all the stops and had banners, posters and t-shirts done. There was another station that had a competition with a *Jazzmasters* golden disk as a prize, which I presented to the winner in San Francisco. Then, there was this track which I didn't have a name for and decided to have this competition for someone to name it. The track was called 'Inner Changes', and the lady who won received an award on stage and a signed copy of the album, which stated that she named the track. She was over the moon.

At the time, CDs had really taken off big time and similar to vinyl records, it was a lovely thing to see, especially when it had your face on it, your name, credits, facts and a story on it. It meant so much, whereas now everyone is on a clicking frenzy, tapping a screen to play a track in a millisecond. Yes, it's progress, but as a result, record signings have now become redundant and fans don't get the chance to meet the artists that close any more.

I have to say, British fans are incredible, but I've found they can be easily swayed by a number of factors in terms of staying with you, including things as basic as the clothes you are wearing, but more so for the format of music you are delivering. However, if you are looking for loyalty, it's really hard to beat the Americans. If they like you, they'll support you for life. It doesn't matter if you are wearing a string vest, a tuxedo or a T-shirt; it's in the grooves that matters to them. The first time I did a signing in America, this guy turned up with all my albums and singles. Even now, they're like that. There are fans that do that in the UK, but the difference is that it's the norm in America. Believe it or not, I sold more records in America and Japan than some of the UK's top-selling artists.

The Japanese were really good at promoting JVC. To take a non-domestic artist and sell about sixty-five thousand albums was incredible. The Post wrote in December 1992, *A single entitled Blue Days taken from the Jazzmasters LP spent four weeks at number one in the Japanese charts, outselling releases by the likes of Madonna, George Michael, Roxette and Elton John.*

We were working our way through these cities and radio interviews nicely. Next up was Dallas, followed by Chicago and then LA. After we finished the interviews in Dallas, we had some hours to kill and decided I wanted to drive down the road President Kennedy got assassinated on Dealey Plaza. I asked my driver to take me down to the exact route Kennedy did on the day he got shot, as I took a load of video film. Then later, I compared it to the actual footage, which felt a bit strange as I started to think about that day in history and what happened.

Later that evening, around eight p.m., we were somewhere downtown in Dallas signing stuff for about five hundred people, with their *Jazzmasters* posters, records, CDs, you name it. After having signed the lot, done a load of photos and press bits, we decided to go outside and have a drink, because it was a lovely warm evening. I'm out there with Les and about five or six other people when all of a sudden, I heard, *BANG, BANG, BANG.* It was like everyone immediately started doing the Oops Up Side Your Head as they hit the floor. I was the only one standing up, saying naively with a smile on my face, 'What's going on?'

Next thing, this massive bouncer got up and almost rugby-tackled me to the ground and said, 'Man! We're being shot at. Stay down.' I didn't realise, but it was a random drive-by shooting and we were only about five yards from the people with the guns. The moment they passed, we all ran back inside and stayed there for about thirty minutes, surreally discussing what had just happened. Most of the people who came out said they owned guns but that they'd never been that close to a drive-by. I genuinely thought it was either fireworks or someone nearby who was shooting a television programme which had a cop scene involving guns. I don't know why I even thought that! Recapping the day – we went to see where Kennedy got shot and then we got shot at the very same night.

Although the gun shooting episode should have left a lasting impression on me, it was actually my first and only dabble with cannabis that left me with a bad taste in my mouth - literally. Unlike these days, where cannabis is legal in a number of States in the US, back then, it was illegal throughout the country. There we were in San Francisco with me, Les and about five other radio promotion people when one of them started smoking a joint and said, 'Come on, Paul. Join in.'

I replied, 'I hate the smell of smoke. No thanks.'

After a few more drinks, they're still goading me and making fun. 'Come on, man. What's wrong with you?

I thought you Brits were up for anything.' I said again, 'I really hate smoke.' But it got to the stage where I said, 'Gimme that.' I picked up a chunk of this skunk and ate it.

Everyone was like, 'Whoa! Yeah!' I didn't feel any different and wondered what all the fuss was about. I didn't get any reaction, so I grabbed another lump, put in in my beer, gave it a stir and drank the beer.

Les then said, 'You need to stop that. You'll fuck yourself up.'

I replied, 'What? It's doing nothing. I'd be worse if I had half a bottle of brandy.' Honestly – I thought this skunk was all a load of crap.

So, I did it again and grabbed another chunk and said, 'Look. It's doing fuck all to me.' The issue was that if I'd have smoked it, the hit would have been instant, but because this going through my digestive system, it was taking a lot longer to set me off. It was basically a ticking time bomb.

We then headed off to do a really important interview with The Gavin, which was a big-name magazine. We're at dinner and we get about five minutes in, with them asking me questions about *Jazzmasters* and whatever else

254

I was working on. All of a sudden, their voices weren't in time with the movement of their mouths. There was a two- or three-second delay, but it was also like a slurry voice which had been slowed right down. Let's say you've got a turntable and it's playing away at 45rpm and all of a sudden, you put it down to 33rpm, everything would slur and become slooooow.

I didn't know where I was or what was happening. Everyone was looking at me, thinking, *What's wrong with him?* as I was not saying anything, just staring at them.

We were all supposed to be going out after to China Town to a club and I mumbled to Les, 'Hotel.'

Luckily, Les quickly jumped in and said, 'Paul's had a really bad virus and he's been given some antibiotics which he was not supposed to drink alcohol with. They've obviously reacted with him and he needs to rest up.' That did the trick and they started being all sympathetic, but I felt so bad about the situation. People made the effort to come and interview me and they couldn't because I was stoned out of my head.

Les took me back to the room at the hotel and he went out with the radio people, which kept them sweet. I woke up the next day to find all the taps on full blast and the TV at full volume, which apparently was my handiwork. Also, in the middle of the night, there had been a raid because a prostitute had been using the room next door and the police had banged the door in. Les asked, 'Did you hear that commotion last night?' I hadn't heard a thing. I felt rough as hell and I'd certainly learned a lesson that drugs weren't for me.

After finishing the American side of the promotional tour, we flew from LA to Tokyo, which again messed with my body clock due to Tokyo being sixteen hours ahead and the flight being eleven hours. Thankfully, the buzz from the tour in America kept us going.

When I landed in Tokyo, I was No.1 in the Tokio Hot 100, which meant I received this incredible greeting from the fans. Parties left, right and centre and the Japanese couldn't be more polite if they tried. JVC came and met us and really rolled out the luxury, which included everything from a flash car to a fantastic hotel in the middle of Tokyo. As we were treated like kings, Les made out like it was all normal, but he was absolutely buzzing. Everywhere we went, I proudly introduced him as *My manager, Les,* which helped him relax as he was apprehensive about what he was there to do. All he really had to do was half listen to what I was saying and back me up, but l made sure he was in every meeting, went to the restaurants, got to meet the people and was never made to feel like a spare part. He did just great.

Japanese culture is incredible. We went with the bullet trains across to Osaka and Sapporo and unlike the UK, where nearly all the trains are late, this thing, which travels at about 200mph, always arrived to the second. I did about one hundred and fifty interviews in one week in Tokyo and I'm genuinely not exaggerating. They all had empty reels of tape in the centre of Tokyo and they'd do the interview and leave, which meant I didn't have to travel everywhere and that's what allowed me to do so many interviews. It's not like nowadays with technology where I can do it on a Zoom call or a really hi-tech line which makes you sound like you're in the studio anyway., back then I'd have to travel to, say, BBC Leicester or BBC Newcastle to do the interview, which meant you'd waste a whole day travelling for sometimes a thirty-minute feature.

It wasn't all work, though. I loved shopping out there and I couldn't get enough of it, especially the electronics. We went down this road called Akihabara, which is their equivalent to Tottenham Court Road in terms of electronics, but with ten times as many shops and all the new stuff that you couldn't find back home. It was like a paradise for me and I would have loved to have bought a video camera but there was a problem with incompatibility. Being a former H-Fi salesman, I was up to date with technology and knew that America and Japan used what was called NTSC format and Europe used something called PAL B. NTSC used far less frames per second than PAL, which meant that I wouldn't have been able to play it back home. However, there was this brand-new Godzilla toy that had come out, which had about twenty-four little motors inside it and every part moved. It was brilliant, but it was also bloody heavy, as I carried it all over Japan afterwards. I decided to buy it for my son, Paul Jr, who was about two at the time and I also got some stuff for Maxine, my daughter.

One thing I got addicted to on that trip was tempura udon, which I couldn't get enough of and ate every day. On the last day, the guy that was taking me around, Yoichi, an absolutely lovely fella, put his head in his hands and said, 'Please, please, please, Hardcastle-san – no more tempura udon!'

I laughed and said, 'OK, OK. Seeing that you've been good to me with my album, today we will not have tempura udon.' He was delighted and relieved, although I did have a sneaky tempura udon later that evening.

We stayed in Japan for about ten days and then headed back to London. All in all, it was an amazing month. BRE magazine wrote in July 1993 referring to my tour, *Like King Midas, everything Londoner Paul Hardcastle has touched turns to gold...Hardcastle has shown that he can deliver quality music capable of scoring in a host of formats.*

Les really enjoyed being my stand-in manager and had picked up quite a bit about the industry on that month-long trip. On the flight back to the UK, he said to me, 'I feel on a bit of a downer now after that whole month. I really enjoyed it, but I'm back to my normal day job.'

I replied, 'Why don't you form your own little label? Get a few artists and give it a go. I'll help you any which way I can. Go for it.' That turned out to be his turning point. He went from working for his dad as a precious metal scrap dealer to scouring the internet and finding his first artist. He went on to get a little distribution deal, signed his first artist and put an album out. It did OK but didn't make a lot of money. However, it also didn't lose any.

From there on, he started working long days and nights looking for new artists that he thought could be something. He'd listen to the radio and if he liked something, he'd contact them and offer them a deal. He initially used to tell them he was working with me to add credibility to whatever and whoever he was talking to, but as he started signing different artists, his label started to get a bit of a name and he became self-sufficient. I'd still pass his details to any up-and-coming artists and then Les would take care of the rest.

At the time of writing, Les is now CEO of Trippin and Rhythm Records, America, the owner of Cutmore Entertainment and Cutmore Records. His label has been going well over fifteen years and is one of the most successful in the new adult contemporary format; and has been voted Label of The Year three times on Billboard in America. Les uses a great promotions man in Jeff Lunt, who used to look after me at JVC America but had actually stepped away from the industry when Les was getting Trippin and Rhythm Records off the ground. Les wanted Jeff on board, got in touch with him and asked if he'd like to come back. They got on really well; Jeff agreed and still works for Trippin n Rhythm. That one phone call, *What you doing for the next month?* changed everything for Les. He's had a lot of success of No.1's with different artists and it didn't take long before I told him, 'You don't need me any more.' I've had thirty-eight No.1's in my career to date and at least half have been on his label. However, music apart, we've remained great friends.

**

At the time of releasing the first *Jazzmasters* album, someone from the promotion department of the American arm of JVC knew someone who worked at the White House. She said, 'Bill Clinton is a saxophone player. You should send him a copy of *Jazzmasters*.'

I said, 'Yeah. Why not!' The person who knew the person made sure the CD got straight to him and then a few months later, in September of 1993, I received two letters. One was a letter of thanks from Bill Clinton where he said,

Dear Mr Hardcastle.

Thank you for sending me a copy of The Jazzmasters. As you know, I am a great jazz fan and I can assure you that I will enjoy listening to your latest release.

I appreciate your generosity and wish you great success with your future recordings.

Sincerely,

Bill Clinton.

Nice one, Bill! The other letter was sent by his PA on his behalf and said if I was ever in the Washington area and wanted to have a viewing of the White House to please contact him. I never did take him up on that and don't even have a good excuse why. All in all, a fun-packed 1993. Roll on 1994…

January 1994

Four Weddings and a Funeral premieres.

British ice-skating championships won by Jayne Torvill and Christopher Dean.

Manchester United legend Sir Matt Busby dies.

Paul Hardcastle gets caught up in a massive earthquake.

Trebles and Tremors

A 6.7 magnitude earthquake struck the region (of Northridge, Los Angeles) at 4:31 a.m. on January 17, 1994. It lasted for thirty seconds or more and several aftershocks followed within minutes. The state said at least fifty-seven died in the earthquake, though a study issued the following year put the death toll at seventy-two, including heart attacks. About nine thousand were injured and the damage costs were estimated at $25 billion.

Fox 11 News

My relationship with JVC was one of mutual respect. They opened the doors to their company and I opened the doors to my house.

A few months after the tour of Japan and America, four or five Japanese guys came over to my place near Ongar. My son, Paul Jr., was about four or five at the time when they pulled up in the driveway in this big black car and we were dressed in matching black jackets and jeans. When they got out, he said to each and every one of them all enthusiastically, 'Hai,' whilst bowing. They thought it was really funny and started speaking Japanese back to him really quickly. He had no idea what they were saying, but he thought it was a lot of fun. I then took them over to my studio and they took a great photo of me and Jr sat on the forty-eight-track desk, with racks either side of us, both holding guitars.

By 1994, I was selling more records in America than the whole JVC label put together. They decided to send me to Los Angeles to make a video for a track called 'Can't Stop Now' and with me making them a lot of money, they gave me the full VIP treatment, including getting picked up by a limo and giving us this gigantic eighth-floor suite at the Sheraton Universal hotel, which was just next to all the fairground rides.

On 16 January, we got a private tour of Universal Studios and went on all the rides, which was so much fun, especially the Back to The Future one. I soon understood why so many people came out to LA during the UK winter months and why it was such an attractive place to visit because of the weather, the ocean and the beach, which were all there for the taking. Me and my wife even started talking about maybe buying a place out there.

That evening, the head of JVC, Kanami Tagima, wanted us to have dinner with him and some other senior staff at the company. The JVC PR guy, who was coming around with me to make sure everything was good, came up to the hotel room to check I was on time for the meeting I had with Tagima downstairs in the hotel lobby. He arrived two minutes before the meeting, which was very Japanese in terms of not too early but never late. Just for a laugh, I said, 'I don't fancy it tonight. Tell him I don't want to meet tonight. I'm tired.' The guy thought I was serious and nearly started crying. At first, I didn't say anything, then after a few seconds, I was like, 'Noooo! I'm only kidding. You know? Joking? Forget it. Let's go downstairs.' The look of relief on his face was palpable as he smoked about twenty fags before we'd got down to the lobby to calm his nerves.

We went to Grauman's Chinese Theatre, which was really close to where we were staying, had some drinks and a lovely dinner. They gave me a little gift, which was cutting-edge technology at the time, which was the size of a credit card and held thirty seconds of voice. It was called a *talking memo,* and it had a little switch on it which would record and then you'd play it back. Obviously, the quality wasn't great, but it was tiny and this one had the Jazzmasters written across it, with a sample of the music on it.

After dinner, we went back to the hotel shortly after midnight. I decided to turn on the telly and flicked to MTV. I remember thinking, *I've come thousands of miles away and look what's on.* They were playing 'King Tut'. We went to sleep around one a.m., then about three hours later, I woke up in what I thought was a weird dream after perhaps having had a bit too much to drink. My wife was shouting, 'Paul, Paul, Paul.' That's when I properly woke up. I just remember these very strange sounds that were like deep rumbles and roars combined with something out of *The Exorcist.* It's a noise I'll never forget. I wasn't sure if we were under attack or in the middle of a violent storm. Then I looked over and saw the television shooting along the sideboard and everything else on the sideboard where the tea and coffee stuff was, moving all around. The whole hotel was swaying like a palm tree and as you tried to walk, you would be thrown off balance. Outside, the sky looked like it was being lit up by lightning, but it was actually electrical explosions due to the substations blowing up. I said, 'What the fucking hell is going on?' That's when it hit me about thirty seconds in that we were in an earthquake, which is a situation I never thought I'd be in.

I now knew we had to get downstairs and out of the hotel as quickly as possible. My wife was looking for her shoes and all this sort of stuff and I said, 'Forget the fucking shoes! Let's get out. NOW!' As we left the room, I had a pair of underpants on and I grabbed a blanket and my wife had a dressing gown on. Before coming out to LA, I'd treated myself to this little portable Sony radio cassette player that could record radio. Don't ask me why, even after I told my wife she couldn't take her shoes, I decided to grab this radio as we were going down the stairs.

As we got out of the room, there were all these people running down the emergency stairs, crying, screaming and some quiet in shock. Then, the rumbling stopped as everyone just stared at each other. Then the rumbling started again and there was ceiling plaster crumbling down, but thankfully, nothing else. I put on the radio and it was talking about the earthquake and this massive dam in the San Fernando Valley that could blow and kill thousands.

We got to the bottom and everyone was outside by this big decorative fountain in front of the hotel, which at this point had water going from side to side, splashing all over the place. I was thinking about what I'd heard on the radio and asked this American woman, 'Where's the San Fernando Valley?'

She replied, 'You're right in the middle of it.'

I thought, *That's not the answer I wanted to hear.*

Simon Harris, who did *Bass (How Low Can You Go)*, was also staying at the same hotel and I bumped into him by the fountain. I said, 'What the fucking hell is going on here?' Then I tried to lighten the mood and said, 'Is this bass low enough for ya?' He struggled to speak as he was out of sorts, as was everybody.

The aftershocks kept on coming and my first thoughts were, *Is the hotel going to collapse?* I was looking at how high the building was in relation to how far away we needed to be to make sure we were safe if it did topple. It wasn't a good situation, to say the least. We were all sitting there on the edge of this fountain and waited until they thought it was safe for us to go in and get our stuff. I went up and like an idiot, went up in the lift, which is not the thing to do in these situations. I got in there, grabbed everything I could into a case, half-shut it and got the hell out of there.

We were supposed to be there for a week, but I thought, *Fuck this. We're going home.* My wife made a phone call and changed the flight relatively easily, which kind of told me they were used to that in Los Angeles with these situations. We jumped in a cab and the driver said, 'Is this your first earthquake, man?'

I replied, 'Yeah and hopefully my last', which he found funny. On the way to the airport, there were whole sections of the Ventura Highway which had collapsed, which made me say to the taxi driver, 'Can you put your foot down, mate?'

I called up the record company from the airport and Denny Stilwell answered. 'You're safe! That's great. We can film the video tomorrow.'

I said, 'No chance. I'm going home.'

He replied, 'Is there anything we can do to get you to stay?'

I said, 'Unfortunately, no. Not a chance.' As we were walking on the runway to board the plane, we had another strong aftershock and I was thinking, *Get us on that plane and take the fuck off.* I hate flying, but on that day, I loved it! The sense of relief from everyone on the plane was evident.

16 January was Martin Luther King Day, which is observed on the third Monday of January each year, which turned out to be 17 January in 1994. The earthquake hit at four thirty a.m., on 17 January and in the first twenty-four hours, almost sixty people died. However, the toll would have been a lot higher if it had been a few hours later as everyone was on their way to work, either getting hit with crumbling debris or driving on the freeways which

collapsed. It also helped that it was a national holiday, which meant fewer people were on the road. New buildings, such as hotels, had been built to withstand earthquake sways, but the smaller residential properties, especially those made from wood, suffered the most casualties. Very sad.

They closed the hotel for a number of weeks, as it was officially condemned due to the damage, but I did go back about a month later to film the video because they said the chances of another earthquake so soon after were very low. Being the tourist I am, I even bought a T-shirt which said, *I survived the 6.7 Northridge Earthquake.* I also went back to the hotel because they'd kept the guests belongings and I brought home the balance of the stuff we'd left, including my wife's shoes.

***

I'm not saying wherever I go, I attract danger, but the year after the earthquake, I was close to another disaster. This time, it wasn't one of natures. I was in Japan in March 1995 with Les, promoting the latest *Jazzmasters* and Hardcastle albums and at the end of the week-long tour, we got to the Tokyo Metro and headed back to Narita Airport.

I was totally oblivious to what had been going on, but when I got home, my wife was annoyed with me and said, 'Why didn't you say you were OK?'

I said, 'OK about what?'

She said, 'That sarin attack on the underground.' It turned out that a few minutes after we'd jumped on the train, some lunatic had set off this poisonous gas, sarin, which killed thirteen people and injured a few thousand. At the time, we could hear emergency services sirens all over the city but didn't think anything of it. Close call.

On the bread-and-butter side of things, I couldn't complain. Rick Ross and Snoop Dogg had used a sample from my track 'Wonderland', which was featured on Jazzmasters II and on the same album, I made history with a track called 'Walking to Freedom', which I played acoustic guitar on.

At the time, we were staying at an amazing place called the Nikko Hotel in Los Angeles, promoting the *Jazzmasters II* album, which was the first time I'd seen a telephone in the room that also allowed you to control the Hi-Fi, the lights, open the curtains and all sorts. We took the album around America and put it on a station in San Diego and the DJ, Kelly Cole, said, 'There's a track here with Paul Hardcastle playing acoustic guitar and he hasn't been playing it very long. See what you think.'

The lady at the radio station had a listen and said, 'Wow!' The funny thing is, I hadn't played much acoustic guitar and I can remember my wife saying to me at the time, 'Why have you bought an acoustic guitar? Why don't you get someone to play it?'

I replied, 'Because I fancy it,' without any real logic behind my answer.

A couple of days after arriving in San Diego, we went down to the lobby of the Nikko hotel and Jeff Lunt made some enquiries about how 'Walkin to Freedom' was doing in the chart as it was its first week live. Jeff came over and put his arm around me and said, 'Hey man. All the stations are playing it at the same time. It's gone in at No.14,' which was a big entry for the Top 100. However, the week after, it went straight to No.1 in the NAC (New Adult Contemporary) chart and stayed there for sixteen weeks, which is a record that still stands to this day.

The balance of 1995 was busy, juggling a number of albums and singles. In the meantime, Simon had signed the Spice Girls, which was great foresight on his side, as they hadn't even released 'Wannabe' yet. I remember Emma Bunton asking me at a launch party for them, just after they'd been signed, 'What's Simon really like?'

I said, 'I promise you will not be disappointed. He's been great with me and no doubt he'll do the same with you.' Their climb to fame happened really fast and thankfully, in the not-too-distant future, I was able to play a small part in one of their productions.

December 1997

Maglev, Japanese train builders, set a new world record of 332mph.

Rover Group produces the final Rover 100.

Elton John on Honours list to receive knighthood.

Spice World premieres, with a little help from Paul Hardcastle.

The Score

From his success in the '80s with 'Rainforest' and '19',
Paul has gone on to create a niche for himself in smooth
contemporary jazz. While each project is different in
name and in style, they are unmistakably Hardcastle.

Pure Music Magazine, Orlando, Spring 1997

In 1996, I released *Hardcastle II*, which included a cover
of 'Money', by Pink Floyd, which I jazzed up a bit. The
album featured vocals from Helen Rogers and Steve
Menzies, but also my daughter Maxine on the track, 'Look
to the Future'. As a ten-year-old, she said things like, 'I
wish there would be no more wars, I wish there would be
no more hate, I wish there would be no more hunger.'
Then, in 2022, I did a remix, age-morphing Max through
the years and the sad part is, the things she mentioned are
still totally relevant over twenty-five years later.

Same year I released Hardcastle II, Allen Kepler came
over from America and visited me at my house. We'd kept
in touch ever since we first made contact in the early 90s
and often talked about everything from music to family to
Chelsea FC. In fact, we even had a kick about with the
football in the garden! We were chatting about music and

he told me how he loved my song, *Maxine*, which came out in 1993. He said, 'That's really cool to name a tune after your child.' Then, a few months after he went back to America, I released a single named *Shelbi*, after his daughter. It was a top hit in 1997 and Allen was overwhelmed with the gesture. However, the most important thing that happened in 1997 was on 25 May, when my third child, Ritchie, was born. He went on to become a good guitarist, but being a musician was not where his heart was. More about him later. In the meantime, opportunity came knocking again.

Shortly after the release of *Hardcastle II*, Simon Fuller called me up. 'Do you think you could do a score for the Spice Girls movie?'

I said, 'Is it going to be a soppy film?'

He replied, 'No and it's up to you how hard or soft you make the music and you can be as creative as you want. However, the movie is running behind schedule and you have six weeks to complete the score. What do you think?'

I replied, 'I turned the Top of The Pops them tune around in two days, so, yeah. Why not!'

The creativity bit is where I enjoyed myself the most. For example, there's this bit where there's an alien craft that comes down and I was able to create a dramatic noise as it landed, or when this guy kept following them around and every time you see this guy, there's a loud mini musical burst which brings his scary presence to the next level. Then, in another scene, there's this bloke driving down the road in a truck and he picks up one of the girls, turns on the radio and a thrash metal track comes on. That was actually a recording of me playing guitar in my studio and I added some mad drumbeats to it. What I designed fitted the film, which was mostly for kids, but they also used a dance track of mine in the movie when they were in an Army training camp. The only thing they did leave out was the music to a scene that featured Gary Glitter performing his track, 'My Gang'. Just as we were getting all the sounds and music together for the final cut of the film, the headlines of Glitter blew up across the media and they removed the track from the movie very quickly.

I couldn't have done too badly with my efforts because the Spice Girls liked what I did, Simon liked it and I won *The Best Score* award from ASCAP (American Society of Composers, Authors and Publishers) for Spice World. More than anything, I enjoyed doing it. I also went on to do the music for the programme, *S Club in Miami and also some music for Simon's 'American Idol*, reality show. A little bit of trivia for you about S Club. Many people think the band may have been called *S* after Simon because he created the band, but that's not true. It's called *S* because it's the nineteenth letter in the alphabet, keeping in line with his subtle homage to *19*.

Capping off the end of the year, I covered Judy Garland's 'Have Yourself a Merry Little Christmas?' with vocals from Alison David. The track went on my album Cover to Cover and was a two-CD compilation mainly aimed at the American market because they go crazy for

Christmas albums, which I just can't do because they bore me shitless. I decided to do that one track, which had a nice vibe and something different and it took almost twenty years before I did another one in 2015. I wrote that one with Becki Biggins and she sang, 'Coming home for Christmas'. That's about it for my Christmas contribution.

1998 came with some interesting opportunities. In late spring of that year, Les Cutmore, my former pretend manager and now boss of Trippin N Rhythm Records, gives me a call. 'There's a guy who wants you to run a record label for him. He wants you to go over to America and meet him.'

I said to him, 'Are you coming?'

He said, 'Yeah.'

I thought, *I doubt anything will happen and it will just be a bit of a laugh.*

I then jokingly said, 'Tell him we want to fly Concorde,' as I laughed.

He phones me back an hour later and says, 'Yeah. That's all booked.' I still didn't believe it until later that day I got a call from America asking which seats we wanted on Concorde. Those seats were about eight grand each, which was a hell of a lot of money back then. The guys who wanted me over lived on Long Island and ran this radio station called Smooth Jazz CD101, which was huge and had a massive reach. It turned out this guy had a number of business interests, including being a massive shareholder in Coca-Cola, which basically meant he was minted.

When we arrived, he had us picked up in some amazing cars and put us up in the most incredible hotel in Chicago, where we stayed for the next four days. He gave me around $200,000 to start setting things up and then all of sudden, about a month later, they decided they weren't going to go into the record business and instead, he was going to buy about fifty radio stations. I said, 'Ah, that's a shame. Listen – I'll get the money sent back over to you.'

He replied, 'Don't worry about it. That's fine.'

I was seriously shocked, but thought after, *Not a bad gig, that!*

Just before Jazzmasters III came out in late 1999, Gavin magazine wrote, *In a positive way, keyboard/composer/producer Paul Hardcastle is your classic British Two fingers up kind of guy. He's not necessarily the bother boy type, mind you, but more along the lines of a stubborn individualist. Whatever the current Smooth Jazz trends dictate, trust Paul to explore an opposite direction.* It wasn't that I was trying to be anti-establishment; it was more a case of me having the vision to do something with a track that retained its unique flavour but put a new, fresh spin on it.

As part of the Jazzmasters III album, I did a cover of America's *Ventura Highway* and Fleetwood Mac's, *Dreams*, both of which featured Helen Rogers on vocals, but around this time, I also started my own record label, Hardcastle Records, as JVC records were closing up shop, concentrating all their efforts on retail items such as their Hi-Fi stuff. I can't have been doing too badly because I picked up *UK Smooth Jazz Artist of 1999*, which was decided by a combination of record sales and radio play.

***

My first published collaboration with my son Paul Jr was on the *Jazzmasters – The Greatest Hits* album, with a cover of the track 'Shine', which we recorded in 1999 and released in 2000. I was working on the track and little did I know that eight-year-old Jr was sitting outside the studio listening. By now, he'd started playing his Peavey Wolfgang Eddie Van Halen Special guitar, which I'd bought him a few months earlier, which had customised pick-ups and lowered strings to the fretboard. I decided to get him in the studio and asked him to play the hook on the track. Well, it ended up on 'Shine' and it went on to be No.1 in the US on the NAC chart, but it was also Jr's first of four No.1's with myself. To my knowledge, we're the only father and son to have had four No.1's together.

However, Jr's fascination with music started much earlier. Just as he was starting to walk as an infant, I bought him a little drum pad, which worked with D-size batteries. Although he couldn't walk, he was hitting this pad with pretty good rhythm and we've even got photos of him in a mint green baby grow with a nappy on hitting these drums as everyone was geeing him on saying, 'Yeah, Paul! Go on!'

He got his first guitar when he was about three. It was called a little axe, like Slash's guitar, with two spikes at the bottom and two spikes at the top. It was powered by a little 9V battery slot at the back and in the hole under where the strings were, there was a little speaker. What a great piece of equipment for a kid. His fascination for music soon became a passion and then a talent which he quickly nurtured, albeit, like his father, he didn't always take the conventional route.

On one occasion, when he was about six or seven, me and my wife went away on a trip and we gave Jr strict instructions not to touch the two alto and soprano saxophones because, firstly, I was using them to record the sax on the Spice Girls movie and secondly, they were very expensive. I'd got the sound calibrated just the way I wanted, with the reeds in a certain way and all that when Jr decided to pick it up and showed his grandmother what he could do. He couldn't play it properly, just get a few notes out of it, but his nan started saying, 'This is fantastic!'

Next thing I get a phone call saying how proud she was of Jr, whereas I was thinking, *Please don't drop them!* I gave him a call in the morning and asked, 'Why was you playing the saxophone?'

He was like, 'Errrrr.' After the film was done, I had a huge change of heart. I decided to give him both saxophones and told him to get some lessons. Funny thing is, Jr still uses those saxes to this very today.

Paul was pretty versatile at that age and played drums, a bit of keyboard, bass and sax. He started playing drums at school and he used to love his drum lessons. Everyone thinks it's just a case of picking up the sticks and banging a drum, but it's a real art to keep in time and follow a melody and it's difficult to make a drum solo as interesting as a guitar or sax solo. Unless you're Buddy Rich or Carl Palmer, then you'll struggle to stand out as a drummer.

After stopping the drum lessons, he started to have piano lessons and hated them. It was all old stuff and by then, he was already into his soul music and a lot of stuff that I was doing. When people listen to Jr's music, many assume he reached Grade 8 on the sax and a number of other instruments, but the fact is, he can't read music. He's pretty much dyslexic when it comes to that. He can do it very, very slowly, but when he looks at music, it jumbles up into a thousand things and it's like everything goes the other way round.

Like me, he's always had a good ear. When I was teaching him, we'd sit there with three CD players plugged into an amp and I'd load three different CDs in and press play on the first one and he would have to get that root note first time and as quickly as possible. If, say, for example, the root note was D on the sax when I pressed play on the CD, then I'd stop that and put the next CD on, etc. It helped him adapt to any key changes as a natural reaction, which is really important for live stuff. I still believe that your ear is the most important thing. You read music if you really want to play other people's music, but to Jr, it was like a maths lesson. I said, 'You'd be better off using your time doing something that you want to do in music.' If you're not into learning crotchets, quavers and semi-quavers, who gives a shit?

Then, when he started playing with other people and they'd start saying in musical jargon, 'We're going to play E Flat and want you to come in with that on the sax straight after.' He didn't have a clue what they were saying, but he knew what part of the song they'd be referring to and waited to hear that note, as he knew he'd be able to react quickly and keep it going.

Once his passion for the sax was lit, there was no stopping him. When Snake Davis used to come over to the house, Jr would sit and listen to a half hour of the session with us, which, again, was a great learning curve for him. Snake, who was the sax player for M-People, was the first person to teach him some bits on the sax and used to show him things to practice to become a better sax player. He was definitely someone who sparked his passion for the instrument.

Apart from Snake Davis and Gary Barnacle, one of Jr's big influences was Rock Hendricks, who also played on the newer stuff of my albums. Rock has the smoothest tone and has played with all the greats like Stevie Wonder, the Jacksons and Marvin Gaye. He's been a massive help to Jr as a musician and I still work with Rock to this very day.

He also had some sax lessons from a jazz great who lived around the corner, called John Altman. He's the guy who wrote the score for *Titanic* and arranged the song, 'Always Look on the Bright Side of Life', for Monty

Python's Life of Brian. John had his own big band, was a really credible old-school jazz musician who would write note by note and he was also an incredibly lovely guy. Jr was friends with his son, Robert, who's a great percussionist and goes under the name of Bobby Sticks.

John was the first person who got Jr playing deep jazz. When they were doing their lessons, he'd be on the piano and he would throw some really strange chords at him and he'd have to solo over them, which really expanded his playing. Jr had lessons with John for about six months and he taught him everything he could to help him continue in the direction that he was going, as opposed to sitting there and writing and reading. It was a big eye-opener, or should I say an ear-opener for him.

My involvement in the music industry, particularly in the last three and a half decades, has meant that I'm not in the public eye, whereas Jr is live on the sax in front of anything from a few hundred people to a few thousand. The best advice I gave him was to stick with live performing for a career because the industry as a whole when it comes down to recording, unless you've got a big following, it's a massive gamble. The amount of time it takes to make an album is incredible and he can get a few grand for maybe four or five hours playing live, whereas trying to get that from Spotify and downloads is a long and sometimes fruitless exercise.

I used to say to him, 'When you're out playing, just pretend you're practising.' The difference is that he now gets paid for *practising* and he's getting better and better.

***

By the late 1990s, my dad had had a couple of strokes, but that didn't stop him. When we were younger, we used to have races in our Ford Cortinas and because I always used to beat him, he went and had his engine looked at and supped up at bit, just so he could leave me standing. Despite being in a nursing home in his last few years, that instinct was still very much alive and he managed one day to get out on his three-wheel mobility scooter and head down to the betting shop, which was about four miles away along a busy road. Unfortunately for him, he got pulled over by the police as he was on the way to place a bet.

Sadly, dad passed away in the year 2000, but he left great memories for the whole family. Christmases were great with him as he'd jump on the piano and sing songs which we would all join in with. We're lucky enough to still have some of his bits and pieces from when he used to perform, like his trumpet. I refurbed it and have since passed it on to Jr and when the time is right, it's something he'll pass down to his kids.

Jr was very close with my dad and after he passed away, Jr found information of my dad's Army papers online. After being born in Cuba, he came to London and then went to the District of Columbia in Washington, America, where he was enrolled into the Army. We've got scans of his passport and it's quite scary how similar we look. My dad kept his accent from the American scene for the whole of his life and whenever he saw Jr, he'd always say, 'Gee, Paul. You're getting big.'

He genuinely was an amazing guy who was always upbeat, had a great positive energy about him and let's not forget that he was a real joker. Everyone loved him. RIP dad.

January 2002

Jennifer Capriati beats Martina Hingis in the Australian Open.

'Foolish' is released by Ashanti.

Mr Bean animated series debuts on ITV.

The Euro currency has been introduced to a further twelve countries.

Paul Hardcastle stops using the Synclavier in place of new technology.

RIP Synclavier

Back in the mid-2000s, music downloads were the birth
of the digital revolution. But the numbers say that the
download era is likely to go down in history as a brief
glitch — a transitional phase between physical products
and cloud-based music that did the industry no favours at
all.

FORBES

I remember watching Star Trek in the 1970s and they had these video handsets and I thought, *Wouldn't it be brilliant if you could actually do that.* Then, about thirty years later, it happened. When Facetime came out in 2010, it was a game changer, but the technology didn't happen overnight.

I got my first mobile phone late 1985 from a shop in Ilford and it was one of those Motorolas which was bigger than two house bricks. I was in my Jaguar XJS one time and I remember ringing up Simon Fuller's office and saying, 'Have a guess where I am.'

He replies, 'No idea.'

I said, 'I'm phoning you from my car.'

I was always joking around with Simon and he said, 'Yeah. Course you are.'

The day after, I went round and took this phone with me and he was like, 'Fuck me!' Within no time, these phones started to get smaller and smaller, as did the batteries. Back then, it was more gimmick value initially, but I wouldn't know what to do without my phone now.

The same applies to music technology in terms of progress. Soon after the year 2000, I started learning Emagic, which soon became known as Logic after Apple bought Emagic and renamed it. I could have bought an SSL (Solid State Logic) desk at the time, which had total recall on it, but it was £200,000 and that made no financial sense.

At the time, the Synclavier made my life so much easier and faster. Having that extra time then allowed me to work on three or four tracks at the same time as opposed to an analogue desk with no memory recall. However, with the Synclavier, I'd be working with a massive mixing desk and as I worked on something, I'd have to move all the knobs for the reverbs and all that. Then if you compare it to now, I can save my work on Logic, go for a meeting and carry on where I left off. With the ability to save and freeze things, I can and do have up to ten things on the go now. That's something I couldn't do without now and in fact, that's why I've been able to make so many singles and albums in the last few decades because I enjoy bouncing from one thing to the other and don't lose any windows of creativity.

The speed at which the physical music itself started to change after the millennium was also incredibly quick. I grew up listening to music on 7" and 12" vinyls. A 7" couldn't hold much more than about five minutes of recording time, whereas you'd get over twenty mins on a 12". There is something about taking a record out of a sleeve and putting it on a turntable and lifting that needle on a good deck. It's an event. Whereas now, I can just shout, 'Alexa. Play Steely Dan,' and it's on within a second. The vinyl market is now a small market with more novelty value than anything else and it will realistically, like all hard copies, struggle to compete with the cloud. There is, however, something nice about having a physical library of music to hand to someone to hold and look at. The artwork for the covers, the intrigue of pulling out the CD, vinyl, or cassette from its cover to then hit play.

Back in the day, people wanted white labels because you knew you had it before the majority of the population. I've still got the original white label of '19', the very first test pressing, to see what I thought. I kept a lot of my white-label vinyl stuff – in fact, three of each for my kids. I also still have the demo of '19', which I took into Chrysalis Records. Yes, downloads are the future, but you can't plop one on a table as a talking point.

At the time of '19', CDs were just coming out and I remember asking Simon in 1986 if my Paul Hardcastle album was going to be coming out on CD and he said, 'Yeah.' That turned out to be my first album on CD and with Simon having bought me a CD player for my wedding present, I now had a reason to use the thing.

Coming back to what I said a few chapters back about recording songs onto cassettes from the radio in the '70s and '80s – some things haven't changed a great deal, as people always find a way of getting free music. The thing is, even if you can get it on Pirate Bay now, what's the point? You can get most of the stuff on YouTube, Spotify, or Amazon Music. At first, everyone in the music business was panicking about Spotify, but years before, Simon Fuller was so ahead of the game and warned that CDs were going down, years before we even dreamed of CDs not being around. He said, 'It's all going to go to this thing called streaming and downloads.'

We all said, 'What's that?'

First time it got my attention was seeing one of my new albums online the same night it was released. To say I was pissed off was a big understatement. The pirates thought they were the Robin Hoods of the industry, making them famous for a few weeks. However, it's true that record companies were charging too much for CDs and also, a lot of people were putting two or three songs on there and the rest were fillers. At least that's one good thing that did come out of it, which was providing quality with quantity instead of taking the piss out of the person buying an album on the back of two or three singles.

In the late 90s and early 2000s, most of the downloads were crappy quality MP3s that had to be stored on some kind of memory device and most of the downloads were illegal. You'll never stop the pirates, but thankfully, the industry now has cleaner selling and distribution channels providing high-quality downloads.

Artists soon started to go through music aggregators, which are companies that help you distribute your music. I was going through a company called The Orchard, which was started by a guy called Scott Cohen. He was a bit of a pioneer of the whole music download revolution and I signed with him a long time back. It was in its infancy then and I remember asking, 'What about all the illegal downloads? How do you we stop people nicking all the music?'

He said, 'We've done enough research to know that if someone wants a really good high-resolution copy, they'll pay for it.' And he was right. If you've got fans who like what you do and you treat them well, there's a good probability that they'll download your stuff. Without them, I might as well just listen to the music on my own.

The buzz is when someone else says, 'I really like what you do.' That's all I want. I never wanted anyone to say you're better than this person or that person, or those are nice clothes you've got on. Those sorts of comments are from people who just want to visit the music business and leave it as quickly as possible after making as much money as possible. They don't do it for the actual pleasure of going into a studio and coming out with something and genuinely liking their creation.

I got good use out of the Synclavier and despite the hefty cost, it more than paid itself back. Apart from all the tracks I used it for, there were also some great memories, such as my son, Paul Jr, who was fascinated by the red-light buttons that used to be featured on the B-52 Bombers. When he was about four, I used to tell him that he couldn't touch those buttons because it could make the machine explode.

Then, the moment I turned the Synclavier on and it lit up, he'd say straight away, pointing to the red buttons. 'Can I push that one, dad?'

Of course, I'd say, yes, then when he pressed it, we'd pretend it was about to launch a missile or something like that and I'd say, 'Noooooo!' Good memories.

I've been working with Mac since 1990. When I'm at the Apple store and I say, 'I've had Macs since the IIfx,' they look at me like I've just landed from a different planet. When I told them it cost me over six grand and only had 80MB of hard drive, they genuinely thought I was joking. That said, with today's technology and the choice of all the bells and whistles, I'm not sure the chorus of '19' would have happened because that was led by the fact of how long I had on the Emulator II sampler, which was only two seconds and me tapping with one finger. To an extent, I owe the success of that track to the restricted technology of the time.

***

Irrespective of which medium of music was being used in the industry at the time, I continued to follow my heart and make more albums. Six years after *Hardcastle II*, I released *Hardcastle III* in 2002, which was the first album I'd released in the UK in ten years. The reception was decent, but obviously to a different type of music market. It took people a while to realise I wasn't going to keep doing remixes of '19' for the one-hundredth time. Also, people still wanted me to do hip-hop stuff and I was changing to the more chill-out side of things. There were no bad comments about it, more people saying things like, 'When are you going to do some more heavy stuff like *Soundchaser* and all that sort of stuff? *Echoes Magazine* in the UK wrote in September 2002, *What happened to him after 19? Ask the Americans. They love him…Paul's blend of dance and urban jazz sounds certainly seems to appeal across the water: he's sold over two and a half million records since the early '90s and regularly outsells the likes of George Benson, Al Jarreau and Pat Metheny.* That kind of summed up where I was at that point. I wasn't trying to alienate my followers in the UK; it's just that my music was more popular across the pond and not so suited to the British pop market.

The year after, I launched Jazzmasters IV, which included sax from Snake Davis and a rapper called Kid Crab on a track called 'If You Knew'. What happened was he wrote to me and then showed me a demo of the track, which was all about his life. I thought it was brilliant and agreed pretty much straight away to put it on the album. However, people were saying, please don't go down the rap route. I replied, 'Yes, it's a risk to come off-piste from time to time, but it does work occasionally. Take a listen.

He wrote this track, which is a story about how tough his life has been, but how he's bounced back and is still carrying on. Give the story a chance.' Eventually, the naysayers came around and even provided positive feedback.

Although I encouraged people to give Kid Crab's track a chance, whenever I was asked to perform '19' live, I always said no. After deciding to go back on my word and perform live in Montreux, I said, 'Never again.'

However, as the old expression goes, 'Never say never again.'

April 2004

Google introduces Gmail.

Brian Lara beats the highest individual score in Test innings with four hundred and not out.

Little Britain wins Best Comedy at the fiftieth British Academy Television Awards.

Usher tops the UK and US charts with 'Yeah'.

30 St Mary's Axe (The Gherkin) opens in London.

Simon Fuller celebrates nineteen years of 19 Mgt.

Uncle Albert

Boomerang Trotter always comes back.

Buster Merryfield

Bearing in mind that I didn't want to perform '19' live on *Top of The Pops* in 1985 because it basically involved me standing there with a keyboard and no vocals, you can imagine what my answer was nineteen years later in 2004 when I was asked to do it at the Albert Hall.

Here's what happened. A lady called Kim Chappell had been working on private yachts down the south of France for a while, looking after all kinds of weird and wonderful people, when she bumped into Simon Fuller around the year 2000, who was working on a deal with Annie Lennox and renting a villa in Grasse. Me and my mate Pete Quinton were guests and that was the first time I met Kim. I instantly jelled with her and she soon became like a mate I'd known for years and we'd be constantly taking the piss out of each other.

Shortly after, Simon persuaded Kim to move back to London to work for him as he had a number of exciting projects going on, one of them being the ninetieth anniversary of 19 Management. He had decided he was going to throw a monumental party on the anniversary and when Simon throws a party, it's a serious paaaaarty. He decided to hire the Albert Hall, throw a concert and he asked Kim to produce it.

It was the first big show Kim had ever done and she was terrified. Simon was pretty cool about it and said, 'Just use these people.' He put her in touch with some brilliant production guys like Kim Gavin and Phil Christensen, who are old-school legends.

It was a really big gig for those in the industry and you couldn't buy a ticket for it. The concert consisted of the majority of artists that had been under Simon's nineteen banner, such as Annie Lennox and Dave Stewart, Victoria Beckham and Emma Bunton, who had branched out to solo careers, Will Young, some of the American idols, some Pop Idols such as Gareth Gates and Cathy Dennis performing 'Toxic' and 'Can't get you Out of my Head'. Most people recognise those tracks due to Britney Spears and Kylie performing them, but very few people know that Cathy wrote those tracks herself.

I actually had the pleasure of being involved with Cathy, signing with 19 Management in the late 80s. Simon said to me, 'I'm looking to manage a new act and wondered if you could give me a hand?'

I said, 'Of course.' We went to the Sound Suite and got six people who 19 Management thought were good and the test song we got them to sing was 'Don't Waste My Time'.

At the end, he asked me, 'What do you reckon?'

I said, 'The girl from Norwich.'

He replied, 'So do I.' That's how Cathy Dennis got signed up.

Back to the Albert Hall. They wanted to open the show with '19' because it was the beginning of everything for Simon. Apart from meeting Kim at the villa a few years before, my next conversation with her was in 2004 when she was Show Director for Simon and she asked me if I would perform '19' on stage at the Albert Hall.

My initial answer was, 'Absolutely fucking not. I haven't performed that song live in a long time. Besides, who wants to see me just standing there with the keyboard? It will be rubbish. No. I'm not up for it.'

We sat and had a drink somewhere in Central London and somehow, by Kim's pure flattery and charm, I agreed by the end of our catchup to take part. However, I had to make sure it would be more than just me on stage with a keyboard. I said to Kim, 'OK. But I'll need dancers, a proper production team and other stuff.' That's when we started on the journey of working out what that performance would look like.

They had the sound stage built in Docklands Arena and everyone was in there for about a week before, rehearsing. I think I started to drive Kim a bit mad because every time we spoke, I wanted to add something else to my bit. On one of the calls, I said, 'I'd like lasers and mirrored gloves.'

She said, 'I also love lasers and am also a big fan of Jean-Michele Jarre's work from the 80s, but with mirrored gloves, we're probably going to blind some members of the audience, which isn't going to make for a very fun evening for them.'

I said, 'Ah. OK.' But I was already hatching a backup laser plan.

I also asked Kim if we could get my daughter Maxine to do the vocals and she said, 'Brilliant idea.' Max was eighteen at the time and when I asked her about the vocals for '19', her initial reaction was no. She used to be quite hesitant with a lot of things because I think she was worried about the reactions of how it would be received by the public, but she's always delivered really well. This time was no different.

Kim knew my concerns about wanting my act to be more than a keyboard performance and it's like she managed to get to my creative switch, flick it on and spark my imagination to the potential of what we could make that performance into. I have to give Kim her dues. She nailed the lot. She knew my love of technology, past and present and she organised for an old reel-to-reel to be put on the stage and put lots of retro kit around me to beef it all up.

The show was produced by Kim Gavin, who was one of the best in the business and had produced for the likes of Take That and had been a major player in the choreography of the 2012 Olympics closing ceremony. For my performance, he'd organised about sixteen dancers, all in camo gear and with black paint streaks across their faces, all choreographed by himself.

Despite the health and safety brief from Kim Chappell, I decided to wear a bracelet that was made up of bits of mirror which picked up all the lights and lasers. The evening was filmed from different angles, which worked great for reflecting and when I saw Kim after she said, 'You little bugger!'

The best bit for me was the start. I was standing on this plinth on a scissor lift underneath the stage and they said, 'We're ready to go.' Next thing it started to rise up and I appeared to this packed Albert Hall. I'd only ever performed the track live at Montreux back in 1986, so nobody knew what to expect or even what I'd play. All I knew was that I wanted to start with something different. Me and Kim Chappell are both huge Pink Floyd fans and I decided to have this long-winding intro using a riff from Pink Floyd's 'Shine on You Crazy Diamond'.

For those in attendance, they didn't know initially what was going on, when suddenly it went, *This is the story of men who were victims of war*... Then the whole place erupted as they knew '19' was about to be performed. I made the start a lot longer and had these helicopters on massive screens with the sound of gunfire coming through quadrophonic speakers around the Albert Hall. Suddenly, the track kicked off and the adrenalin started pumping as all the dancers started doing their thing. I was playing bass synth live and a couple of other bits and Maxine did a fantastic job on vocals. It really was a lovely father-and-daughter moment.

Also, there's nothing quite like having a concert where everyone has a common thread. People knew each other within this concert and were incredibly supportive, enthusiastic, happy and euphoric, which led to the most extraordinary energy in there. That concert was not open to the public, yet it totally packed out the Albert Hall. People still talk about the ninetieth Anniversary Party to this very day because it was pretty spectacular between the pyro, lasers and dancers. Simon did, however, pull out all the stops to make sure everyone felt a part of the production, albeit some were a bit worse for wear the day after. As a boss, Simon is incredibly generous and he gave nineteen tickets to every member of staff, all the suppliers and all the people who helped 19 Management along the way. He was very much one for acknowledging that the success happened as a team effort. You went into your box and there was loads of food laid out and somehow, Kim had struck the most extraordinary deal with Mumm champagne, which meant everybody got a lot of free bubbly. Let's just say it was a very well-lubricated crowd, to say the least.

A full house at the Albert Hall was incredibly special, but how would it compare to a stadium full of fans?

May 2011

Oprah Winfrey airs the last of a twenty-five-year-long chat show.

Manchester United got their ninetieth top-division league title.

Osama Bin Laden is killed.

Paul Hardcastle gets permission from Marvin Gaye's family to mix a classic.

Tell Us, Paul. What's Going On?

He was an all right player who could certainly score a goal, but don't let Hardy kid you that he was a great player. He was a smaller player, bandy-legged, bit older than me and I'd say I was probably a bit above the players on the estate at the time, but he was certainly a lot better than me at music, that's for sure. The whole area was aware that Hardy and DJ Steve Walsh, who we grew up with, loved their music and you could always hear the sounds pounding out of Walshy's flat, in particular on the Tachbrook Estate. However, we were never, ever sure of how far they would get. When Hardy started to make it big time, everyone from the estate would be like, Oh, yeah! Hardy – I used to play with him. It was like everyone was his best mate from then on in. I always followed his career and as they say, When the local boys do good, were all so proud.'

Tony Gale

I earned the nickname *Curly* when I used to play football (or *soccer*, for the American readers) as a kid on the on the Tachbrook Estate in Pimlico. I was a goal poacher and used to have an extremely accurate left foot, even though I'm right-handed.

My nearest club to where I grew up was Chelsea and as a kid, my footballing idols were Peter Osgood, Charlie Cooke and Ian Hutchinson because of his really long throws. With the ground being within walking distance, it was a no-brainer that I became a blue. Roll the clock forward to August 2001 and the Chelsea TV channel had just been launched. Shortly after they started, I received a call from Gina and Dave from Chelsea FC, asking if I had any music, I could let them borrow for the channel. I went over and met them with my son Jr and they explained that they had this new weekly programme called *Blue Tomorrow* coming out and if I could do an intro for it. I said, 'Yeah. No problem.'

To help with the promo, they got me to do a photoshoot in the middle of the pitch, wearing the new kit that was coming out. There was a ball there and the presenter from Chelsea TV said, 'Go on then. Show us your skills.' I ended up scoring a belter against an open goal and then did a Vialli, running with my arms out. Zola was my hero at the time and it was an honour to meet him and interview him on the channel. I also enjoyed interviewing Peter Osgood. In addition, I interviewed a few fans, which was great, because, similar to music, without them, there's no football club.

I didn't charge Chelsea anything because, at the time, they didn't have a lot of cash and were nearly going under. However, my efforts didn't go unrecognised and they did give me VIP treatment for the next few years. I got a lanyard with my photo and name saying that I was staff for Chelsea FC, which I wore with pride. I got to meet all the players I wanted and managed to invite some friends over with me into the player's lounge, such as my childhood mate, Gary Stewart. We got to meet some great players like Le Saux, Zola and Lampard, but it got even better when I had the opportunity to actually play on the pitch against some of these legends.

I played in the Soccer Six tournament a number of times and of course, the number on my back was nineteen. A lovely chap called Mark Abery, who ran a company called Cup Promotions, ran the tournament and I interviewed him for Chelsea TV. I mentioned jokingly that I'd like to play in the tournament and he said, 'No problem. We can sort that out.' I was over the moon.

The first time I played was at Chelsea, in front of about forty thousand people. Ron Chopper Harris was on the same team as me, with Peter Osgood as our manager. I asked Peter if he'd play, but he said his knees were stuffed and he couldn't even kick a ball. There were the likes of George Best, Lennox Lewis and a load of others, but playing at Stamford Bridge was incredible from a purely fan perspective, not to mention I got Bestie to sign my shirt. I scored a halfway decent goal in my first game against Chris Eubank in goal and I remember saying to my old mate Tony Gale at a later date, 'I can understand the buzz football players get playing at these stadiums and seeing the ball hit the back of the net, having friends and family there and hearing the roar of a crowd.' Jamiroquai also played that day and he wasn't bad! After the game, we had a little chat about music and I remember telling him that I was a fan of *Return of the Space Cowboy* and that it was one of the tracks that always gets me up dancing.

I also played at the old Boleyn Ground at West Ham, Elland Road in Leeds, Anfield in Liverpool, Goodison Park at Everton, Reading and St James Park in Newcastle alongside the likes of Peter Beardsley, Kenny Dalglish, Ian Rush, John Aldridge, who I really looked up to. It was a bit surreal and despite being in the presence of greatness, I did mix up Rush and Aldridge because they looked very similar with their hair and taches. I was on the massage table and next to me was Ian Rush.

I said, 'All right, Ian.'

He replied laughing, 'No, Paul. I'm Aldo!'

I've said all embarrassed, 'Ahhh, shit. Sorry mate!'

The game at Elland Road was painfully memorable. Brendan Ormsby, Jaki Graham's brother-in-law, who used to play for Aston Villa, was on the opposite side and he came in with this massive tackle which had me had me up in the air. Brendan's a really nice guy, but his old instincts kicked in that day.

I really enjoyed the Soccer Six tournaments, but in the end, because of my old motorbike accident, my knees gave in and I couldn't do it anymore. I decided to stick with music, which was a little less painful.

The mid-2000s was a busy time for me. I released the *Jazzmasters V* and *Hardcastle IV* and *V* albums and became No.1 in Contemporary Jazz 2006 on the Billboard charts, as well as No.1 in the Top 10 Smooth Jazz Artists of 2005 and 2008. The most popular tracks, 'Northern Lights', 'Lost in Space', 'Desire', 'Shine and Serene', led to me picking up the Billboard Smooth Jazz Artist of the Year Award in 2008, which was a massive honour. Smooth Jazz Network wrote, *The 2008 year-end edition of Billboard Magazine has officially named Paul Hardcastle as Smooth Jazz Artist of the Year. ...Hardcastle is also a nationally syndicated radio host on the Smooth Jazz Network, heard on more than twenty-five radio stations across the United States.*

Same year, Simon Fuller got married. Simon had recently been named the most successful British music manager of all time by Billboard magazine and unsurprisingly, it was a multimillion-dollar wedding in the Napa Valley, California, with a massive Who's Who in attendance, like Annie Lennox, the Spice Girls, Claudia Schiffer and Leona Lewis. After the ceremony, the guests sat down to dinner and Mark Ronson's sister, Samantha Ronson, provided the music as the resident DJ with this state-of-the-art sound system.

There was a dance area set up me and my mate Pete got on the dance floor and started shaking a leg before it became crowded. Nigel Lythgoe, who was a professional dancer and choreographer, was also there and somehow, we ended up having a bit of a dance-off. I'll admit, there was a little bit of an edge there as we were trying to trump each other with our moves, but for everyone else looking, we were providing great entertainment. To cap it off, Simon put up his guests at the Auberge du Soleil, which cost about three grand a night back then. All in all, a good night had by all, including Simon – I think.

2008 was a fun-packed year between topping the charts and Simon's wedding, but 2009 had some ups and downs, with the lowest point being when my daughter Maxine was viciously attacked by Louis Glover. I wasn't at home when it happened and when my wife told me, I couldn't get my head around why it had happened. Maxine was a lot smaller than Glover, very slight and had never been involved in a fight in her life. It was a one-sided beating and she sustained a broken nose as well as having clumps of hair removed from the attack. As the trial unfolded, I was at court with Max most days, which in itself was a horrible experience for her to have to go through, especially as the media were constantly hovering around her. In the end, Glover was given a thirty-week suspended sentence for assault occasioning actual bodily harm.

***

I'm proud to say that I've been able to work on a number of tracks with my children, which have had notable success. With Paul Jr, the first was 'Shine', the second big hit we did together was called, 'The Circle', which featured on an album called *The Collection*, in 2009 and reached No.2. Then in 2010, *The Jazzmasters VI* track

'Touch and Go', featured Jr on sax and reached No. 1 on the US Billboard Jazz songs chart, becoming my tenth number one on the Smooth Jazz chart, in addition to being awarded Billboard's *Best International Musician* and *Best British Artist*.

There's a track on the Jazzmasters VI album called, *One Chance*, and it was from an interview. The long version says, *We've got Paul Hardcastle in the studio today and he's now just gone to number one this very day and it's his tenth in the States,* etc.

He asks me, 'What's your take on life?'

We did the interview and the track started off and I said, 'That's a good question.' Then then it goes into the song.

> *This life is no rehearsal*
> *One chance to live our dream*
> *Here today, gone tomorrow*
> *Can we fulfil our destiny?*
> *...The chance you missed*
> *The time you'll not forget.*

I was basically saying, don't look over your shoulder in resentment. Take all the opportunities you're given.

Talking of opportunities. In 2011, I did a remix of 'Rainforest' for the Hardcastle VI album. However, this one was special because it was mixed with the legendary Marvin Gaye's signature song, 'What's Going On?' I need to give credit to my dad, though, because shortly before he died, he was the one who gave me the inspiration for the track. My dad loved Marvin's music and I played him a few bits. I was messing around with '19' and he said, 'Maybe mix in some Marvin Gaye, 'What's Going On'?'

My initial reaction was, 'What on earth are you talking about?' However, years later, it made total sense.

Marvin was obviously dead by 2011, but I'd managed to get permission from his family to use his voice and that was all down to 'Rainforest' because apparently one of his brothers was a massive fan of the track. It gave him confidence knowing the sort of music I'd been doing with all the new adult contemporary stuff and that he wouldn't be handing the track over to some kid who was going to throw a load of heavy beats at it and turn it into a techno track.

I'd done a slow version of 'Rainforest' previously to see if it worked and something either has to smash you in the face or make you feel sad. The music I put to it was a really nice backing track. I took all the bass away and cut it up a little bit and I thought, *This might actually work.* Then I found a sample of Marvin's vocal and spent a hell of a long time working on the track because it needed to be brilliant, or else his family was going to tell me to fuck off. I decided upon an Army drum to start it off, the sound of a helicopter, then it came in with a bit of sax and then Marvin before going straight into the track. I also had Paul Jr playing on the track, which added that little something extra.

The label sent off the track to Marvin's family and they came back and said, 'Yeah.' However, it wasn't a done deal until I'd gone through all the red tape. I had someone trying to do the legal stuff for me and after a long time, I got an e-mail from this lady who ran a clearance company in LA.

She said, 'We've got the rights sorted out. We have legal clearance.' To say I was happy was an understatement. That goes down as a milestone moment for me, the same as when '19', became No.1 and when I was on Top of The Pops for the first time.

***

In 2012, my son Paul Jr was over in Ibiza and was talking to someone who said he was in the music business. Jr mentioned that I was also in the trade and the guy said, 'Yeah? What's his name?'

He said, 'Paul Hardcastle.'

The guy replied, 'You're fucking kidding? Would you mind if I contact him?'

Jr said, 'No problem.' Next thing I got an e-mail from this guy and he asked if I'd be interested in making an album for Pacha.

I thought, *I've been doing smooth jazzy stuff for a while,* and replied, 'Yeah. What sort of stuff are you thinking?' The result was an album called Perceptions of Pacha VIII and it did really well. It's funny because it wasn't long after that my daughter Maxine became resident DJ at Pacha.

Then, the year after in 2013, over fifty years after attending Rutherford school, me and my old mate Eric decided to do go back and have a few photos outside the gates, for nostalgia's sake. The school is no longer called Rutherford, but some academy and there were building works going on in the playground. It was about six p.m. and we decided to pop our heads in when, next thing, the deputy headmaster came out and asked what we were doing and we said, 'We used to go to this school back in the 70s and we wanted to have a look around.' He was actually quite nice and showed us around the school building, the playground, down all these long corridors and the old hall where we had assembly, which was strange as it was like it was frozen back in time. After reminiscing, we went across the road to this real spit and sawdust place and had a quick sherbet, but after a couple of minutes, some guy recognised me and wouldn't stop talking, so we headed off home.

As the old expression goes, *Every day is a school day,* and the next chapter of my life was exactly that.

February 2014

Same-sex marriage is legalised in Scotland.

Jay Leno hosts *The Tonight Show* for the last time,
with Jimmy Fallon taking over.

XXII Winter Olympic Games are declared open in Sochi,
Russia.

Revolution begins in Ukraine.

Paul Hardcastle becomes Chairman of NUA
Entertainment.

Music Is the Answer

I'm always looking for a new challenge. There are a lot of mountains to climb out there. When I run out of mountains, I'll build a new one.

Sylvester Stallone

Neil Utley is one of Britain's most successful businessmen, but before I met him at a friend's party around 2012, I didn't know anything about him. We immediately got on very well and I said, 'We'll have to get together and have a beer or something.'

He replied, 'Yeah. Sounds good.' Then, one day, I received this invite to his fiftieth birthday from his secretary and that was a real eye-opener.

At his house, there was a collection of his cars and there was this Marilyn Munroe-type person singing 'Happy Birthday to You,' and she had this model of a Bugatti Veyron. She then stops singing and says, 'This is from your friends. I'm sure you can add it to your toy collection.'

He looked at the model and must have thought, *Piss-taking bastards!* Instead, he said, 'Thank you very much.'

Then Marilyn says, 'And your real one is outside.' Two of his mates had come together to buy him this car, which cost over £1 million. I thought, *Bloody hell!*

Early 2014, Neil asked me to be the chairman of his record label, NUA Entertainment. He'd just sold Hastings Direct for a good sum and recently bought Posh and Becks old manor for over £11 million, but he also did a hell of a lot for charity, which I respected him for. However, as a music lover, he'd always wanted to get into the music industry, whereas, from my side, I wanted to get more involved with the business side of things in terms of management, so I accepted.

I soon started to realise that the man who wanted everything had everything. He did it all, from travelling everywhere by helicopter to hosting great parties, with the most memorable being for the 2014 World Cup, where there were about 2,000 guests at his house. Then, just when I thought I couldn't be more gobsmacked, I went to his stunning house in Washington, which overlooked the Potomac River and included a glass swimming pool which went over the river. However, one thing he didn't have was a fully functioning record label.

He'd created Nusic Sounds and I remember saying to his team, 'You mean Music?'

They said, 'No. Nusic.'

I said, 'Everyone is going to think what I've just said.'

I said to Neil, 'That name needs to change.' That's how NUA (Neil Utley Artists) Entertainment came about. The first release on NUA was with Charlie Simpson, who used to be the front man of Busted. He had moved away from the pop side of things and was concentrated on the songwriting for his next album *Long Road Home*.

At the time, I had just finished the *Jazzmasters VII* album and decided to go with NUA as I thought it might add some weight to the list of artists but also give them some visibility on the global scale. Thankfully, *Jazzmasters VII* entered the Billboard Jazz chart in the USA at No.1, giving NUA their first No.1 Album.

A couple of months in an old friend of mine, Steve Betts, came up with this idea of hosting a reality TV show. We had a chat and came up with *The Next Big Thing*, which was something like a mini-X Factor. You had to send in your demos and if successful, you'd get a recording deal of around £100,000, which included studio fees, promotion and all that, which meant you probably got around £20,000 in your pocket.

Steve Betts used to work at Warner Brothers and had great contacts in the media. I got to meet Steve through a mutual friend in America after signing with Universal for a couple of albums and he was involved in that. Together, we took the idea to Terry Underhill, group program director at UTV, who loved the concept, which added a lot of weight in terms of visibility as NUA and UTV joined forces. Despite UTV being a Northern Ireland-based channel, it had radio stations outside of its immediate geography, including places such as Stoke, Swansea and Liverpool. They got great advertising from it and we got great marketing.

The final was held at the Cavern Club in Liverpool, which was great, but I had about fifteen hundred videos to watch in advance. Here's an example of some of the stuff I had to trawl through. This girl comes on the video and says, 'Hello guys. I've just got in.' Straight away, you could tell she was pissed. She then says, 'I've applied to the *X Factor*, but if I win this one, I'll come with you lot.' Then she started singing this song and it was awful and about two-thirds of the way through, she stops, puts her hand to her forehead and says, 'My fuckin head,' referring to her hangover.

The minimum entry age was supposed to be sixteen, but there were a few under that age who applied and really did try. Instead of dismissing them, I sent them a message back saying, 'You're only young and starting out. Keep at it.' I got a lot of parents coming back to me saying thank you for that. My equivalent was trying out with Direct Drive in 1981. If someone had said I was shit, I may never have continued my career. No harm in giving a few words of encouragement. It costs nothing.

The panel was made up of me, Steve Betts and radio DJs from the stations we were working with. After getting together a shortlist, we then chose about six contestants until we got to the winner, which was all great fun. The guy that won it was called Pete Gardiner from Northern Ireland and he was a brilliant lyricist. There's a video on YouTube that I made with just a small camera, going around London with Pete and a young guy who was my assistant. The track we'd put together was called *Idols*, and we had so much fun doing that, mainly because I was out and about instead of being stuck inside the studio. That video got more views than any others he did with proper producers.

I also filmed him on a bridge singing as all these people were walking past and despite not being allowed to film on the Underground, we did. Pete was as brave as fuck and walked up the carriage, playing to everyone and in the end, they were all clapping and laughing. Then we went to Trafalgar Square and there was a group of about ten girls and I asked, 'Can you make a circle around him?'

They said, 'Yeah,' as they started clapping around him while he was singing. Fantastic day, but, for whatever reason, Pete didn't click with radio and it never really happened for him, unfortunately.

Despite being chair at NUA, the rest of 2014 was packed solid on my own music front. *Jazzmasters VII* reached No.1 in the US Jazz charts and I was voted *Best Smooth Jazz Artist of All Time* after the general public voted on Ranker. I had no idea about any of this until sax player Rock Hendricks sent me a link on the internet and I was obviously very happy, but if I have to be honest, I don't see myself as that in any shape or form. It's like some people have said they think I'm a better bass synth player than Stevie Wonder, but I don't think I am. It's all very flattering, but it's just perceptions. What was more important that year was when I won Smooth Jazz Artist of the Year on Billboard and a few years before, when I won UK Jazz Artist of the Year, also on Billboard. That was ranked against other live artists from the year, based on sales and radio. Those awards had some substance to them, as opposed to people just giving their opinion on me being the best jazz artist of all time, with very little significant weight behind their opinion.

Then, randomly at the same time, I was also a DJ for my local radio station, Time FM, where I was given permission to choose exactly which tunes I wanted, which was basically whatever I liked from the 70s, 80s and 90s. I'd be playing English groups like Light of the World, Hi-Tension, Freeez and all that sort of stuff, but also an eclectic blend of anything from Eva Cassid's 'Somewhere Over the Rainbow', to 'Dancing on a Smooth Edge', which was a ballad by Whitney Houston on the B side to 'The Shoop Shoop Song'. Hardly anyone knew the track and they'd be like, 'Wow. I never knew that was Whitney's.' For me, I think that's her best track.

***

I went on to do a number of remixes of '19' over the years; however, for the twenty-fifth and thirtieth anniversaries, I was inspired by something other than money and fame.

In 2010, there was an English sergeant major on telly and I heard him say, 'The average age of my guys is nineteen. I'm taking boys to war in Afghanistan.'

I instantly thought, *I was talking about that twenty-five years ago.* I didn't feel we'd moved on that much. My son, Paul, who was nineteen at the time, said to me, 'Did you know that a friend of mine died out in Afghanistan and he was only nineteen?' His name was George Sparks and he was hit by an RPG (rocket-propelled grenade).

I decided to contact his family and said, 'I'm doing a new version of *19*. Would you mind if I put George's picture in the video?' They were over the moon, more than anything, because they felt he'd been forgotten. They'd been promised by the local council that they'd get a park named after George; then, a couple of weeks before it was supposed to happen, they went back on their word.

I said to them, 'I promise you; I'll keep George's name alive and his memory.' That was the main reason I did it. Also, Richard Hunt was the two hundredth soldier to die and I spoke to his mum, Hazel and she said the same sort of thing and that she'd love for him to have his picture in the video.

I decided to take '19' from 1985 and added all the new bits to it and let the public know that part of the profits went towards soldiers with PTSD. I wrote the new lyrics with a view of a soldier being sent out there. I honestly wish I didn't have to put the new lyrics in it because that would have meant that we'd made progress and the world was a much better place. Unfortunately, history keeps repeating itself and there's one phrase in there that says, 'Does this all sound too familiar?' and I think it really does. That's the problem.

The track instantly picked up loads of media attention and I was on ITV News, in newspapers, magazines and I also did an interview with ABC News, America. The only thing that hindered sales and more poignantly, awareness was the release date. We already had the date organised a long time in advance and then there was the General Election in the UK, which meant all the press releases and articles fell through the floor.

Then, in 2011, '19' unexpectedly re-entered the UK top 40 charts after a twenty-six-year absence when Manchester United fans banded together to try and get the single to No.1 after celebrating their ninetieth English division title in the topflight. I knew nothing about it when all of a sudden, my social media accounts started going mad and I received hundreds of messages an hour from Man U fans. I donated all of the income from this unforeseen chart success to Scotty's Little Soldiers, which is a Norwich-based charity that supports the children of parents who were killed while serving in the British armed forces.

That same year, I made my first appearance at the Apple Store on Regents Street, talking about my knowledge of Logic. I took Maxine and Paul Jr with me and we had a backing track with us, which Max sang live to and Paul played the sax.

Moving on to 2015, I released *The thirtieth Anniversary Mixes* of *19* under the NUA label to raise awareness of British serving officers with PTSD. On speaking with the charity, *Talking 2 Minds*, they hit me with a line that stuck in my head. *More people are committing suicide on returning from war than actually out on the battlefield.* That was the one thing that made me think, *Wow.*

They also said, 'Out of every two soldiers, one of their partners will get it by proxy as well.'

I asked soldiers what it was like to have PTSD and they said it's like a shaking blur or a jelly, so I tried to interpret what someone with PTSD would have in the video. The Daily Mirror said the remix was *The most disturbing video for a pop song ever.* The first time around, it was mainly focused around the kids being so young at nineteen, whereas this time, it was about PTSD. I did all the remixes and did the video all myself and every penny raised went to *Talking 2 Minds.*

Baroness Molly Meacher, an absolutely lovely woman, hosted a reception at the House of Lords, supporting the great work of Talking 2 Minds in their quest to help people overcome PTSD. That was the first time I'd been into a parliament building and I remember showing Molly the video before everyone got there and she mentioned to me that her son had PTSD. I did warn her the video was hard-hitting and after, she said, 'I didn't realise it would be that impacting, but it is.' Similar to back in 1985, I received a number of letters from soldiers saying thank you for the video and a few said, 'Thank you for saving my life. I was close to taking it.'

Me and Neil presented a cheque for £10,000 to the CEO of the charity, Rob Paxman, in the hope that PTSD could be better recognised and appreciated and that more relevant and structured support could be put into place, similar to what *Talking 2 Minds* was doing. We can only hope for future generations.

***

My following in America had given a great deal of positive feedback about my show on Time FM and as a result, it eventually became pre-recorded and came on at ten p.m. to accommodate the American audience. However, despite really enjoying my three-year stint on the radio station, I had to stop in 2017 because it was a commitment which I couldn't fully dedicate myself to.

On the subject of commitment. After opening an account for Paul Jr with Santander building society in 1991, in 2017, it came to my attention that £2,900 had come out of the account without either my or Paul's permission. The terms of the account only allowed a maximum of £500 to be withdrawn without the account book and the last time any money had been taken out was nine years earlier, in 2008, when Jr passed his driving test. On that occasion, I took out five grand and needed to show the book, my driving license and a credit card for ID to release the cash.

Rolling forward to 2017, I got in touch with Santander and told them that I believed fraud was going on. They said they had no CCTV footage or any other evidence and the Financial Ombudsman got involved and leant in favour of Santander because of the time that had elapsed. They might have thought the case was over, but I certainly didn't.

I decided to let the press know about what had happened and if the money was reimbursed, I would be donating the lot to a charity called Teens Unite Fighting Cancer, which was especially dear to my son Ritchie, after a best mate of his called Robbie Lee Raymond died from leukaemia. I also threatened Santander with court action and even said I'd get the bailiffs sent to their head office to reclaim the money.

My social media followers were all behind me and *This Is Money* did a great article about the case. Then, would you believe it, soon after, Santander decided to do a U-turn and sent a cheque to Teens Unite for £3,011.85, which was a little over £100 more than went missing, or the equivalent of about 3.5% of lost interest over the years of the cash going missing.

I'm glad to say that through Neil Utley and NUA, I managed to do more than just shout at Santander for Teens Unite and the charity world. Due to his lifestyle and the circles, he mixed in, you'd naturally meet very influential people just being around him. We went to one international charity function called Mercy Ships, which deploys hospital ships around the world, offering free health care to some of the poorest countries. People were offering auction prizes, saying things like, *you can come on my boat for three hours*, or tickets for such and such and I thought, *What can I offer?* I went to the auctioneer and said, 'I'd like to offer an auction prize for a day in the studio and they can make their own record.' It ended up getting the highest bid on the day by a long way. The people that bought it were obviously well off, but were really nice people with it. They'd followed my music and I gave them a demo of what sounds they could use and they made this track and went home as happy as Larry.

Back to Teens Unite. There was a ball in aid of the charity and the CEO, Karen Millen OBE, was there, along with Co-Founder Debbie Pezzani. I got talking to Karen and I said, 'I'd like to contribute something to the charity, but don't want to overstep the mark. How about if we get between six and ten of the kids with cancer and I make a track and put some lyrics to it and we get them over to Neil's studio?' She was over the moon. I told Neil about the idea and he was very supportive and generous to make sure it happened. He provided the studio with full refreshments, which included a few alcoholic beverages.

The teenagers who turned up were all shy at first and I knew it wouldn't be fair to write a song for them because I had no idea if any of them could sing and didn't want to put them in a compromising position. However, their voices were very important and I thought to myself, *I've made records with people talking before and they haven't done too badly!* That's what we did. We recorded a track about living with the disease but with their direct input.

What a great day! From my side, I was there for one main reason – to record a track with them and make sure they had a great experience. I walked in, introduced myself to everyone individually and then said, 'We're here to make some music. So, let's go make some music!' Their faces lit up and as they all got up to go to the recording studio, I said, 'You look like a rowdy bunch. I'll have my hands full here.' And they all started laughing, which was brilliant.

The music came out really well and I made up a little chorus, which Maxine sang, but everybody took part in. *Teens Unite. Where we feel free to fly. Teens Unite. We keep our heads to the sky.* It wasn't the greatest of lyrics, but it worked incredibly well. Then they each took turns in either singing or talking a line of the song and between what I wrote and what they brought to the table on the day, I weaved it all in together and we made the track. The lyrics were very touching and seeing the expression on their faces as they read out lines such as, *To be strong is just far from physical. It takes endurance of heart and strength of mind for you to find who you really are. To act as if you're tough is far from being brave.* This was followed by the chorus. The song came out very well and I just hope that for those few hours, they were able to look at life from a more positive angle and also to have some fun because, in the end, what's life without a little bit of fun?

Then, in 2018, I did a video for dementia in collaboration with The Utley Foundation, which was launched at the House of Lords. One of Neil's friends, a guy called Tony, wrote the script and filmed the video, which had me walking all over Central London wearing this big overcoat, shivering away because it was absolutely freezing that day.

The video really hit home, hitting the audience with some hard-hitting facts, such as – around a million people in the UK who have been touched by dementia in some form and it costs the country's economy about £100 billion over three years, at the time of writing. The point of the video was to show that music really does help. Music doesn't discriminate age, gender, race or creed and it's always there for everyone at any time. It helps reduce tension, depression, agitation and anxiety in people with dementia and it can help to retain memories, connect with loved ones and even delay the onset of symptoms. However, only a small fraction of care homes in the UK use music therapy for those with dementia. Music not only helps those affected by the disease but also the carers. Bringing together so many talented, capable people to help address this fundamental need in society is essential and is something that needs to happen continuously and increasingly. Something as simple as personalised music from our past helps us connect to the present.

On the NUA front, I also managed a band called Beattie Heart and was able to get them a deal in America on Harvest Records, which is a massive label. The likes of Pink Floyd and Deep Purple had been with them and Beattie Heart went over there, did some promotion and when they got back, they said, 'We don't want to do this anymore. We're splitting up.' That was that!

My last indulgence in managing someone was with a guy called Joe Whelan, who'd got very far with *X Factor* with a cover of Led Zeppelin's, '*Whole Lotta Love*'. Joe was a fantastic guitar player, great vocalist and very looking guy with an incredible physique due to all his kickboxing. I thought this guy had it all.

He came over to the house and we did a demo of 'I've Been Waiting for A Girl Like You', by Foreigner, which came out well. He came up with a lot of stuff and then I went to see a guy called Chris Briggs, who was working at Sony at the time. Normally, you'd only get about ten or fifteen minutes with a top A&R man, but I was in there with him for an hour and a half. Chris had been involved with the likes of Def Leppard and Robbie Williams and said, 'Joe's really, really gifted, but his songs sounded like Bon Jovi B sides.' I didn't repeat that to Joe, but I did try to explain that he needed to come up with something a bit more current, which I think he took a bit of offence to. Although we made an album, it didn't go anywhere and I didn't want him feeling that I didn't want him to succeed because he genuinely had a great deal of talent. I ended up having a chat with him and said, 'I hope you do well with your career, but I really don't think I can help you. I wish you all the luck for the future.' That was me done with managing artists.

I ran Neil's label for four years and we had some great fun, but we'd said from the beginning that if either of us weren't fully enjoying it, we'd just say and that would be it. Working on the management and business side of things was a great experience, but it also made me realise that my main passion was being in the studio making music. We parted on great terms and are still mates now. Through

Neil, I had some great experiences in the charity world, furthered my knowledge of the music industry and met some incredible people, which is what life is all about. Like the track 'One Chance' on the *Jazzmaster VI* album, you need to seize the opportunity because you never know what's the corner.

March 2020

All news headlines point towards Coronavirus Disease 2019 (COVID-19).

Contagion

Nothing in life is to be feared; it is only to be understood. Now is the time to understand more so that we may fear less.

Marie Curie

A lot of things happened in 2020, with some events taking more than others to bounce back from. *Hardcastle IX* was released, the divorce from my marriage went through and the world changed as a virus became the main topic of conversation.

When the virus started hitting the headlines regularly in January 2020, my first thoughts were, *What's all the fuss? It's just another cold or flu that everyone gets around this time of the year.* But when I started to see the figures on the telly, I was like, *'How many died? How many new cases?'* Then, when lockdown was announced, pretty much everyone realised it was serious. I'm fortunate to say that the pandemic didn't affect me financially, but I was very aware of the hardship so many people were having, living on the breadline, losing businesses and struggling to live day to day.

COVID – na-na-na nineteen. You wouldn't believe the number of people who asked me to do that track during the pandemic. I decided that if I did that track, the proceeds would have gone to the NHS, but I didn't know what to do. Would I base it on the original? It's not like The Commentators, where it was jokey for the cricket; the pandemic was a very serious subject and so many people either died or were affected in some form by the virus. I didn't want the press to then say, 'He's just done this to get back in the charts and be an opportunist during the pandemic.' This could have been very offensive to so many people. Also, you had Captain Tom Moore, who soon became Sir and he did the *You'll Never Walk Alone* mix and raised loads for the NHS. There's no way I was going to try and steal a piece of his thunder. In the end, I decided to give it a miss.

I did, however, make a track called *Thank You*, which had a video of all the doctors and nurses on it, which was warmly welcomed by many people in the NHS and members of the public. Then, when I went to the hospital a couple of years down the line for a blood clot in my leg, a couple of the nurses came over and said, 'We saw that thing you did for us on Facebook. Thank you very much.' That was humbling.

The pandemic made us live differently. I understand the enforced rules that the government made us follow, even if they didn't follow themselves, but it was all very grim and factory-like. There was the washing and sanitising of your hands until you barely had any skin left, but one of my first memories from the initial lockdown was the shopping experience. Seeing about one hundred people outside a shop wearing facemasks, with security keeping control of the queues, was all very tense. Then, when you got inside the shop, everyone was looking at each other to make sure nobody was getting too close. I'm surprised there weren't more fights from people space invading. It created new mindsets, which took a while to get out of.

Then there was all that stuff on the floor in the supermarkets. The *Keep two meters apart* graphics on the floor reminded me of the motorways when you see, *Keep two chevrons apart*. You were shopping and worried about how many people in the queue had it.

Not seeing people out was weird. There was that aura of, *We're in the shit*. I might not have wanted to go across the road to the pub, but the fact that I couldn't was hard to accept those restrictions and I had no idea of when it was all going to end. I felt like I was in that film *Contagion*.

The people I spoke the most with were my kids and about five long-term friends, but it wasn't the same. I found myself number-watching on the television, which wasn't good and when it went over a certain figure, we'd either go into Lockdown or carry on with the current Lockdown. Then, when the figures went down, there was a mix of fear from some people to get out again and get the virus and joy from others, purely based on freedom, which was my sentiment.

I didn't go in the studio for a couple of months because I was deflated and lethargic and when I did go back in initially, it was like walking into a morgue because I had no enthusiasm for anything at all. I fell out of love with football after someone missed a penalty for Chelsea and during the matches they played fake crowd noises for reactions because the stadiums were empty. In fact, I've struggled to get back into my football since.

The pandemic nullified my interest in a lot of things. A lot of people did video calls, but I didn't, simply because I didn't feel like talking to anyone. The priority was to just get through another day and hope the one after was going to be better. As restrictions dropped slightly after the first wave, me and my mate Arthur, would cycle to tiny little shops in Romford and get a sandwich, which was like a massive outing and big treat, but that was about it.

It was a very strange time and it genuinely affected me. Before lockdown, I'd tried Buddhist meditation for about six sessions just to slow myself down a bit and improve my sleep pattern because I'd be looking at the telly while looking at a manual, having my dinner and trying to speak to someone on the phone. My brain would then be nonstop before going to sleep and I found the meditation class was helping. But when it came to doing it on my own on a video call during lockdown, that didn't work. In the end, I went down the chemist and bought some Nytol and that did the trick.

I even went to see a doctor and he asked me if I was depressed and he gave me some tablets to take. I opened the box, read the leaflet and it said, 'Warning. These tablets may cause depression.'

I thought, *'What the fuck? Is the doctor taking the piss?'* I binned them and realised the only thing that was going to get me rolling again was me.

It took me about two months to get back into my studio to start and make music again, but when I did, it was a great form of healing. In fact, the first couple of tracks I made were related to Lockdown. One was called *Earthquake Lockdown* and the other was *Spaced Out*.

Spaced Out was the first track that got me back in the studio and here's how that came about. I went into the studio and did a drum track, which very quickly made me forget everything that was on the outside, whether it was the weather, the pandemic or anything really. The reason I did a drum track is because it's the easiest thing I could do and that would help me to spark my passion again. I did the track and then started to add some chords and bass and it started taking shape. More importantly, I was enjoying it. Bearing in mind I thought I'd be in the studio for about forty-five minutes to an hour, I ended up spending about eight hours in there. When I came out, I was a different person. I was now someone who was chomping at the bit to get back in there the next day. I didn't give a shit about the pub or anything else I felt I was deprived of. It reminded me of when I first started out in music and I would live in my studio and wouldn't leave it for days. I think it was just getting used to not having the choice to leave and see my mates when I wanted to when COVID was on, but music was the solution for me and made the days pass so much quicker.

I then called a mate, Mark Dover, who's in charge of Time FM, who I used to do the show for. I got him to do the intro to *Spaced Out*, saying, 'The latest government research figures on the COVID-19 pandemic suggest that many people feel frustrated and isolated and have a lack of motivation. Many other people have described it as a sense of being spaced out.' Then the music and lyrics start. The tracks have never been released, but they will be one day.

Music got me centred again and made me realise how lucky I was. I didn't have to get up at seven a.m. and jump on a packed train and worry about getting the virus and then being in an environment, like maybe a coffee shop or an office, where I could get infected. Before lockdown, I liked to get out, produce other people, go to studios, go to meetings and all that social stuff, but that was no longer a fun prospect or even possible.

***

At the time, my son Ritchie lived on site but in his own separate flat. We were part of a nominated bubble, like many other people who lived on their own, which was great. Otherwise, you'd go crazy not having human interaction.

Towards the end of the first lockdown in July 2020, my *Hardcastle IX* album was released. I'd actually started recording it in 2019, put it on hold because of COVID, went back into the studio in May 2020, finished the album in June and released it in July 2020. *Hardcastle IX* generated four NO.1's including 'Latitude', but the one track on the album which holds a special place in my heart is 'Tropicool' and involved Ritchie.

I had a riff in my head and showed it to him and said, 'Go and practice that.'

He came back the next day and I said, 'That's pretty good. Do you fancy playing it on a track of mine?'

He said, 'Yeah!' I put the machine on record and took about ten takes because sometimes you do one take and it's fantastic and other times the first note is great and the rest is rubbish or the other way round. You always get something from being able to choose the best. It may be one word from a singer or one note from a guitarist. If I'm using a sax player or a singer, I always record when they first go in there and start playing to it and some of those pieces, I've used more than you would believe because of the excitement they've got when first entering the studio, that positive energy as they're trying all kinds of different things they wouldn't normally do, because they're worried about getting it wrong. If it's the first time they've done it, they let themselves go. I always push *record*, whatever. It's no different to a camera or cine film or video because half the time, you do catch things by mistake. That's the same with music.

We were in the studio for about an hour and I said to him, 'That sounds really good. I'll keep that.' And he was happy as a sandboy. The track got as far as No.3 and it was touch and go if we'd hit the top spot because there were a few new tracks which had just been released by well-known artists who would eventually be going on tour and would be going around to the radio stations, whereas I don't do that much these days. Also, I'm British, whereas nine out of ten people in that chart are American.

I phoned up my promotions man, Jeff Lunt and said, 'Give this track your all, mate. I don't care if my next ten tracks don't get anywhere, but this one is important.'

He e-mailed me not long after and said, 'We've got a really good chance. I'll let you know later on tonight. Not counting our chickens, but I would say there is a very good chance of you overtaking the No.1 spot.'

Well, it did. When Jeff called to say, 'You've done it.' I couldn't wait to tell Ritchie. That's the beauty of music. It doesn't need to be anything overly complex; it can just be something that goes with a rhythm or a beat. Being able to tell his own kids one day that he did this track with granddad would be something magical.

Ritchie never got jealous about how many tracks Paul and Maxine had featured on or what they'd achieved in music because they both worked full-time in the music industry. He gets that. However, he'd been asking for a while if he could be on a track, but he was always going away on trips, skiing or work and it just didn't happen. He's proud of that track and he did really well. I'd even go as far as to say he can play the guitar better than me. There's actually one track which involves all three of my kids, called *No stress at all,* on Hardcastle VII. Ritchie was doing a little bit of picking on the guitar, Paul was doing the sax and Maxine was doing backing vocals.

Out of my three children, Ritchie is the least associated with music in the public eye, but that doesn't mean to say he has no interest or talent, far from it. From a young age, he'd meet people from the trade coming to the house, such as Allen Kepler, not to mention he'd see me constantly working in my studio at the back of the garden. Did I want him to get into music? I won't lie, semi-yes. I say semi because the music industry was a bit up in the air with downloads and all that going on. Not to mention, it can be a suffocating industry to work in if you don't know how to correctly distance yourself. I never forced it on Ritchie. I let him try a few things out and then it was up to him if he wanted to pursue it to the next level. If you force anything on anyone against their will, it's a recipe for disaster on so many levels.

From a young age I taught him how to play guitar and one of the first things I told him was, 'The strings will hurt your fingers after a while.' I was basically explaining that you get callouses on your fingers. It was a little bit of a life lesson that if you stick with something, you work through it and get better at it.

I taught him how to play 'Samba Pa Ti' by Carlos Santana, Deep Purple's, 'Smoke on the Water' and 'Twinkle Twinkle Little Star', which made him popular at primary school. When he was seven years old, he entered a talent competition and played 'Samba Pa Ti', wearing a little leather jacket and looking like a proper little rocker.

Well, he only went and won the competition. As he walked off stage, they gave him some sweets for winning, which made him happy as Larry and that guitar is still very much alive in the front room.

There came a point, though, like many typical teenagers, that your parents want you to do things and you naturally gravitate the other way. When Ritchie was at secondary school, it's not that he detached himself from music; he just didn't pursue it as much as, say, Maxine and Paul Jr. He had aims of gaining a degree and knew which interests he wanted to pursue, which he achieved. I'm very proud of him for that. However, left to his own devices, he eventually came back around to music and started to enjoy it again because he was doing it at his own speed, with his own motivation, which, in essence, was for enjoyment, as opposed to making music with the pressure of making money.

***

Another good remedy for getting through the monotony of COVID was laughing. A few Jimmy Carr videos certainly cheered me up a bit. I met him a couple of times before the pandemic and every time he was hilarious, but one of the most memorable was at a charity function around 2014 at the Barclays building up in London.

Ritchie was with me and the function was called the BGC day. Every year on 9/11, in conjunction with the Cantor Fitzgerald Relief Fund, they would remember the hundreds of work colleagues who were killed in the Twin Towers whilst raising money for good causes around the world. They invite loads of celebrities and get them on the phone to do some trades and give the profits to charity, which is an amazing thing and an incredible day for us to be a part of.

Vicki Michelle from *'Allo 'Allo!* was on our table and was a really lovely woman, but when you looked around it was like a who's who of entertainment. There was Paul Merson, Keith Richards, Steve Davis, Tony Hadley, loads of big names. Ritchie was like a kid in a sweet shop. Dad. Look, *It's David Hasslehoff!* Being quite shy back then, I went over to the Hoff and asked if he could have a photo with Ritchie and he warmly agreed.

Then Ritchie points and says, 'Look. It's Jimmy Carr!' I didn't know him at the time, but we went over so Ritchie could have a photo with him and said, 'Hi Jimmy. I'm Paul.'

He replied, 'Hiya. How you doing?'

Without letting on that he knew who I was, he then turned to Ritchie and said, 'What's your name?'

He replied, 'Ritchie.'

Jimmy then said, 'How old are you?'

He replied, 'I'm seventeen.'

He then said, 'You've got two more years to catch up with your dad, haven't ya?' The speed he answers things and how quickly he can rip someone a new one is a serious talent. Within about fifteen seconds of me saying hello, he destroyed me and everything relating to the number nineteen. I was pissing myself while Ritchie just stood there, totally starstruck and had no idea what to say to him.

Then, about three years later, I randomly bumped into him again. Every year at Christmas, me and my old mates from the 1970s go to a restaurant called Roka in Central London and I bumped into Jimmy in the loo. He was on the way to do some show and we just had a quick exchange. I said, 'Do me a favour. On the way out, you'll see where I'm sitting near the door. I'm with some mates and was wondering if you could insult them for me?'

He said, 'No problem.'

He comes over and we did this whole fake chat of, 'Hi Paul. Fancy seeing you here!'

He then said, 'Who are these reprobates you are with?' They were all staring at him in awe for a few seconds before he started laying into them and everyone started pissing themselves laughing.

From one joker to another, that reminds me about Boris Johnson around this time. I was invited to go up to City Hall and meet Boris when he was Mayor to discuss how the Mayor's Office could give buskers more leeway. Back then, Ritchie was really into politics (before Boris was PM) and was a fan of his. As you can imagine, Boris, being an incredibly popular bloke, was absolutely swarmed and surrounded by people while everyone was trying to get his attention. Ritchie tried his best to make his way over there but couldn't find a way to get his attention. I wasn't fussed about Boris, but knew how much it meant to Ritchie to meet him and grabbed him his hand and said, 'Stay with me.'

We made our way near the front and I said, 'Hello, Boris.'

He didn't recognise me, but the guy next to Boris, who was one of his aids says all excited, 'This is Paul Hardcastle.'

The second he said that, Boris suddenly came to life and started saying, 'Ah! Na-na-na-nineteen! Bloody great record.'

I said, 'Yeah. Anyway. Can we do a quick snap with my son Ritchie?' Ritchie managed to have a quick chat, a photo and then we headed off.

***

As we came out of the pandemic in 2022, I released *Harcastle X*, which included three tracks with my son Paul Jr. He did a great version of 'Smile', which had a lovely nostalgic twist to it. About twenty years ago, I did a compilation video of the kids smiling and faded it in on the track for 2022. There's a bit where Jr crashed his little quadbike and it went into the pond and you could see him crying. There's a bit in the song where it goes, *Smile. What's the use in crying* and it cuts to him crashing the quad into the pond, which he bawled his eyes out at the time, but now we all watch it and die of laughter.

There's a crossover between part of the theme with *19* and the COVID-19 pandemic in terms of PTSD. The long-term effects of that virus, both physically and mentally, will be around for a long time. It's how we handle the future and use the lessons we've learned, which is important; otherwise, like war, history will repeat itself again.

January 2023

Pop Benedict XVI dies, aged ninety-five.

Wrexham A.F.C., co-owned by Ryan Reynolds, draws 3-3 against Sheffield United in the FA Cup.

Novak Djokovic wins the tenth Australian Open and twenty second Grand Slam.

A French nun becomes the world's oldest person to die at one hundred eighteen.

Paul Hardcastle starts penning his autobiography.

One Hit – I Wonder?

Despite the fact that dad was working from home, he took his work so seriously because he wanted to give us, his kids, the best life he could. I remember waking up in the morning and him being in the studio and I'd get back from school, even after after-school activities like swimming or karate and he'd still be in there. Now that I'm a young man, I look back and see why he threw himself into his music so much. He wanted to give us, his kids, the best life that we could possibly have and I think it would be safe to say, a life that he didn't have when he was growing up. To be frank, I can put everything I have down to my dad and his hard work.

Ritchie Hardcastle

March 2023, my phone goes and I see it says, *Mac Camilleri.*

I answered, 'Hello, Mac! How you doing, mate?' But it wasn't Mac. It was another one of his friends who had his phone and they were at Mac's sister's.

His sister came onto the phone and said, 'Mac had a heart attack last week and there's nothing they can do for him due to his arteries being furred up. He doesn't have long left.'

I'd be lying if I said I wasn't choked up. Mac was a good friend and a bit younger than me. I asked, 'Where is he?'

She replied, 'Harefield Hospital.' Which is one of the best places in the world for heart specialists.

My thoughts were, *if they can't save him, nobody can.* I knew I needed to get up there quickly because he had a matter of hours left.

Mac's son, Paul, whom Mac had named after me, was now a senior university lecturer in theoretical physics with a focus on quantum fields and string theory, whatever that means. At a guess, I'd say it means he's bloody clever. I called him up and said, 'Are you able to make it up to the hospital?'

He replied, 'I'm in Ireland and won't be able to make it back in time.'

I said, 'Record a message for your dad and make it exactly what you're thinking right now because this is going to be the last time he'll hear your voice.' Paul was obviously nervous about doing it, but thankfully, he did it immediately after we came off the phone.

Shortly after I left my house, I was at Liverpool Street station and I got a call from Paul who said, 'They're giving him a couple of hours.'

Mac's sister was there and I called and said, 'Make sure you tell them not to turn that machine off before I get there because he needs to hear Paul's message before he goes.'

She said, 'OK.'

I rushed like a blue arse fly trying to get to Harefield hospital and when I got there, I gave him a hug and he half flickered his eyes.

I said, 'Mac. It's Hardcastle, mate. Listen. I've got a message here from your son Paul.' I put my phone next to his ear and played it to him and you could see his eyes flickering rapidly, which was a really emotional moment.

I stayed for about half an hour, then said, 'I'm going to go now, Mac.' Knowing his sister and the doctors wanted to turn the machine off because it wasn't fair keeping him in that state. As I was leaving, the nurses came in and turned everything off, but at least he got to hear his son before he went.

When I got home, I had the idea to take part of what Paul had said in the message, cut it up and put a really nice piece of music to it, with the intention to send it to Mac's sister for her approval. I hate it when people play that horrible organ music at funerals. You go in there keeping your emotions together and then you hear that and you're through the floor. At my dad's funeral, I put my dad's voice into one of my tracks called 'Feel the Breeze' when they brought him in, which was a nice, uplifting tune. In the eulogy, I told the story about our two Ford Cortinas, how we used to race and how he got his souped-up to beat me. Then, when we left, we played another track from the *Jazzmasters* collection. It kept the spirits and mood of people nice and positive, which was then reflected straight after as we were joking and laughing about various episodes relating to my dad.

I think it's essential to have music which is a celebration of a person's life, not a grim send-off. Same went for Mac. He was a very good friend and a fun guy and he deserved a nice send-off. I sent his sister what I'd done and she said, 'It would be a very fitting thing to play at the end and the fact that you did it would have made him so happy.'

As you can imagine, at the funeral, people became very teary-eyed as the music started to play because the words were very poignant. It was very, very sad. His son, Paul, had written a really lovely poem about his dad and asked, 'Would you read it out at the funeral.'

I said, 'Of course.' I've done a number of eulogies, including my own parents and I've been lucky to have done them without crumbling. In the eulogy, I read out the poem and also explained what a great job Paul did with the message he left his dad and that I was going to play a track which involved part of that message.

At the end of the speech, I said, 'Oh. By the way. It's available in all good record shops from Monday.' There was a second's silence followed by laughter.

Funerals do make you stop in your tracks and make you realise what's important in your life. The year before Mac passed, I had a blood clot on the lower part of my leg, which made my leg blow up grotesquely. It could have been related to the motorcycle accident, but it's nothing in the grand scheme of things, as I'm still here. I now take a little blood thinning tablet and that seems to work. I've also got a condition called central serous retinopathy. Sometimes, you can get a small hole behind your eye and it makes very strange things happen. I've never touched hallucinogenic drugs, but from what people tell me, I'm getting that experience for free with the distortion I experience. Objects that are dead still will start to rotate back and forth in front of me, which makes it interesting for me when I'm in a restaurant and my napkin starts moving around slowly as I'm about to grab it. I go to Moorfields Hospital and if it doesn't get better on its own, then I'll need to have some operational intervention. It doesn't affect my day-to-day work; it's just a bit weird! All in all, though, it's all manageable.

One thing about life – it goes full circle. You're born knowing that one day, you'll kick the bucket. That's why I get so much pleasure in seeing my children enjoying and progressing so well in their lives, even if I might not get to spend as much time with my beautiful grandchildren, which is not by choice.

I'm asked all the time how my very young grandchildren, Paul Jr. and Penelope, are doing. I'm happy that people genuinely care and are interested but it's a bittersweet situation. I wasn't going to delve into this sensitive area, but I may as well end this book being open as I have throughout. The honest answer is I have only ever seen them once since they were born. Yes, just one time and at the time of writing. They are now over two years old. I asked politely and to quote, 'Hi ***. Please can you let me know when it will be convenient for me to pop over and see Penny and Paul?' I never received a reply from anyone. That was two years ago. It's not just for myself, but child access has also been stopped for my ex-wife and daughter.

Unfortunately, their mother and Paul Jr separated due to irreconcilable differences, but for reasons unbeknown to me, she and her family took a lot of their problems out on myself. Perhaps I was seen as the person who should pay for everything? When I got married, my future in-laws were poor and I had no problem whatsoever picking up the bills for everything. But that's not the case with Paul Jr's in-laws. They are not living on the breadline. I guess it was just all too easy to expect me to be the cash cow.

I could go a lot deeper into this, but I think you get the gist. In my own personal opinion, people who use young children as a way of gaining some kind of retribution or revenge and using them as pawns, is really scraping the bottom of the barrel, not to mention the impact that this will inevitably have on the twins.

In terms of a full circle, my son Ritchie ventured over to Los Angeles in September 2023 for what can only be described as a passing of the torch trip as he went to meet my old mate, Simon Fuller.

The purpose of the trip was for him to learn more about the music industry, given that he's getting more involved in the family business, but not on the production side of things because that's mainly Paul Jr's bag. Ritchie is more interested in the business side of the music industry and how that works, but he was also looking to expand his network of connections.

Despite me telling Ritchie so many good things about Simon over the years, this was the first time he was going to be meeting him face to face. Before going out, Ritchie was understandably a little bit nervous, but mainly because he knew how incredibly packed Simon's schedule was and how everyone wanted a piece of him all the time.

I said to Ritchie, 'The moment you sit down with Simon and have a proper conversation with him, you'll be at ease. He's one of the nicest people you will ever meet.'

Despite Simon's hectic schedule, he made time to get Ritchie into his office and the pair had a good old sit down, catching up about how our family was, what Ritchie been up to in terms of his own personal journey, where he thought his future might be and how Simon could help.

In Ritchie's own words, 'Within minutes, I felt like I'd known him my entire life. He's genuinely one of the nicest, most warming, kind-hearted people I've ever met.' Ritchie mentioned his interest in the business side of the music and entertainment industry in general and how he was trying to find a niche in insurance within the industry. Simon was very encouraging, giving him great advice in terms of the future. They also spoke about Simon's journey and he told Ritchie that he'll always be grateful of the fact that I helped him with his first big start in life, on the management side of things. Despite the fact that Simon always looks into the future, because you have to stay very current in music and entertainment, he still recognises the origin of his story. Hence, the company name XIX (nineteen!) and hence the first thing Ritchie saw before walking through the reception area was a '19' vinyl on the door.

Ritchie also met up with a number of top people from the music industry during his trip, including Olivier Chastan, who runs Iconoclast. They basically acquire people's catalogues, managing the intellectual property of some of the most iconic artists and brands. Ritchie had lunch with him, and Olivier told him his story and how Iconoclast was formed, which Ritchie found particularly interesting. As with Simon, he learnt a lot from Olivier.

One thing that stuck with Ritchie was a nice comment from Simon. 'Ritchie. I could genuinely see you doing very well as a business manager on the music side of things in the future.' Who knows, eh?

**

At the time of writing, a new album has been released by Chrysalis Records called *Nineteen and Beyond*, which is basically a compilation of my best stuff with them from 1984 to 1988. It's crazy to think that it's almost been forty years since '19' and the journey that came with that track. That number will never be far from my thoughts and will always be the number many associate me with and I'm fine with that, even if some people are oblivious to what I've gone on to achieve since then. I remember getting a call in the late 2000s from a lady at VH1 who was conducting research to help with a show they were doing on *One Hit Wonders*. I initially thought she was calling to ask if I could do a theme tune for it, but she said, 'The show will be about artists who had a No.1 but never had another one after in their careers and disappeared from music.'

I didn't want to make her look silly because, at the time, I'd already clocked up around twenty-five No.1's, so I just said, 'Thanks, but it's not for me. Judging from your criteria, I don't think I'm eligible.' I didn't want to embarrass her because she obviously hadn't done her research, but at the time of writing, I'm proud to say, including '19', I've had thirty-eight No.1's, or 2x19 in total!

As opposed to creating music for record labels before on request, I'm now content with being in the studio and making albums, which I feel I want to do. If somebody wants to listen to it, then great, but for now, it has to be good fun for me. As long as I've had good fun doing it, the rest doesn't matter. I still occasionally get asked to remake or mix tracks, but once again, it has to be something I'm interested in, as opposed to years gone when I just asked what the brief was, churned out what they wanted and then moved on to the next project. For example – I was recently approached by a company which owns lots of big stars catalogues and they asked me about redoing some of their artists work, including Whitney Houston and Luther Vandross. I'm currently working on the demos and although nothing has been signed contractually to move the tracks forward, let's see. If it happens, it happens and if it doesn't, I won't lose any sleep over it.

It's scary to think that I'm in my fifth decade of making music and sometimes wonder where the music industry could go in the future with the rapid progression of formats and technology. In 2023, it took me three months to convert all my vinyl, tapes, cassettes and CDs to digital, just in case the music caught fire or was stolen. The cloud has benefits, but with the push for minimalist aesthetics, history seems to disappear to an extent, which is a little bit sad. Also, technology sometimes goes too far. You can get programmes that write tunes for you now, which I think defeats the object. You can have the fastest computer in the world and the most expensive guitar and keyboard, but if they're sitting there dormant and you don't do something with them, they're not going to whistle over to me and say, 'Oi, Paul. Make a track with us.'

I've got no problem people not liking what I do and that's not arrogance; it's just everyone's personal taste. I don't like The Beatles music, but I like Pink Floyd, Black Sabbath and Hawkwind. If the Birdie Song can go to No.1, then good on them. I think back to the time when '19' was No.1 and I felt like I was in a goldfish bowl. You see a number of disgruntled pop stars that feel that they can't be left alone and that, to me, says it all. It's not what it's all cooked up to be. You need to ask yourself, *do you want to be taken seriously as an artist or merely be famous on the telly for a short burst?*

One of my fans in America called, Dorothy, was one hundred and three and she liked listening to my music. I did a birthday message for her one hundred and fourth and she was over the moon.

I've had people saying, 'Thank you for saving my life,' 'Thanks for giving me hope,' and 'Thanks for the memories,' all through my music. I'm not sure what people's ambitions in life are, but that's now far more satisfying for me, knowing that I've been able to positively impact a few than getting some lines in a paper and a photo.

If my life ends tomorrow, it's been a very good one. Some people have it hard throughout the whole of their lives and they look over their shoulder and say, 'Bloody hell. What happened to me?' and that's not mocking anybody because some people are born into hardship or make a few wrong turns in their lives. At the time of writing, I've lived sixty-six years of doing what I wanted instead of living to ninety and dying miserably, never having chased any dreams. Everything from here on is a bonus.

Am I done with music, though? Stay tuned…